# CABIN
# FEVER

# CABIN
# FEVER

by Addison M. Conley

2023

Butterworth Books

**Cabin Fever**

This trade paperback original is published by
Butterworth Books, Nottingham, England

Cataloging information
ISBN: 978-1-915009-30-2
CREDITS
Editor: Nicci Robinson
Cover Design: Nicci Robinson
Production Design: Global Wordsmiths

# Acknowledgements

*abin Fever*, my fourth novel, was first conceived three years ago and owly began to take shape. We've all been through some turmoil since the art of the pandemic. Luckily, I haven't lost anyone to the virus. If you have, end my deepest condolences and hugs.

This book would not have been possible without my developmental ditor, Nicci Robinson, also known as the wonderful author Robyn Nyx. hank you so much for allowing me to torture you. LOL. You're awesome. n sure you LYAO at a few of the things I wrote. Remember the bees uzzing whenever you need a laugh.

Hugs and a huge thank you to my beta readers, particularly K. McIntosh, n Bowen, and LHK. LHK has been a dear friend for years and was a enior analyst who kicked my ass when editing my reports and grilled me efore I briefed senior executives. She's never held back punches, and I ank her dearly for her brutal honesty. Her suggestions have made me a etter writer, and our conversations have made me a better person.

I send you a gigantic hug to ARC reviewers. And dear readers, thank you o much for purchasing this book or reading it on Kindle Unlimited. I hope ou enjoy it. If you like my work, please consider writing a short review on mazon, Goodreads, or another major outlet. A review, even the tiniest ne, helps enormously.

Lastly, feel free to drop me a note or ask a question at addison.m.conley. uthor@gmail.com. I'm also on Facebook at AddisonMConley.Fiction. uthor

# Chapter One

*April*

KATE MINTON SAT WITH her legs crossed, sipping her water and staring at the Chicago Tribune. Outwardly, she tried to project calmness, but her stomach sloshed around like melting Jell-O. Being called to the managing partner's office at ten a.m. was not good news. Would they dare fire her over her harassment complaint?

Her paralegal job once meant more than a paycheck. But everything changed when the mega-firm gobbled up her old law office. The extra hours and demands became insane, and the subtle misogyny was irritating. After reassignment to a new team—all from the new firm—the team's boss groped her and exposed himself in private.

"He will see you now, Ms. Minton." The receptionist gestured toward the doors.

She folded the paper and dropped it on the coffee table. Her legs slightly quivered with every step toward his office, but she managed not to stumble as she made her way inside. "Good morning, Mr. Atkins."

"Lovely to see you, Katherine. Have a seat." He motioned to an oversized wingback chair.

She took in her surroundings. A colossal desk dominated the huge office, a reflection of his ego. Two walls of glass gave a stunning view of the skyline. God, how she wished she was outside enjoying the sunshine and the cool breeze on this gorgeous afternoon. But she was trapped on Willis Tower's hundred and first floor, like a mouse about to be eaten by a tomcat.

He cleared his throat. "Katherine, you've been indispensable. I've heard so much about you and all of the cases you've helped to make a success." He smiled, but it looked insincere.

"Thank you, sir." She was determined not to crumple under his scrutiny.

"Unfortunately, we need to trim the ranks and realign our budget.

We're eliminating your position."

He leaned back and gave her a cold, hard gaze that hit like a laser beam. A tidal wave of nausea mixed with anger washed over her. How could they do this? *Breathe.* "Interesting timing."

"I've had several conversations with the former managing partner. He thinks very highly of you, and he's insisted that we offer you a generous severance package with the separation agreement."

"I see. And what are the details?" She held his gaze.

He slid the folder across the table. She didn't pick it up, wanting him to give her the news.

"A general release of liability and other standard paperwork. We agree to provide you three months of pay in exchange for an agreement not to make any claims, file a lawsuit, or accuse us of age discrimination. You'll also be able to file for unemployment."

*I'm forty-two, not senile.* "Lovely, considering your lawyer assaulted me."

"I'm sorry, but we have been unable to substantiate either case since you were the only two in the room. And truthfully, we're overstaffed now that the firms have merged. The package reflects that. Also, as you know, Illinois law allows us to terminate our working relationship at any time, without reason or cause." He rocked in his chair.

With nothing to lose, she stiffened her spine. "I've built a career here, and I've stayed for over twenty years because everyone was honest, hard-working, and fair. A lot has changed since the merger." One by one, employees of the old firm were either quitting or getting fired. She'd half-expected to be the latest casualty.

He stood and tapped his finger on the desk. "Today is your opportunity to go elsewhere. You'll find all the paperwork is in order. Legally, you have the right to consult with an attorney. Plus, you have twenty-one days to consider the agreement, and seven days after signing to revoke it. With those protections, I'd like you to sign it now." He placed his Montblanc fountain pen on the folder, pushed it further to the edge of the desk, and sat back down.

She twirled the expensive pen while examining the documents. Although she was well aware of the standard paperwork, she shuffled, scanned, and circled passages as her mind whirled, and her stomach threatened to empty her breakfast. How was she going to pay her bills?

ast month, she'd moved a substantial amount of savings into her 401k
etirement fund. If she touched it now, the IRS would charge her an early
withdrawal fee.

"Ms. Minton, you're wasting my valuable time. I'm more than happy to
withdraw the package if you prefer to fight."

With no witnesses to her assault, a lawsuit would hurt her more than
ne firm, and he knew it. Her only hope was that other assaulted women
would step forward, and there was no guarantee of that. Many sexual
arassment cases were lengthy and brutal, consuming time and money
nd draining everyone's emotional stamina. If she signed and left, they'd
lk about her for a while, but eventually, the gossip would dwindle.

She scribbled her name across each required line and tossed the
older back. While maintaining eye contact, she put the cap back on his
Montblanc pen and slowly placed it inside her jacket's breast pocket.
A little extra compensation. Are we done here?" Kate would give the
en back if he objected, but she suspected he wouldn't. While she was
etting fired, the jerk lawyer would likely only receive a verbal reprimand.

"I guess it's true what they say about you being a little fiery. It must
e the hint of red in your brown hair." He laughed and flicked his wrist,
ismissing her. "Keep the pen and gather up your belongings. Just be out
y noon."

Her legs were shaky and heavy, but she held her chin high and strolled
oward the door with as much grace as possible. When she paused
nd turned at the door to meet his gaze, he grinned and winked. Acid
reeped up into her throat. She jerked the door open and shut it harder
nan intended, causing the receptionist to look up, a glint of sympathy
nown in the young receptionist's eye. Kate marched on.

She grabbed a half-empty box from the copy room and turned it
pside down. The packs of paper thudded as they hit the table, just like
er life was crashing from a high to a low. *Breathe.* For a brief moment,
ne squeezed her eyes shut to hold back the tears before entering the
ramped office space to face her coworkers.

"How did it go?" Tiffany asked.

"Not good."

"But you're fantastic at your job."

She froze at the unexpected comment. "Thank you." Out of respect for
nhat she thought would be a just process, Kate hadn't mentioned a word

about the assault to any of her coworkers. But her team had learned all about it through the gossip chain. Oh, how wrong she'd been to expect fairness under the new management. On the bright side, she wouldn't have to work with the jerk or the others who protected him. Why did powerful men always seem to escape justice?

The work phone blinked, indicating voicemail. That wasn't her problem anymore. She needed to calm down, and the best way for her to do that was to go home, slip into comfy clothes and stroll through the park before the unseasonably warm day disappeared. First, she needed to send one last email. Immediately after typing her password into the computer, a screen message popped up with a countdown clock: "You have eight minutes before your access is terminated. Security."

*F'ing jerks.* She attached critical notes involving her cases to the email, changed the address to the entire firm, and typed, "I regret to inform you that I am no longer an employee. I wish you all the best. Kate." With the countdown under one minute, she punched the send button, then dug her cell phone out of her purse and turned it on.

"Kate, you know all personal cell phones are to remain off until an employee leaves the building."

"Yep. Check your email." She cranked up the volume on "No" by Meghan Trainor and cleaned out her drawers. Halfway through the song, her phone chimed with several text messages, all from her half-brother Joel.

*Father's in the Evanston Hospital and wants to see you.*

*His cancer has returned.*

*He may not make it this time. Kate, hurry.*

She hastily brushed all her desktop items into the box, snatched up her purse, and ran for the elevator. Downstairs, she yanked her badge off, threw it at the guard like a baseball, and stepped through the turnstile door. One taxi driver passed her by, ignoring her hand waving and loud whistling, but the second one stopped.

"Evanston Hospital." With the traffic, it would take at least thirty-five minutes. She slumped in the seat, and tears welled up. This time, she was powerless to stop them.

She shouldn't *be* crying over him. It wasn't like he'd been an affectionate father. Sometimes, she'd put that down to him being over fifty when she was born, stuck in his ways and too old to be the dad she'd needed

# CABIN FEVER

Other times, she thought it was because she was his only daughter and a disappointment to him. Whatever it was, her mother didn't put up with it for long, and they soon divorced. She had hoped their relationship would improve as she grew older, but a level of irritation continued between them.

The taxi lurched to a halt, snapping her back to the present.

"We're here, miss," the driver said.

She fumbled through her purse for her wallet and stuffed the bills into the driver's hand. "Keep the change."

The hospital lobby was as bright and modern as any, but she had hated hospitals since her mother died while undergoing surgery. Isaac was always in and out of the hospital, but it never seemed to slow him down—until now. Sadness, dread, and anxiety flooded her as she inched toward the ICU waiting room. She dropped the box on an empty chair and waved at her half-brothers. Roger barely put up his hand, and Karl nodded.

"There you are." Joel walked toward her with open arms.

They didn't speak as he gently rocked her. All of her half-brothers were twenty-plus years older, with Joel being the youngest. He was affectionate, but Roger and Karl were just like Isaac, stiff and all business. If you didn't talk about cars or the stock market, they acted like you almost didn't exist.

Joel kissed her forehead. "The pain medicine makes Father doze on and off. Only one of us can stay in his room, but I'll walk you back."

"Just give me the room number and point me in the direction."

He nodded. "1204."

She covered her mouth with her hand and stifled a cry when she entered. She hadn't seen Isaac for four months. The contrast between then and now was horrific. His skin draped over his bones like he hadn't eaten in weeks. His chest barely rose. If it weren't for the lights on the monitors, she might've thought he was dead. She tiptoed over and sat on the chair by the window.

Tears rolled down her cheeks. Kate never completely felt understood, and she didn't feel valued like her brothers. He'd never disowned her, but he often said that her "lifestyle" was a hard choice. Now, her father, this shell of an old man, would die as he lived, a mystery man who rarely showed his true self.

"Katherine?"

"Yes, Father." She wiped away her tears. When he raised his trembling hand to reach for her, she scooted forward and delicately wrapped her fingers around his bony hand.

"I'm sorry. I wish I had been a better father. I love you." He squeezed her hand with surprising strength. "Please forgive me."

"It's okay. I love you, too." She gently squeezed back.

"I was wrong, and I can't say how sorry I am. I hope you marry the woman of your dreams."

Her breath hitched in her throat. "Thank you, Father." Why had he never said those words before? More tears threatened as she gently rubbed her thumb over the back of his hand.

"You were a spunky girl who questioned everything." He smiled. "That used to irritate me to no end. It's made you into a strong woman. Don't give up."

"I'm sorry for being a bit too much of a pain at times."

*He coughed and struggled to breathe.*

"I should call the nurse."

"No." He coughed a little more before his breathing leveled out. "You look like my Grandmother Rosemary, but your spunk is undeniably like Mother Emmeline."

Kate was speechless. He never spoke of his family.

"I'm tired. I love you." He closed his eyes.

So many years had gone by, and he'd waited too long to be the loving father she'd always wanted. It was too much. She patted his hand and turned to look out the window. After drying her tears, she glanced back at him. He seemed at peace. Maybe they would talk about his family later. It was never too late to try, was it?

The sound of the ear-splitting monitors rocked her senses. Two nurses rushed in and pushed her to the side. Everything blurred as they frantically worked on him. She watched as her father's life slipped away despite the nurses' efforts. The line on the heartrate monitor remained flat. Her hope that they might finally talk, and that they could begin to build a real relationship faded into the ether.

Another nurse rushed in. "Please. You need to wait outside."

Kate stumbled back, and the nurse closed the door. Unable to stop the flood of sorrow, she inched down the hallway. A brightly lit stairwell sign caught her attention despite her blurry vision. She ducked inside, slumped down on the cold metal stairs, and sobbed.

# Chapter Two

KATE RESTED HER HEAD against the glass of the apartment's enormous picture window and gazed at life below. It was another bright sunny day with boaters taking advantage of a calm Lake Michigan. From her vantage point, the joggers and walkers looked like tiny dots as they exercised on the lakeside path.

Her eyes filled with tears. What the hell was she going to do? Earlier, she'd contemplated picking up a chair to smash the window, then hurl herself to the pavement thirty-eight stories below. But she was a chicken, and her beanbag chair, the only furniture left in the room, wouldn't crack the tempered glass.

The chime for her door security app sounded, and she swiped the phone screen to open the video. "Ah, it's you. Come on up." She forced her limbs to get her to the front door. The thump of the deadbolt sounded ten times louder than normal. She pushed the door wide open and trudged to the breakfast bar. The cold granite chilled her skin as she leaned against it for support.

Moments later, the elevator dinged open, and she rubbed her temples at the sound of her best friend's stiletto heels clicking on the building's hallway marble floor. God, she should have called Sherry, but the truth was, she was too embarrassed and wrapped up in self-pity.

"Jesus, what the hell happened?" Sherry glanced around the empty room.

"Welcome to the party." Kate grabbed the half-empty wine bottle and took a big swig, then wiped her mouth on the back of her sleeve.

"Classy. You're drunk."

"No, just pleasantly buzzed." She held out the paper plate. "Cheese and crackers?"

Sherry took a deep breath and crossed her arms.

"Fine. Don't have any of my appetizers, but you can't have my main meal." She dropped the plate on the kitchen countertop, picked up a tub of theater buttered popcorn and hugged it to her chest.

"When was the last time you ate something real?"

Kate shrugged and crammed a handful of the snack into her mouth. Several kernels fell to the floor. Sherry rolled her eyes and walked around, surveying the apartment. The wooden floors and empty rooms amplified the sound of her footsteps.

"Shit, Sherry. Stop stomping around." Kate tossed the bucket down, and it almost tipped over.

"Wow, you got dumped bad."

"Yep." Kate shuffled back to her perch by the window, plopped into the beanbag, and gazed at the skyline for the millionth time. After the death of her father and losing her job, the last thing she expected was for her girlfriend to dump her.

"When did Audrey leave?"

"Yesterday afternoon." She took another gulp of wine.

"Why didn't you call me?" Sherry cocked her head.

"I was too fried and needed some alone time." *To stop feeling like such a pathetic loser.* She knew it wasn't true, but her crumbling world hurt so bad.

"I'm sorry that so much slammed into you over the past few weeks, sweetie. I know your relationship had always been feast or famine, but I thought things were getting better."

"So did I. Apparently, Audrey had planned to end it the day Isaac died but put it off out of sympathy. Isn't that sweet? Then on her way out the door, she dared to call me a boring workaholic. Talk about twisting the knife." She swung her arm and wine sloshed onto the floor.

"Sweetie, put down the bottle." Sherry brushed a box off and sat.

On days like these, Kate wished they'd been able to make it work in college, but their friends with benefits gig didn't fit either of them. The friendship that grew from that remained one of the startlingly few highlights in her life. "Sorry. You know I normally don't drink this much. The day started okay, but another firm turned me down. Then I re-evaluated my bills and cash, and it went downhill from there." Despite years of excellent performance appraisals, her last five job applications had been unsuccessful, leading her to believe the groping, asshole lawyer had trashed her reputation. Almost twenty-one years of hard work, and it all seemed lost.

"Maybe this break will do you some good. You're not boring, but you are a tiny bit of a workaholic." Sherry raised her hands, and her many bracelets jingled. "Think positive. You'll find another job. Besides your talent, you never give up. And when you're ready, a wonderful woman will come into the picture."

Typically, she was a glass half-full person, but this relationship ending was like someone had body-slammed her in a pro-wrestling match, and it had knocked every ounce of optimism from her. "Even if I find a job, this damn condo is too expensive. I need to move out of Chicago." She rubbed her eyes with the palm of her hand. "God, I don't even own a car."

"I'm sure your brothers will cut you a deal."

"More like cut my throat."

Sherry flicked her wrist. "Joel's not that bad. You can sleep in our spare bedroom while you look for a job. Max could use help with the garden, then she'll have more time for me."

"I don't want to be a third wheel. And when are you two getting married? After four years of living together, isn't it about time?"

"You're welcome anytime. And I'm happy with our current arrangement, but if Max ever asks, I won't say no. She just better buy me a big-ass, gorgeous engagement ring." Sherry stretched out her hand as if she were imagining the ring. "Now, tell me what happened at the reading of your father's will."

"I didn't attend." There was little point. Her father never allowed Kate a glimpse into the family businesses because she was a girl.

"What?"

"I'm sure Isaac left the car businesses to my brothers."

Her older half-brothers were involved in everything. Anger and inferiority peaked in her teens, and it wasn't until the middle of college that she learned to hold back instead of lashing out. She might have been able to quell the rage over the years, but the hurt lingered under the surface like a deep abscess. And painfully, everything had popped at once.

"How do you know he didn't leave anything for you?"

"Why would he start helping me out now? Isaac was Mr. Business day and night." She grabbed the bottle but put it down when Sherry arched her eyebrow. "Remember the burnt-orange Gremlin in college? Paying him monthly for that beat-up car made it hard to buy food. And it took me twelve years to pay back the damn loan that supplemented what my scholarship didn't cover."

"You've told me this a thousand times. I'm sorry your father wasn't as loving and affirmative as you wanted, but he was there for you. He had a weird way of trying to show you the value of earning a dollar, but so what? Most people have to make their own way in this world."

Kate huffed and looked back out the window.

"And yes, he was unhappy that you weren't into men, but he never kicked your ass out. And remember when he first met me?"

Kate grinned. "The shock on his face was awesome."

"How many white fathers would take their daughter's Black girlfriend out to dinner? Isaac may not have rolled out the red carpet and sent out announcements, but he treated us kindly." Sherry smacked Kate's knee. "It was over twenty years ago. You need to let it go. Don't let the past define your future."

More tears trickled down Kate's face. She had made progress with her father over the years, but he remained rooted in some old-fashioned ideas, and she couldn't figure out why. And now he was gone. She grabbed a wad of tissues from a nearby box and buried her face. "Shit. Why did he have to wait until his deathbed to show his love?"

Sherry gently pulled Kate's hand down and looked her in the eye. "Now is the time to start fresh. What's your next move?"

"I have half a notion of saying screw it and starting over somewhere totally different." She dabbed tears away, blew her nose, and dropped the tissues into the small waste can next to her beanbag chair. "Maybe I should apply to one of those TV shows like *Alone*. Imagine what I could do with a half-million dollars."

"Sweetie, you'd never survive a week on a wilderness reality show. You're more the glamping gal."

"Ha, I'll show you someday." The security chime sounded again, and she glanced at her phone. "Excuse me. The History Channel is calling me to audition for the next season of *Alone*." When she opened the app, she saw a man in a business suit standing in the building foyer. "Can I help you?"

"Ms. Katherine Minton?"

"Yes. What can I do for you?"

# CABIN FEVER

"Hello. I'm Mr. Oliver Travis. We spoke on the phone the other day. I'm so sorry you were too ill and couldn't attend the reading of your father's will. I was in the neighborhood and was hoping to get the matter settled. May I come up, please?"

"Sure." She hit the button to let him through the security door.

"Can't be all that bad if he's coming here in person. I'll step out for coffee and let you two talk." Sherry began to rise.

"No, wait. I need to clean up and change clothes. And whatever it is, I don't want to hear it alone. Please stay."

"Okay, but don't take too long in the bathroom."

Kate had difficulty getting out of the bean bag and finally rolled out on all fours. When she stood, the sudden movement created a brief dizzy spell. She swayed and put her hand on the window to gain her balance.

"Thank the Lord you drank white wine and don't have red-stained wench's teeth." Sherry smirked and motioned toward the bathroom. "Go."

Kate hurried off, shimmied into her last clean pair of jeans, and slipped on a short-sleeve blue shirt. After washing her face and gargling with mouthwash, she popped a mint into her mouth. There was little time to tame her hair except to brush it and spritz her unruly curls with hairspray. Except for her red eyes, she looked half decent.

She paused at the sound of Sherry speaking; her unique, charming, and professional tone was mesmerizing. That voice and her intellect were the reasons why Sherry had become one of the top public relations managers in Chicago. Behind that polished figure stood a strong, independent, and kindhearted woman. Kate was lucky. Not many relationships ended well, let alone blossomed into a lifelong best friendship.

She stepped back into the living room. "Hello, Mr. Travis. I'm sorry I can't offer you a place to sit. I'm moving out. If you'd like to leave the paperwork, I can read it later and get a notary to witness my signature."

"You of all people should know I can't do that." He smiled and snapped his briefcase open. "Proof of identity, please."

She pulled out her wallet and handed over her driver's license.

"Thank you."

As the papers passed into her hand, a wave of nausea washed over her. So much had gone unsaid between her and Isaac. The stack's thickness wasn't surprising. Unlike his personal life, Isaac always spelled everything out in his business deals.

"Your portion of the estate begins on page thirteen," Mr. Travis said.

*Lucky thirteen.* Kate slipped on her reading glasses. On most days, she could get by without them. Today was definitely not one of those days. Instead of starting where he indicated, she skimmed the entire document, wanting to know her brothers' shares. Her body trembled inside with the flip of each page. She'd expected as much: everything to them. But his words at the hospital had given her a glimmer of hope. How could he do this to her?

"To summarize, here is the check for fifty thousand dollars." Mr. Travis passed her an envelope. "Mr. Howard Jacobs will deposit the second fifty thousand dollars in a local bank account once you've spent thirty days in the cabin. Oh, and remember to arrive within sixty days from now, or the first check is the only inheritance you will ever receive. Then—"

"This doesn't make sense." Kate waved the papers at him. "Why do I have to live in this cabin?" Out of the corner of her eye, she saw Sherry raise one of her meticulous, manicured eyebrows.

"I have no idea, Ms. Minton. I'm only here to execute the will."

She dropped the papers onto the countertop and crossed her arms. "And when do I get the final payment?" It was written in the will, but she needed to hear it to believe it.

"The deed and the half a million dollars will be transferred to you *only* after you spend three hundred sixty-five consecutive days in the cabin."

Sherry's eyes widened, and she mouthed, "Holy shit."

Kate understood the contents of the will perfectly, but that didn't make Isaac's bizarre wishes any less confusing. It was all too much. Her stomach churned from the mixture of emotions and alcohol.

"And where is this restored pickup truck?" She couldn't believe Isaac was giving her another used vehicle. It wouldn't be one of the expensive antiques her brothers had inherited. And why on earth was it a pickup truck?

"I spoke with your brother, Mr. Joel Minton, yesterday. He will have it delivered after the body shop crew finishes. If you have no further questions, sign here." He held out a pen.

She took it, rolled it between her fingers, and looked at it from different angles. It was a Grayson Tighe, one of the most expensive pens in the world. The sculptured overlay of a naked woman over topaz was exquisite. She'd never be able to afford such a luxury, or maybe she would if she could survive this ridiculous challenge of Isaac's.

"It was your father's. Once you sign, it's yours. The rest of the collection was divided between your brothers, nieces, and nephews."

Kate sucked in a deep breath. She remembered Isaac's fountain pen collection but had no idea that it included a Grayson Tighe worth thousands of dollars. As her brain's common sense screamed at her to sell the pen to cover her debts, a powerful memory sprung forward, and her heart whispered to her to keep it. Isaac rarely let anyone touch his precious collection. When Kate was young, she'd snuck into his home office and somehow managed to open the massive display case. She'd admired the gleaming pens for a long time before reaching out to touch one. At that instant, he'd caught her. His growl caused her to break into a shaky sob. When she'd rattled on about writing a letter to Santa, he melted like a teddy bear and consoled her. He sat her on his lap and showed her how to use the pen, praising her as she wrote. It was the last Christmas they'd had together as a family before her mother left him.

Mr. Travis cleared his throat. "If you would please sign, I can be on my way."

She gripped the pen and scribbled her name on each required line.

"I'll have the signed documents copied and mailed to you overnight. Good day, Ms. Minton, and good luck."

Once the door clicked shut, Sherry spun toward Kate. "What was that all about?"

"Short version? My brothers got the businesses and the antique car collection worth millions, and I have to hike my ass off to Idaho and spend a year playing pioneer living in a cabin."

"Your wish came true then. You get to start over somewhere totally different. I'd sleep in a cabin for a hundred thousand, let alone five hundred. How nice is the cabin?"

"I don't have a clue. Isaac never mentioned anything about Idaho to me." Kate drummed her fingers on the kitchen countertop. Maybe Isaac's family lived there.

"Oh!" Sherry made an exaggerated horror face. "Don't they have snakes, wolves, and bears? You'd better stop at a gun shop and pick up a shotgun or whatever you need to protect yourself."

Kate rolled her eyes. "I've never shot a gun and would likely end up shooting myself."

"There's probably a class you can take from a big burly man. I doubt there are many lesbians around."

Yeah, Kate doubted that too. And while she didn't have any visions of dating soon, she wouldn't say no to the company of a gorgeous woman. She'd have to make some new friends if she was going to survive this.

"Are you driving, or are you going to sell the truck and fly?"

"I'm thinking a road trip will clear my head." She waved the check in the air. "One thing's a given; if I have to live out in the boonies for a year, I'm replacing the carpet, decorations, and fixtures, and I'll be buying a giant TV."

# Chapter Three

RILEY ANDERSON YAWNED AS she placed the last of five boxes in the hardware store's back room. She picked up the barcode scanner as Aunt Lilly strolled through the door. "Morning. I have to leave soon, but Nathaniel will be in soon to cover for you and Tom."

"Did you finish cleaning and supplying the cabin?"

"Yep, I did it before going to Pocatello." Riley quickly scanned the items. "I also told Mr. Jacobs about some additional repairs that need to be done."

"Can I have your attention, please?"

She placed the scanner on the shelf. "What's up?"

Lilly crossed her arms and narrowed her eyes. "What took you so long in Pocatello? Why did you spend the night?"

"Oh, I caught a glimpse of the high school rodeo at the fairgrounds." She smiled and resumed the inventory.

"Really? How'd you do that since the rodeo final was last weekend?"

*Shit. Now I've done it.*

"Was this the reason?" Lilly stuck a beer coaster with a rainbow logo in front of Riley's nose. "Girl's Night Out?"

Riley grumbled. "And what were you doing rifling through my pockets?"

"Your jacket had fallen off the hook. When I picked it up, the coaster fell out."

"I'm a grown woman."

Lilly tossed the coaster on the shelf and patted Riley's cheek. "Yes, you are, and I wish you'd find a nice girl around here instead of at a bar miles away. Surely, there's someone in your meet-up group that caught your attention."

"Again, it's none of your business." Riley cringed at the sound of her harsh tone.

"You're right, but the next time you go to Pocatello, don't lie. I love you and only want the best for you. I just wish you weren't looking for a girlfriend in a bar."

It was odd how Aunt Lilly enjoyed wine but didn't like bars. Riley guessed her attitude came from her religious upbringing. "The dancing is good."

"Uh-huh. With as many as you've enjoyed recently, I'd say you could win *Dancing with the Stars*." Lilly hugged her then held her at arm's length. "Dear, you need to find a partner that you can connect with emotionally, and you're not going to find her in a bar. I know you've been hurt, but please don't give up."

Riley clenched her jaw. Lilly rarely brought up her sex life and hadn't since she was in her wild early twenties. Dammit, she was forty, and she could do what the hell she pleased.

"Morning, ladies. What's the schedule like for today?" Megan, Riley's best friend, came into the room. She looked back and forth between them. "Did I interrupt something?"

"Just greeting my dear niece, who waltzed in at six this morning after spending the night dancing away in Pocatello. Enjoy your day, ladies." Lilly picked up the coaster and handed it to Megan before she left.

Megan chuckled. "It's amazing how she puts up with you."

"When I finish this, we need to drive out to Tuckers' ranch. They want an addition built on the barn. Hayley says they'll complete the screened-in porch today at the Thompson's. So, we'll swing over there next."

"Ah, doing what you do best. Changing the topic."

Riley shook the barcode scanner at Megan. "I don't need it from both sides."

"I thought you liked two women at once."

"Shut up. That's not funny." She regretted telling Megan about the threesome with Beth and another woman whose name Riley couldn't remember. "That year with Beth was a poor lapse in judgment that I promise never to repeat again."

"Sorry. I was out of line." Megan folded her arms. "But seriously, aren't your casual hookup days over?"

"Hayley was with me. We had dinner and stayed for the dancing. I swear. We were too tired to drive. And no one slept in my bed but me." The thought of picking up a woman had crossed her mind, but she wasn't going to admit it.

Megan tilted her head to the side. "Okay. Now, tell me about this city slicker coming into town. Hunting permit restrictions are tight this year."

"She won't be hunting."

"She? A woman from Chicago is going to stay up in the cabin?"

"Yeah, I just hope she isn't a tourist hiker that thinks she can scale Mount Borah dressed in shorts and carrying one bottle of water."

"Interesting. Wonder if she's cute. For you, not me."

Riley put the scanner down and shook her finger at Megan. "Knock it off with your sad jokes. Besides, your love life isn't anything to brag about."

"Got a third date with a woman from Idaho's Department of Fish and Game." Megan wiggled her eyebrows. "Need any tips?"

"Zip it. And stop doing that thing with your eyebrows. It creeps me out. Let's go. I'll finish the inventory later." She headed for the door.

A few hours later, Riley sat in the cramped storage room that doubled as an office and chewed her sandwich. She'd been going since four this morning and finally had this moment of peace at three o'clock. Tom was at the front desk of the store, and Nathaniel was out on a delivery. The lumberyard staff ran like a well-oiled machine, Megan was going strong as her right hand in her home renovation company, and Aunt Lilly had a booming business on the grocery side. And while Tom managed the hardware store, Riley liked to work the counter now and then. It gave her the chance to interact with a lot more folks.

She took a big swig of her soda pop and thought about Isaac Minton. He was an out-of-town recluse who rarely smiled, except around Aunt Lilly. But that wasn't hard. Everyone loved her. His passing wasn't a surprise. Good God, the man was as old as the hills and had to be close to one hundred. And his daughter must be in her late sixties or seventies. What the hell was an elderly single woman planning to do in a rustic cabin for a month? Howard Jacobs could have quickly settled the estate in Idaho.

She shook her head. Kate Minton would be in for a huge surprise. Although the cabin was cleaned up, the roof was in terrible shape. Mr. Minton hadn't visited for several years, and his handyman obviously hadn't cared for the place. Riley didn't have time for a thorough inspection, but she reckoned it'd be a miracle if the roof lasted another six months.

Her phone vibrated, and she read the display: unknown caller with a California area code. *Beth?* The bite of sandwich Riley had just taken lodged in her throat. She had blocked Beth, but the woman never gave up and often used friends' phones. After three years, she should've gotten the hint, but rich little Beth didn't like to hear the word no.

Riley didn't give a damn about relationships anymore, but a good roll in the hay hadn't recently satisfied her either. She just felt numb in the love department. And why was Aunt Lilly mentioning finding a partner nearby? Riley knew every lesbian in the county—half of them worked for her. And the only lesbians she knew that rode ATVs, fished, hiked, cycled, and snowmobiled were her friends or employees. Dating any one of them made her shudder. For now, work and sports made Riley happy, and that would have to be enough.

She wadded up her sandwich wrapper and tossed it toward the trash can. It hit the side and bounced off. "Just like my love life. Best to stick to building things."

# Chapter Four

"IT'S A GOOD THING I only stayed a week. I think I gained five pounds." Kate put the last of her bags by the door. She was blessed to have good friends.

"Sweetie, you know it's no trouble at all." Sherry hugged her. "You can stay a bit longer."

"I already messaged the Idaho lawyer. But thank you."

"You're welcome. And I believe in karma. There'll be a good reason your father gave you the cabin."

Leaving the big city for a backwater town had Kate seesawing between excitement and anxiety. But with no job, no place to live, and barely any liquid cash, it seemed like the best option. And with a half-million up for grabs, she was prepared to tolerate almost anything. "Joel called last night and wished me good luck. He said Father's hunting and fishing trips included Idaho, but he didn't know about any property or relatives."

A horn sounded outside, and Kate groaned. "And I can't believe he gave me a truck."

"It can't be as bad as that old Gremlin." Sherry laughed.

Kate stepped onto the front porch and froze at the sight of a beautiful, dark cherry-red pickup truck in the driveway. She couldn't believe Isaac had planned such a wonderful gift. It was even more remarkable that he'd remembered her favorite color.

"Good morning, Ms. Minton." A young man from the body shop stood next to the truck, smiling. "Your 2000 Ford has a rebuilt automatic engine and four-wheel drive. The custom interior is the best part. Hop inside."

In a daze, Kate wandered over and slid behind the wheel. She ran her hands over the supple gray leather seats and glanced around at the fancy interior. But why did she need such a large, powerful truck? Just how remote was this cabin?

"Seat covers are tucked under the seats. They'll protect the leather when you need to haul anything dirty," he said.

After showing her the various features, he helped Max load things up. Kate stood in silence with Sherry, then lowered her head and turned away.

"Ah, don't you cry, or I'll start." Sherry rubbed Kate's back.

"I was looking forward to a fresh start, but now, I'm not sure."

"You'll be fine. It's going to be an adventure." Sherry held her until her tears stopped.

"Hey, I need a hug too."

Kate drew Max in for a group hug. "I'm going to miss you guys."

"We'll always be a phone call away," Sherry said.

"And we'll plan a visit and a camping trip." Max winked at her partner.

"I'll sleep on Kate's sofa, and *you* can camp." Sherry pinched Max's cheek then kissed her.

Their back-and-forth banter made Kate laugh. She'd miss it. "You better visit soon." After another round of goodbyes, Kate drove away. Her chest heaved with deep breaths, and she tried to control her emotions. She'd spent most of her adult life alone; she could handle this. If someone had told her months ago that she'd travel out west to a cabin that no one in the family knew anything about, she would've thought they were bonkers. Her father's words echoed through her brain: *You're spunky. It made you into a strong woman.* Hopefully, through this trip and the cabin, she'd learn more about him and maybe even a little about herself.

\*\*\*

After another long day of driving, Kate had seen enough flat farmland and prairie grass to last a lifetime. To break up the monotony, she took the northern Wyoming route through the Grand Teton National Park. The roads were clear, but the amount of snow on the ground surprised her. She pulled off into one of the park's scenic overlooks and gazed up at the majestic, snow-capped mountains. They looked like dragon's teeth jutting out of the earth.

Kate's muscles ached, and exhaustion fogged her brain. Dinner had only heightened her drowsiness, but she couldn't resist a soak in the hotel's secluded, adults-only hot tub. She slipped down into the hot, soothing water, grateful to be the only one present. Her muscles relaxed, and when she looked up, a gazillion stars shone like diamonds in the moonless night sky. Never before had she seen so many.

That night, she slept like a baby and didn't seem to mind the alarm that woke her at five-thirty a.m. With only six hours of driving to her final destination, Kate hurried to pack but froze at some strange sounds from outside, and they were growing louder. Her heart pounded as she tiptoed to the balcony's sliding glass door. The rising morning sun glistened off a thin layer of freshly fallen snow and illuminated a meadow filled with countless bugling elk. It was a wondrous sight. She'd only seen such majestic animals in books and on the internet. Grand Teton was one place she'd return to someday.

It wasn't a far drive to Idaho. When she entered, the terrain changed drastically descending down the mountains. Irrigated farm fields spread out like a blanket around the Snake River and the city of Idaho Falls. Further west, the land became arid and all vegetation disappeared, wiped out by endless black lava flows. Kate had read that the volcanic activity of the Craters of the Moon National Park was fifteen thousand years old.

The black landscape that stretched for nearly twenty miles along the highway soon bored her. Further west, she welcomed the sight of vegetation and the splash of color from roadside wildflowers. The rounded mountaintops appeared eroded by weather over time but rose to new heights as she headed north.

Relief washed over her when she reached the city of Ketchum. Only an hour left to drive. She'd read that the city was the home of the first American ski resort. She looked up at the patchy snow on the mountain; the ski runs looked challenging. Too bad the season had ended. Maybe she'd give skiing a try next winter.

"Shit." She slammed on the brakes, and almost rear-ended another vehicle that had stopped to turn left. The long trip had dulled her senses, and her body ached. She'd come back to Ketchum another day. Right now, she only had time to briefly stretch her legs and grab a coffee.

Further north, splashes of pretty purple and white flowers dotted the roadside. The winding road narrowed, the evergreen groves thickened, and snow covered the ground. Kate blinked back driver fatigue that even coffee couldn't erase. Four long days had taken its toll, but when she crested Galena Summit, excitement tingled down her spine. The broad

Sawtooth Valley stretched out below, framed on each side by mountains filled with trees. *Her* cabin was tucked away somewhere in those beautiful mountains. Maybe twelve months here wouldn't be so bad.

The fuel gauge warning light blinked rapidly, and her pulse quickened. She did *not* want to breakdown in the middle of nowhere. Like a mirage, a gas station and the town came into view. But unlike Ketchum, Kate could probably throw a stone over Merrick. Dear Lord, it looked so tiny.

"Welcome to Merrick. Fill 'er up?"

She jumped when the cheerful attendant appeared at her window. "Yes, please." She motioned to the back of the truck. "And could you fill those up?" Thankfully, Max had hounded her into buying a small electric generator, but she'd need fuel for that too.

"What brings you to town?"

"I'm staying at the Isaac Minton cabin off Baylor Road for a while." She handed him the cash when he'd finished.

"There's a cabin past Lilly Smith's house. You have to go further up Falcon Creek. The road's pretty rough." He took off his cap and scratched his head. "I thought that was Christensen's land."

"Thank you." Kate figured the young man was confused. There'd been no mention of the Christensens.

"Nice wheels," he shouted as Kate drove away.

Several small shops dotted Main Street. A quaint library and Nancy's Diner and Bakery caught Kate's eye. "Coffee, pastries, and a good book. What more can a person want?" Kate shrugged. "Okay, I'd take a good woman who gives great massages, but I have a feeling I'm going to be celibate this year." She nodded when she saw a full-service laundromat. "Wow, I didn't expect that."

The law office was the last business at the far end of the town. She parked, but as she neared the door, a tall man in a business suit flipped the window sign to *Closed*. He turned and grinned. Dimples formed on his cheerful face, and his eyes shone brightly. With slightly graying hair around his temples and round-rimmed glasses, Kate guessed he was about the same age as Joel.

"Why, my dear Lord. You must be Kate. I'm Howard." He held out his hand.

"That's me." Kate shook his hand and returned the smile.

"Come on back."

"If it's not too much trouble?"

"No trouble at all. We can get the basics done. Although, you're lucky to catch me. I didn't mention that I close early on Tuesdays because I thought you were arriving tomorrow."

"I made good time."

She followed him into a large conference room with a long mahogany table. Gorgeous landscape oil paintings, so vivid they almost looked like photos, hung on the walls. There were no windows, and a closed door in the left corner presumably led to his private office. Oddly, a bank vault was on the right.

"Have a seat." He retrieved a document from a filing cabinet and placed it in front of her.

"Did my father give you a picture of me?"

He grinned again. "No, but your features tipped me off."

Kate assumed he was referring to her ice-blue eyes. People often asked her if she wore colored contacts.

"I recall your father's pride in you. He loved your unique eye color, but it was your spirit that he often spoke about."

She blinked several times. Not once had she ever heard her father say he was proud of her.

"When you called, I had Riley Anderson drop off supplies and thoroughly clean the place. Once you get your bearings, you may want to pick up more." He confirmed her directions and handed her the key.

"Thank you."

"You owe Riley nine hundred and fifty dollars, but you can take care of that later."

Kate raised her eyebrows. "Is it a month's worth of supplies?"

"My dear, it would have cost less, but the mice had made a nest in the old bed. It had to be replaced, and the walls had to be patched too."

She smiled and nodded. "Okay. A fresh mattress sounds good." She hadn't thought of it before, but who knew how long it had been there or who'd slept on it. As far as she knew, Goldilocks and her three bear friends might've had a sleepover.

"We don't overcharge our neighbors here. But the cabin needs other repairs before winter. When you pay Riley, ask her to give you an estimate. She's part-owner of the general store, and she runs a home renovation company."

"All right." Maybe this cabin wasn't going to be quite as idyllic as she'd imagined.

"Now, it's almost dinner. I recommend you go over to Nancy's. Rainbow trout is the special tonight. Try to get up to the cabin before nightfall. Luckily, the last bit of snow melted a couple of days ago, but the road is a little rough. In the next few days, you can get back to me. I have some papers and a few more things to go over with you."

"Thank you." She paused to look at the paintings one more time. "These are so lifelike. Who's the artist?"

His face lit up, and he smiled widely. "Mary Jacobs-Dawson, my grandaunt. She was also an avid photographer." He pointed to some pictures across the room. "Her career took off after she married and moved to Boise. Still, many thought she shouldn't even have a career since she was a woman. Her husband was a well-to-do physician and thankfully, he supported her." Howard hooked his thumbs in his suspenders. "Not many women hyphenated their last name in those days. She was a proud suffragist. She also gave free art classes at a local school for the deaf."

"My friend Max taught me basic sign language. Her sister is deaf." Kate smiled at the coincidence as she gazed at the paintings. "I love Mary's work."

"She was your grandmother's friend."

Kate sucked in a breath, and curiosity filled her, but exhaustion overcame the urge to ask more details. It'd likely be a long conversation best saved for another day. "I'd like to talk to you about that one day, but I should get going. I *am* hungry, and Nancy's sounds perfect."

"It was a pleasure to meet you finally. Have a great evening." He walked her to the door.

"Likewise." She got back in her car and set off. Nancy's Diner looked full as she passed, so she didn't bother. Hopefully the supplies Riley Anderson had left would tide her over until tomorrow, and she ached to get to the cabin to try out that new bed.

# Chapter Five

"BAYLOR ROAD ISN'T BAD," Kate muttered. The asphalt road ended and became gravel, with sections of washboard ripples that shook the truck. A low thud startled her as the front side dipped. "Okay. One gigantic pothole I didn't see." She squinted at moving black objects on the road and off to the side. "No way!" Four cattle stared at her for several minutes before moseying along to the stream. "Wouldn't want to hit one of those."

Several miles down, she jumped at the sound of her GPS beeping, alerting her to the road leading to the cabin. She veered left, and the road's condition deteriorated and narrowed to one and a half times the width of her truck. She skirted the best she could around the ruts and chunks of rocks, some the size of a volleyball. Boulders littered the shoulder, and there were few turnouts and level spots. Her hands ached, and her knuckles were white from gripping the steering wheel. It had been a long time since she'd changed a tire, and she didn't want to reacquaint herself with the process right now.

The road continued higher on the steep mountainside, and she slowed the truck to a crawl while her breathing and heart raced. There was no metal guard rail. When her nerves got the best of her, she stopped and rolled down the window. She glanced over the edge and judged the drop-off to be at least two hundred feet down to the stream. It wasn't a sheer cliff but rolling the truck over the side certainly meant serious injury or death.

After two switchbacks, she rounded a corner and a meadow stretched before her, gradually sloping up to the cabin and a huge barn. She parked and took a few minutes for some deep, cleansing breaths, thankful to be in one piece, then quickly walked around the cabin's perimeter. The key worked, but the door stuck. Kate threw her weight against it. She lost her balance as it popped open, and she fell ass over teakettle. After brushing herself off, she turned on her phone's flashlight and searched along the wall for a switch.

"No. Freaking. Electricity. You've got to be kidding me." She put her hands on her hips. After more calming breaths, she glanced around the one room cabin. Three boxes and an old-fashioned lamp were on top of a square table in the center. Two rocking chairs, a coffee table, and a potbellied stove were to her right. Storage cabinets, a chair, a washbasin, and a bathtub were to her left. A bed and dresser were in the back left corner and a rough kitchen in the other corner. A fancy red stove separated the kitchen and the bed. What she didn't see was a washing machine and dryer. Kate panicked, remembering a strung-up line behind the cabin that she'd almost strangled herself with.

The cabin looked like just another catastrophe in her life waiting to explode. "Fuck." She sank into the chair and buried her face in her hands. Alone and unwatched, Kate broke. Her body shook as the tears flowed. The pain of feeling abandoned by her father, the years of working her ass off only to be shown the door, and her failure at relationships hit her all at once. She couldn't stop the tidal waves of heartache.

The sobs tore through her. She pulled a pack of tissues from her pocket and wiped away her tears and the oh-so-attractive snot. Her meltdown subsided, leaving her with a stuffy nose. The memory of her mother, her strongest supporter, jumped into her mind. During Kate's sophomore year of college, she'd organized a team to advocate for a campus gay straight alliance and immediately came under attack. Emails and some verbal exchanges were extremely vicious, and two professors seemed to lean on Kate harder than before. She wanted to quit college, but her mother's encouragement pushed her through.

*Oh, Katie. Don't quit and give them the satisfaction of driving you out. I know you can rise above this and make it through with flying colors. You're stronger than you think.* Her mom had lifted her chin with her index finger. *I'm proud of you. Never forget that.*

"I miss you so much, Mom." Tears clouded Kate's eyes once more, but she didn't break this time. She drew in a deep breath and exhaled. She could survive a month while she considered the year-long exile challenge.

The chair scraped along the floor as she quickly rose. She lit the lamp and held it up so she could see better inside the boxes. One contained two additional lamps with fuel bottles, matches, candles, and cleaning supplies. The other two boxes had canned goods, dehydrated food packages, dried fruit and nuts, granola bars, apples, lemonade mix, powdered milk, and powdered eggs. The contents looked better suited for a trip to the moon rather than a stay in the woods. Dinner wouldn't be extravagant. And there was no coffee. What kind of a person left supplies with no coffee?

Kate whipped her head around the cabin. "Shit, how do I cook?" She stared at the red stove. A teakettle and skillets cluttered the top with wood stacked next to it. She puffed up her cheeks and blew out a breath. She was no chef, and she had no idea what to do with a wood-burning unit.

She turned toward the kitchen window and saw a note attached to the kitchen sink faucet.

**Dear Ms. Minton,**
**I left six five-gallon stackable water containers for you because your old generator broke. You'll need a new, heavy-duty generator to run the well. And since I didn't know when you'd arrive, I didn't put ice in the icebox. Stop by the general store, and we can fix you up.**
**Sincerely,**
**Riley Anderson**

"No running water!" She stared at the six large plastic containers to the right of the kitchen cabinets. *Icebox?* Was that Idaho speak for refrigerator without electricity? She opened the biggest door of a tall wooden cabinet and found it lined with tin. She shook her head. Chilling wine was going to be a problem. She turned around again, and it hit her. No toilet.

She took several long strides, stood over the wooden chair next to the washbasin and lifted its lid. "Great, a chamber pot like I'm living in the 1800s." She smacked her forehead with the palm of her hand when she realized the tool shed outside the cabin must actually be her toilet.

A contraption suspended above the clawfoot bathtub caught her eye: a bucket with a garden hose protruding from.the bottom and a nozzle dangling at the end. She was supposed to shower with *that*? She was trapped in a gigantic camping trip nightmare. A few more tears fell, but she went back outside to inspect the outhouse. No one had sat on the throne for some time by the mild odor, and the pit looked almost empty. Hand sanitizer and toilet paper sat on a side shelf.

A giant woodpile was next to the barn. Someone else would have to chop that up. She didn't venture into the barn since one end looked like it might collapse. Halfway back to the cabin, she stopped and whipped her phone out of her back pocket. "No service. Double shit."

Kate dropped onto the ground and hung her head between her knees. She wasn't sure she could handle a day of this, let alone a month or year. What the hell was her father's logic behind all of this? His comments about her great grandmother, Rosemary, and grandmother, Emmeline, made her curious, but what would she find out about him and why he left Idaho?

Sadness settled in her chest as she thought about her predicament for the millionth time. No job and no cash left her with little choice, but she had a decision to make: stay a month, take the hundred thousand dollars, and go back to Chicago, or stay a year for the big jackpot. Staying meant spending money to fix the cabin, but that should still leave her enough to live on. Wouldn't it? "My life is a fucking mess. All I do is survive."

As painful as it all seemed, Kate wasn't going to take the easy route anymore. Positive change would only come if she faced the difficulties head-on and made things happen. Sitting around feeling sorry for herself wouldn't help. She squinted into the setting sun and forced her shaky legs to stand. It was cold at nearly eight thousand feet elevation, and the temperature would plummet soon.

"Time to get busy. Too damn bad there's no wine to drink." She hurried inside. It took a few tries, but she soon had a fire in the potbellied stove and a can of soup on the cookstove. After dinner and a sponge bath—she definitely wasn't ready for a jungle shower—she made the bed and collapsed.

The howling in the middle of the night cut right through the walls and woke Kate, making her feel like a victim in a Stephen King movie. Somehow, sleep finally overtook her for a few fitful hours. When the sun poked up, she pulled the covers over her head. The cabin was freezing. She scurried out of bed, dressed, and tossed firewood into the stoves.

Her stomach grumbled loudly, so she rifled through the supply box. "Screw it. I can't think without coffee." She snatched her keys and jacket and stepped outside. The frigid morning air chilled her to the bone, and she wrapped her arms tight around her body as she hustled to her truck. She fired it up. "Thirty-two degrees!" She cranked the heater dial up to max and hoped to God it was efficient.

Kate pushed through the door of Nancy's Diner and Bakery at eight a.m. Her gaze settled on a woman standing in front of the baked goods counter to her immediate right. She wasn't wearing a coat, and her flannel shirt sleeves were rolled up, which defied logic given the outdoor temperature but revealed a nice display of well-defined biceps. Her honey blonde hair was tied in a ponytail and contrasted with the rough and tumble look of her baggy jeans and clunky work boots. When she turned, Kate swallowed at the sight of her tight-fitting T-shirt beneath the open flannel shirt.

"Here's your Wednesday éclair and coffee," the woman at the counter said. "And please remind my husband to get home early. Have a great day."

"You too, Nancy. And I promise to kick Tom's butt out the door by three."

The cute woman paid then strolled toward the door and stopped in front of Kate. Her brown eyes had gold streaks that were almost like caramel melting with chocolate.

"Good morning." She smiled broadly.

"Hello." Kate could admire those stunning eyes all day. "Judging by the crowd, this must be the best breakfast place in town."

"It sure is."

Kate looked down when she realized she'd stared for too long. Her breath stilled at the sight of a gun strapped to the woman's belt. *Damn, this is the Wild West.*

"Excuse me, but you're blocking the door."

"Oh, sorry." Kate backed into the coat rack as she stepped aside. "Oops." She caught a glimpse of the woman's toned butt before she left.

Another woman with short, dark hair dressed in jeans and a T-shirt tipped her baseball cap and smiled at Kate as she walked by. The smell of a breakfast sandwich wafted in the air from the bag she carried. Maybe Kate wasn't the only lesbian in town after all. A rebound relationship was the last thing she needed but looking didn't hurt. She pivoted and headed toward the last unoccupied booth.

A woman with salt and pepper hair, maybe in her early sixties, came to Kate's table. "Welcome to my diner. I'm Nancy. My, my, you look like you could use an entire pot of our dark roast."

"Sounds like heaven." Kate breathed in the strong coffee aroma wafting in the air as the tall, stocky woman poured her a cup.

"Any questions on the menu?"

Kate shook her head. After stirring in some sweetener, she raised the mug to her lips and took a quick swallow. The robust coffee had a rich, smooth taste. "I'll have some toast. White bread, please." Audrey's parting words popped into her head. *Every morning, you have toast, which is just like you: dry and dull.*

"Sure thing." Nancy left the mini pot on the table.

Kate enjoyed a long gulp of the black nectar and tried to push away Audrey's presence from her mind. Sure, she was a bit of a workaholic, but Audrey was no saint. Still, the sting of Audrey's words cut deep. She'd said Kate was afraid to do anything adventurous. Ha, what would Audrey think of what she was doing here? But was she just running away from Chicago, her failed relationship, and the loss of her job? Kate rested her head in her hands and closed her eyes. Maybe losing her job *and* Audrey was precisely what she needed. It was time to forget about the what ifs and move forward.

"You okay, sweetie? Maybe you need something more substantial to go with that toast. You look a little pale."

Kate opened her eyes. *Fuck Audrey and fuck toast. I'm hungry, and I'm not boring.* "I'll take an omelet with bell peppers, diced tomatoes, onions, and spinach, and a side order of hash browns and ham, please."

"Coming up."

Kate opened her phone and googled the price of land in Idaho and found that it varied widely. It dawned on her that she'd never asked about the acreage, nor could she recall seeing the amount in all the paperwork. She'd ask Howard later. Surprisingly, the county had a decent website which listed the ethnicity as ninety-seven percent white, half a percent Native American, and the rest Hispanic. That was pretty much what she expected. She skimmed further down the page to the town statistics.

"Population six hundred and fifty-seven. You're kidding me?" She stared in disbelief.

"That's our little town."

Kate jumped. She hadn't heard Nancy approach.

"Ah, I didn't realize Merrick was so charming for such a–"

"Dinky town." Nancy smiled and placed the meal in front of Kate, along with a glass and a jug of water. "What we lack in size, we make up for with quadruple heart and kindness. Eat up, sweetie. Ketchup and hot sauce are behind the napkins."

"Thanks. I don't need them." But Audrey's words rattled her brain again. "On second thought, it might wake me up." She grabbed both bottles and squirted plenty over the eggs and potatoes.

Nancy chuckled and walked off. Kate stuck a hefty bite into her mouth. "Not bad." Seconds later, the burn finally registered in her throat, and she gulped a whole glass of water. When she caught Nancy's gaze, Kate grinned and raised the empty glass in thanks.

Nancy came over with another plate. "Here's some more toast on the house. It helps absorb any excess acid."

"Thank you." The next bites weren't so bad. A tall man with gray hair and a beard came in, and everyone waved. Nancy threw her arms around him and kissed him. Kate smiled. At least, the town folks didn't seem uptight. And if lunch and dinner were as good as breakfast, she'd be coming here regularly. The stove at the cabin wasn't up to much, and if she was going to stay here for the full year, she'd be eating out a lot. She silently cursed her father for tossing her a crazy challenge. But for half a million, she could last a year. *How hard can it be?*

# Chapter Six

A LIGHT DRIZZLE FELL while Kate ate breakfast, and it hadn't let up. With no umbrella, she hastened her steps from the diner to the bank. Opening an account and depositing the first inheritance check should be quick, but the woman helping Kate wouldn't shut up.

"The gentle rain is wonderful. We rarely get much precipitation during the spring and summer, but oh, my Lord, we get slammed with snow in the winter."

The last thing Kate wanted was a lengthy conversation on the weather. She handed the first inheritance check to the teller.

The woman leaned over the counter and whispered, "There's already an account under your name. Mr. Jacobs transferred fifty thousand dollars the first thing this morning, but there's a thirty-day hold. Never seen that before. Would you like me to check with the manager?"

"No, it's okay." Kate smiled, hoping the excessively chatty woman would take the hint.

"Please check your address, and I need a copy of your driver's license." The woman swiveled the screen around.

Kate scanned the screen and handed over her ID.

The woman made a copy. "Okay, hon. You're all set." She handed Kate a booklet of complimentary checks and pointed toward the window. "The rain has stopped. Have a great day."

"You too." Kate exited the bank and glanced at her phone. "Yes, three bars." She posted a couple of pictures and tagged Sherry: *Home, sweet home. Outhouse and no electricity, but I'll fix it up.*

Sherry responded immediately. *OMG. Should I call you Grizzly Mama?*

*Funny. The only cell service is in the town, and it's eighteen miles away.*

Sherry sent a shocked ghostly face emoji. *In other words, I shouldn't assume you've joined a fundamentalist religion and become someone's twelfth wife if I haven't heard from you in days.*

Kate sent a face emoji with a stuck-out tongue. *I have to go. Love ya. Back atcha.* A smiley face and hug emoji followed.

Seconds later, her phone rang. "Hey, big brother."

"Hi, Katie, baby."

She rolled her eyes. "How's the family?"

"Good, but I'm working a lot. The businesses are a mess. What's the cabin like?"

"Rougher than I expected, but nothing I can't handle." She hoped.

He chuckled. "I don't doubt that. How's Merrick?"

"Quaint."

"I wonder if our relatives traveled on the Oregon Trail. I hope you're able to figure out more about the Idaho connection and our grandparents. Maybe we have cousins in Merrick."

Kate stopped in her tracks. Isaac was old, and his will only listed Kate and her brothers. She assumed there weren't any immediate relatives nearby, but distant cousins were a possibility.

"I'm sorry, Kate. Gotta go. Love you, sis."

"Love you too, big brother." She hung up and headed to the law office. "Good morning. Is Howard free?"

"Hello, Ms. Minton. I'm sorry, you just missed him. He left to handle a family emergency in Portland, Oregon." The secretary looked ashen. "His cousin was in a car accident and was rushed to surgery."

"I'm so sorry. Please give him my best wishes. Did he leave any paperwork for me?"

"No, but he still wants to sit down with you."

Kate made a tentative appointment, then walked over to the general store.

A short older woman smiled and greeted her. "Hello, welcome to the Anderson and Smith Store. I'm Lilly Smith. How can I help you?"

"I need a few groceries." Kate perused the aisles and picked up a few favorites and a big tin of coffee.

"Howard mentioned you'd pop by," Lilly said as she totaled up the cost. "It's a shame his cousin is in the hospital. We pray for her."

*Damn, word of mouth really does travel quickly in a small town.* "Yes, I hope she recovers quickly. Oh, please excuse me for being so rude. I'm Kate Minton." She extended her hand, and Lilly wrapped both her hands around Kate's. She thought Lilly was going to come around the counter and hug her.

"And I'm so sorry for your loss, dear. Isaiah, I mean Isaac, was such a nice man."

*Isaiah?* "Thank you. He certainly lived all ninety-four years to the fullest." The name Lilly used struck Kate as odd. Perhaps it was an old historical name for Isaac that was common around here.

"I live down the road from your cabin with my niece Riley. Don't hesitate to stop and visit or ask for help."

"Thank you. Is Riley around? I'd like to thank her."

"You're in luck. She's in the hardware store today." Lilly thumbed over her shoulder to a set of wooden swinging doors.

"You have hardware next to groceries?"

"We're a small town. Don't worry, the dirty stuff is in a separate building, and our lumber yard is a block away."

Kate pushed through the wooden doors and looked around. It was unlike any store she'd ever seen; kitchen gadgets and a display of appliances were on one side, and woodstoves and hand tools were on the other side.

A customer was standing at the counter talking to the woman Kate had ogled earlier at the diner. She deposited her grocery bag on a round table displaying product pamphlets and catalogs. When she looked back, Riley removed a long gun from a glass display case full of guns. *Jesus, how many guns does one small town need?*

"Here you go." Riley handed the gun to the customer along with a small box.

"What do I owe you?"

"No charge for the minor repair. Seven dollars and ninety-four cents with tax for the shot. You know, you'd save more money by buying a bigger box of shells."

"This will do for now. Thanks, Riley."

"Sorry about the loss of your cow."

The man shook his fist. "If that damn lion comes back again, I'll give it an ass full of lead."

"You stay safe, Pete." She waved goodbye then glanced at Kate. "Can I help you?"

"There are lions out here?" That explained the plethora of guns.

"Yep. Canada lynx, mountain lions, and bobcats."

"Oh, wow." Kate lifted her hand in a weak wave. "So, I'm Kate Minton, and you must be Riley Anderson. I wanted to thank you for everything you did at the cabin."

"You're welcome. We could shake hands, but you're standing nearly twenty feet away."

"Oh, sorry." Kate moved closer.

Riley stepped out from behind the counter and held out her hand. Surprisingly, it was soft and not rough as Kate had imagined.

"Can I have my hand back now?" Riley grinned.

Kate laughed and released her. "What other items do you think I'll need?"

"The water containers I dropped off should last at least a week if you're frugal. You can pick up more from the store or have some delivered." Riley casually leaned back against the counter. "There's nothing wrong with the well. It's over six hundred feet deep, but the old generator gave out. I have a dual-fuel one in the back that would work nicely. You'll need it for renting. August and September are the months for elk and deer hunting. But there are—"

"I won't be renting. I'm going to live there."

"Pardon?" Riley blinked, and her mouth hung open. "I thought you were only going to be here a month."

"Nope." Kate laughed. Goosebumps crawled over her skin under Riley's stare. "I need the cabin hooked up to electricity. How soon can you do that?"

"Impossible."

"Excuse me?"

Riley cracked her knuckles. "The closest electric line ends at our house, and that's eight miles from your cabin. The power company charges twenty-five dollars per foot to run a line. If you want electricity, you'll have to buy an off-grid solar power system with a hefty battery bank."

"How soon can I get one?"

Riley motioned to the table. "Let's sit down."

The chairs scraping across the wooden floor along with Riley's abrupt change in manner didn't sit well with Kate. "Is solar expensive?"

"Yes, but you need to consider more urgent repairs."

"Such as?"

"When I fixed the hole in the wall, I noticed the roof leaks and sags.

Luckily, we don't have much rain this time of year." She gestured outside and shrugged. "Today's a little unusual."

"So I've heard." Kate drummed her fingers on the table.

"We have lots of snow in the winter, and some days, it's heavy wet snow. I don't think the roof will take another winter. You need to do the repairs, or you'll have more than mice getting in."

*Dammit.* At this rate, she'd be spending all the money to make the cabin habitable. "What other preparations will I need for the winter?"

"Supplying fuel for the generator isn't a problem in the summer, but there's no way in hell—"

"Watch your language," Lilly said as she walked through the swinging doors. She came over and handed Riley a note.

"Yes, Aunt." Riley read the note and placed it on the table, face down. "Your father shut down the cabin from November through April. If you stay, you'll need a snowmobile with a sled to haul fuel and supplies. Otherwise, a storm could leave you stranded for a week or more. If you run out of generator fuel, you'd better have water in containers."

"I've never ridden a snowmobile."

"It's not hard. Do you have a gun?"

Kate crossed her arms. She acknowledged there were dangerous animals wandering around, but that didn't mean she had to be the one to shoot them. Nancy's husband entered through the back door and settled behind the counter. He opened a thick catalog and put on reading glasses. Kate looked at Riley. "No. I don't like guns."

"Ms. Minton, you're alone next to the Sawtooth National Forest. Besides the big cats, we also have wolves and western rattlesnakes. And that's just a few animals we have here that you don't have in downtown Chicago. If you won't have a gun, don't ever go out at night. Use the chamber pot. Oh, and don't ever approach a moose."

That wasn't desirable, but it was better than going against everything she believed. "When can I get everything scheduled? And can I have the cost, please?" Kate crossed her legs.

Riley rested her elbows on the table and clasped her hands together. "Are there any other amenities you want?"

"I need a modern refrigerator and freezer. How old is that icebox anyway?"

Riley tilted her head. "It's a reliable White Mountain Grand, circa

1900."

The way she said it made it sound like Kate was being unreasonable to want modern technology, but she didn't want a hundred-and twenty-year-old machine responsible for keeping her food from spoiling. "I also need a new electric stove and a bathroom. Nothing fancy. There's plenty of open room. Oh, and a small stackable washer-dryer combo." Kate looked down at her nails for a few seconds to gather some courage. There was no way she could live in the cabin for a year in its present condition. When she realized Riley wasn't talking, she looked up.

Riley stared at her coldly. "Your present cookstove is the best modern wood-burning stove available. I wouldn't recommend replacing it with an energy-hogging electric stove."

"Oh."

"For a bathroom, we're talking interior plumbing, a water storage tank, a tankless water heater, two or three one-hundred-pound propane cylinders, possibly a higher capacity well pump, and a septic tank."

Riley's attitude grated on Kate's nerves. What did she have against Kate? It wasn't her fault her crazy father had stuck her out here to earn an inheritance. "Why do I need propane if I buy a solar-powered system? Won't that do?"

"Batteries are expensive and only store so much, and a storm can block out the sun for days. You'll need propane." Riley shook her head. "Also, you need insulation to keep the heat from escaping. Unless you like frozen pipes."

Silence filled the room for a few agonizing seconds. Kate felt like crawling under the table but didn't want to appear weak.

"Installing insulation also means you'll burn less wood, unless you like getting up in the middle of the night to add more wood to the stoves." Riley leaned back and rested her arm on the back of the chair.

Kate ran her hand through her hair. This was turning into a nightmare. Maybe she should just grab the money and go. But her mother and Sherry had always said Kate's persistence was second to none. No, she wasn't going to give up this easily. "How much do you think all of this will cost, and how long will it take?"

Riley cracked her knuckles again. "You're looking at two months of construction, and if we run into problems, that timeline could stretch to three or four months. I'll need to take more measurements and examine the damage properly for an accurate estimate."

"This place is under a thousand square feet, and you've already seen it." Kate remembered Howard Jacobs saying that they didn't swindle their neighbors around here. Maybe Riley hadn't gotten that memo.

"I believe it's thirty-five by thirty, which equals one thousand and fifty square feet, and that doesn't include the porch and barn, both of which need repairs. And you shouldn't go into the barn's southside extension. It's about ready to collapse."

Kate tamped down the anger that brewed in her belly. "If I were to hire you, how soon could you start?"

"Not until September."

"What?" A sickening feeling fell over Kate.

"Ms. Minton, I'll do what I can, but I can't guarantee anything. My crew is booked."

"How much do you charge for an estimate?"

"Nothing."

"Fine. Please write one up, Ms. Anderson. Thanks for your time." Kate stood and grabbed her grocery bag.

"Anything else? How about satellite service? Maybe an outdoor hot tub?" Riley grinned.

"Yes, satellite service. And I'd appreciate it if you could call me the day before you come out."

"Yes, ma'am." Riley gave a mock salute.

*Damn arrogant woman.* Kate turned and walked toward the door. The news wasn't good, and the closer she walked, the more her body shook.

"Oh, Ms. Minton."

Kate stopped and looked over her shoulder. "Yes?"

"There's no cell service at your cabin so I can't call you. I'm free Saturday afternoon. Can I stop by around three?"

Kate nodded and marched out. When she got back to her truck, she rested her head on the steering wheel to catch her breath before driving off. A few blocks down, she pulled over where there was still cell phone reception and searched the web for contractors in nearby Pocatello. With a population of over fifty thousand, the city likely had more experienced professionals. Plus, a second estimate was sensible. After several calls, only one contractor was willing to come out for a fee of five hundred dollars to make the five-hour round trip. It was pricy, but they were able to start the renovation next month.

Staying in the cabin for a full year was looking less likely but giving up and moving back to Chicago would be admitting defeat, and she was done with that. And she had half a million dollars at the end to keep her hope alive.

The sooner the repairs were completed, the better. God help her if she had to work with Riley. Kate couldn't imagine what it would be like to work with the hot woman. *Hot?* Kate had to admit, Riley might be a pain in the ass, but she was gorgeous.

# Chapter Seven

RILEY TURNED TO SEE Tom at the counter and winced. She didn't know how much of the conversation he had heard. "Sorry about that."

"You were a little harsh. That's not like you."

Tom was a good guy who had been with the store since her dad and Uncle George opened it years ago. After Aunt Lilly, Tom and Nancy were like her parents. "I'll smooth things over later. I'm going in the back to do paperwork. Call if you need me."

He nodded, and Riley went to the dinky office/storage space off the main storage room. She rarely showed her frustration in public, let alone with a customer. She shook off her lousy attitude and reassessed the situation. Isaac's daughter wasn't an old woman at all. Riley guessed she was about her age, and she was sexy with nice curves. Kate was nice to look at, but Riley knew better than to get involved. Flings with customers never ended well, and Kate didn't have a clue about living out here. Hell, she probably got winded after a quarter-mile hike.

Riley laced her fingers behind her head and stretched. She'd acted like a jerk and would apologize later. Kate had gotten under her skin, and Riley boiled over when Kate ignored her for a few seconds to examine her perfectly polished, deep red fingernails. It reminded Riley of Beth and her feigned indifference. Kate didn't look anything like her, except they were both feminine with an incredible chest and those damned manicured nails.

Personality was important, but she loved a woman's softness. Whether it was her poor choices or bad luck, her relationship with every femme she'd dated ended because their interests never aligned or things had crumpled into an utter disaster.

She thought back on the worst of the bunch. She dated one woman for three months. One night, the woman confessed she had done jail time for stealing from her ex-husband but claimed it was a misunderstanding. No thanks. Riley didn't need that kind of trouble. Another was into BDSM, and Riley was out of there when she pulled out handcuffs and a whip. One was political and spent most of her time in Boise: the long-distance didn't work, and Riley found politics boring as hell. And all of them hated the outdoor sports that she loved.

Then there was Beth, her last catastrophe. Beth's only outdoor passion was downhill skiing. But for each hour on the slopes, Beth partied for two. Riley couldn't afford the endless hours of partying. Her body screamed from lack of sleep, and her businesses suffered.

Nope, she'd had too many disasters, and Kate was off limits.

She picked up Uncle George's old leather ledger. Although roughed up around the edges, she couldn't bear to part with it. She missed him and her dad so much. They were such good souls and would give their last loaf of bread to anyone. She took a deep breath and sighed. Her dad and Uncle George would have helped Kate. She should too, but Kate looked like a woman that needed her hand held twenty-four seven. Riley didn't have the time or patience for that.

Aunt Lilly came into the office and smacked her upside the head.

"Ouch. What was that for?" Riley rubbed her head.

"Why were you so rude to Kate?" Lilly glared at her.

"I'm sorry, but she doesn't know a flipping thing about living off the grid."

"So, teach her. You and your crew refurbished my house and decked it out in all the bells and whistles. And we're her closest neighbor. Helping her is the Christian thing to do."

Riley broke eye contact and folded her arms. "I offered, but she didn't seem too excited."

"What do you expect? You were disrespectful."

Riley knew Aunt Lilly was right but something felt off. Why did Kate leave the comforts of her city life for a world she didn't understand? "I don't want to lead a calf to the slaughterhouse. She shouldn't be here."

"Well, she is, and you don't know her situation." Lilly leaned in and pointed her finger inches from her nose. "And it's not your place to judge. Later, why don't you drive it up to Ms. Minton's cabin and do the estimate?"

Riley sighed. "I made an appointment for Saturday."

Lilly raised her eyebrow.

"She doesn't have phone service. I just can't show up unannounced, and I'm busy. The measurements will be done on Saturday. I promise."

Lilly nodded and left.

Riley rested her head in her hands. She'd taken on too much lately between the various renovation projects and bookkeeping. Yet, she wouldn't mind seeing Kate so soon, even if she was off limits.

\*\*\*

By Saturday, Kate still had trouble with the stove. She either got it too hot or took forever getting it up to a reasonable temperature. Her cooking attempts were nothing short of a disaster, but at least she didn't screw up the coffee. After breakfast, she layered up and set out for a hike, figuring she could make it back before her appointment with Riley in the afternoon. She hoped their conversation would go better this time.

Kate took off with a confident, swift stride. After only thirty minutes, her legs burned, her heart pounded, and she gasped for air. Damn, the altitude was kicking her butt. Her eyes widened at the sight of vibrant wildflowers, and a sweet smell filled the air. She snapped a few photos with her phone then sat cross-legged and drank some water, taking it all in.

The beeping of her watch alerted her to return to the cabin. As she crested the hill that overlooked the cabin, she saw a tall, lanky young man leaning against an ATV, playing with his phone. He didn't seem to notice as she approached. "Hello."

"Hi, ma'am. I'm Nathaniel Stevens." He slipped the phone in his back pocket and tipped his hat. "Riley apologizes that she can't make it. She sent me out to take measurements and pictures of the damaged sections. Could I do that now?"

"Sure. Just come inside when you're done." A part of her was relieved not to face Riley so soon, but her muscles flexing wouldn't be so bad to see again.

Kate shrugged off the notion and pondered what can of soup or other processed delight she'd have for her next meal. The roof boards and ceiling joists creaked loudly, and she glanced up. The area above the bed bowed inward. That wasn't good. The kid couldn't weigh more than one hundred and forty pounds. There was more bowing and creaking as he crossed to the other side. When he tapped the door minutes later, Kate was relieved that he hadn't crashed through the roof.

"Can I start inside?"

"Please." She stepped aside and let him in. She relaxed in the rocker and started reading.

"Almost done." He tripped over a storage box but caught himself before crashing into the center table.

"I'm sorry. I should have moved that."

"No harm. That reminds me. Before your renovation begins, you'll want to move things into storage. Don't worry about heavy furniture; we can do that. Looks like you have a nice-sized barn in decent shape, except the south side is dangerous."

"I'm aware." A wave of panic hit Kate. Where was she going to stay during the renovation? A hotel would be astronomical. She'd have to find something cheap.

"All finished. I'll get these to Riley. It'll take her a couple of days, but she'll personally deliver your estimate. Is Tuesday good?"

Riley's no show and now having to wait longer irritated Kate, but it wasn't Nathaniel's fault. "Sure. Can I offer you a glass of lemonade before you go?"

"Thank you, ma'am." He scribbled in his notebook.

She poured a glass and handed it to him. "What cell phone company do you have? I saw you on your phone earlier."

He laughed. "No service reaches out here. I was playing a game. But don't worry, Riley will get you a sweet deal on satellite service. The only thing you'll have to worry about then is downtime during bad storms."

"Did you grow up in Merrick?" She wanted to take her mind off the cabin *and* learn more about the town.

Nathaniel finished his drink and wiped his mouth on his sleeve. "My father and I moved to town after Mom died." Nathaniel rolled the empty glass on its base. "He sold the farm. Said it was too big to run without Mom. Said he wanted to walk me to school. Everyone knew the truth about his boozing, but when it's your old man, it's hard to swallow."

"I'm so sorry." Kate hadn't meant to be nosey. Although she'd only been in Idaho for a few days, she was bored of talking to herself. And Nathaniel was chatty for a young man.

"He's been sober the last four years. We get along okay. I can forgive, but I can't forget. I was ten when he almost burned the rental house down. That's when Aunt Lilly and Uncle George took me in."

46

"You're Riley's cousin?"

"Oh, sorry. I'm not a blood relation. It's just they were there for me when my real dad wasn't. I was so young, and the Smiths were so kind that I started calling them aunt and uncle. Riley's my boss but kind of like an older sister, and sometimes like a strict mom." He blushed. "I shouldn't have said those things. Please don't tell her."

"Your secret is safe with me."

"Lilly is Riley's dad's sister. His name was Richard Anderson. Did you know that he built the store with George?" Nathaniel grinned. "They built it with their own hands, then made it into a success." A shadow of sadness passed over his face. "They're both gone. Mr. Anderson died before I was born, and Uncle George passed about five years ago."

"I'm sorry for your loss." Kate refilled his glass. It sounded like Nathaniel's life with George and Lilly Smith had been a life-saver for him. His story also made her sad thinking how much she had wished for such a close family.

"Anyways, I learned a lot by watching and listening to Riley and Uncle George. They'd talk about how to fix things and what materials they'd need. They usually agreed, but even if they didn't, they were always polite. And they were super patient with me." He laughed. "Well, Riley not so much, especially the one time I hid under the truck bed cover after getting in trouble with Aunt Lilly." He chuckled.

"What happened?"

"Aunt Lilly grounded me for skipping school. I got up around sunrise the next morning and sat on the tailgate of Riley's truck. When she came out of the house, I quietly slipped under the bed cover and shut the tailgate. She started driving, and I thought she was going to Nancy's for a pastry. I figured I'd sneak out and visit my friends once she got there. It was September, and the morning was chilly, so I wrapped up in an old blanket. It was good that old wool blanket was back there because Riley drove clear to Idaho Falls. By then, I was frozen. She parked, and I hopped out at the speed of lightning. Boy, did I scare the crap out of her." He held up his hand. "Sorry for the language, ma'am."

"Sounds like an adventure." Kate smiled.

He laughed. "That was only the beginning. There were tons of people and rainbow flags."

Nathaniel clearly had no clue that he had just outed Riley. But that tiny fact made Kate smile wider. Perhaps surviving this adventurous ordeal wouldn't be so hard after all. Maybe Riley's arrogance was all for show, and Kate had judged her too quickly.

He took a drink then kept talking. "I was fifteen. Riley made me promise to raise my grades and not skip school. Then she called Aunt Lilly and told her I was helping her pick up supplies. She apologized for forgetting to mention it. It's the only time I've ever heard Riley tell a lie."

"Ah, it was only a little white one."

"I've worked with Riley at the hardware store since the middle of high school. I like it, but I really love computers. Riley and Aunt Lilly helped pay for my computer repair degree. I do that on the side. So, if you need anything, please let me know."

"I will." This kid was a talker, but Kate enjoyed his stories.

He downed the second glass of lemonade and stood. "Thank you, ma'am. I'll tell Riley you'll expect her Tuesday."

Kate walked him out and watched him drive away. She sat on the porch rocker and thought about Nathaniel's stories. Lilly had a personality that immediately made Kate feel comfortable, while Riley seemed to be a rough outdoorswoman who thought a little too much of herself. Thanks to Nathaniel, Kate now saw a different side of Riley, a softer, caring side. She needed to give Riley a chance. Maybe they could become friends after all.

# Chapter Eight

"WELL, I'LL BE DAMNED." Riley recognized the truck when she pulled up to Kate's cabin. The Pocatello Company was expensive, and they cut corners. If Kate was going to get another estimate, she should have called someone closer. Ketchum and Sun Valley were larger than Merrick, and the contractors located there were reasonable. The other contractor waved and drove away as Riley hopped out of her truck.

Her anger vanished when she looked at Kate. She wore blue jeans and a purple V-neck sweater that highlighted her nice body. Riley looked up at Kate's smile, but it didn't match the look in her eyes. Riley swallowed. She needed to focus on the job and not how Kate looked or felt. *She's just another customer.*

"Good afternoon. Aunt Lilly packed you some goodies including some ice for your icebox." Riley set the cooler down and adjusted her satchel before it slid off her shoulder. "And I have your estimate."

"That's extremely kind." Kate peered inside the box. "Oh wow, two ribeye steaks, a casserole, and fresh vegetables." She shifted on her feet. "I'm embarrassed, but I don't know how to operate the wood-burning cookstove fully. I'd be grateful if you could show me. And please stay for dinner."

"Ah, sure, but I need to go afterward to feed Hank."

Kate blinked. "Oh, in that case, show me how to use the stove, and you can have dinner with your boyfriend."

"Hank's the best boyfriend a girl can have. He's my high-energy, fifty-pound Siberian husky." Riley grinned. By the look on Kate's face, maybe she wasn't so straight after all and just gauging Riley's gayness. *You wish.*

"Then, please join me."

She followed Kate inside and placed her satchel on the table. Riley was suspicious when Aunt Lilly had asked her to wait and deliver the estimate in the early evening. Then she'd thrust the cooler in her hand and said, "It never hurts to make friends."

She knew exactly what Aunt Lilly meant, but it was wishful thinking. Yeah, Kate was attractive and an ultra-femme, but she was most likely straight. And by the look of her hands, she probably considered buffing her nails a sport. Damn, it'd be nice to date a femme that could run her nails down Riley's back during sex and still enjoyed outdoor sports. She doubted that was Kate. There was no way she'd make it through the winter. Then she remembered Aunt Lilly's words right before she left for Kate's cabin: "Be on your best behavior and apologize."

"Um, Kate, I'm sorry for the other day. There's no excuse for my rudeness."

Kate finished filling the icebox and turned to face her. "Thank you. I want to apologize for being impolite too." She shook her head. "No, scratch that. I was a bitch to you for demanding an estimate and storming out. I'm sorry. I'm really not like that."

"You were a touch irritated, but you're not familiar with living here or construction. I should've been more understanding."

Kate gave her a small smile. "Sounds like we're both a little argumentative." She turned to the cookstove. "I haven't used this contraption except to heat soup and fix coffee."

"You haven't eaten anything else for days?"

"Nope. Except the times I've been to Nancy's."

"Okay. Let's get you started." Riley pointed to the stove. "This is a cream of the crop Rosa XXL made by La Nordica, an Italian company. Porcelain steel with polished cast iron doors and façade. It's gorgeous and functional."

Kate raised an eyebrow. "Are you secretly a saleswoman for the company?"

"I ordered two, one for myself and one for a customer. The customer changed her mind before they arrived. It sat in the store for several months. Your father was in one day, and I offered it to him at a deep discount. Guess he knew the quality because he snatched it up right away."

"What do you like to cook?"

"I make a great pizza. One of my other favorites is cooking homemade soup on top while baking bread below. Aunt Lilly has a great no-knead bread recipe that's quick and easy." Riley swung the firebox open. "Your wood goes in here. If the stove is cold, it's important to build a fire slowly. I also find it easier to regulate the temperature by building a fire gradually."

# CABIN FEVER

"How do you control the temperature?"

"These air intake levers. You want to push the lever to the left a fraction after the fire catches, and it gradually gets hot. Heat it up before you go to bed, and you'll have a nice bed of coals in the morning. That'll make breakfast easier and faster."

"By the way, how dangerous is it around here? I've heard howling at night. Do people have a problem?"

Riley clenched her jaw. Kate needed to understand the reality and danger of living out in the mountains, but Aunt Lilly would be mad if she scared Kate to death. "Occasionally. One night last winter, a woman in town saw her forty-pound dog fighting with something about the same size. When she separated the stray by the scruff of its neck, she found herself holding a juvenile mountain lion instead of a dog."

"What happened?"

At the sight of Kate's wide eyes, Riley's slight irritation receded. She was so cute. "Her husband came out and killed it with his handgun. Luckily, she only suffered some scratches. Juveniles don't look like adults. They look cuddly with black fur, and brown spots, and rings on their tail, but they still have good-sized teeth."

"I had no idea."

"Most of the time, wildlife will leave you alone. The key is to be aware of your surroundings. If you see a predator, don't run. And like I said before, don't go out at night alone." Riley pointed to the canister of lemonade on the countertop. "I'm thirsty. Do you mind?"

"God, I'm a terrible host. I should have already offered you a drink." Kate poured Riley a glass. "I'm curious. Why didn't you leave me some coffee when you first stocked the place?"

Riley shrugged. "I didn't know if you were a Latter-day Saint."

Kate blinked. "You mean Mormon."

"Uh-huh. Most don't consume caffeine."

"I definitely drink coffee. Are you a Mormon?"

"No." Riley dug through her satchel. The last thing she wanted was to get into a conversation on religion. Her mom had shoved enough of that down her throat. "Let's talk about the cabin. You have a lot to think about." Riley spread out her drawings on the table. "Here are two options for staying within the existing framework. They both cost forty thousand dollars, provided we don't run into any problems."

"Really? The other company showed me a similar plan but wanted thousands more dollars. Were they trying to rip me off?"

Although Riley didn't like the other company, tearing them to shreds would be unprofessional. "They're driving farther, and you want a short timeline." Riley rolled a pen in her hand. "My plans include a couple of propane tanks, a generator, a septic tank, driveway grading and gravel, and a twenty thousand dollar solar-powered system."

Kate sat up rigid. "Why so much for solar?"

Riley shook her head and smiled. City people had no idea what it cost to bring their everyday urban luxuries into a place like this. "The price includes state-of-the-art solar panels, wiring, labor, and most importantly, the battery bank. Batteries are expensive but necessary to store electricity when storm clouds block the sun. But you still need to be conscious about what you're using. Everything but the fridge needs to be shut down when you run a washing machine. Same with the TV."

"I had no idea solar was that restrictive," Kate said softly.

"Unfortunately, you don't have a choice since you're off the grid." Riley had taken the time to prepare options, so she pushed ahead. "In this layout, we build a bedroom with a closet off the back. We'd spruce up the kitchen and build an island. More room is a good resale feature for the future." Sure, Kate had said this was going to be her home, but she hadn't experienced a Merrick winter yet. Riley had no doubt Kate would be hightailing it back to the Windy City soon enough. "This plan is fifty thousand. The barn would be a separate five thousand, but you could put that off until later." She sipped her lemonade. "You should also plan a five to ten percent margin for hidden problems."

Kate looked ashen. She swallowed and looked down.

"I believe we're a better company, but if the Pocatello Company can get the job done sooner, then I understand." Riley handed Kate the papers. "You can keep these for reference."

"I never expected it to cost this much." Kate buried her face in her hands and sniffled.

God, Riley hated to see a woman cry. When Kate looked up, a chunk of wall around Riley's heart fell. "Look. If you're desperate..." She silently kicked herself for her poor choice of words. "I mean, you could save money by cutting back on solar, but you'd have to drop satellite service and your major appliances."

Kate grimaced. "I'm a wimp. I need a connection to the real world. And how would I wash and dry clothes in the winter?"

Riley offered her a pack of tissues as tears continued to fill Kate's eyes.

"Thank you." Kate dabbed her eyes. "I'm not sure I can do this."

Riley placed her hand gently on Kate's, and her heart squeezed when Kate's sad eyes met her gaze. She appeared so fragile. Surely Kate had considered getting a loan, unless her property was already mortgaged. Then again, maybe not. Riley cleared her throat. "Using the property as collateral for a bank loan would be an option."

"The cabin's practically falling apart, and the small plot of land probably isn't worth much. Maybe I was crazy for thinking about living here." Kate's hands trembled as she raised her glass of lemonade to her lips.

Riley frowned. "Didn't you inherit all of your father's Idaho land?"

"Yes."

"And how much land do you think you have?" Did she not even realize?

Kate shrugged. "I don't recall. I was supposed to go back and talk to Mr. Jacobs, but I didn't get the chance before he had to leave town. Why?"

Riley leaned back and smiled. "I'm sure the bank would happily accept part of your fifteen hundred acres as collateral."

Kate choked on her drink. "Pardon? How many acres did you say I own?"

"One thousand five hundred."

Kate looked suitably dumbfounded. "How do you know?"

"The county's database has all the parcel maps, along with their owner's information, posted online. The last time your father sold any land was to Mr. Peterson for cattle grazing and another small section to Aunt Lilly."

"Wow."

Riley was amazed that Kate didn't appear to have read the legal papers thoroughly. But most people skimmed through the legal mumbo jumbo language, and she had just lost her father. "So, congratulations. You're one of the few that still has land mostly surrounded by the national forest."

"Trees are beautiful, and we need less deforestation in this world," Kate said. "What's your best guess on the land value?"

Riley rubbed her forehead. "Your land is remote. Don't hold me to it, but I'd say somewhere around two million."

Kate's mouth hung open.

"Don't get your hopes up. Sales move slowly around here. Sometimes it takes a year or more before you find a buyer." Riley squirmed in her seat. Why did she care if Kate sold or not?

Kate pointed to the most expensive plan with the addition. "Let's get things moving as quickly as possible."

Riley couldn't believe her ears. One minute, Kate looked like the world was disintegrating, now she was charging ahead. "We need twenty percent down. You can cut me a check for the deposit once the bank approves the loan."

"I have enough money for that now. I just didn't think I'd spend it so quickly. But the cabin will be worthless if I don't make repairs. Let's do it." Kate pulled out a checkbook from her bag.

"Now? You want to sign now?"

"Yes."

Riley scratched the back of her head. "Okay. Please read the contract carefully." She studied Kate's face and posture as she read the pages. Her body was relaxed, and the sadness was gone. She was puzzling, and Riley found herself inexplicably drawn to her. "We'll get you fixed up before winter hits."

They shook hands. Feeling the softness of Kate's skin was intoxicating, and Riley hung on a bit longer than she should have.

"Thank you. I have to admit that I'm not looking forward to winter."

Riley cocked her head. Kate had an enormous learning curve ahead, and she didn't want her faltering on her own. "Don't worry. I can get you a great deal on a used snowmobile, and I'm a member of a club. We can teach you."

Kate's smile grew, and Riley melted. But she still couldn't envision Kate living in the country long term. Instead, her mind conjured up Kate wearing a tight business suit that accentuated her curves and heels that showed off her legs. *Where the hell did that come from?*

They chatted as Kate cooked the steaks in the cast iron skillet with a bit of olive oil. The cabin filled with the smell of wonderful food, but it was the delicate floral scent of Kate's perfume and her smile that further chipped at Riley's hard exterior. *Damn, this job was going to be hard.*

# Chapter Nine

*Memorial Day*

AFTER TWO WEEKS IN Idaho, Kate was unhappy with the cabin, but she was over the shock, especially with the potential to net a couple more million. She headed to town for supplies and to visit the County Clerk's Office and the library.

Everywhere, flags and decorations marked Memorial Day. Next to the library, she noticed a simple monolith she hadn't seen before. Flowers and small flags surrounded its base. She stepped closer and read the names of fallen soldiers from World War One to Afghanistan and Iraq. For such a small town, Merrick had sacrificed dozens of its citizens.

Kate's cell rang. She rummaged around her bag, whipped it out in the nick of time and answered the FaceTime call. "Hi, Sherry. Good to see you." Kate waved and sat down on a nearby park bench. "Good thing you caught me. I was about to leave town."

"Back into no-man's-land?"

Max appeared and kissed Sherry's cheek, then captured her mouth for a deep smooch. Sherry moaned.

"Maxine, I can't see your hands. Can't you wait?"

They broke off their kiss, and Max narrowed her eyes. "We had an agreement—no full names. Or did you forget, Ms. Katherine Louisa Minton?" She gave Sherry a peck on the cheek and waved. "Bye. I'm playing in the garden while my sweetcakes works."

Sherry's five-foot-eleven-inch honey, Max, looked more like an androgynous model than a botany college professor. Her hazel eyes against her dark skin were gorgeous. Their combined, polished power couple look melted away on the weekends when they became the most down-to-earth couple that Kate knew. "What's happening in the suburbs of Chicago?"

"I switched companies." Sherry twirled in her chair.

"What?"

"I was offered a modest raise. The best part is I can work from home half of the time. What's going on with you?"

"Congratulations! That's great news." Kate gestured around her and did a three-sixty with her phone. "I'm getting to know the area. The library, diner, and general store are the biggest forms of entertainment for me. An older woman name Lilly runs the general store. She gave me a cookbook and some tips on woodstove cooking." Kate rolled her eyes. "I'm trying my best, but I'm not holding my breath for a Michelin star anytime soon."

Shery laughed. "Are you staying for the month or the year?"

"I'm going to tough it out for the year." Kate swallowed. "Oh, God, Sherry, I hope I made the right decision. I signed a contract to renovate the cabin that's going to eat up most of my cash."

"Well, for heaven's sake, you need electricity and a few amenities. And the half a million at the end is sweet, but are you sure? I had no idea it was so rough."

"I needed a change. The people are friendly, and the mountains are gorgeous." Kate looked away as she teared up. Sure, Idaho had a unique beauty, but she was out of her element and way over her head.

"Don't you dare cry on me. I can't hug you."

Kate pulled a tissue from her pocket and wiped her eyes. "It's not bad out here. It's just lonely without you guys." She choked out a laugh. "I have plenty of company if you're talking about the animals. You were right on the money about all the critters."

"Oh, sweetie, maybe they'll let you cancel the renovation contract. You can stay with us for as long as it takes to find a new job and apartment."

"Nope. I was see-sawing between cocky confidence and scared shitless, but I'm committed now. Turns out, there's more money in the property."

"How much more?" Sherry looked excited.

"After the first contractor scared the hell out of me, Riley showed up with a realistic one, and she told me there's more land than I thought—a lot more. I just confirmed the acreage at the County Clerk's Office." Kate grinned then did a little drum roll with her fingers. "I could potentially net two million from selling the land."

"So that'd be two million on top of the half-million in cash?"

"Yes. I'll tough it out, then I'm selling and getting out of Dodge."

Sherry whistled. "That changes the whole picture. I don't feel sorry for you at all now."

"You should. I still need your sympathy. I'm having to pee in a chamber pot, and my toilet is outside."

"Ew, that would *not* be for me, not for all the money in the world. Are you sure you want to do this? Hell, money isn't everything...although two and a half million for a year's discomfort is a hell of a payoff."

"I needed a change from my dreary life. Well, you guys weren't dreary, but my job sucked. Even before the merger, the hours were long." Kate took a deep breath and let it out. "And I don't know why I stayed with Audrey for so long. We were polar opposites. Sorry for spilling my guts. I'm sure you have better things to do than listen to me whine."

"You know you can always talk to me. And forget about Audrey. Are there any lovely ladies in town? Who's Riley?"

"You go straight for the throat." Kate chuckled. "Riley is the woman who owns the renovation company. We got off on the wrong foot, but we're mending fences now."

"Is she attractive?"

"Yeah, but I'm not looking for anything on the rebound."

"Forget about the past. Think about asking Riley out."

Kate rolled her eyes. "I don't think that's a good idea. *And* she carries a handgun. It's common around here, but you know how I feel about guns. And I'm her customer. It's not a good combination."

"Could be exciting for a change. You haven't dated a butch for some time." Sherry arched an eyebrow. "Maybe if you sweeten the pot, she'll give you some freebies."

"Yeah, right. I'll pin her against the wall or something."

"That's a start. Make her see some of your power, then submit to her." Sherry laughed then her eyebrows scrunched. "Sorry, an email just popped up. I have to answer it before my online meeting. You take care, and when your cabin is refurbished, we might just pay a visit."

"I'd love that. Congratulations on the job again."

"Bye, sweetie. And ask Riley out."

"You're hopeless. Bye."

Kate tossed the phone into her bag. Riley had shown a softer side to her personality when she'd delivered the estimates, a more appealing side than the cocky, abrasive one she'd first portrayed. And there was no denying that Riley's muscular frame caused her to tingle. But silently admiring Riley's physical beauty was one thing. Asking her out was crazy. Look but don't touch was Kate's new motto for now. She climbed back into her truck, turned on her iTunes playlist, and headed toward the cabin. Ani DiFranco's "Overlap" played. Kate had always imagined sitting in a bar with that song playing in the background as she locked eyes with a woman that made her heart skip a beat. As she conjured up that image, she saw Riley. Instead of her usual baggy clothes, she wore tight-fitting skinny jeans with a shirt unbuttoned down to her cleavage.

"Oh, no, no, no. No rebound romancing."

# Chapter Ten

*June*

KATE HUMMED WHILE MOVING around the kitchen. Her cooking had improved and, to her amazement, she enjoyed putting in the effort. In one week, she'd tried ten recipes in Lilly's cookbook. It was such a huge change for her. In Chicago, breakfast was toast and coffee, lunch was typically a protein bar or yogurt drink, and she and Audrey usually went out for dinner or ordered takeout. Kate had cooked more this week than in an entire year in Chicago.

After taking the bread out of the oven, she turned her attention to the six boxes near the bed and began the hunt for warmer clothes. The nights and mornings were surprisingly chilly for the first week of June. She stuffed one dresser drawer with long sleeve shirts and sweaters. In the next drawer, she found an old towel wrapped around something. She lifted it out and opened it. Inside was an antique black and white photo of a large family. Some young children sat on the floor and behind them sat three women and an older man with a weathered face. His white hair and long beard contrasted with his dark suit and blended in with his light shirt. Three young adult couples and a single woman stood in the back. All of them had expressionless faces except for the sad-looking young woman at the end, who stood alone cradling a toddler that seemed to be crying. The women wore dresses to their ankles, and Kate guessed it was from the 1800s, but the one tall young man standing in the center of the back row suggested otherwise. He wore a military uniform, and the woman to his right hung on to his elbow.

She studied the older adults in the middle row. Was this a husband with three wives? She thought all Mormons lived in Utah. The wife closest to the husband had cheekbones and wavy hair similar to her own features. Kate held the photo closer and squinted. The longer she looked, the more she was convinced of the resemblance.

She flipped it over and read the inscription: "In the year 1917, we celebrate the Gideon Christensen family of Merrick, Idaho. My son, Elijah, stands in the center back row next to his wife. His sisters and their husbands stand on each side. It is the day before Elijah departs to serve our country. Our Heavenly Father, please guide and protect him. In the name of our savior, Jesus Christ, Amen."

Her father must have left the photo for her to find. She recalled hearing that last name before but couldn't remember where. A knock on the door drew her out of her daze, and she gently put the picture back.

The wind gently blew, filling the air with the scent of wildflowers. Riley waited for Kate to answer the door, and a tingle of anticipation ran down her spine. She pushed it away, not wanting to entertain thoughts of Kate's appeal. But damn, she was a good-looking woman.

Just as she was poised to knock again, the door swung open. "Good morning, Kate. I hope it's not too early."

"It's almost ten." Kate laughed. "I may have grown up in the city, but I don't sleep in that late. Please come in. You're just in time for coffee and fresh-baked bread. I tried Lilly's no-knead bread recipe. My cooking's improved, and I promise not to poison you." She pulled Riley inside.

Heat flashed through her body at Kate's touch, and the sight of Kate in a dress that hugged her chest sent a blaze straight to Riley's core. She missed the touch when Kate dropped her hand, but the sway of her hips made Riley want to follow her inside. "I just wanted to drop off some info on windows."

While Kate sliced the bread, Riley thought about how thrilling it would be for Kate's delicate hands to touch her. Her gaze traveled up to Kate's breasts. She looked up when Kate pushed the plate to the center of the table. Kate's smirk and the sparkle in her eyes said it all; she'd caught Riley checking her out.

"If you don't mind me asking, what's the story behind you and the cabin? I mean, it's night and day compared to Chicago."

Kate's smile dropped, and her eyes cast down. The short silence was awkward, and Riley wished she hadn't asked the question.

"My parents divorced when I was ten. They remained friendly, but my relationship with my father got worse. I felt abandoned. Things improved a little in college, and he came around more after my mother died when I was twenty-four. But I never seemed to meet his expectations like my older half-brothers did." Kate threw her hands up. "For some unknown reason, he decided to give me this cabin in his will. I just wish he would have spent more time with me."

"I'm sorry."

Kate shook her head. "Don't be. Isaac was an enigma who treated everyone equally—as in, everyone and everything was a serious business deal."

At least Kate had a father. Riley missed her dad and cherished the moments when Aunt Lilly shared stories about her big brother and all the shenanigans they pulled when growing up.

"Did you know him? Did he ever come into the hardware store?" Kate asked.

"Occasionally, but mainly the grocery store. He seemed friendly, but that's not too hard with Aunt Lilly. She puts everyone at ease and draws out the good."

Kate smiled. "I agree. She's very positive and friendly. You're lucky to have such a good aunt."

"Yes, I am."

Kate pushed the plate of bread toward Riley. "Are you afraid to try it?"

"Not at all." She buttered a big slice, tore off a piece and popped it into her mouth. "Yum. I think this is better than Aunt Lilly's, but don't tell her I said that."

"You put enough butter on it." Kate's smile widened before taking a bite of her own piece.

"That's my weakness. I love butter, cheese, and any sauces with butter and cheese." She took a drink. "And good coffee."

"After the renovation, I'll have to make you some gnocchi with potato and cheese in cream sauce."

"Oh, I'm in trouble now. That sounds delicious."

"What about your parents?" Kate asked.

The question shouldn't have caught Riley off-guard since they were already talking family. She wet her lips and swiped her index finger back and forth along the edge of her coffee cup. "I was a daddy's girl. He died when I was eight."

"That's so young. I'm sorry."

If Kate stuck around long enough, she'd hear the gossip. "My mom remarried and moved to Arizona. We're not close." Riley leaned back and folded her hands in her lap. "They consider me a sinful abomination since I'm a lesbian. End of story." She gritted her teeth and stiffened her spine. For years, she hadn't cared what others thought about her, but for some reason, Kate's reaction mattered.

"Well, they sound like homophobic idiots. That's their problem, not yours."

Kate's eye contact didn't waver, and Riley looked away. She stuffed another piece of bread in her mouth and said nothing.

"My mother was much younger than Isaac. I don't know for sure, but I believe they had an affair, and I was an accident. My mom would never answer my questions, and she never spoke ill about Isaac. He was more like a strict grandfather than a father to me."

"Did you always call him Isaac?"

Kate grinned wickedly. "I used Father to his face unless I wanted to piss him off, which was most of the time as a teenager. But he was always Isaac when I was talking to my friends."

"It sounds like the two of us could write a TV drama with our weird family histories."

"Yeah." Kate took a sip of her coffee. "Isaac never talked about his family until the day he died. He said I looked like his grandmother and had 'spunk' like his mother."

"Spunk? Yeah, I can see that."

Kate shook her head. "I visited the library yesterday. There's no Minton family in the valley, and there were none in the past."

"Maybe you're looking for the wrong name."

"What do you mean?" Kate frowned and pinched her eyebrows together.

"I think your dad was part of the Christensen family. They were one of the early pioneers of this county." She ate the last bite of her bread.

"Oh, shit." Kate's eyes widened, and she jumped up so suddenly that her chair wobbled. She rushed over to her dresser and pulled something out. She placed an antique picture on the table in front on Riley.

"This is the Christensen family from 1917. Could this be my grandparents and great grandparents?"

"I'm sure Howard Jacobs would know. His ancestors were in the first wave of immigrants that settled here too."

Kate blew out a breath. "He's still in Oregon. Would Lilly know something?"

"Possibly."

"I need to see her." Kate bolted to the door.

"Wait a minute." As Riley hustled to catch up, Kate spun around and smacked into her, almost knocking her down.

"Oops, sorry." Kate grabbed her handbag and keys.

"Easy. We don't want an accident. I'll drive."

"Oh, I need to get the picture." Kate almost knocked her over again as she grabbed the picture off the table.

"Slow down, or you're going to drop it and shatter the glass everywhere." She sighed as Kate dashed to the truck with the picture clenched to her chest. From their previous conversations, she shouldn't be surprised at Kate's interest in learning about her family. But Kate's excitement was Riley's dread. The picture showed one husband and multiple wives. That made Riley's stomach tie into pretzels and her mind race. How long before Kate found out about her family?

# Chapter Eleven


RILEY HAD BARELY PARKED her truck when Kate jumped out. She hurried after her and caught the door as Kate swung it wide.

Aunt Lilly looked up and smiled. "Good morning. Did Riley give you an update on the construction progress?"

"Was my father a member of the Christensen family?" Kate asked.

The bell jingled as Riley shut the door. Aunt Lilly glanced at her for an explanation, and she shrugged.

"I'm sorry. I found a picture," Kate said. "Whether it's good or bad, I want to know about my father's background and his family."

"Let's go sit down." Riley draped her arm around Kate's shoulders and guided her to the back of the store. Kate trembled under her touch. "Nathaniel, could you please keep an eye on the grocery store. Where's Tom?"

"Did you forget? Aaron called in sick, so you sent Tom to the mill."

"Okay. Call Megan for me. Tell her I won't be making the rounds today." She didn't stop at the table but pushed Kate toward the back, and Aunt Lilly followed. "Have a seat." She hopped onto a stack of rugged wooden boxes. "Sorry. It's crowded but private."

"It's okay. What about your work?"

"No worries. Megan will take care of it. You'll meet her when we start the cabin renovation. She and I tag team as supervisors."

Aunt Lilly sat in the other seat and took Kate's hands in hers. "Why don't you start from the beginning, dear?"

Kate handed Aunt Lilly the picture. She talked with her hands as much as her voice, and the gestures showed her flustered state.

"How is my father related to them?"

"He was the son of Elijah Christensen," Aunt Lilly pointed to the young man in uniform, "and his wife, Emmeline."

*Damn.* Riley had never heard that before. How much did Aunt Lilly know?

Kate blinked several times. "Why did he change his family name?"

"Let me put your mind at ease by telling you that the Christensens are a very respectable family."

"Which makes changing his name even more peculiar, doesn't it?" Kate's eyebrows rose.

"I don't know why your father never told you." Aunt Lilly caressed Kate's cheek gently. "All I know was some sort of falling out happened years ago after your father came back from World War II. Isaiah moved away—"

"What?" Kate shook her head. "You called him Isaiah." She wrinkled her brow. "I thought that's what you'd called him before. So, he changed his full name?"

"Yes, but I don't know why. It might be about the feud with the Jacobs."

"Howard Jacobs' family?" Kate bolted upright.

Another fact that Riley didn't know. This was getting weirder by the minute.

"Maybe feud is too harsh of a word, and it's all town gossip. I shouldn't have said anything."

"Tell me, please."

Aunt Lilly wrung her hands together and sighed. "Your grandfather and Howard Jacobs' grandfather were best friends who had a falling out, but I don't know what it was about. And, honey, you have to realize that Merrick has a few loose cannons that like to gossip. It's an old story that's been exaggerated over the years."

"Howard is still out of town. Is anyone around that knows the history of the Christensen family?"

"Probably Dr. Allred. He's one of our town's doctors and a history and genealogy buff."

Kate stood. "Let's go see him."

"Whoa." Riley hopped down from her box seat. "There's plenty of time." She tapped her watch. "It's almost lunch. Why don't we relax and eat at the coffee shop, then see if we can get some more information? And maybe go to the library."

"I'm not hungry. We just had bread and coffee."

Riley put her hands on Kate's shoulders. "One slice of bread is not what I call lunch, and with your rapid-fire questions and wide eyes, I'm afraid you're going to have an aneurism and become Dr. Allred's patient before you ask any questions."

"She's right, dear. You need to calm down a smidgen," Aunt Lilly said softly.

"All right." Kate looked at Riley. "But will you go with me after?"

"Of course she will." Aunt Lilly nodded and moved toward the door. "Enjoy your lunch. Kate, I'm sure you'll get all your answers in time."

"Oh, Lilly. One more thing. Were the Christensens Mormons? They, um, looked like it."

"The preferred term by the church is Latter-day Saints. I'm not that formal. And yes, they were Mormons. So was my family, the Andersons, but I converted to the Episcopal Church a long time ago to marry George Smith." Aunt Lilly smiled and left.

"I'm hungry." *That* was a conversation Riley didn't want to have.

"Isn't Lilly your dad's sister?"

"Yes." She clapped her hands and moved toward the door. "A club sandwich and fries sound good. You should eat something; you only had one bite of your bread."

"You were a Mormon?" Kate placed her hand on Riley's arm.

"I was a kid. No big deal." She waved the question away. "Let's go to lunch."

"How old were you when you left the church?"

She dropped her hand from the doorknob. So they *were* having this conversation then. She sighed heavily and turned to face Kate. "After my dad died, my mom became ultra-conservative." She clenched her jaw. All these years later, and the anger still brewed deep down. "Her second husband was a fundamentalist. You know the type, the crazies that want to go back and live like in the mid-1800s." Bitterness slid down Riley's throat, and she bit back the pain. "Thanks to Aunt Lilly and Uncle George, my whole life changed for the better. End of story. Let's go to lunch." She pulled the door open and walked away briskly, hoping Kate would get the hint.

"And no one in the Anderson family was angry at Lilly changing religions?" Kate followed her to the back door and outside.

"The important thing is Dad wasn't mad. George was Dad's business partner and best friend. Aunt Lilly hit the jackpot with a handsome, hardworking, kind, and generous fellow." She looked for traffic, then crossed to the middle of the street. The tactic to shut down Kate's curiosity failed.

"It seems like everyone in the community likes you too," Kate said as she rushed to her side.

She pulled Kate across to the other side of the road and stopped. "There are a lot of good Mormons and Christians living in Merrick, and most aren't homophobic. But a few still hide their distaste behind a smile. The LDS Church's position is that same-sex attraction is not a sin unless the person acts on their desire. Then they view it as immoral behavior and banish the person from the church. They don't recognize same-sex marriage. So, a few people see me as sinful, a wayward soul to save. And some refuse to do business with me." She rubbed the back of her neck. "Like most of the country, things have improved in the last twenty-five years, but there's still room for improvement."

Kate smiled. "I'm guessing you're in your late thirties, maybe forty?"

Riley smiled. She couldn't help it. The change of topic and the brightness in Kate's face didn't hurt either. "I'm forty. And you?"

"Forty-two."

"Ah, my elder by two years." She motioned down the street toward Nancy's. "I'm hungry. Can we please eat now?"

A truck with a large trailer piled high with lumber pulled up beside them and Tom leaned out of the window. "I just wanted to let you know there was a problem at the mill. I argued it was their mistake and won. But the cost of lumber has skyrocketed by about fifteen percent."

Riley shook her head. "Okay." She turned to Kate. "This is Tom, Nancy's husband. Tom, this is Kate, Isaac Minton's daughter."

"Please to meet you, ma'am. If you need any help, just let us know. Around here, we're all family." He extended his hand out the truck window, and Kate shook it.

"Nice to meet you."

"We're going to lunch. Anything you want me to tell your wife?"

Tom's smile widened. "Tell her I love her, and I'll see her tonight with ribs for the grill." He waved and drove off.

At Nancy's, she had the club sandwich and Kate had a small salad. In between bites, she mentioned all the fun outdoor activities that were all within a two-hour radius of Merrick. Thankfully, Kate didn't ask any more uncomfortable questions. Riley liked her past shoved to the back of her mind, where it belonged.

# CABIN FEVER

She held the door for Kate as they left. "I've lived here my entire life, and I haven't hiked all the trails or fished all the rivers."

"Hiking and rafting sounds like fun, but I'm not into fishing." Kate wrinkled her nose.

"I'll have to show you the best hiking trails and teach you to fish. It's relaxing and rewarding. The water is so clear, and the scenery is unbelievable."

"I'm positive the poor fish wiggling on a hook doesn't find it relaxing."

"Don't you eat fish?"

"Okay. You got me there." Kate threw her hands up.

"Give it a try. I'll take the fish off the line for you. Cross my heart." She made the sign over her chest and smiled.

"Maybe." Kate shrugged, then grabbed Riley's arm and tugged her toward the crosswalk.

"Easy, champ. You're about to pull my arm out of its socket."

"Wimp." Kate swatted her arm gently. "Howard's car is parked out front. He must be back. I know none of this is your business, and you've done plenty already to help me. Thank you." She motioned toward Howard's office. "I can take it from here so you can get back to work."

"You're welcome." Riley hesitated for a moment. She wanted to be there for Kate in case she got bad news, but it was best to leave, especially since religion was bound to come up in the conversation. She didn't want any more questions tossed her way. "Howard might have more info for you than Dr. Allred."

"I'd still like to meet him and learn some about the local history and where I'm from."

She nodded. "I'm going back to the store. When you finish, come on down, and I'll drive you to Dr. Allred's."

"Thank you for calming me down earlier." Kate leaned in and kissed Riley's cheek.

Riley flushed at the touch of Kate's soft lips. "Glad to help. Maybe we can have coffee another time."

"I'd like that." Kate's bright smile lit up her eyes.

Riley smiled back as her body pleasantly tingled from Kate's delicate kiss. "Okay." She waved and walked backward a couple of paces just to grab a few more moments of Kate before she turned around and headed to the store. A half a block down the street, she looked back. Kate was still in front of Howard's office, watching her. They waved, and Kate stepped inside.

*It's just coffee.* Helping Kate was one thing, but if she didn't watch it, she'd fall helplessly into Kate's gorgeous eyes. *Dear Lord, why does she have to be so adorable?*

# Chapter Twelve

KATE STEPPED INSIDE THE office after finally tearing herself away from watching Riley. "Hello, Mr. Jacobs. I need to talk to you. Do you have a minute?"

He looked up from the copying machine. "For you, of course. And please call me Howard. May I call you by your first name?"

"Please. How's your cousin?"

"She's doing much better. Thank you for asking." He pulled out a chair for her at the oversized conference table and poured them glasses of water. "Kate, your property is gorgeous. The beauty of the forest and the stunning mountain peaks with the backdrop are amazing."

"Why did my father change his name from Isaiah Christensen to Isaac Minton?"

Howard's face fell. He closed the door to the conference room but didn't sit. Instead, he clasped his hands behind his back and peered at the artwork on the wall. After a few seconds of silence, he pointed at two.

"These are oil paintings of the valley leading up to your property. You can see the cabin in this one. It's tiny in the backdrop, but it's there."

"They're truly stunning." Kate rose and stood beside him. "Almost three-dimensional." They stood in silence, admiring the paintings for a few minutes. Kate decided on a different approach since he hadn't answered her abrupt question. "I was ten when my parents divorced. Father would come around for a few hours on my birthdays and at Christmas. When he wasn't there, it was only Mom and me and maybe a few of her friends. She was estranged from her family. Isaac was never much for conversation outside his business, and neither were my three older half-brothers. And only one of them talks to me. When I was twenty-four, Mom died. I felt adrift, like I had no family. Now Isaac is dead. Please talk to me, Howard."

"I'm sorry," he said softly.

"Howard, no one knew about the cabin or a family connection in Idaho. But my father has given me this property. Why?" She turned toward him.

"I heard your grandfather and my grandfather, Elijah, were once best friends but had a falling out. I can't help but think there's a connection. Please, tell me what you know."

He nodded. "Just remember, my dear, when we dredge up the past, we don't just find good old stories that will melt our hearts. We're also sure to find some surprises and unsolvable mysteries that might make us unhappy. Are you prepared for that?"

"I'm willing to take that chance. You know, my persistence comes from my mother's side. And it appears I inherited my pigheaded stubbornness from my Christensen side."

He laughed, and his head bobbed. "Yes, you're right about the stubbornness, at least from what I've heard. Let's sit down."

The cheerfulness drained from his face as if he was about to tell her a truly awful tale. She sipped her water, while he gulped his.

"There have been different versions of the story over the years, and those with first-hand knowledge have passed. My father said the men just stopped being civil and began to ignore each other, and the women would only give a polite nod and maybe say hello." He pointed to the paintings. "Grandfather's sister, Mary, stayed friends with your grandmother, Emmeline."

"Good for her. Women are more level-headed. Then again, I guess I'm a little biased. Tell me about the Jacobs' and Christensens."

"My family was wealthy and developed several businesses, including the mines. Elijah owned a smaller share of those businesses. When the fighting began, my family bought your grandfather out. Then the Great Depression and Dust Bowl era hit. My family rode out the hard times, partly because of luck, but mostly through their wealth. Your family was struck hard. When your great grandparents passed, Elijah sold the valley farm to survive."

"Do I have relatives nearby?" Goosebumps rippled over Kate's skin. Maybe she wasn't as alone as she thought she was.

He shook his head. "Your two aunts and three grandaunts moved west where their husbands could find work. They're spread out from Washington to California, with some in Utah. My family moved too and settled in Boise and Portland, Oregon. Your father, being the only boy, inherited the property in the end. No one else has a rightful claim to the land."

# CABIN FEVER

Kate rubbed her forehead. "I can't help but think that the feud has something to do with my father changing his name. Why all the secrets around his family? And why did he give the property to me and not my brothers? I just don't get it." She searched Howard's eyes for an answer.

"I really don't know." He twisted the empty water glass on its base. "The answer may be in a locked box that your father left for you."

All the air seemed to leave Kate's body. Bewilderment swirled within her as Howard got up and went into the vault. She rubbed her temples and tried to process everything.

"Use my office for privacy." He handed her a large, wooden box and opened his office door.

Kate moved around Howard's cluttered desk, sank into the cushioned sofa along the far wall, and placed the box on the coffee table. She stared at it for several wild heart beats before opening it. Inside, a letter and a small case rested on top of several leather-bound journals.

She snapped open the case and gasped at the two vintage Waterman fountain pens. The sterling silver overlays were tarnished, but when she removed the cap, the gold nibs were in excellent condition. She set them aside gently and removed the letter.

My dearest Kate,
My dream is for you to have the same opportunity for love and happiness as anyone else. I love you, and I'm sorry I was slow to change.
You have a spark of spontaneity to get out and make your own way. I used to think that was a weakness, but now I see that's not the case. And believe it or not, I admire that in you. The problem is, your spark is dying. There's more to life than work. I found that out far too late. Please don't make the same mistake as me.

Kate's breath hitched. Damn, her father had paid a lot more attention than she'd thought.

After my heart attack four years ago, I decided on this course of action. I wanted you to have the cabin. I decided to lure you with the money to get you to visit in hopes you'd stay. There was too much of a risk that you'd turn it down otherwise, but I know you're full of curiosity and never seem to back down from a challenge.

She hung her head and let the pages dangle in her hand. It dawned on her that he'd been planning this for years. What she wouldn't give to turn back the clock and have those years with him.

I was born Isaiah Christensen in Merrick, Idaho to the family of Elijah and Emmeline Christensen. They were devoted Latter-day Saints and patriotic. WWII changed me. I came home, and Father insisted that I marry a local girl. I refused, and we had a horrible fight. He claimed my beloved mother had cheated. The knife through my heart was when Father said I was the son of Jeremiah Jacobs.

"What!" Kate reread the last couple of sentences. "Holy shit!"

Mother was crying and said it wasn't true. Still, Father threw me out. I moved to Chicago and changed my name. Only Mother would see me the few times I came back to visit. She always denied a relationship with Jeremiah but confessed that she was not free of sin. None of us are.
Father refused to talk to me, even at Mother's funeral. I came home to mend fences when he was dying and brought you with me. You were four. I swear the years of pain and bitterness melted away the minute he saw you. Kate, you look so much like his mother, your great grandmother, Rosemary. Your beautiful wavy, dark-chestnut hair and sparkling light blue eyes match hers.

Now there was no doubt in her mind which woman was her great grandmother in the black and white photo.

But as you grew up, you began to remind me of my mother, Emmeline. I found the cedar box with her diaries years after she had passed. Although she always denied having an affair with

Jeremiah Jacobs, she wrote in the journals about being in love with JJ. I've tried to make sense of it all, but I'm old and might be mistaken.

I have cried many times knowing that Mother loved someone else, and that love put a wedge between them, and between my father and me. I once made a roaring bonfire, but when I took the diaries outside to burn them, my hands trembled as I inched toward the flames shooting into the sky. I couldn't destroy them. I tried to forget about them, but like a spirit, they called to me. I feel in my heart that Mother wanted you to have them. You're smart and can figure things out. If I'm right, you'll understand why I gave you the cabin. And I hope her journals give you some peace.

Even on paper, she still couldn't understand what he was saying.

The fountain pens belonged to her. Mother taught me to write with those pens. Father's reading and writing were barely enough to get by, but she was from a wealthier family who believed women should learn more than cooking. But they also expected well-behaved, obedient women. Like you, she had trouble with that. It's not always a bad thing.

I find it so hard to express my emotions. And because you and I tend to disagree at times, I thought a letter was the best way to tell you.

Love,
Father

Kate would open the journals another time. Right now, she could barely handle the torrent of information and the whirr of emotions. Tears threatened to spill as she placed the letter and pens back inside the box. She closed the top, and her fingertips trembled as she traced a small heart carved on the top. After several minutes that seemed to stretch to eternity, she rose to leave.

"Did you get your answers?"

She blew out a long breath and nodded. "I have something, but there's still a big mystery."

"I hope it goes some way to making you feel better. Let me get the door."

"Thank you, Howard." She forced a smile.

He opened the front door, and Kate left as fast as possible. She quickly walked to the town's small park and sat on a bench. Although she wanted to meet Dr. Allred, her sullen mood wouldn't be a good first impression. What she needed now was to go home and rest.

She dug through her handbag and pulled out her phone just as a chime alerted her to a text message.

*Hi, sis. How's it going in Idaho. Have you met any relatives or figured out why Father gave you the cabin?*

She stared at the screen for a few seconds before finally shifting out of her daze.

*I'm okay, Joel. We have distant cousins from Washington to California, but no one around here. Meeting with the local genealogy expert. Sorry, can't talk now. Bye.*

It made her feel crummy to lie, but the letter and contents of the box had left her shaken. She wasn't ready to talk to anyone right now.

*Cool. Send me a copy of the family tree when you make one. Bye, sis.*

Her thumb hovered over the phone before calling Riley.

"Hello, this is Riley Anderson. How can I help you?"

Just hearing her voice made Kate feel a little better. "Hey. Could you please drive me home? I'm in the park, and I have a headache." Kate cringed at another lie.

"Sure. Give me fifteen minutes."

***

Riley parked and waved, then leaned across and opened the passenger door. Kate placed a large wooden box on the floorboard and slid into the seat. Her eyes were puffy, and the sadness that shone on her face suggested her meeting hadn't gone well. Riley was curious but didn't pry. "Aunt Lilly packed a few extras in your grocery order. The cooler's in the back."

"That's sweet of her. Please thank her for me," Kate said quietly.

"I've found some appliances that will fit your budget and easily fit inside the cabin. We can sit down, and I can explain the details and show you other options to consider."

Kate shook her head. "I trust your judgment."

"I also talked to Dr. Allred. I didn't give him any details, except to say you needed help with family research. He said that you can catch him at the library on Monday and Friday afternoons, and he'd be happy to assist you."

"Great."

Kate's clipped answers weren't her style, but Riley figured if Kate wanted her to know what had happened, she would tell her. Maybe a little music would help. She stopped at the only light on Main Street and pointed to the radio. "Do you mind?"

"Nope."

Riley tuned the satellite radio to a classic rock station. The music was the only sound in the truck cab through several songs.

"I figured you'd be more into country music."

Riley relaxed a little when Kate finally spoke. "Nah, I'm a rebel." She grinned, cranked up Joan Jett's "I Love Rock and Roll," and sang along. Kate gave her a tiny smile. Pleased with her effort to chase some of Kate's dark mood away, Riley launched into the next song, "Sweet Child O' Mine." The line about eyes, skies, and rain fit Kate's current mood. Why was she so sad after meeting with Howard?

"Here you go. Home, sweet home." Riley got out and ran around to Kate's side. The large hand-carved box looked heavy. "Do you need any help getting inside?"

"I'm okay. Thank you again, and please give my thanks to Lilly for a delicious dinner. You can set the cooler on the porch. I know you have things to do." Kate placed the box down and took out her keys. "I'll be fine, Riley. Go on and enjoy the rest of your day."

"All right. Let us know if you need anything. Aunt Lilly and I are fantastic listeners."

"Thank you. Bye, Riley."

Riley got in her truck and drove away but looked back in her mirror a couple of times. Kate hadn't hung around to wave this time. Why were Kate's emotions affecting her so much?

She had to maintain boundaries, but her unconscious mind knew Kate had made an indelible imprint, and Riley was already too deep.

# Chapter Thirteen

ALTHOUGH IT WAS ONLY three p.m., Kate felt like a herd of wild ponies had trampled on her body. She probably should crawl into bed early, but the desire to read her grandmother's journals won out. She took a deep breath, unlocked the box, and picked up the top journal. An envelope tucked inside fell out. She read the letter to Emmeline from her mother. The leatherbound set was a gift because Emmeline loved to write. Her mother had suggested Emmeline write her feelings and thoughts down to help her see the wisdom in the union to Elijah Christensen. The letter said that Father believed that Elijah was a man of integrity and faith and that their dear daughter will be happy and bear fruit.

"Holy shit. It was an arranged marriage," Kate said to her empty cabin. She scanned ahead and stopped on an entry dated June 24, 1915. Days before the marriage, Emmeline's mother instructed her never to disobey her husband. On the wedding night, Emmeline was to lay still and not object or cry. They would isolate for the "blissful week" that followed the wedding in hopes that Emmeline would become pregnant.

A few pages further in, Emmeline wrote that Elijah was gentle and friendly, but that there must be something wrong with her because she found no joy in her "wifely duties." She also talked about how it physically hurt. Kate drew her knees to her chest and cried for her grandmother—a sixteen-year-old girl to whom sex had never been explained, a girl who was probably frightened to death when her parents forced her into marriage.

The initials JJ, written toward the bottom, caught Kate's eye. "JJ visited today. I cried for the first time." Emmeline's feelings for Jeremiah Jacobs must have been there for years. She put the journal aside and set out for a walk to clear her mind. After an hour, she returned and watched the sunset from her porch. The vibrant shades of yellow and crimson dancing over the treetops were magnificent, but they did little to lighten her mood. She went back inside to fix dinner and figured she'd read another day. But the short references to JJ drew her back into the journals like a magnet.

After the "blissful week," daily and weekly chores resumed. Emmeline wrote how she dreaded wash day and described how her hands became raw from the lye soap as she scrubbed to get the blood out of the bedsheets. The passage hit Kate in the gut. She pinched the bridge of her nose and squeezed her eyes shut for a moment before continuing. On the date July 23, 1915, Emmeline wrote, "JJ VISITED TODAY. My heart burst with joy," but no further juicy details.

Kate continued to read rapidly, but it was all mundane description of day-to-day life that made her grateful to have been born years later. Dropping off her laundry and then going to Nancy's for breakfast was a luxury compared to what her grandmother and other women had to endure back then. Washing clothes by making several trips to the stream was far from appealing, and the bucket and rippled washboard combination didn't hold a candle to the washer/dryer combo Riley had ordered for the cabin. Taking five minutes to throw a load in the machine was far superior to an entire day spent hand-scrubbing clothes with lye soap.

A growling sound from Kate's stomach made her look at the time, nearly eight o'clock. She put the journal away and prepared something to eat. It was too bad that she hadn't learned more about the western states in high school. Her history teacher had spent an enormous amount of time discussing the transcontinental railroad, and how it changed the economy and improved travel. The boring teacher glorified westward expansion and talked about how the men were brave. He never talked much about the women's sacrifice, or how the railroad companies and whites confiscated Native Americans' land and destroyed their homes.

Another punch in the gut. The very land her cabin sat on once belonged to the Shoshone and Bannock tribes. Did Kate's European ancestors fairly compensate the tribes? Probably not.

No longer hungry, Kate shoved aside her meal. Tomorrow would be better. Right now, she was fried from the overload of information and emotions.

After placing the leftovers into the icebox, she washed up and shuffled to bed but tossed and turned. She needed to think positive, and the first thing that popped into her mind was Riley. Even though Riley was clearly slammed with work, she had been wonderful to Kate. And her body. Oh, my heavens, her sculptured arms and perfect muscles made Kate dream about the rest of her body under those clothes.

Kate's hand slipped below her pajamas. It wasn't long before she tipped over the edge with the most self-pleasure she'd had in the longest time. And if that was only a fantasy, what would the real thing be like?

# Chapter Fourteen

A COUPLE OF DAYS had passed since the discovery of her father's letter and her grandmother's journals. Kate busied herself by cleaning the cabin and reading Emma Donoghue's *The Pull of the Stars*. It surprised and delighted her that the Merrick library had the book. Still, her grandmother's journals called to her.

After showering, Kate drove to town with a bag full of laundry and several of the journals in her backpack. Just as someone had on her first visit, a member of the staff gave her an overview of their services and emphasized that horse and animal blankets were washed in separate machines.

"Can't find that in Chicago." Kate laughed and headed to Nancy's Diner. As she swung open the door, her mouth watered at the smell of fresh-brewed coffee, baked goods, and other delicious aromas. One of the waitresses filled up a coffee cup and placed it on her table.

"Thanks, that will do me for now. I'll order in a few minutes." Time stretched on as Kate read more journal entries.

"Hi, honey. What are you reading today? That book looks old and fancy."

Nancy topped off her coffee, leaving just the right amount of room for the extra cream that Kate loved. She was noticing little things like that, where people remembered her preferences. It made her feel seen. "It's a history book." She didn't want to share the truth with anyone just yet.

"You need to eat something. You've been drinking coffee for an hour. I don't mind you hanging out, but heaven forbid you pass out from lack of food." Nancy chuckled. "What can I get you?"

"Give me a few more minutes to finish this chapter, and I promise to order."

Nancy put her hand on her hip. "Ten minutes. No more."

Kate opened the book where she had left off. Now and then, she'd found an exciting passage, but most often, the entries described hardships.

She skipped ahead to January 1916 where Emmeline mentioned JJ came to stay with her after Elijah had gone hunting for elk because they were running out of meat and hungry.

"It is cold, and the snow is high, but JJ arrived with trout. We had a feast and kissed for the first time. My body awoke with pleasure."

Her grandmother had lived on the edge of danger. Perhaps her father was right, and Kate *was* like her. Moving out to a cabin in the middle of BFE, where she was surrounded by lions and wolves, was damned dangerous too.

***

The brochures on the solar-powered system had been sitting on Riley's desk for days. She needed to get them to Kate but had been avoiding her since Kate had discovered the picture and the truth of her paternal relatives. Riley wished they hadn't been Mormons. But she most wished that Aunt Lilly hadn't told Kate how she was raised. It was hard to be mad, but that little slip-up would likely bring more questions when Kate had recovered from her own bombshell.

Riley grabbed the printouts and headed to Nancy's for a tall cup of coffee. She hung up her jacket by the door and noticed Kate sitting in one of the booths reading an oversized leatherbound book that looked a lot like Uncle George's ledger. She approached and cleared her throat. "That must be some interesting reading. Your mouth is gaping."

Kate looked up. Her eyes were tinged with sadness, and the sight nearly buckled Riley's knees.

"It's one of my grandmother's journals," Kate whispered. "That's what was in the box Howard gave me."

"Oh, wow." Riley adjusted her cap. "I was worried about you yesterday. You seemed to be in shock."

Kate pressed her lips together and nodded. "It was jarring, that's for sure. Not knowing a damn thing, and then it all drops in my lap." She motioned to the empty bench across from her. "Will you join me for breakfast?"

*Don't sit. Don't you dare.* But Kate made her heart flutter. "Okay. I'll happily join you if it helps erase those worry lines on your forehead." She sat and found it hard to take her look away from Kate's lovely face.

"Riley, dear, you're late. Do you want your usual?" Nancy asked as she approached their table. She sat a massive mug of coffee in front of Riley, refilled Kate's cup, and set the pot down.

"Morning, Nancy. I'm good." Riley sipped the coffee. "Yum, the best in the state."

"I'm ordering." Kate bumped Riley's hand. "Coffee creamer doesn't count as food. Or do you not believe in eating breakfast?"

Nancy laughed. "Oh, she can eat. Donuts every Monday after dropping off Lilly, then it's an éclair on Wednesday. If she doesn't order her usual, I assume she's not well."

"Okay, okay, okay." Riley threw her hands in the air. "I'll have eggs sunny side up over corned beef hash."

Kate smiled. "I'll have the omelet with bell peppers, spinach, and cheese, and can I get some fruit on the side, please?"

"Sounds like you're developing a favorite too." Nancy winked and walked away.

"We'll both have my usual Friday apple fritter after our meal too, please, Nancy."

Nancy's laughter echoed throughout the diner. Riley eyed Kate's book as she sipped her coffee, then looked up at Kate. She still looked sad. Riley couldn't ignore the journals since Kate had brought them up. And maybe it would do her some good to talk about them. "Do you care to tell me about your grandmother?" She tapped her index finger on the hard leather book.

Kate looked at Riley over the rim of the cup. "They're mostly boring entries about chores."

"If it's all boring stuff, then why the long face?"

Kate's cup rattled as she set it down, and coffee spilled over the edge onto the table. Riley grabbed a napkin and wiped it up before it could reach the journals.

"My grandmother had an affair."

Riley paused, then she tore more napkins out of the holder and finished wiping up the mess. "Some conservatives say that everything was different before the fifties. They preached that everyone was once super religious, totally chaste, and only had sex to make babies. We both know that's bullshit. Most adults reach out to one another for love, comfort, and sexual pleasure, not just to have kids. That's true as it has been true since the dawn of time." Riley tossed the wet napkins down and rubbed her forehead. "I don't know your grandparents' situation, but it was pretty rough back then. Some women were treated as property, and their every move was planned by a male family member or their husband. Any woman who had an affair probably did so because she was unhappy in her marriage. Your grandma's lover likely treated her better."

"I know." Kate sighed. "It's just a bit of a shock, and it adds a bit of apprehension that my grandfather may not be my actual grandfather. My father said in his letter that my eyes and hair matched my great grandmother's. But who knows..." Kate stopped as Nancy approached.

"Here you go, ladies." She placed the platters in front of Kate and Riley and hurried off to another table.

Riley seasoned her eggs. "It was taboo for our grandmothers and great grandmothers to write about sexual feelings. I think most diaries written back then were boring. But that might just be me." She grinned. "I have to admit that I like women-loving-women mysteries and sci-fi books with a little romance and sex."

"Really?" Kate arched an eyebrow. "I bet you have a hard time finding those in the library."

"My smartphone loaded with eBooks is all I need for a little relaxation." *What the hell am I doing flirting?* "Anyway, these are the brochures on the solar-powered system that we plan to install at your cabin. I think a ground-mounted system would be best. It'd be easier to brush the snow off."

Kate smiled. "Can you recommend any good lesbian novels about living off-the-grid?"

The flirt took Riley by surprise, and she wasn't sure if Kate was serious or joking around. She shrugged and tried to focus on the work. "The solar-powered system is going to be around twenty-two thousand dollars. I wanted to make sure that was okay before I ordered it."

"Thanks for checking. Yes, please place the order."

Kate placed her hand on top of Riley's. Her skin was soft, and the sensation shot through Riley, sending tingles rippling down her body.

"I'm sorry, again. I came into town pitching a fit over construction like a spoiled brat."

"You apologized once. We're good." Riley extracted her hand to hold her coffee cup. She gripped it hard as she tried to hold on to her last shred of professionalism.

"When I read about the hardships my grandmother endured, I realized how lucky I am. My grandmother survived through all that, so I'm going to try my damnedest to make this place work for me."

Riley breathed a sigh of relief at the shift in conversation back to the cabin. "I have good news. We can start on your place in July ahead of schedule because another customer postponed his project. The road crew will be at your cabin Tuesday through Friday next week. Will that be okay?"

"Fantastic." Kate glanced down at her plate.

"Is something wrong? A funny look just crossed your face."

"My grandfather, Elijah, hunted and fished for food, but it was my grandmother, Emmeline, who had to gut and clean it." Kate grimaced. "It's going to be heaven to have a modern refrigerator and a more spacious cabin."

Riley smiled widely. "What's wrong with fishing? It's peaceful. You really should try it since you like trout. There's nothing like fresh steelhead, caught and cooked over the fire on the same day. Why the arched eyebrow?"

"You keep mentioning fishing. I can eat fish, but I can't stand the thought of catching one, and the cleaning is just gross."

"Hey, if you go with me, I promise to clean the catch."

"Ah, I'm not sure."

Riley faked an exaggerated pout. "Please."

"I might go with you sometime and sit on the bank, but I'm not going to guarantee I'll do any of the fishing."

"Deal." Riley extended her hand.

"Dear Lord, what have I gotten myself into?"

They shook hands, and Riley reveled in the feel of Kate's skin. *So much for boundaries.*

\*\*\*

After chatting over the meal, Kate was sad to see Riley go. She watched Riley strut across the street through the picture window. Her rugged, confident personality no longer rubbed Kate the wrong way. Instead, it was a turn-on. She shook her head and went back to the journal. By the middle of 1916, the kissing and touching between Emmeline and JJ had increased. Emmeline talked about her longing to be with JJ. She underlined the words "I dread my wifely duties." Although Elijah couldn't read and write very well, she'd had to find a new hiding place for the box because Elijah had become suspicious.

"More food or coffee?" Nancy asked.

"It was all scrumptious as usual, but I'm stuffed." She pushed the plate with a half-eaten apple fritter to the side.

"Okay. Let me know. If you stay here much longer, it'll be lunchtime."

"Oh, gosh, I got carried away." Kate glanced at her phone. "I need to go to the library."

Nancy put her hand on Kate's shoulder and squeezed lightly. "I don't mean to rush you off."

"No. It's all good. Thank you, Nancy."

After she'd paid, she walked to the library. She sank into the old mauve-colored love seat behind the back of the research books and pulled out another journal written in 1917. Kate skipped ahead because reading everything would take too much time. There was less about Emmeline being unhappy over chores and life's hardships, and more about the town's history, the mountains' beauty, and JJ. She described how thrilling it was to hold hands and kiss when walking in the woods, but she was terrified about getting caught. The entry ended with "JJ completes my life."

Emmeline and JJ were living on the edge, but it was baffling. Some of their outings were in town. Surely people noticed their subtle displays of affection. And why did her grandmother go on and on about intense feelings but not describe JJ? Kate glanced at her watch. Her first meeting with Dr. Allred was a half hour away, so she skimmed further ahead to entries written in April.

Her eyes zeroed in on the wording, "JJ entered inside me. My breathing and heartbeat drummed like a galloping mare. The world around me ceased to exist. JJ didn't stop. My body quivered and shook in pleasurable ways I had never dreamed of. It is the most incredible thing in my life. I love JJ."

*Holy shit.* Her grandmother had just described her first orgasm and pronounced her love for another man. But something was off. She should have been knocked up every year with all this extra sex she was having.

# CABIN FEVER

Maybe she had difficulty getting pregnant, since her father was born years later in 1925. Kate wondered if her grandfather was even around. She googled World War I and found that the first draft registration didn't occur in the US until June 5, 1917.

Kate slipped the journal and her phone into her handbag when she caught sight of a white-haired man walking toward her. His black shiny shoes, black slacks, and a short-sleeved white shirt with a blue and red striped bow tie made him the most dapper dressed man she had seen in town. She rose to greet him. "You must be Dr. Allred."

"That's me." They shook hands. "I've booked a conference room for privacy. Please follow me."

After discussing the library's collection, Dr. Allred explained DNA testing accuracy and the different genealogy websites. When Kate told him that she'd ordered test kits from three companies, he smiled and said he'd done the same for his testing.

He patted her hand. "It's exciting when DNA matches come back and link you to distant relatives. It helps fill out your family tree."

A desire now burned deep inside to identify as many ancestors as possible. There had to be distant relatives still alive. Perhaps she could even meet some of them.

"Well, that does it for today. Do you have any questions for me?" Dr. Allred asked.

"I've been reading historical accounts from women pioneers." Which was true, but he didn't need to know that they were her grandmother's. "I was um...wondering..." Kate bit her lower lip and looked away.

He put his hand over hers. "My dear, I'm a physician. There's not much I haven't heard. Nothing embarrasses me, and I have always upheld the medical and ethical oaths that I've taken. Whatever you say to me or ask about will remain in private. Please, go ahead."

Kate nodded. "Families were large when settlers moved west. I've read about the period after the wedding being referred to as the 'blissful week.' Or wording like, 'I rested in—'" Kate cleared her throat. She didn't want to say JJ. "'I rested in my husband's arms,' but nothing that mentioned sex." Heat spread from her neck to her face.

"You're correct. Most people didn't write about sexual desires and fulfillment, especially women. That's why the topic was often cloaked in flowery words."

"What if a spouse loved someone else and wanted a divorce?"

"That was frowned upon. Anyone who did that was disowned by their family and the church. If a woman was viewed at fault, the husband or his family would take the children away. The punishment was far harsher on the woman, and a man's word was usually never questioned. Sadly, women were typically blamed for the affair."

"Did anyone ever get away with a slap on the wrist, like if they were wealthy or prominent?"

He arched an eyebrow, perhaps at the specificity of her question. "I'm sure that occurred, and wealthy families certainly had the means to cover most things up. But the court and churches didn't act if the offended spouse didn't press charges."

"But the rumor mill—"

"Would have been vicious because of the hardships of living in small, isolated communities. Any other questions?"

"Not for now. Thank you."

"You're very welcome." He wrote a number on the back of his business card and gave it to her. "This is my home number if you have additional questions. The office number is on the front. Riley mentioned you were new in town and needed to find a local doctor. I'm not taking any new patients, but Dr. Alice Hubert is top-notch." He smiled. "I was Riley's doctor from birth until six years ago when she switched to Dr. Hubert. If anyone can get past that thick skull, it's Dr. Hubert. Riley has a history of not following doctor's orders, like when she broke her leg and planned to go back to work earlier than Dr. Hubert's recommendation. Dr. Hubert paid her a visit to chew her ear off. Riley's a good person but a tiny bit stubborn." He laughed. "I hear she's going to work on your cabin. In construction, stubbornness pays off. She's good, and fair, and won't settle for anything half-baked."

"Good to know." Kate wasn't sure why he'd launched into Riley's medical history—it certainly wasn't professional—but they did things differently out here compared to Chicago. Perhaps it was a generational thing. He had to be in his mid-seventies. Whatever his motive, Kate was pleased at his sincerity. After Riley said her stepdad didn't want a "sinful abomination" around, everyone in town probably knew she was a lesbian.

Outside the library, she called Sherry and told her everything. There were a lot of OMG statements and expletives. Kate didn't know when or even if she'd discuss the journals with Joel. He seemed caught up with Roger and Karl in straightening out Isaac's business issues, so he probably didn't have the time for family stuff.

Without thinking, she called Riley.

"Anderson and Smith. This is Riley. Can I help you?"

"Hi. If you're not busy, want to grab a coffee or something? I can tell you all about my meeting with Dr. Allred." God, she sounded like a lovestruck teenager.

"That sounds good."

Kate smiled. "See you soon."

The line between customer and contractor had officially blurred. They were becoming friends, and who knew where it would go from there. She wouldn't push, but Riley was a good listener, and Kate enjoyed her company. That would do for now. Well, that and a few lustful nighttime fantasies.

# Chapter Fifteen

KATE SAT AT THE table in the center of the room with her head propped on the palm of her hand, staring at the austerity of the cabin. She had adjusted to sponge baths, stoking the woodstoves, and even the cooking but living in the cabin was lonely. Over the past week, she hadn't seen Riley or Megan and wouldn't for another week. They were busy trying to catch up before leaving for a conference.

She glanced down at the bills on the table. Not taking out the bank loan had been a poor decision. And on top of that, her gas-guzzling truck cost a fortune to fill up. In Chicago, she could hop on a bus or the L train and be almost anywhere in the city for a cheap rate.

Last week, she reduced her town trips to twice a week, hoping to save money. Not seeing people for stretches on end was driving her nuts and talking to herself had become so frequent that she had also begun to answer herself. There were good days and bad ones. Today was shaping up to be the worst.

"I'm screwed. What am I going to do in the winter?" She covered her eyes with her hands. Riding a snowmobile into town didn't seem realistic, even if Riley trained her. She'd have satellite internet and TV once the cabin was done. Video chat from a warm living room and watching the snow fall outside sounded nice. But she never was much of a homebody and certainly didn't want to turn into a couch potato glued to the TV.

An owl hooted loudly outside. "Jesus. It sounds like you're sitting on my front porch. Better an owl than a lion, I guess." The sounds from the past week had woken her several times in the night, and she'd had trouble getting back to sleep. She'd dozed off twice in the day while reading and was too tired to think about much of anything else.

"Suck it up." She shuffled over to the rocking chair. Her dinner plate remained on the coffee table. "The bonus of living alone is I can be as messy as I like." Kate choked back a rising melancholy at the many cons of living alone. "Maybe I should get a dog or some cuddly pet. I wouldn't sound so crazy talking to myself."

Deciding to stay for a couple million dollars had seemed like a no-brainer, but, as Riley had pointed out, land moved slowly around here. The thought of getting stuck with the property sat like a rock in her stomach. Tears welled in her eyes. To add more misery, she had no job prospects.

"I'm in the middle of bloody nowhere. What the hell was I thinking?" She grabbed the box of tissues, and her crying grew to sobbing. After a while, she kicked the coffee table, and the plate crashed to the floor and luckily didn't break. "Fuck. It's too late to change my mind now." She cleaned up the mess and wandered to the kitchen. A rancid odor drifted up as she opened the rubbish bin. Twilight wasn't a good time to take out the trash with all the nighttime prowlers around. But she couldn't ignore the horrible stench. The trash had to go out tonight.

She pulled the bag out and stepped out on the porch. Something had gotten into the outdoor bin three nights ago and scattered trash all over the ground. That same something could be waiting for a fresh bag. She swiveled left to right, looking for any danger as she walked forward. "Chickenshit, get your damn life in order." She tossed the bag inside the large trash can and secured the new lock. A slight movement caught her attention, and she jumped. A tiny kitten waddled toward her, looking cold and frail.

"Where's your mommy?" She scanned the area but couldn't see anything, then bent down to examine the furball, whose eyes looked barely open. Then the poor thing let out a hungry growl and dropped onto the ground. "Poor baby, you're starving." She gently picked it up. It extended its claws and let out another cry. "I'm not going to hurt you, little fellow. I can feel your bones. You're so scrawny." She looked around again, but even the kitten's cry hadn't brought out its mother. "Damn, if I'm food for the lions, something's going to make a meal out of you." She stroked it and then hurried back inside.

Kate had another restless night as the poor thing cried on and off for hours, tearing her heart apart. With heavy eyelids and her large coffee travel mug, she drove to the nearest pet store early in the morning. Not knowing the kitten's age, she picked up milk formula and a syringe, pâté for young cats, and several toys. It would have to do as the vet didn't have any appointments for three weeks. They told her to call back immediately and bring him in if his condition worsened. Kate figured that'd cost a pretty penny.

She tried the formula first as the saleswoman had assured her it had the most nutrients. The little bugger scratched her a couple of times but greedily drank what Kate squirted in his mouth.

"What are we going to call you, little buddy? How about Muffin?" She wiped his fur off with a warm moist rag. He growled back at her but didn't scratch this time. "Someone's grouchy, but you're all clean." She stroked his fur, and he seemed to calm a little. "You're going to have to wait to meet Riley. She's been busy, and tomorrow she leaves on a trip."

Kate had dinner with Lilly one night at the diner, and Riley was supposed to show but didn't. Lilly explained that Megan was as cool as a cucumber, but Riley was running around like crazy trying to get things done before leaving for the International Green Building Remodel and Construction Expo. The expo ran for three days, and Megan booked them a room for a week. When Kate found out the expo was in San Francisco, she almost begged to go. It was a fun city. But truth be told, seeing and being around Riley had become the highlight of her days.

"God, I'm thinking like a music groupie and not a grown woman. Plus, I wouldn't have you, little buddy, if I'd gone."

Muffin dug his back claws into her leg as he jumped to the floor.

"Ouch. For a little shit, you sure do have some sharp claws."

Over the next week, Muffin ate vigorously, both the milk from the syringe and the pâté. His strength and weight grew, and he became more playful. Just watching him play with his toys was entertainment. He'd make his unique meow and hiss before pouncing on them and batting them around. It made her laugh.

She picked him up and played with the dark fur trim around his tan-colored ears. "You have the cutest little ears." She stroked him gently. He'd grown less afraid of her and hadn't scratched her since the first couple of days. But she wore long sleeves just in case. He might've had tiny claws, but they were damned sharp and painful. "Do you want to stay with me?" She kissed the top of his head, and he looked at her with his beautiful round eyes. "I have to admit that I'm a lot happier with you around."

The sound of gravel crunching alerted Kate to an approaching vehicle. Muffin catapulted from her arms, and his claws pierced through her long sleeves. "Ow, you little shit."

She opened the door to Riley. "Hi." She gave Riley a hug and held on longer than usual. Riley's body tight against hers was warm and comforting. She stepped back to put distance between them. "It's great to see you." Oh, that tight California T-shirt looked good on her. "How was your trip?"

"Good morning. The conference was good, but I like being home. Here's some cinnamon bread that Aunt Lilly baked for you." Riley flashed a grin. "Are you going to let me in?"

"Sorry. Please come in." *I was just ripping your T-shirt off.* She stepped back and motioned Riley inside.

"Ready for the cabin renovation?" Riley sank into a rocker.

"Sort of but I came across a surprise that might be a small logistical obstacle."

"What?"

"I found a kitten right before your left, and I've grown attached to the little hellion. I've named him Muffin. I can't take him to the bed and breakfast that I've booked." She grinned. "You have a dog. How about a little sibling?" When Riley didn't answer, Kate waved her hand. "Sorry, I'm sure you and Lilly don't need another pet messing up the house. I'll take him to the shelter. It's a no-kill shelter, right?"

"Where did you find this kitten?" Riley raised her eyebrow.

"By the garbage bin." Kate went over to the bed and looked underneath it. "Come on, Muffin. My friend won't hurt you." She scooped him up, ruffled his fur, and sat back in the rocker. Muffin let out one of his healthy half meow-half growl sounds.

Kate smiled. "Want to pet him?"

Riley bit her lip and shook her head. "So, you're an animal lover?"

"Yep. What's not to love about this little guy? I couldn't leave him outside to be eaten by wild animals." Muffin crawled up on her shoulders, and Kate winced. "Easy, buddy. He's shy but so cute. I like his ears the best. Maybe I should have named him Two Tone Tommy." Kate laughed. "You're one of a kind, aren't you, little guy?"

"Um, you can't keep Muffin or take him to the animal shelter."

"Why not?" Kate pulled him out from behind her head. He clung to the cushion with his claws, but they retracted as she placed him on her lap and petted him. "Besides being so freaking adorable, he's curious and smart. And he loves affection."

"Have you ever seen a cat with such unique ears? And ear tufts like that? And with such a fat stubby tail."

"That's what makes him so adorable." She picked him up and nuzzled her nose against his face. His claws popped out, but he didn't swipe her. She sat him back on her lap and looked at Riley. "Are you only a dog fan?"

"Please don't get your face that close to," Riley cleared her throat, "little Muffin again. You have to do something now before this relationship between you two becomes too toxic for him."

She pouted. Why was Riley being so obtuse? She enjoyed having him around, and he was great company. He'd brightened her days over the past week. "What are you talking about?"

"Kate, you don't have a kitten."

Muffin snuggled into Kate's belly, and she continued to pet him. "You're not making any sense."

Riley leaned closer. "Muffin is a wild bobcat."

She stilled her hand then looked down at the bundle of fur. Muffin's saucer eyes peered up at her, and he made that unique sound again. "Damn. I was wondering why his meow sounded like a cross between a screech and a growl."

Riley shook her head. "Let's drive to Lilly's and call Zoo Boise and see if they have room. Not all wild animal rescue places take predator cats. If you wait too long, he'll get attached to you and won't be able to learn how to hunt. He'll grow to twenty-plus pounds in no time, and his claws and teeth will become sharper and thicker. No matter how gentle you think a wild animal is, it can still pose a danger. And the last thing you want is to have to put him down."

"I had no idea. I never meant any harm."

"I know." Riley smiled. "Think of it this way: you saved the little guy from being another predator's meal."

Kate's heart ached. It was the right thing to do, but she'd miss Muffin's company. "Tell me about your trip on the way to Lilly's."

Not seeing Riley for days had created a depth of loneliness within Kate that was unlike any other she'd experienced, and they weren't even dating. But just hearing Riley's voice relaxed Kate like a lullaby. Now she needed to get gutsy enough to ask Riley over more often without sounding lonely and desperate.

She bit down on her lip. She was crushing big time. But if Riley had the same feelings, she didn't let it show.

# Chapter Sixteen

*Fourth of July*

THE JAUNT INTO TOWN cheered Kate up. Howard offered her a part-time job, and she happily accepted. It required online research and for her to coordinate with other law offices across the state. The offer saved her sanity, and she sure could use the money. She entered the general store with a smile, excited about the much-needed dose of mental stimulation. "Good afternoon, Lilly. Happy Fourth of July."

"Hello, Kate. Did you enjoy the parade?"

"Yes, I did."

"It's too bad we can't have fireworks, but the chance of starting a wildfire is too high with the drought."

Kate missed the big display of fireworks that she'd watched every year at the pier in Chicago. As a child, her mother told her the fireworks were a special occasion to mark her birthday month. But she didn't want Lilly to know. She didn't want to be a bother to her new friends. What was there to celebrate about being over forty anyway? Good God, she was going to be forty-three.

"It's such a lovely day." Lilly said. "When I get home, I plan on relaxing on the back porch with a good book and a glass of iced tea." She tapped her finger on her chin. "Or maybe a glass of wine."

That tiny revelation surprised Kate. With the exception of one bar in town, she thought the county was dry. "I planned to pick up veggie burgers, bread, and marmalade, but wine sounds better. Do you sell wine here?" She enjoyed wine but hadn't drunk any alcohol since Chicago, the day everything slammed into her.

"No, they only sell alcohol at the bar. But you don't want to go into that cowboy joint. I order from a store in Ketchum and have a small collection. I'll bring some to your cabin the next chance I get. What do you like, red or white?"

"I enjoy both, but most of all, I'd enjoy your company." She didn't like to drink alone and knew what that led to.

"You're sweet. How have you been?"

"Sad since Muffin left, but I just got a part-time job with Howard, so I'll be in town more often. Being at the library, diner, general store, and seeing my favorite people—I can't think of anything better." Kate smiled.

"Oh, the job sounds exciting."

"And Riley's crew finished installing the septic tank yesterday. Things are looking up."

Days ago, Kate had tucked the box with the journals into storage. Since taking Muffin to the zoo, she'd focused on what lay ahead. There'd been enough emotional surprises for a while. They turned at the swoosh of the swinging door that separated the groceries from the hardware side, and Riley rushed in.

"Aunt—oh, hi, Kate—I was inspecting the construction of the Fraziers' new sunroom. Mr. Frazier wanted me to give you this grocery list for pickup tomorrow." Riley plopped the list on the counter and swiftly pivoted toward the hardware store.

"Just a doggone minute, young lady." Lilly smacked her hand on the countertop.

Riley stopped frozen halfway through the door and turned her head. "What'd I do wrong?"

"Take a break and chat with our neighbor and friend." Lilly motioned to Kate.

Kate suppressed a giggle at Lilly's not so subtle, "Where are your manners, young lady?" Riley came closer and leaned against the sales counter.

"Hello, Kate. How are you today? Have you been happy with the work so far?" Riley's tone was soft and measured.

"I'm fine, thank you. Now that the septic tank is in, I can't wait for demolition and construction to start. A real bathroom instead of an outhouse will be heaven." She smiled.

"Good."

The door swooshed again, and Nathaniel came in. "Hi, everybody. Riley, I'm back early. I'll relieve Tom at the counter. Bye."

Lilly shook her head. "And there he goes. Everyone's running like a chicken with their head chopped off. My Lord, I can't keep up with you all.

I guess things are hopping on the hardware side."

"Can't complain. Sales are good, and I just booked another renovation to begin after Kate's place. Being busy makes the day go by faster." Riley opened the beverage refrigerator and turned her head to Kate. "Want a pop?"

"Pop?"

Riley held up a can of Coke. "Or would you prefer something else?"

"I'll have a Sprite, please."

Riley handed Kate the drink, gave Lilly two dollars, then chugged a good quarter of the cola before Kate had hers open.

"So, ladies, when does demolition start?" Lilly's eyes sparkled.

"Part of the supplies are being dropped off tomorrow with demolition beginning soon. I'll see what else we need from there." Riley turned to Kate. "I did my best shifting the schedule to July."

"And I'm so grateful for that. Thank you for everything. I had no idea it would be this complicated." Kate smiled at the bashful blush that tinted Riley's face. The new look amused her.

"You're welcome."

"Where are you staying?" Lilly asked.

Kate shrugged. "I'll camp out for a week. Then I've booked a bed and breakfast." It was above her budget, but she had no choice. Sleeping in a tent wasn't ideal either, but the B&B didn't have a vacancy right away.

"Oh, dear, that won't do." Lilly scrunched her face, and her eyebrows formed a deep V. She leaned over the counter. "I'm sorry, dear. Camping and cooking outside alone isn't a good idea. And I'm sure the B&B is beautiful, but that will be expensive."

"It'll be okay." Kate put her hands in the back pockets of her jeans and forced her biggest smile. Sure, camping scared the living daylights out of her, and the canvas wouldn't offer much protection against mountain lions or wolves. Just hearing howling from inside the cabin was enough to raise her pulse, but she wasn't going to admit to being afraid.

"Night-time in the summer isn't too cold with the right sleeping bag. And I bet sleeping under the stars is beautiful." Kate turned to Riley. "I read that all areas should be two hundred feet apart: my tent, cooking area, the washing area, and where I hang my food. And all food and trash have to be at least fifteen feet off the ground." Her research hadn't fooled anyone by the look on Riley and Lilly's faces. Hell, she hadn't even convinced herself she was up to the task.

"Yes, and you should have a gun," Riley said softly. "I can help you set up."

"Nonsense. She's not camping out alone." Lilly lightly smacked the back of Riley's head.

Kate suppressed most of her laughter, but a slight giggle escaped. She put the Sprite can to her mouth, hoping it would cover the lingering smirk she couldn't control. It might look harsh to the outside observer, but she could tell that Lilly's tough love didn't bother Riley. Although a smart, forty-year-old woman, Riley was a teddy bear who rolled with the punches thrown by her aunt. The unintended pun that sprung up in her mind made Kate cough to hide more laughter. Riley looked at her with a raised eyebrow but a hint of a smile.

"There's only one solution. Come stay with us, dear." Lilly smiled.

Kate nearly choked on the drink. She glanced at Riley's gaping mouth.

"It will be so much fun with you two and Hank." Lilly came out from behind the counter and pulled them into a hug. "Now, don't you worry. Riley's bedroom and the guest room are on the opposite side of the house from me. The noise you and Riley make can't possibly disturb me."

Riley's eyes bulged, and Kate bit the inside of her mouth to hide her reaction to the double entendre, which she was sure Lilly didn't mean. Kate cleared her throat. "I appreciate the offer, but I don't want to impose."

"It won't be any trouble. Riley can share her huge bathroom with you, which means no more sponge baths."

That put the offer into perspective. Oh, to have a regular bath again. "That would be lovely. Are you sure?"

"Of course." Lilly smiled. "You deserve a break after roughing it with no electricity for this long."

Kate didn't want to disappoint Lilly, who looked like an excited girl having a sleepover. "Your offer is so generous, but I wouldn't feel right staying for free."

"I'm not worried about you paying. But I could use help twice a week at the store, and I'd pay you just like any other employee. That is if you can work it around your new schedule with Howard."

"I'd love to help, but I couldn't take your money."

"Young lady, if you work here, I will pay you." She looked at Kate over the top of her glasses.

"You might as well say yes, or she'll will pester you to death."

Lilly swatted Riley's shoulder. "Don't pay any attention to her." She rolled her eyes. "Okay. There might be a hint of truth in what my dear niece says, but it would be delightful to have you join us."

"Thank you. I'd love to be your guest." Kate grinned. In one day, she'd gone from boredom to having two part-time jobs and somewhere real to stay. And she could use the money since the cabin renovation was eating her initial windfall. It would be a long time before she saw the rest of the inheritance.

"Riley, dear, I can catch a ride with Tom and Nancy. Why don't you take off early and show Kate the house?"

"Uh, sure."

"And please stay for supper, Kate. I'll get out that wine."

"Excellent company and fine wine. What a treat. Thank you, Lilly." Kate grinned, but Riley's expression was unreadable. She'd have to be careful to give Riley her space.

"Now, you two go on. I'll see you soon."

Lilly grinned as if she was sending them off to the school prom. Realization struck Kate. *Oh, God. She's trying to fix us up. Relatives meddling never worked.* She swallowed her doubts, waved to Lilly, and headed toward the door.

Riley rushed to open it for her. For a split second, their gazes met, and nervous excitement tingled down Kate's spine at the slight smile on Riley's face. Resisting falling for her was going to be hard.

# Chapter Seventeen

Riley turned off Baylor Road and onto Hawksbill Creek Road. She looked in her rearview mirror. Kate was following at a respectable distance. What the hell was Aunt Lilly thinking? Kate was too cute, and Riley didn't need the distraction. She took a deep breath and parked.

Kate got out of her truck with a huge smile. "Your house looks amazing from the outside. I love the wraparound porch."

"Thanks. First, we need to walk Hank." Damn, that gleaming smile. What was wrong with her? Every time Kate gave her that warm look, she turned into a quivering mess inside. *Focus on Hank and not the hottie.* They stepped through the door, and Hank rounded the corner at full speed, sliding sideways on the polished wood before rushing toward them. Kate took a step backward.

"Sit." Riley pointed in front, and he stopped precisely where she indicated. "Good boy. Did you miss me?"

Kate laughed at Hank's response. "He sounds like he's trying to talk."

"Huskies like to mimic human sounds." Riley kneeled down. "Shake." Hank stretched out his paw. After shaking, she vigorously rubbed his jowls. "Oh, you're such a good boy." She held out a treat, and it disappeared after a couple of chews. He howled again. "You have to work for your treats, buddy. Kiss." He licked the side of her face, and she rubbed her cheek against the side of his head. Riley stood and looked at Kate. "Step forward with the palm of your hand up and let him sniff and lick your palm. Then you can pet him like I just did."

"Can he sense that I'm afraid?" Kate said with a shaky voice and wide eyes. "He's big."

"Huskies love everyone, especially Hank. Go ahead. He's a gentle boy."

Kate inched forward. Hank made more soft noises and thrust his head toward her as if to say, come on, but he remained sitting at attention. When the tip of Kate's shaky hand finally was under his mouth, he bathed her palm in kisses.

"Don't be afraid. Now, give him a good rub and scratch."

When Hank stepped forward and nudged his nose against Kate's face, she flinched.

"Back." Riley held up her hand, and Hank did as he was told. She motioned lower, and he lay with his snout on the floor. He looked up and back and forth between them. Riley smiled. "Good boy." She turned to Kate. "He likes you and was only trying to kiss you."

"I've never been around dogs much, but I trust you." Kate sighed gently. "He's got adorable eyes. He looks like he's begging for forgiveness."

Riley cupped her hand over Kate's ear and whispered some commands. In the process, she inhaled Kate's vanilla perfume. No wonder Hank wanted to kiss her. She did too.

"Are you sure he'll listen to me?" Kate looked hesitant.

Riley nodded.

Kate cleared her throat. "Up." She raised her hand palm up. Hank stood. "Spin," Kate twirled her index finger, and he turned three circles. "Sit." She pointed to the floor. "Wow. He's well trained."

The scent of Kate's perfume lingered in Riley's nose. As Kate bent to rub Hank's cheeks one more time, Riley envisioned running her fingers through Kate's hair. *I have to stop this. Crushing on our gorgeous houseguest will only lead to trouble.*

\*\*\*

Kate laughed at Riley and Hank as they ran big loops around her. "You said we were walking him. I didn't think you meant running. Now, I understand why you changed into sweatpants and running shoes." She was no longer afraid of Hank and was beginning to look forward to being Lilly and Riley's houseguest.

"Huskies like lots of activity, especially running. Aunt Lilly can't run, so we always run ahead then back and around her like a game. She gives him a treat every so often, and we do it all over, again and again."

"Like a wacky oval racetrack."

"Yes. Today, you're Aunt Lilly." Riley reached in her pocket and held out the bag to Kate. "Last one."

"You're such a handsome boy." Kate bent down, giving Hank his well-deserved salmon treat. When he finished, she petted him. Hank turned and whined.

"Spoiled brat. Now, he wants his back rubbed."

Kate giggled and ran her hand along his back, then massaged his hips. He vocalized what sounded like a sigh of pleasure. When she stopped, he nudged his nose into her hand. Kate glanced up. A cocky half-smile played on Riley's lips.

"Okay, that's enough, attention hog. Sit." Riley shook her head.

Hank whined but finally sat.

"He's a big lovable baby." Kate smiled.

"Yep." Riley stretched her arms above her head, and her T-shirt rose, giving Kate a glimpse of a toned, flat stomach.

"Is something wrong?"

"Ah, no." The heat spread from Kate's center to her face. How long had she stared?

"Time to show you the house."

Kate could think of plenty of other things to see, betting that more of Riley's body was ripped with strong muscles. God, she had to stop mentally drooling before she really embarrassed herself.

By the time they got back, Lilly was home. Hank pranced over to her, and she lavished him with love.

"I started dinner because you were out longer than normal." Lilly turned from Riley to Kate. "How do you like your room, dear?"

"I haven't shown her the house yet. We gave Hank some extra exercise."

Lilly pointed upstairs. "Plenty of time before dinner."

Beyond the kitchen and a breakfast nook, a large living room jutted out into the yard. The picture windows let in tons of light. "Is that a greenhouse?" Kate asked.

"Yep, Aunt Lilly's pride and joy."

The remainder of the downstairs consisted of a formal living/dining room with a woodstove, a library, and a bathroom.

"There's another woodstove in the basement. Both are tied into the ductwork."

Kate laughed. "I have no idea what you're talking about, but I'm guessing it means the house stays warm in the winter."

Riley nodded.

They climbed the stairs to a landing. Family photos covered the entire wall.

"That's Uncle George, Aunt Lilly, and Dad." Riley pointed to the picture, and a bittersweet look flashed across her face.

Kate nudged her and pointed to another picture. "Is this you?"

"Yeah. I was six. It was taken here in the backyard. Aunt Lilly and Uncle George didn't have any children, and most of our relatives lived out of town, so we visited a lot."

Young Riley had an adorable grin. It was something Kate hoped to see more often. As she studied the photos, she saw plenty with Riley's dad but none with a woman who might be her mother. Then she spotted one. "Is this your mother?"

"No." Riley jammed her hands in her pockets and frowned. "It's Uncle George's sister."

By the tone of Riley's swift reply, Kate had hit a nerve. She pointed to some pictures of a young boy. "Who's this?"

"Nathaniel when he was a little runt. He's no relation, but I think of him like an annoying much younger brother. His dad dropped him off one day at the grocery store and didn't come back for several years. Aunt Lilly and Uncle Harold talked about adopting him, but Nathaniel's dad wouldn't let them. The asshole's still around, but Nathaniel just tolerates him." Riley's frown deepened.

Kate's heart ached. Now she understood their relationship better.

Riley pointed to the left. "That side is Aunt Lilly's bedroom, craft room, and private bath." She walked in the opposite direction. "On this side, the front room is filled with keepsakes. And the next one is the guest room." She motioned for Kate to enter.

Kate didn't know how Riley was able to push aside such sad feelings so easily but clearly, switching topics was one of Riley's defense mechanisms. She went with the flow and tried to keep the conversation light. "It's large yet cozy. Oh, I love that crocheted afghan." Kate brushed her hand over the intricate pattern of the forest green blanket covering the bed. "Did Lilly make this?"

"Yep. She made two for every bed, one for the summer and one for the winter."

"She's talented."

When they reached the bathroom, Kate was in awe of the spacious layout which rivaled any fine hotel. The huge room had a double sink, a storage cabinet, a toilet, a soaker tub, and a shower large enough for a couple. *I wonder how many girlfriends have showered here?* A soft click caught her attention. Next to the light switch was a wall-mounted device displaying a temperature reading. "A heated tile floor is going to spoil me. I may never move out."

"Lilly's is also heated. They're our only energy hogs. My room is in the very back of the house." Riley led her toward her space but stopped at her doorway, partially blocking Kate's view. "I'd show you, but it's a mess. Whenever I make the bed, Hank messes it up. He sleeps in his doggie bed sometimes, but he likes to cuddle. The extra warmth is fine in the winter but not so good in the summer."

"Now, the truth comes out. Mama likes to spoil her baby." Kate snickered. "And speaking of Hank. Where is he?"

"Sitting and watching Aunt Lilly cook and waiting for scraps."

Riley closed the door, and they stepped outside onto a balcony. Pine trees surrounded the yard to the west and north, and an array of solar panels faced south.

"The deck stretches from Aunt Lilly's end and wraps around my side. Feel free to come out and sit at this table anytime but be careful if you walk around the perimeter. We're not used to guests and may forget you're here. You might get an eyeful of something you don't want to see."

"Got it." She suppressed a grin. Seeing Lilly naked would be embarrassing, but she wouldn't mind seeing Riley in the buff. She followed Riley around to a breathtaking view.

"That's Castle Peak in the distance. At nearly twelve-thousand feet, it's the tallest in this valley."

Kate squinted to see the top of the peak over the trees and terrain before them. "Is that the one near my cabin?"

"No. The one closest to you is Blackmon Peak."

"The views are lovely, and so is your house."

"It was Uncle George's childhood home. His sister moved to New Mexico, and his brother lives in Montana. We visit occasionally. They've got a boatload of kids and grandkids. Everyone's friendly. They even told me to bring a girlfriend next time."

"You don't have any cousins or siblings nearby?" Heaviness settled in Kate's chest when Riley frowned, and a dark look settled over her face.

Kate wished she could remove whatever pain was deep inside Riley's heart.

"Come on down for dinner," Lilly yelled up the stairs.

Riley swiftly turned. "Let's go. You don't want to miss Aunt Lilly's famous cooking."

After Lilly said a prayer, they passed around plates of chicken, mixed vegetables, and mashed potatoes. The meal was a welcome sight compared to the basics Kate cooked. A bowl of mixed greens rounded out the meal.

Lilly passed her a bottle of red wine. "Help yourself. It's my favorite shiraz from Australia. Light and snappy, bursting with cherry, raspberry, and herb flavors, followed by a silky finish. It goes well with any meal."

Hank sat nearby looking like a poor, unfed pup. Kate took a bite of the vegetables. The zucchini, onions, red peppers, potatoes, and carrots were seasoned to perfection. "Incredibly delicious. Did you grow all these?"

"Yes. That's the fun part, but canning is a necessary chore for winter."

"I used to help my friends in Chicago with their garden. I've never canned, but I'd love to learn."

"That'd be wonderful." Lilly puffed her cheeks and smiled.

Kate settled in a little bit more at Lilly's wonderful welcome and sighed. This felt...like a real home. "Your house is lovely."

"Thank you, dear," Lilly said. "Riley and her crew finished the updates two years ago."

Kate nodded toward Riley. "Impressive."

"Thanks." Riley looked a little coy.

Although Lilly and Kate talked constantly throughout dinner, Riley stayed quiet and reserved. Kate wasn't sure if her earlier question had anything to do with Riley's manner. As dinner wrapped up, Lilly insisted on cleanup so Riley could escort her home.

"Thank you for everything. Your offer to stay here is so gracious." Kate stepped forward to kiss Lilly on the cheek, but she wrapped Kate in a bear hug.

"I'm already looking forward to spending time together. You should move in over the next couple of days." Lilly handed Kate a key, then hummed a tune as she went back into the kitchen.

"After you." Riley opened the door.

# CABIN FEVER

Driving in the dark freaked Kate out. As she followed behind Riley's truck, she gripped the steering wheel tightly, and scanned the blackness for elk and other animals. Relief flooded her body when they pulled up to the cabin. The one positive thing about the night was the twinkling stars. "Words can't describe the awesomeness." Kate folded her arms to stay warm, and she gazed at the sky. They stood in companionable silence for several minutes. She turned toward Riley. "It's colder than I expected. Thanks for the escort. Goodnight."

"Goodnight. I'll wait until you're safely inside before I leave."

"Thanks." She hugged Riley and was delighted at the returned affection. Their arms fell about the same time, and when Kate leaned away, her lips accidentally brushed the side of Riley's soft cheek. A thrill shot through her, and for a moment, she desperately wanted to kiss Riley.

"I have to get to work early. Let me know if you need help moving in." Riley walked backward toward her truck. "I had a great evening."

The near kiss appeared to have taken Riley by surprise and brought Kate's simmering desire to the surface. "I'm looking forward to seeing more of you."

Riley smiled. "See you soon."

Seeing her smile filled Kate with happiness. She waved and stepped inside her cabin. While she tidied up for bed, she thought about how kind and generous Lilly was. Riley rarely let her guard down, but a softer, caring side poked through when she did. And Kate liked that side a lot.

But Riley seemed to be hiding a secret which had something to do with her mother. Families typically displayed a wall of pictures. Oddly, not one at Lilly's house showed Riley's mother, and when Kate asked, Riley's expression turned sad. She didn't mean to hurt her. Whatever the reason, she should shy away from asking questions. Perhaps, she'd find the answers in time.

# Chapter Eighteen

SEVERAL LESSONS AND LOTS of encouragement from Lilly grew Kate's confidence in her cooking. Last night, Lilly had suggested that she bake a surprise for the construction crew. When Kate joked about not poisoning them, Lilly giggled and patted her cheek and told her she'd be fine.

As Kate removed the second raspberry coffee cake from the pan, she smiled. Being around Lilly was beginning to fill the void inside. After her mom died, the only person she could turn to was Sherry. Her father had been next to useless. And there hadn't been any contact with her mother's family since she was a young child. "I need to be thankful for what I have. And right now, it's time to taste the fruits of my labor. God, I hope it's edible." She popped a piece of cake into her mouth and moaned as the flavor of the sweet cake and the tart raspberries burst on her tongue. "Not bad."

She sliced and wrapped the two large cakes and placed them inside a picnic basket next to plastic mugs and two coffee thermoses. She was meeting the crew for the first time today. It was the second day of demolition, and she was curious to see the results and discuss the next steps with Riley.

Hank sauntered into the kitchen with his frisbee in his mouth and bumped Kate's leg. He dropped the disc and stood back with a pleading look in his eyes. "Your mommy took you for a run at dawn, and I just walked you an hour ago. I know you miss her, but she says demolition is too dangerous for a doggy." He leaned on his front paws with his butt in the air and whimpered. "Okay, bud. A few more minutes in the backyard, and that's it." He followed her outside. The game of toss and retrieve worked overtime on Kate's shoulder.

She pulled her phone out of her back pocket and shook her head at Sherry's text. *Happy 43rd birthday. You really should get laid or at least get to second base.*

*Thanks for the wishes. The sun shining is all I need. And my pink vibrator.*

*Boring.*
*I'm leaving soon for the construction site.*
*Oh, to see Riley?*
*NYB Bye.*
*Just saying. Don't want you to die with only a pink vibrator. Bye, sweetie.*
"Hank, it's time to go in." He whined, but she was having none of it. "Hank, inside now." Like a sullen child, he wouldn't budge. She went inside and closed the curtain but peeked out to see his reaction. He came to the door and whined. She slid the door open and let him in. "I think you're spoiled." She patted his back. "I'd love to be in your skin for a day and have Riley lavish and spoil me."

She shook her head, silently scolding herself. Constantly being around Riley, even just a few hours in the evening, was doing a number on her heart and head. And Sherry pushing her didn't help. Time to put her lust aside and carry on.

\*\*\*

Riley and Megan carried the last piece of the kitchen cabinets out to the dumpster. While the front faces were salvageable, the frames weren't. They passed by the work crew taking a break on the porch.

"What color is your girlfriend's truck?" Charley asked.

Riley didn't respond immediately. After tossing the cabinet into the dumpster, she glared at Puck, the likely culprit of the rumor. "She's not my girlfriend. And it's dark cherry. Why?"

Charley pointed into the distance. "She's on her way up the hill."

"Everyone, be on your best behavior, please." Riley wiped the sweat off her brow with her shirt sleeve. She noticed that Kate didn't drive too fast up the hill. Riley had already chewed out two others this morning. The new gravel wouldn't last long if people sped up the driveway.

Kate parked behind their vehicles and hauled out a giant picnic basket.

"Well, if she's not your girlfriend, then I'll take her. She's bringing food, and she's cute." Charley smirked.

"Zip it." Riley glared at Charley and made a mental note to talk to her and Puck later. She rushed over to Kate. "Let me help." A zing went through Riley as their fingers touched when she took the basket from her.

"Thanks. I hope you don't mind me popping by."

"Not at all." With reluctance, Riley tore her gaze away from Kate.

Kate's daily routine baffled Riley. She rarely rose before seven. After breakfast, her energy zoomed into high gear, almost like a flipped switch. Riley snapped out of those thoughts as the swing of Kate's hips caught her attention. She turned toward the makeshift lunch table and placed the basket on top, hoping no one had noticed her staring.

"Hello, everyone. I baked some raspberry coffee cakes." Kate moseyed up like a shy young girl.

Loud whistles and grateful cheers came from the crew. When the ruckus died down, Riley made introductions. "The most important person for you is Megan. Besides being my best friend and project manager, she's studied structural engineering."

"Don't forget awesome fishing guide." Megan gave a warm smile and stuck out her hand. "Pleased to meet you, Kate."

"Hayley specializes in masonry. Puck's a carpenter. Her nickname is from her love of hockey. Then there's Charley, another carpenter. Pete is the electrician, and Dylan does foundations."

"Those two are our token males," Puck said.

"Well, someone has to watch over you," Dylan said, then turned to Kate. "Good thing my wife isn't jealous of you, ladies."

"And Charley gets called Charlene when she messes up. She's our baby dyke." Puck grinned.

"Shut the fuck up." Charley hopped up and lunged toward Puck.

"Relax." Hayley held her back.

Riley narrowed her eyes at Puck. She had irritated Riley too many times lately. If she weren't so good at her job, Riley would have fired her long ago. "Please excuse my crew's manners. I promise they're top-notch, skilled professionals."

"Does the cabin have a foundation issue?"

Kate's concerned voice drew Riley back into those crystal eyes.

"No," Dylan said. "You're good to go, ma'am."

Kate's perfectly timed question eased Riley's nerves.

"Why do you need all these specialists if you're only tearing out stuff and replacing it?"

"We need to get the demo done swiftly. That way, we can adjust for any problems." Riley gestured for Kate to step inside. "Take a peek."

Kate shuffled to the center, and her mouth gaped.

"We removed most of the back wall to replace the rotten timbers and to make room for the new bedroom. There was no insulation, but we'll put in spray foam. It'll keep in the heat and prevent any critters getting in."

Kate glanced around then faced Riley. Her face was ashen, and Riley swallowed.

"The best news is your structural beams and foundation are solid. That would have cost big bucks and time if it wasn't." Riley stomped her foot on the floor. "And the thick solid ponderosa pine on the floor will look gorgeous and new after we sand and refinish."

Kate pointed up at the sky as her shocked gaze remained on Riley.

"That's sort of the bad news." Riley cleared her throat.

"Sort of? Where's the roof?"

Riley forced a smile. "We still need to take the rest down."

"Huh?" Kate's eyebrows furrowed.

"We found too much rot." Riley smacked her hands together and rubbed them back and forth. "But there is a bright side to the situation."

"I can't imagine what." Kate didn't sound convinced.

"You asked once about improving the lighting."

"Do you plan on making the roof one big skylight?" Kate placed a hand on her hip.

"Oh, that's funny," Puck said from behind them.

Riley turned and glared at her.

"I'm just taking these bags out." Puck picked one up.

"Do that later. Leave us alone, please." After Puck was out of earshot, Riley turned back to Kate and softened her tone. "I'm not going to sugarcoat this. What we saved in the foundation and floorboards, we lost in the roof." She picked a piece of wood out of one of the trash bags and handed it to Kate. "Push your thumb into it."

Kate did so, and it pressed inward.

Riley handed over a hammer. "Now, hit it with this."

The wood crumbled, and Kate's eyes widened. "Could it have caved in?" she whispered.

"Some spots were close."

"Why would my father fix the foundation but not the roof?"

"Water can seep in and create big problems in a short period of time." Riley rubbed the back of her neck. "Your father's usual handyman is a nice guy, but he's in his late sixties. I suspect he hasn't been on a ladder for some time."

"How the hell does this improve things?"

The stunned look on Kate's face showed her vulnerability, and Riley fought the urge to soothe her with a giant hug. "You don't have much ceiling height in this old cabin, and the windows are dinky. It'd be a shame to put up a whole new roof without modernizing. If we raise the sidewalls and pitch the roof higher, we can create a cathedral ceiling and install larger windows. That will make the cabin brighter."

Kate rubbed her forehead as she looked around. "That'd be a lot of space to heat."

"Yes, but it'd increase the value. Also, you'd have the option to install a loft."

"How much total are we talking with a loft and the barn?"

"Seventy thousand dollars." Riley held her breath, expecting Kate to blow up.

Kate crossed her arms and glanced around. "That's a hefty increase. And all because of a freaking rotting roof."

"I'm sorry the roof couldn't be patched."

"But it did feel like a dark cave in here. I'm in this deep. Go for it." Kate sighed, then pointed her finger at Riley. "Provided you can stick to that dollar amount. And if you can't, I want you to stop immediately. I can't sink another penny into this place."

"Understood." Riley showed Kate a rough sketch and was pleased her drawing made Kate smile.

"Are you sure you didn't take art classes?" Kate asked, sounding a little brighter.

"It's not too hard to draw straight lines." Riley shrugged, but Kate's compliment warmed her.

"Oh, yes. How much extra time?"

"Not much. More luck came your way." Riley bounced on her toes. "The materials are available. I'll schedule delivery ASAP, and I have a friend in Challis who's looking for additional work. He and two buddies will be joining my crew. We'll have the exterior completed sooner than expected so that we can focus on the interior." Riley smacked her hand to her forehead. "I almost forgot. There's an old horse-drawn passenger buggy in the barn."

"I knew something was under the dusty canvas cover but didn't peek.

Is it worth anything?

"It's not a typical farm buggy. It's a stylish two-person ride with leather seats and four red wheels. I sent the pictures to the county museum. It'd be worth about three thousand after you refurbish it. But if you donate it, the museum will spruce it up for free, and you'd get a tax break."

"Sounds reasonable."

Riley put both hands on Kate's shoulders. "This cabin will be top-notch, and you'll be toasty during the winters. We'll get it done right." Despite her reassuring words, Kate looked more worried than convinced, and without thinking, she pulled Kate into a full hug. With Kate nestled into her chest, Riley's body flooded with warmth. Realizing she lingered longer than was reasonable for friendship, she pulled back. "Trust me."

Kate nodded and smiled. "I've heard all good things about you and your workers. Are you going to try my coffee cake?"

"Yep." Riley grinned. "I'm impressed with how you've gone from canned soup for days on end to baking your own cakes."

"Thank you." Kate blushed at the compliment.

By the time they stepped outside, the crew had already torn into the cake.

"OH. MY. GOD. This is awesome. Can I marry you, Kate?" Puck's mouthful of food muffled her words, but her volume was loud, as always.

"Sorry, you're not my type."

Puck shrugged and took another piece of coffee cake. Riley wondered if Kate dated women and what her type was. *Why am I thinking this way?* Thoughts of Kate arose more frequently, and every time, Riley's body throbbed. But Kate was a customer, and that meant Riley had to keep her crush under wraps—at least until the construction was over. After that, all bets were off...

# Chapter Nineteen

*August*

KATE HAD THE WINDOW down, enjoying the breeze as she rumbled along the gravel road in her truck. Today was her weekly meeting with Dr. Allred, whom she'd come to adore. Building a family tree was far more time-consuming than she'd imagined, but it was rewarding in a way she'd never expected. Uncovering historical tidbits and finding pictures of her ancestors gave her a sense of belonging, as if missing puzzle pieces were finally snapping into place.

She'd been fortunate. Moving in with Lilly and Riley six weeks ago had been a blessing, despite her early misgivings. A peace she hadn't felt for quite some time had settled over her. Lilly was a darling and had taught her so much about cooking. And Riley loved to share her pizza and BBQ recipes. Kate never thought that cooking would become one of her hobbies.

And surprisingly, she was thoroughly enjoying the part-time work for Howard and Lilly. "Oh, my God." Kate laughed. "I'm having fun working." Everything here was so different from Chicago: a slower pace, lots of coffee breaks to chit-chat, happy interactions with customers, no skipping lunch, and no excessive daily hours or crazy demands.

She thought about Riley. Kate had been popping by the construction site when she didn't see her at the general store. Thank goodness the renovation was moving swiftly without any additional problems. She enjoyed seeing the progress and catching glimpses of Riley. Whenever Riley talked about construction, her eyes sparkled, and a big smile danced on her lips. Kate giggled at the thought of Riley's hand gestures and expressions that came to life as if she was painting a masterpiece in the air.

Ah, those hands—supple and soft yet so strong—and Riley's smile caused Kate's pulse to race whenever she stood nearby. If Riley knew the effect she had on Kate, she didn't show it. And Kate tried her best to hide her growing attraction for fear of potentially hurting their new friendship, not to mention the contractor-customer complication that she didn't need.

"Shit." She hit the brakes hard as a deer jumped out in front of her truck. Her eyes widened at the massive rack of antlers as the buck bolted away. She took a deep breath and moaned, hoping the sudden stop didn't hurt her computer. She looked around for her bag. It wasn't on the seat or on the floorboard. No bag which meant no wallet, no computer, and no notes. She sighed and turned the truck around.

When she got back to the house, Riley's truck was in the drive so Kate assumed she hadn't left for her trip to Boise yet. Kate opened the front door, and Hank bolted down the stairs to greet her. She braced herself for his onslaught of kisses. "Are you having a lazy day off too, boy?"

He yelped a reply, gave her another kiss, then ran up the stairs and waited at the landing, his tail wagging furiously. Kate climbed the stairs, and at the top of the landing, Hank looked up at her with pleading eyes. She turned her pockets inside out. "I have no treats on me. Sorry, boy." He didn't move and blocked Kate from stepping onto the landing. "Come on, move, Hank." He wagged his tail but remained in place. "Hank, move." After a few seconds, he jumped up and ran off. "Crazy, lovable dog." Kate rounded the corner, and the bathroom door popped open. Riley stepped out with only a towel wrapped around her. Hank blocked her way.

"We already had our run, and you got a treat," Riley said, not noticing Kate.

Hank howled, and Kate was tempted to do the same. She swallowed at the sight of Riley's bare shoulders and legs. The towel scarcely covered her butt. Hank whined some more.

"You're a big baby. Move." Riley waved him away, but he jumped up on her, and her towel fell to the floor.

Kate's core caught fire at the sight of Riley's body. She took in every inch and curve—firm breasts, a flat stomach, and those incredible legs. Kate's mouth watered. She looked back at Riley's gorgeous breasts, and her pulse shot through the roof. Riley had now seen her and was staring, but she'd made no attempt to retrieve her towel.

"Ah, sorry. I, um, forgot some things." Kate shifted from foot to foot but didn't avert her gaze.

Riley leaned against the doorjamb, crossed her arms, and faced Kate. "Well, I guess you'd better get them."

Paralyzed with embarrassment and excitement, Kate's pounding heart nearly leapt from her chest. Several long seconds of silence followed before Riley kicked the towel back into the bathroom and walked down the hall. Her glorious ass and hips gently swayed. She glanced back from her bedroom door before disappearing inside with Hank.

Kate slumped up against the wall and took a deep breath. She hadn't seen a body in such amazing shape for a long time, and oh, the things it made her want to do to and with Riley. She pushed away from the wall and headed to her room to gather her things, smiling and thinking how fortuitous it was that she'd forgotten them in the first place.

\*\*\*

Riley stretched out naked on the bed and placed her hands behind her head. It was warmer than usual, but not bad with the breeze coming through the window screens. Hank sprawled out at her feet. He rested his head and one paw on her leg. "You're such a bad boy. Did you knock my towel off on purpose?"

He looked at her with sad eyes as if he understood every word.

"She didn't look away. Guess she liked what she saw. What do you think? Was she shocked or turned on?"

Hank's moan sounded like he'd said, "I don't know."

Riley grinned. "You're the best dog I've ever had, but your advice is a little rusty. Shame the situation wasn't reversed. I would've loved seeing her naked, especially to get a glimpse of her breasts. They fill out her shirts and dresses beautifully."

Hank moaned.

"Ah, you agree." Riley couldn't deny the physical attraction, but it was more than that. She admired Kate's determination to move to Idaho and give it a try. But Kate leaving her job in Chicago to live in the middle of nowhere didn't add up. Were there other factors besides the inheritance that had influenced Kate's decision? Whatever the reasons, it was none of Riley's business.

Riley took a breath and sighed. Fantasizing about getting involved with Kate was insane, especially when Riley sucked at relationships. Every woman she'd ever been with had left her, after unsuccessfully pushing her to move from "boring Merrick." Even if Kate was interested, she probably was no different. It might only be a matter of time before she gave up and headed back to civilization.

And what would happen when winter arrived? Yes, Kate would love all the renovations, but Riley bet that one good winter storm would cause her to re-evaluate her situation and hightail it out of town. Even if she made it through a storm or two, Riley doubted Kate could cope with the loneliness of living alone in the mountains. *Nope. I need to put distance between us.* A knock on her door disturbed her thoughts.

"Sorry, Riley. My truck won't start. Could you help me?"

She bolted out of bed. "Give me two minutes, and I'll be down."

Hank rolled over on his back while she hustled to get dressed. She scratched his belly. "Are you coming, or are you going to snooze all day?"

He tilted his head and gazed at her then jumped down, snatched her tennis shoes up into his mouth, and dropped them at her feet. She slipped them on and smiled. Kate blushed easily. Riley couldn't wait to see how she reacted now that she'd seen her naked.

\*\*\*

While Riley inspected the engine of her truck, Kate doodled in her genealogy notebook. Anything to distract the continuous thoughts of seeing Riley's gorgeous naked body that still sizzled in her brain.

"Dammit. I don't know what's wrong." Riley wiped her hands on a rag. "I'll give you a ride into town, and we can get the garage to tow it."

"Oh, no, that's okay. You've been working extra hours. I don't want to inconvenience you on your day off. I'll reschedule." Kate flicked her wrist.

"It's okay. I'll review some records with Tom and go to Boise another time." Riley hopped into her truck and motioned for Kate to get in. Hank jumped in the back seat and poked his head between the front seats. Along with running and playing, he loved truck rides. He howled his approval when they started moving.

Kate couldn't figure out what to talk about, and their silence hung heavy in the air. Should she make a joke out of it so they could just move past it? She looked toward the mountains and berated herself. Their friendship had grown in the past weeks, and she admired Riley. But more and more, her meandering thoughts were not so platonic. The sight of Riley's toned and beautiful body had only amplified her feelings. That pleasant buzz down low had spread throughout her entire body. She needed to open up another topic, something neutral and safe.

"Tell me about valley farming." Kate motioned to the fields. "All the irrigated farm circles look strange next to the brown, dry backdrop. And how do the evergreen trees growing up higher get enough rain? It's all a little weird and so different from the trees and farming outside of Chicago." She laughed.

Riley looked over at her like she was nuts, but it worked. After talking about the valley, Riley enthusiastically went back to her favorite topic, the Sawtooth National Forest and Recreation Area. "My favorite are hikes to the alpine lakes. We have over four hundred that were carved out from glaciers receding. And the lakes are stocked by the Idaho Fish and Game Office."

Kate could care less about what fish was in what lake, or what time of year a person could fish. And she definitely didn't want to catch her own meal. "Oh, I read Idaho has hot springs. Which ones are the best?"

"Our natural hot springs are awesome, especially Goldbug. I'll have to take you sometime. Would you like that?"

"That'd be nice." Kate relaxed, and they soon arrived at the library.

"Come to the store when you need a ride back."

"Will do. Thanks, Riley."

Hank licked Kate's cheek and tried to crawl out with her.

Riley grabbed his collar. "Stay."

At the library door, Kate turned and watched Riley's pickup disappear down the street. Oh, dear Lord, remembering what was underneath Riley's baggy jeans made Kate's mouth water again. She shook her head and tried to focus on the task at hand, but all bets were off tonight. The image of Riley in the buff would be Kate's guilty pleasure and fuel luscious fantasies for months to come. The question would be whether or not she could keep her emotions bottled up.

# Chapter Twenty

Days passed, and neither Kate nor Riley spoke about the naked incident. In fact, Riley seemed to go out of her way to not spend time around Kate. They still had friendly exchanges but not as often as before, and Kate missed them. She returned home from shopping in Ketchum and for once, Hank didn't come running. Kate headed toward the kitchen.

"I think you should ask Kate." Lilly put her hands on her hips.

"But—"

"Sorry. I didn't mean to interrupt." Kate turned to leave.

"Oh, you're fine, dear." Lilly laced her arm in Kate's and pulled her in. "Riley's meeting up with some friends tomorrow for cycling. I thought you might enjoy getting out."

Riley's facial expression spoke volumes. Kate wasn't welcome.

"Now that my truck is back from the garage, I thought I'd take a relaxing drive then go to the library. Besides, I haven't done any mountain biking for years. I'm not in shape like Riley."

"Nonsense. You're fit as a fiddle. Riley will take it easy on you. And tomorrow's weather will be splendid." Lilly glared at Riley.

"I have an extra mountain bike, and some shorts that might fit you." Riley crossed her arms. "Can you ride an intermediate trail?"

Kate arched her eyebrow at the implied challenge. "I've ridden a few intermediate trails on vacations to Wisconsin, Michigan, and New York, but I was thinking about taking it easy tomorrow. Lilly, maybe I can help you in the greenhouse."

"No, I can take care of the plants. Go with Riley and enjoy yourself." Lilly patted Kate's shoulder and left the room.

"We need to leave by seven. See you at six for breakfast?"

Kate nodded.

"I'll put the shorts by your door for you to try on tonight, and I have an extra CamelBak, so you don't have to load up with water bottles. We ride for at least four hours, and we have a late lunch at a nearby restaurant.

You should bring a bag with clothes you want to change into after the trip. Okay?"

"It's all right. I don't have to go."

Riley eased her stance and gently touched Kate's arm. Her fingers lingered and warmth spread throughout Kate's body.

"Sorry, I'm grumpy. Tomorrow's weather is supposed to be lovely, and cycling is one of the best ways to enjoy the mountains. It'd be great to have you along. Please. Again, I'm sorry."

Riley's attitude pissed Kate off, but maybe it was some work-related thing that had her on edge. Whatever it was that got her so worked up, her apology sounded sincere, and her warm brown eyes melted the last of Kate's annoyance. "Okay. Thank you."

"Great. See you in the morning."

Kate turned partially and watched Riley head down the hall with Hank on her heels. Thanks to Hank, she now frequently thought of Riley's toned backside. She waved when Riley rounded the corner to go up the stairs. Yep, one of tomorrow's highlights would be seeing Riley in tight cycling shorts. She stiffened, and goosebumps rose on her arms. If Riley's friends were as buff as her, Kate might not be able to keep up with them. It was too late now. The best she could hope for was not to make a fool of herself.

\*\*\*

Kate was half asleep through breakfast and on the drive to Hailey, Idaho. When they arrived, Riley introduced her to six women, all of whom looked like seasoned riders, which only heightened Kate's apprehension. Although she was usually good with names, she struggled to remember them all.

A short-haired blond arrived. "Hi, everyone. Why are we doing Croy Creek? I thought we were going to ride Greenhorn Gulch Adventure."

Riley rubbed her neck. "I'm not feeling up to an all-day ride of twenty-three miles and steep grades. I've been working a ton, and I keep getting leg cramps. Let's ride the standard seven-mile loop, and people can add Two Dog if they want an extra workout." Riley gestured to Kate. "This is my friend Kate. She and I will bring up the rear today. Kate, this is Penny."

"Pleasure to meet you." Kate shook her hand.

"Same here." Penny eyed Kate's bike. "Riley's old bike? Nice to know it's getting some use."

Kate smiled, feeling terrible that Riley had modified their plans to accommodate her. But there was no turning back.

Penny turned to Riley. "What are we doing once we finish the course?"

"I'm thinking of relaxing at Juanita's, grabbing some tacos, and having a beer," Riley said. "If anyone beats me at pool, I'll buy their lunch."

"Okay. I'm in. Let's go." Penny hopped on and took off.

The trail gradually increased in difficulty, and by the third mile, Kate's legs burned. Her breathing grew heavier during a steep section. *God, what was I thinking?* She wished her excuses had worked. *Don't pass out. You can make it.*

"Let's stop here," Riley said, as if she'd read Kate's mind.

She didn't argue. They were far behind the other riders.

"You, okay?" Riley asked.

"Yeah." Kate motioned to the landscape. "The summer wildflowers are gorgeous," she managed to say between huge puffs of breath.

"You look a little pale."

Kate put her hands on her knees.

"No. Straighten your back and put your hands behind your head." Riley pressed her hand against the middle of Kate's back while she gently pulled her arms up. "Research of professional athletes shows it improves oxygen consumption compared to dropping your arms to your side or resting your hands on your knees."

Kate frowned at the mini lecture. "Really?"

"Scout's honor."

Within a couple of minutes of holding the position, Kate felt better. She breathed in the clean mountain air and looked out over the meadow below at Mother Nature's colorful palette of reds, yellows, and browns. "What are the small blue violet, bell-shaped flowers? And the white ones?" She pointed to an area just below where they stood.

"The blue ones are Scottish bluebells. The white ones are sego lily."

"Stunning." The flowers were gorgeous, and Kate was impressed that Riley knew the names. Riley continued to surprise her. "Why did we stop here and not with the others?" Kate took a sip of water from her backpack tube.

"It's a tight space, and I thought you might be more comfortable away from the crowd."

"Let's face it. I'm not as ripped as you guys. Maybe I should turn back."

"No. You're doing great." Riley placed her hand on Kate's shoulder. "Don't worry about what anyone else thinks."

"I bet they're talking about the rookie you're helping out."

Riley grinned. "Probably not. They're more likely gossiping about how I met my new girlfriend."

Kate sputtered the tube from her mouth. "What?"

"You know what friends are like, desperate to know all your business."

Riley smiled her easy smile, and Kate relaxed a little. It seemed like whatever she'd done to upset Riley, she'd gotten over it. "Thanks for choosing the easy trail for me. Can we sit for a few minutes and look out at the meadow?"

"Pick a spot, honey." Riley put up her hands and laughed. "Sorry, just kidding. Don't worry, I'll make sure everyone knows we're only friends."

*Only friends.* They had become friends, but somehow the words stung. Since seeing Riley—every glorious inch of her—it had taken all of Kate's strength not to conjure up that image on a daily basis, and even more not to pine after her.

"Would you like some almonds?"

Kate nodded, and Riley shook some out in her hand.

"Thanks for looking after me."

Riley turned toward her. "I'm sorry for being rude last night. I wanted to do the killer route we planned. But I was an ass. I can ride that another time."

Kate shrugged. "No need to apologize. Lilly seems to like pushing us together."

"She means well, and I love her to bits."

"You're lucky to have a relative that cares that much. My attitude about my father is changing. The more I learn about his background, the more I understand him. I wish we could've had that reckoning while he was alive."

"Aunt Lilly is wonderful, but she's always on my case about dating." Riley wrapped her arms around her knees. "She acts like I'm not putting myself out there." Riley picked up a rock and threw it. "I'm not the best dating material."

"Sounds like you're too hard on yourself. I'd be flattered if such a smart and handsome person asked me for a date."

Riley looked up quickly and grinned.

# CABIN FEVER

Kate pointed up the hill and got to her feet. "The other bikers are taking off. Looks like it's time to go."

\*\*\*

Kate's words hung in Riley's mind like a bug in a spider's web as they each mounted their bikes. Was she just teasing, or would she go on a date with Riley? The thought of taking Kate out distracted her. The section with intense rollers, berms, and tabletop jumps lay before them. Shit, she'd forgotten to tell Kate about the route and what to expect before they started. She slowed down to observe Kate who yelled out, "Yippee," then caught air on a big tabletop jump and screamed, "Yahoo," on the landing. Kate never lost control of her bike. Instead, it was Riley that hit the course at breakneck speed and almost fell.

Kate's fearless attack of the technical section surprised Riley. She picked up speed and performed her own tricks. Kate skidded the bike to a stop at the bottom, forcing Riley to do the same. She almost ran over her but didn't have the heart to get mad. Kate's enthusiasm had blossomed as the ride went along, and Riley was having more fun than she'd thought she would. She'd expected Kate to take everything super slow.

"This is a fabulous trail." Kate grinned. "The technical part is my favorite."

"It's in the top twenty mountain bike trails inside the Bureau of Land Management. I have to admit that you're a good mountain biker."

Kate shoved her lightly. "Hah! I have you fooled. I probably won't be able to walk tomorrow."

"Hey, you two," Penny said as she approached.

"We can hear you, and so can everyone else in the next county over." Riley crossed her arms.

"Are we doing Two Dog?

"Nah, we're going for lunch."

Penny pointed to the clear sky and its random collection of fluffy white clouds. "But it's beautiful."

"You can if you want, but I want to relax," Riley said.

"All right." Penny patted Kate on the shoulder. "Nice jumps."

"Thanks." Kate beamed from the compliment, and Penny waved and rode off.

"How much further?" Kate took another drink.

"Only one more mile."

"Good. Let's earn our beer." Kate took off like a rocket.

Riley grinned. So, Kate wasn't entirely a damsel in distress. Sure, she didn't know a lot, but she asked questions. And when she failed, she always gave it another shot—that impressed Riley. The temptation to ask Kate on a date was growing, and she wasn't sure how much longer she could resist.

# Chapter Twenty-One

ANOTHER WEEK PASSED, AND Kate couldn't wait to tell Dr. Allred the good news. Just outside the library, her phone dinged with a new text message from Sherry. They texted back and forth, then Sherry's favorite topic of Kate asking Riley out popped up. Ever since Kate had admitted her attraction to Riley, Sherry had pestered her about dating. The more Kate resisted, the more Sherry poked. Kate ignored the question and told her about playing with Hank, the cycling trip, and an upcoming hike instead.

*Okay. Have it your way, Womanless in the Wild.*

Kate laughed, typed goodbye, and went inside. "Good morning, Dr. Allred."

"You look happy."

Kate nodded and grinned. "The renovations are on schedule. Riley says it's her smoothest job yet. And when I'm not working at Lilly's or Howard's, you're feeding my new addiction to genealogy. My DNA matches are starting to pay off." She took out her phone and swiped to open her family tree on the genealogy app, then opened one of the profiles and pointed to a picture. "This is Frances. She's a second cousin and a high school history teacher in Portland. We've corresponded a couple of times. The other day, I chatted via video with her and a couple of her students about the Oregon Trail. We talked privately afterward, and she gave me information on how the Christensens traveled from the east to Utah, then into Idaho and Oregon."

"That's splendid news." He put the newspaper back in the rack and guided her back to the conference room.

Kate had no idea why, but she had come out to Frances, who was a Mormon. Surprisingly, Frances immediately said, "Good. Love is love," and mentioned being a member of the Mormons Building Bridges group, a national coalition of ally and LGBTQ LDS church members. Dr. Allred was also a Mormon. What would he think?

He sat across from her with a wide grin. "I made excellent progress searching the county courthouse records back to 1890. I found records where your great grandfather established mines with the Jacobs. I also retrieved twelve marriage certificates, forty-eight birth and death certificates, and various land transaction documents. By 1954, everyone had left the region except your grandparents, probably because neighboring states had better job opportunities." He handed Kate a thick folder and a thumb drive. "You can link them to your tree on the computer."

"Wow." The folder thickness and the number of documents astounded her. Somehow, knowing something about her family background made her feel less alone. Yet, most of the information was along the male lineage. She hoped to find more about the women in her family. "How much do I owe you?"

"The courthouse records weren't much at all. Donate a little something to the library, and we'll call it even."

"That's so kind of you, thank you." Her words didn't seem adequate. Her history was coming to life with his help.

Someone knocked on the door.

The librarian, whom Kate had not formally met, smiled from the doorway. "Doctor, there's a phone call for you at the desk."

"Please excuse me, Ms. Minton."

After Dr. Allred departed, she offered her hand. "Hi, I'm Lena."

"Kate."

Instead of leaving, Lena took Dr. Allred's seat. She looked about Kate's age, and she wore a conservative dress with the hem halfway down her calves.

"It's so courageous of you to move out here on your own. I'm happy that we can help you find your family roots." Lena smiled sweetly.

"Thank you. The library's collection is impressive."

"We don't have the money to pay Dr. Allred, but he loves the research so much that he morphed into being the curator. And he's donated countless books."

"He's fantastic." Kate finished writing a brief note, but still Lena lingered.

"Our winters can be brutal, and the road down your way often shuts down after snowstorms."

Kate nodded. "I'll be prepared."

Lena pulled her chair closer to the desk and to Kate. "I hear your cabin is being renovated with a solar-powered system and the works. How's that working out?"

Lena scooting her chair closer was odd, and the expression in her eyes looked alarming. What was Lena trying to do? Kate put her pen in the notebook and closed it. "Yes. Riley Anderson and her crew have been terrific. It's exciting watching the transformation."

"And you're staying with her until the work is finished?" Lena stared, unblinking.

An unnerving silence filled the room. Whatever the woman was fishing for, Kate wasn't going to bite. "Yes. Riley and Lilly have been wonderful hosts. I regard them as friends." Kate grinned as wide as she possibly could.

Lena leaned closer and whispered, "You know Riley's a..." her lips puckered as if she was tasting something sour, "lesbian. And so is most of her crew. The men say she does a good job, but you need to be careful."

"How so?" Kate cocked her head to the side, daring Lena to go further.

"You're an outsider who might be vulnerable. She might try to put the moves on you." Lena made the puckering gesture again.

"Oh, really?" Kate leaned back, crossed her arms, and narrowed her eyes. "I'm not sure how I'd take that."

"Exactly." Lena smiled, looking far too pleased with herself.

"It'd certainly be interesting either way."

"Interesting? What do you mean?" Lena's eyes widened.

Kate leaned over and drummed her fingers on the table, enjoying making her wait for her answer. "It would be a fabulous compliment. And I'd have a dilemma; would I remain her friend or explore my options?" Kate batted her eyelashes and grinned. "She is a rather stunning butch."

Lena recoiled backward. "Oh, dear Lord. I pray for you, Ms. Minton."

"Thank you. I'll pray for you too." Kate smiled warmly at Lena, whose disdain was written all over her face.

The door opened, and Dr. Allred returned. "Now, where were we?"

"I need to get back to work." Lena practically jumped out of his chair and was gone.

"What was that about?"

"Apparently, Lena is concerned for my soul and believes that my friendship with Riley will tarnish my reputation." Kate leaned back, crossed her legs, and draped her arm over the back of the chair. "I don't judge my friends by who they love, and I expect the same from others. Lena and I won't become friends."

"I see. Lena is extremely religious. So am I." He sat and placed a large, wrapped package on the table. "Matthew 7:1 says, 'Judge not, that ye be not judged.' And Joseph Smith later said, 'Judge not unrighteously, that ye be not judged; but judge righteous judgment.'"

Did that biblical tongue twister mean he supported Lena's view or not?

"Kate, the problem is, what is one person's righteous judgment may not be another's. People are imperfect and frequently make mistakes. Therefore, I believe the Lord is the only one who can see clearly and judge perfectly. People who try to judge often make the situation worse." He placed his palm flat on the table and shook his head. "Lena and her small group of friends are right of center. They gossip, but my advice is to pay them no mind. You'll find that most people in town don't judge or mistreat anyone with different views or lifestyles. Most care more about finding common ground."

"It's good to hear you say that, because Riley is my friend." *A really hot friend.* Kate cleared her throat. "And I'm also a lesbian."

He nodded. "Diversity is good for a community."

His compassion and forward-thinking astounded her.

"Now, I have a present for you."

With a gleaming smile and sparkling eyes, he pushed the package in front of Kate. "Open it." He looked like a child at Christmas.

She ripped the paper off to find two framed pictures. The first was a portrait of a young woman, maybe sixteen or seventeen. The brown wavy hair and pale blue eyes were unmistakable.

"That's your great grandmother, Rosemary Barton. She was the first wife of your great grandfather, Gideon Christensen. It was painted the month before their wedding in 1887."

Seeing a color rendition instead of a late nineteenth-century black and white photo took her breath away. She traced her great grandmother's jawline with her fingertips. The resemblance was astonishing. "Thank you. I'm at a loss of words." Kate put the painting aside. The next one was a black and white photograph of two young women and two men standing next to a horse and buggy.

"This is your grandfather, Elijah, and your grandmother, Emmeline Davis in 1914, a year before they were married. Also in the picture are

# CABIN FEVER

Jeremiah Jacobs and his sister, Mary. Jeremiah was Elijah's best friend, and Mary was Emmeline's best friend. Jeremiah is Howard Jacobs' grandfather."

Dr. Allred hadn't raised the rumor about Jeremiah and Emmeline, and she wasn't about to. "They look so young."

"The girls were fifteen, and the boys seventeen."

Kate studied their faces. Each bright smile looked full of happiness, but it wouldn't be long before Emmeline became an unhappy bride. Did she know that her parents planned to marry her to Elijah when the picture was taken? It would be several years after the marriage that Elijah discovered Emmeline's betrayal. What ate at Kate was the unknown. Was Jeremiah her real grandfather? She figured it unlikely since she shared the same unique eye color as her great grandmother, Rosemary. She put the picture down delicately, hoping Dr. Allred didn't see her hands shaking. "Thank you so much."

"You're very welcome. No matter what faith, we gather our strength from the Lord and our family. We must celebrate our accomplishments of the past and work hard to live an honest, fulfilling life. There's so much life to live without looking backward at unhappy times." He placed his hand gently on top of hers. "If your great grandparents and grandparents were here, I'm sure they'd be proud of who you are and what you're doing with the cabin."

She teared up, and before she could think, she got out of her chair and hugged him. He welcomed her embrace and patted her back.

When they sat back down, he handed her another document. "From my research, Rosemary's parents built the cabin for her and Gideon as a wedding gift. They gave it to Elijah when he married Emmeline, then Elijah willed it to your father. The way I see it, you were meant to live in that cabin."

She considered how amazing it was that she'd come so far. The fear that had initially taken hold had receded. Now, curiosity and the grit to make it roared within her. "The cabin feels more like home, and I'm getting to know people well. Merrick is a charming community."

"Good. Welcome home, Kate."

Kate loved the company of Lilly and chatting with Dr. Allred, Nancy, and others, but it was Riley who lit her fire—an all-consuming fire of desire. It surprised her how fast her feelings had developed, and she couldn't separate lust from deep affection. It just all seemed to muddle together when she was around Riley. Her plan to sell the cabin next year was still in place, but that looked more remote than ever before. Yet, doubts and questions lingered. Should she date Riley? Kate wasn't interested in a friend with benefits. Or was she?

# Chapter Twenty-Two

RILEY CLOSED THE CASH drawer, wrote down the balance, and tapped her pen on the ledger. She stared at the narrow profit for this month. Perhaps they had to consider increasing prices. A few phone calls to remind folks who were behind on payments wouldn't hurt. Maybe they'd be more likely to pay on time if they charged a late fee like other businesses, but Uncle George never had. He always believed in helping those in need. She sighed. There had been lean months before, and they always managed to get through. The front door slammed, and she jumped.

"Riley!" Nathaniel smiled widely. He skidded to a stop and fidgeted from foot to foot, not in a nervous way but like a kid at the county fair waiting to collect his prize.

"Yes, Nathaniel?" She'd lost count of the times she'd told him not to slam the door. She didn't feel like arguing today.

"Riley!" He turned around like a spinning top.

"Nathaniel! You won the lottery? Did you buy a new truck? Are you and Brooke getting married?"

"Heck, no. I'm only twenty-two."

Riley shrugged. "I give up. You're late from a delivery, and I'd like to go home."

"Oh, good. Nathaniel's back." Aunt Lilly walked in and pulled on her coat. "My side is locked up. Let's get going."

"I need to talk to Riley for a minute," Nathaniel said.

Lilly adjusted her purse strap on her shoulder. "In that case, I'm going to Nancy's. See you there, dear."

When she left, Nathaniel said, "Oh, my God, I didn't know she was still here."

Riley rolled her eyes. "Now, why are you so worked up?" She was hungry and irritated. More grinning. "Nathaniel, I'm not going to stand here and guess all night. Spit it out."

He leaned over the counter. "Kate was at the library around lunchtime.

Lena had a very fascinating talk with her."

"I'm sure she did. Kate's researching her family. They were part-founders of the town."

"Really?"

"Yes. Focus, Nathaniel. Why is this conversation so important?"

"Lena has told everyone, and I mean everyone." He opened his arms wide.

"About what?"

"She warned Kate about you being a lesbian."

Riley gritted her teeth. Lena irritated Riley to no end by pushing religious literature to "save a person's soul." Now poor Kate would be bombarded. But why was Nathaniel grinning?

"That's not the best part." He beamed.

"There's a good part to this story?" Riley tried to maintain a neutral face.

"Yes. Kate said she would be flattered if you came on to her. Kate's gay! Isn't that great? You should ask her out."

Riley froze for a split second, then tossed the financial ledger into the drawer and locked it. Inside, she was doing a happy dance. The teasing during the cycling trip had Riley's mind spinning and her body abuzz, but she hadn't been sure how Kate identified. "Don't repeat that, Nathaniel."

"Why? It's all over town. And you don't talk about it, but everyone knows about you."

Riley sucked in a deep breath and let it out. "It's disrespectful and downright rude to be talking about other people behind their backs. Did Kate talk to you personally?"

"No."

"If Kate told you about her sexuality and said she didn't care who knew, then you could blab. But she didn't, so don't repeat it." She wanted to make sure he understood. Nathaniel's immaturity and goofiness often got him in trouble, but he had a big heart. "Look, dude. I know you don't have a problem with me, but some in this town do. Lena is a busybody and probably exaggerated the whole thing. Don't repeat a word she says. You don't want to be a part of any misinformation, and I know you don't want to hurt Kate's feelings. End of story."

"I'd never hurt Kate, but there are tons of people in this town that don't care who someone loves, and I can only think of a handful of people that don't like you because you're gay, and—"

"Stop!"

He dug his hands into his pockets and hung his head. "Yeah, okay. I'm sorry. I won't say anything, I promise." He looked up and grinned. "But you should still ask her out."

Riley crossed her arms.

"We want you to be happy, and Kate's lit."

Riley frowned. "Huh? Kate's what?"

"Lit. She's awesome and really pretty." He wiggled his eyebrows.

Damn, he'd picked up that creepy gesture from Megan. "Let's go home." Riley slid on her lightweight jacket, stepped out from behind the counter, and motioned toward the door. "I'm hungry."

"Riley?"

Her hands dropped, and she craned her neck at the ceiling. "Now what?" She put her hands on her hips. "I'm waiting."

"Your shirt inched up when you put on your jacket, and I caught a glimpse of your gun. A long time ago, you said it was for protection against wild animals when you're alone visiting construction sites. But I can tell when it's holstered on your belt, and you have it on even when you're in the store. Why? The break-ins happened in the middle of the night with no one around."

Riley sighed and looked into his eyes. "Leaving it on is easier since I go back and forth between the store and construction sites. I'm just being prepared, whether it's a wolf or a man."

"But this town is full of good people."

"A lot of people pass through." Riley put her hand on Nathaniel's shoulder and squeezed gently. "And I do believe that good people outnumber the nasty, crazy assholes in this world." She patted the gun underneath her shirt. "But I'm all that Aunt Lilly has left. And right now, she's waiting for me to take her home."

"Okay." He hugged her and didn't let go. "Thanks for giving me a job and teaching me all kinds of stuff."

"You're welcome. You know we're in front of the store window. You'd better let me go, or Lena will be gossiping that I'm taking advantage of an employee half my age."

He laughed and stepped back. Outside the store, he said, "You're not forty-four."

Riley nearly dropped the keys as she locked up. "You know I just turned twenty...for the second time. Now, go home before I kick your ass."

He walked backward. "Okay, old lady."

She shook her finger at him.

"I mean, yes, ma'am."

"That's better. Have a good evening." Riley took her time walking to the diner. Nathaniel had probably never heard of the murder of Matthew Shepard over twenty years ago. She swallowed against the bile rising in her throat. She'd been to so many bars and talked to complete strangers. What if she'd gotten into a car with a woman, thinking she'd gotten lucky but instead, she ended up tied to a fence, beaten, and set on fire? Tons of good people lived in Idaho and neighboring states, and so did a few white supremacy groups. She patted her gun. If some homophobic asshole took up their shit with her, she wouldn't go down without a fight.

Riley entered the diner and saw Lena in a corner with her friends. *Fantastic.* Thankfully, Aunt Lilly had chosen a booth on the opposite wall.

"Sorry, I was getting hungry and ordered supper. I hope country-fried steak, spinach, and butter beans are okay for you," she said.

"Fine, but let's take it home."

Aunt Lilly raised her eyebrow and sat up a little straighter. "Our meal will be cold by the time we get home. And I don't want to give them the pleasure of making us leave."

"Sure." Riley plopped down.

"Lena's mother is right wing too. We used to be friends until I left the church to marry George."

"Ah, I didn't know that."

"It's all in the past." She squeezed Riley's hand. "I love you. I don't know what I'd do without you."

Nancy arrived with their salads.

"And you're perfect just the way you are," Aunt Lilly said. "Isn't that right, Nancy?"

Nancy smiled. "Absolutely. Your aunt is precious and wise. Jess will bring your meal. I'm heading home. Tom's cooking me supper."

"So, Tom's a secret master chef? When can we expect some grub?" Riley asked.

Nancy giggled and headed out the door.

But Lena and her friends kept eyeballing and pointing in her direction.

The whispers and giggles were getting under Riley's skin. She jabbed her fork into her salad.

"Stop looking over there."

"Sorry." Riley clenched her jaw. Lena and her gang hadn't changed since high school. She could handle their annoying ways, but what she didn't like was that Lena seemed to be setting her sights on Kate.

Lilly placed her hand on top of Riley's. "Ignore them."

By the time Riley finished her salad, she had blocked them out of her thoughts. They took their time and ate in peace. While they waited for the check, Riley showed Aunt Lilly the revised drawing for Kate's cabin. "Take a look at this. Megan found a killer bargain on Western Red Cedar to give Kate a back deck. There's enough left over in the budget to pay for the material but not labor. Megan and Hayley offered to help me build it. What do you think?"

"She's going to love it."

"We thought it'd be nice to surprise her with this and a few other perks. But she keeps checking up on our progress. We'll build the deck last. Can you keep her busy the last couple of weeks?"

"*We* thought?" Aunt Lilly smiled. "No problem. I'll give her some extra gardening and cooking lessons." Aunt Lilly clapped her hands together. "If I didn't know better, I'd say you were warming up to the lovely Kate. Maybe her staying with us wasn't such a bad idea after all."

"I'm just being friendly."

"Whatever you say, dear."

Riley looked out the window. "Should be nice weather tomorrow." *Brilliant comeback.* Sure, Kate was attractive, but Aunt Lilly would skin her alive if she messed around with Kate and broke her heart. And Riley's long-term commitment track record wasn't too flipping fantastic. Not to mention, the complications with dating a customer would probably be a headache. Still, Riley couldn't shake the yearning that filled her body and soul every time she saw Kate.

# Chapter Twenty-Three

*September*

ALTHOUGH SOME OF RILEY'S friends participated in Rebecca's Private Idaho, one of the top cycling gravel events in the world, she had decided not to race. Instead, she spent the Labor Day holiday weekend working on Kate's cabin.

By the second weekend in September, the renovations were shaping up nicely, so she suggested a road trip and hike. Her heart skipped a beat when Kate said yes without hesitation. She was still trying to stay professional and not crush on Kate, but her body didn't listen to the logical side of her brain.

Along Trail Creek Summit Road, Riley pointed out landscape features and explained the gravel road that stretched between Sawtooth Valley and the Big Lost River Basin was part of the racing course. Kate had gasped at the drop-off cliffs, saying she was happy they were on Riley's side. They passed by Mount Borah, the highest peak in Idaho, and traveled south. Riley briefly glanced at Kate, whose smile stretched wide. That and her bright personality warmed Riley through. "What do you think of the scenery?"

"The mountains in the Lost River Range are incredible. I just can't get over how dry the lower terrain looks, except around the middle of the valley. Is it because of a drought?"

"Yes, but this valley is more arid than the Sawtooth Valley. We're going to Bear Creek Lake. It's a moderate hike and one of the best in this valley."

South of Mackay, Riley turned east to head into the mountains, and Kate burst out laughing.

"What?"

"Back there." Kate thumbed over her shoulder. "A cow had its mouth over one of the irrigation spigots while the others drank from a trough."

Seeing Kate so cheerful lifted Riley's spirits to a new high. Along the way, they encountered more cattle grazing. At one point, she had to stop as eight cattle blocked the road and stared at them for several minutes before moseying away to graze.

Riley pulled into a parking spot. "The trail is a moderate hike about five and a half miles roundtrip, and it's gorgeous."

Hank jumped up and stuck his head between them. He nuzzled and licked Riley's face then Kate's. She threw her head back and laughed again, which made Hank bathe her in more kisses.

"Come on, Mr. Romeo." Riley opened the back door, and Hank jumped out. His tail curled in excitement.

"I checked out the map last night," Kate said. "The route looked shorter over the gap between Warren Mountain and Bear Creek Lake."

Riley grinned. She'd have to give Kate a map lesson on how to read contour lines. "The gap is strenuous, and the side facing the lake is too steep—unless you're part billy goat. Or are you into ropes?"

Kate's eyebrow rose slowly. "Aren't we a little early in our friendship to be asking those types of questions?"

"Ah, I didn't mean it to sound like that." Riley's cheeks burned at a naughty mental image.

Kate snickered. "Sorry, I shouldn't tease you. You get enough of that from Puck."

"Don't compare yourself to Puck. She goes for the throat to embarrass me in front of other people. Your private teasing is mild horseplay." Riley liked Kate's casual joking. A lot. That was the real problem. Every interaction seemed to lower Riley's defenses and brought Kate closer. And Riley couldn't seem to deny her anything—that's how they'd ended up here. "Let's get going and take maximum advantage of the sunlight." Riley slung her backpack over her shoulders. She clipped a leash on Hank's collar, and Kate gave her an odd look. "Yeah, he isn't fond of being leashed, but it's a national forest rule."

"What's the elevation gain?" Kate leaned her trek poles up against the tailgate and adjusted her pack.

"We start around seven thousand feet, and we'll climb up to 8,800 feet. Where's your jacket?"

"In my pack. The sweater and my hat should be enough right now."

"Are you layered up?" Without thinking, Riley reached over and gently peeled back Kate's sweater.

"Would you like to undress me to verify?" Kate grinned mischievously.

"Um, sorry. I just don't want you to get cold." Riley looked away and pointed toward the trail. "You'll heat up as we hike, but the wind up here can whip up unexpectedly."

"I'm a big girl. I know when to put on and take off clothes." Kate took off at a brisk pace. She glanced back over her shoulder with a broad smile. "What are you waiting for?"

Hank vocalized his excitement and took off after her, yanking Riley along. "Easy, boy. You almost ripped my arm out."

"He's loving it." Kate patted his back.

Other than Hank's howling and their occasional chit-chat on the cabin's progress, they moved ahead in relative silence, soaking in the comfort of nature. As the hike became more strenuous, Kate's breathing grew more labored. Riley gently tugged on Kate's arm. "Hey, let's stop here for a break. It's relatively flat compared to what's ahead."

"Sounds good." Kate slipped off her pack.

Riley tied Hank's leash to a small tree and took out her water bottle. She poured some into a portable dish for him, and he licked it up with gusto. She quenched her own thirst but not the metaphorical one that resulted from admiring Kate's figure. Riley closed her eyes and silently chanted, *She's only a friend.*

Hank whined an unusual sound, and Riley opened her eyes. Kate had wandered off the trail and was snapping pictures with her smartphone. Riley ran toward her. "Watch out." Just as she did, Kate stumbled over a rock. Riley lunged and caught her in the nick of time. Kate wasn't too close to the edge, but even a short tumble down the rocky hill would have caused severe injuries.

"Thanks." Kate looked at Riley with wide eyes. "I'm sure a face plant would have hurt."

"You're welcome." Although the danger was over, Riley still held on, and Kate didn't move.

"I guess I need to pay better attention."

"It's a fabulous day to take pictures. The sky is gorgeous." *And so are you.* Kate's gray hat contrasted against her soft hair, framing her beautiful face. Riley dropped her arms. "I'm just thankful you're okay."

"So, you don't come to the Lost River Range much?"

"I haven't for some time. Sawtooth National Forest has so many trails to choose from."

"It would be lovely to go with you on more hikes. I promise to be more careful."

"Sure."

Hank whined. Kate giggled and ran over to him. "I love you too, boy."

He jumped up, stretching fully, and licked her face.

"Bad boy. Get down." Riley looked at Kate and shook her finger. "And your giggling only encourages him. He's like a lovesick puppy around you."

They drank more water and had a snack, and Riley described how to distinguish between the different trees. Hank lay down and rested as Riley rattled on about the forest. "We're lucky the Big Burn of 1910 didn't come this far south."

"That sounds like a horrible forest fire."

"Over three million acres burned. The wildfires stretched from eastern Washington across northern Idaho and into western Montana, and north into British Columbia, Canada. Some parts of the forest have never recovered."

"Did you study forestry?"

Riley kicked some dirt with her boot. "I studied natural resources conservation at the University of Idaho in Moscow but didn't finish."

Kate took Riley's hand and squeezed gently. The connection zipped through Riley.

"What happened?" Kate softly asked.

Riley shrugged and looked toward the mountains. "Moscow's on the border with Washington, almost nine hours away. I didn't have a car and couldn't come home often. Also, I felt out of place on the sprawling campus. It's like a mini town in rural Idaho. My classes had tons of excursions, which I loved, but the dorm and the indoor classrooms felt suffocating." She kicked the ground again. "At the end of my sophomore year, I was beginning to feel at home, but Uncle George had a stroke." She looked up into Kate's eyes. "He never fully recovered. He was my idol and mentor after my dad's death."

"I'm so sorry." Kate took Riley's hand again and didn't let go.

"He downplayed the stroke and tried to push me to go back to school. But I just couldn't. They needed extra help, and I wanted to come home. Secretly, I worried that he'd have another attack and die while I was away." Riley struggled to push the last words out of her choked-up throat. "Besides, the store and home improvement business grew on me."

Kate drew Riley into her arms, and a comforting wave of warmth rushed through Riley. When Kate withdrew, Riley missed her body, the smell of her light perfume, and her silky skin against Riley's cheek. A couple minutes of silence went by as they looked out over the forest.

"Uncle George never did have another stroke, but the physical restrictions from the one were bad. But you'd never see him sad. He was always a cheerful guy with a razor-sharp mind. He died five years ago from a damn rare cancer."

"Thank you for sharing your personal story with me. I'm sorry for your loss." Kate brushed the back of her hand over Riley's wet cheeks.

Kate's touch was comforting, but Riley struggled to control her tears. "I'm sorry."

"For what? It's good to cry sometimes."

"It's not something I do. Before and during Uncle George's funeral, I tried hard to be strong for Aunt Lilly; she was devastated. But after, I locked myself in my room and curled into a ball and sobbed." She sighed deeply. "I haven't cried since." Letting part of her defenses collapse in front of Kate was like opening an enormous flood gate, allowing her grief to spill out and be carried away.

Kate hugged her. Their bodies together felt so good, but if she lingered in Kate's embrace too long, the balance between their friendship would be blown to smithereens. Riley pulled away and walked back to Hank. It was all too much. "We should get going. There's steeper terrain ahead." She slung the pack over her back and tugged Hank's leash. She had to tuck her feelings away, or she'd lose control.

When they reached the lake, Kate peeled off her boots and socks at its edge. Hank stretched out on the rocks next to her and somehow made himself comfortable.

"It's cold."

"I can take it." Kate glanced up and grinned. She dipped her toes into the water. "Oh, you weren't kidding. It's chilly but refreshing. By the way, when are you going to teach me how to fish?"

"I thought you weren't interested in fishing."

"I enjoy learning about your hobbies. Maybe I should give it a try." Kate bit her lip. "Just promise me that you'll take care of the bait and hook and any squirmy stuff."

There was no mistaking the tone of Kate's flirt. Heat flashed through Riley's body. She couldn't imagine what would happen if Kate had touched her skin. "Next day off, I promise."

Kate held her gaze for a second then looked around. "When I first arrived, I couldn't fathom how anyone could live here. These mountains are so different than the Tetons. The forest seems to barely cling to life on the high jagged, crumbling peaks." She put her socks and boots back on.

"You've been to the Tetons?"

"Yes. I passed through on my trip to Idaho. The field outside my hotel was filled with elk. I'd like to go back someday."

"Maybe we can take the trip together." Riley wandered back and helped Kate stand up. "Each range has a rugged beauty all its own. I like the contrast. In the summer, the snowmelt turns the mountainside and meadows into a thing of sheer beauty. Red, pink, purple, blue, and yellow wildflowers grow everywhere. I like the White Cloud Mountains where we live. It gets more rain than this range. But I have to admit that the Tetons are pretty awesome."

Hank rubbed his head on Kate's leg and looked up at her with soulful eyes.

"You're such a lovely boy." She hugged him.

"He's buttering you up for food."

They found a spot to have lunch and sat in companionable silence for a few minutes.

"Riley, I'm glad we became friends. Our beginning was a little rough. I'll be honest. I viewed you as a tough female 1800s pioneer, but you do have a soft side. You won't disappear on me when the cabin is done, will you?"

Hank lunged forward, and Riley grabbed Hank's leash and wrapped it around her hand.

Kate turned to look around and back at Riley. "What is it?"

Riley leaned in toward Kate and pointed.

"Oh, wow. They're beautiful," Kate whispered. "Are those bighorn sheep?

"Uh-huh. Easy, Hank."

"Would he go after them?"

"Yes."

# CABIN FEVER

Despite their hushed words, the sheep scurried over the ridge to the other side and Hank relaxed.

"What hike do you want to do next?" Riley asked.

"I thought we were going fishing." Kate laughed and looped her arm through Riley's.

The tingle from Kate's touch spread to Riley's core like a speeding train. She placed her other hand on top of Kate's. "Anything you want."

"Anything?"

They were so close, but before Riley got the nerve up to kiss her, Hank squeezed between them, and Kate withdrew and rubbed his ears. The pleasant hum within Riley turned to doubt. Maybe she had misread Kate. After all, she was friendly to everyone, always smiling and laughing with little touches here and there.

Riley walked over to the lakeside, kneeled, and splashed water on her face. Instead of clarity, the multitude of feelings overwhelmed her, and uncertainty settled like a boulder in her gut. She needed to be back in control. "We should head home." She sprung up and threw on her pack. Kate gave her a funny look, and Riley realized the flimsy excuse didn't provide much cover for hiding her feelings. *Think.* "We'll have plenty of sunshine hiking, but I don't want a long drive in the dark."

"Oh, good point, given those crazy cliffs." Kate quickly threw on her pack and started down the trail.

Riley leashed Hank and followed. For now, everything was back on course, but they had to get through the drive. *God help me if she touches me in the truck.*

# Chapter Twenty-Four

KATE WOKE BEFORE THE sun because Riley promised a new adventure but groaned when Riley thrust a fishing pole in her hand. "I remember now, but do we have to go so early?" She blinked at the outdoor thermometer attached to the window. "It's thirty-six degrees."

"And two months from today, winter begins."

"Oh, that's just mean. It feels like winter already." Kate exaggerated a shiver.

"Relax. The sun will warm things up to sixty-two."

"When? By three o'clock?"

Riley cocked her head to one side. "I promised to teach you, and you promised to try. And it's the best time of year. Are you a chicken?"

"No, but it's cold and barely daylight. What about breakfast?" Kate crossed her arms. Seeing Riley so chipper in the morning perked Kate up, but she wasn't going to admit it.

"Nothing like a good cup of coffee on the river." Riley laughed and grabbed a thermos. Walking backward, she shook it at Kate. "Food is already in the truck."

"You're a tease." Truthfully, she looked forward to their outings and with each encounter, she lost a piece of her heart to Riley.

The day started with Riley practically pushing her into the cold river waters, but by the end, Kate had a blast. Her newfound love of outdoor sports was all due to Riley's enthusiasm, but it didn't hurt that Riley looked smoking hot when her muscles flexed.

At the end of the day, Kate followed Riley inside to the kitchen, lagging from exhaustion. Her eyes drifted down to Riley's cute, tight butt. "What a day."

Riley twisted around, and Kate was slow meeting her gaze.

"Were you staring at my ass?"

"Ah, no."

Riley grinned wickedly and leaned toward Kate. "Sure. Just like the day Hank tore off my towel, except I bet you don't like my jeans hiding the view." She winked.

Kate's mouth dropped open. Heat spread across her face and went straight down to her core. Over the past couple of days, Riley seemed more relaxed, and her teasing mood today was a total turn-on. Did Riley feel more? Good Lord, what would it be like to have Riley's arms around her? Her eyes dropped to Riley's lips. The thought of those lips all over Kate's body made her wet. Riley's laughter dragged Kate from her daydreaming.

"I wish I'd filmed you today, but I didn't want to risk dropping my phone." Riley snickered and mimicked Kate reeling in a trout. "'Oh, my, this one's big.'" She made an exaggerated shiver with a dumbstruck look to match. "'What! I'm not touching that thing. You get over here.'"

Riley chuckled so hard, she made herself cry. Soon Kate was giggling uncontrollably too and didn't notice Lilly standing in the kitchen doorway.

"Sounds like fishing was a success. How many did you catch?" Lilly asked.

"I caught three." Kate proudly pointed to herself and smiled. "Riley only caught one."

"Yeah, but my one outweighed your three."

Kate stuck out her tongue. "Spoilsport. You could have let this rookie bask in her glory for a little bit."

"I'm happy you two had a good trip. I'm especially looking forward to you two rodeo gals cooking me supper. But," Lilly wagged her finger, "you know my policy, Riley. Clean the fish outside."

"But the wind's picked up." Riley threw up her hands.

Lilly pointed to the door. "Outside, now. Kate can shower and have a cup of tea with me while you're busy. Go!"

Riley gathered up the fish and left.

"I haven't heard her laugh that hard in years." Lilly's eyes sparkled. "It's wonderful to see her so happy."

Kate liked seeing Riley that happy too, and she especially liked Lilly's implication that it was her doing. "We started off in the pits but ended up on the mountain top. She's a good friend." But an insatiable itch inside her told her they were more than friends.

Lilly stepped forward and sniffed the air. "I'd hug you, but you smell like fish."

"Your darling niece took my first trout and rubbed it on my shirt and jacket. She said it was an initiation ceremony." Kate laughed, remembering how she tried to run away, but Riley had chased her with the fish.

"Go on upstairs, lickety-split. I'll make us tea."

"Thanks." Kate paused. "Lilly?"

"Yes, dear?"

"I miss my mother. You remind me of all the good times with her."

"Oh, what the heck." Lilly bear-hugged Kate. "Riley's like the daughter I never had, and you're fast becoming my second."

Kate's eyes misted over as she relished Lilly's affection. "Thank you for everything. I should shower." She thumbed over her shoulder. "If Riley beats me to it, she'll hog all the warm water."

"That she will. Go on, child."

Lilly's term of endearment wrapped around her like a warm blanket. Moving here was turning out to be one of the best things Kate had ever done. And with each day that passed, she thought less and less about moving back to Chicago.

\*\*\*

Kate's alarm woke her from a lustful dream. She smiled, but a few seconds later, her smile faded. Today's big reveal of Kate's newly renovated cabin would be bittersweet. She was unsure about living alone after enjoying Riley and Lilly's company for so long. Regardless, this was her life path and she'd have to deal with it.

She dressed and quietly hurried downstairs to cook breakfast. The first rays of sunshine painted the sky with lovely hues of gold and pink. She was almost finished by the time Lilly walked into the kitchen in her robe.

"Good heavens, what is that delicious aroma filling the air? And what time did you get up?" Lilly's eyes were wide.

"About an hour ago. I wanted to cook something special as a thank you for letting me stay." Kate smiled and poured Lilly a cup of coffee. "I have a spinach quiche and seasoned potatoes in the oven."

Lilly laughed, and she wiped her eyes. "You're well on your way to being a first-class country chef and outdoorswoman. I'm proud of you."

"Thank you." Kate gave her a one-arm hug, careful not to spill Lilly's coffee.

"Morning." Riley came in, rolling her shoulders. She wandered over to the coffee pot and poured some into a large travel mug. "I think I'll double-check the cabin before you two head over at ten." She sniffed the air. "What's cooking?"

"Kate made us a quiche." Lilly grinned like a proud mother.

"And it's almost done. You need to stay and eat. It's not good that you skip breakfast and eat junk half the time." Kate poked Riley's stomach and went to pull out the quiche.

"No way am I saying no to that."

"To Kate or the quiche?" Lilly grinned and sat down.

"I need a little extra cream." Riley buried her head in the refrigerator, apparently ignoring the question.

Kate had the notion to slap Riley's butt but restrained herself.

"I could use a little extra cream myself," Lilly said.

Kate glanced at Lilly, who was studying her. *Shit. She just got caught me ogling Riley.* Kate turned back around and plated the quiche along with some fresh strawberries.

"Thank you, dear." Lilly smiled when Kate placed her breakfast before her. "I'm going to miss having you around every day for breakfast and supper."

Kate squeezed Lilly's shoulder. "I'm going to miss you, but you're welcome at the cabin anytime."

"What about me?" Riley faked a pout.

"I'll miss you too." Kate lightly smacked Riley's arm.

"How about you stay for supper on the nights you work in town? Then you won't have to worry about rushing home and cooking, and I still get to enjoy your company." Lilly smiled brightly.

"I might just take you up on that once a week."

"You should give Aunt Lilly a set of keys to your cabin." Riley rose and grabbed the salt and pepper shakers from near the stove.

"That's a good idea in case of an emergency."

"I was referring to your kitchen. Once she sees your place today, she's going to want to cook supper up there all the time." Riley sat down, blew on her fingernails, and polished them on her shirt. She looked directly at Kate. "My fine architectural sense and artistic interior flair will blow you over and wow the pants off of you."

Kate gulped some coffee, which did nothing to cool her down or stop the heat emanating low and spreading throughout her body.

Riley stopped midway through chewing. She blinked rapidly then poked at the quiche with her fork. "This is great, but I've gotta go." Riley hopped up and wrapped up the rest of the slice. "I really need to check on the cabin. See you later."

"She needs to slow down." Lilly shook her head as the door shut. "Eat up, Katie, dear, then take your shower and finish packing. I'll do the dishes."

As they finished breakfast, she and Lilly indulged in some small talk. Kate nodded, only half-listening. She should be happy to move back into her own space but couldn't shake off the tinge of sadness. It settled on her chest like a heavy X-ray blanket. She was going to miss seeing Lilly and Riley every day.

# Chapter Twenty-Five

LILLY WAS STILL TALKING about plans for a winter garden in her greenhouse as Kate drove them to the cabin. Kate nodded now and then, but excitement and jitters swam in her stomach. The cabin was ready, and she couldn't wait to see it. "Almost there." Kate rounded the last corner.

Lilly's hands flew up. "Oh, my. It looks wonderful from the outside. They screened in the front porch."

"And no more leaking roof." Kate smiled. "I haven't been up here for a couple of weeks." She glanced at Lilly. "Seems someone had me busy in her greenhouse and cooking up new recipes."

"Why, for heaven's sakes, child. I don't know what you mean." Lilly's cheeks reddened.

Riley rushed up and helped Lilly out of Kate's truck, then turned to Kate. "Welcome to your new home."

"Did my new living room furniture arrive?" Kate motioned to the rocking chairs on the front porch.

"Yes, and I gave these beauties a new coat of paint yesterday afternoon, but they might still be sticky." Riley opened the front door. "After you, ladies."

Kate stepped through and glanced around, slowly taking everything in. She could hear Lilly gasp behind her. Then Kate turned in a circle like a kid. "Oh, my God. I can't believe the difference. It's so beautiful. And the windows are awesome." She clapped her hands and brought them to her mouth. It was beyond her dreams. "What type of wood is this?"

"The inside is stained pine, and we used Douglas fir to trim around the windows for that two-tone look." Riley pointed at the ceiling. "The beams are all Douglas fir and so are the new vertical support posts. It has an excellent strength-to-weight ratio for building and is the best choice for homes prone to storms, high winds, and earthquakes."

"Just what I expect from you. Builder lingo." Kate laughed. "But it's nice to know it would stand up to an earthquake. Thankfully, we don't have to worry about those."

Lilly's eyebrows rose almost to the top of her hairline, and an uncomfortable silence settled over the room.

"Idaho doesn't have earthquakes, right?"

"Well, dear, we do have some," Lilly said.

She swung around to face Riley. "How bad?"

"Most are minor, but the 1983 Borah Peak Earthquake registered 7.3 on the Richter scale and damaged parts of downtown."

"Then last year's quake measured 6.5," Lilly said.

"Yeah, but the center was deep in the forest and didn't cause much damage." Riley held up her index finger. "And we always build sure and steady."

"And you never thought to tell me this before?"

"Sorry. I thought you knew. You moved here." Riley jammed her hands in her pockets.

"You're right. I'm just," she drew a deep breath, "astonished." The earthquake detail knocked some of the wind out of her. "Okay. Let's finish the reveal. I love the kitchen island."

Lilly brushed her hand along the countertop. "You picked out a lovely granite."

"Thank you." Kate smiled. "But it's quartz. More economical."

"I couldn't tell the difference," Lilly said. "And I love the base cabinets in light gray and the top cabinets in white. It brightens the room."

"Best of all, they don't look a hundred years old."

"It figures you'd care most about the kitchen." Riley grinned.

"Well, dear, it's the best part of a home. And from your appetite, I'm guessing you agree." Lilly patted Riley's stomach.

Kate laughed. "Speaking of eating, I now have a dining room. The center table leaf is amazing."

"Hope you don't mind. I had a local craftsman cut the original in two and insert the leaf."

"Not at all. It matches perfectly." Kate smiled.

"He carves everything by hand, including the flowers on the side."

"Wow." Kate turned toward the new loft. "The spiral staircase is a work of art." She eyed the handiwork. "I thought it was going to be a basic ladder-type thing."

"Don't you like it?" Riley sounded concerned.

"I love it." Kate ran her fingers along the wood. It would be rude to ask the price, but she imagined the gorgeous one-of-a-kind staircase cost a pretty penny.

"It's a gift from me. The same guy who did the table built it."

"Riley, it's fabulous. Thank you." Kate tucked her hair behind her ear and smiled. Affection ran through her like an electric current, and she wrapped Riley into a hug. "Thank you, thank you, thank you."

Besides the truck and cabin from her father, no one had given Kate such a thoughtful gift in ages. And although she meant the hug as an act of gratitude, she hung on a bit longer, enjoying the feel of Riley's body tight against hers. Remembering Lilly was present, Kate stepped back. "Let's go upstairs."

"You go up, dear. I get enough knee exercise at my house," Lilly said.

The loft was the size of a small bedroom. Kate looked down at Riley. "It's cozy."

"You have room to put in a desk and a sleeper sofa or a full-size bed," Riley said. "Ready to see your new bedroom and bath?"

"Yep." Kate hurried down the steps.

"Goodness gracious, dear. Don't go so fast. It would be nasty if you fell," Lilly said.

Kate didn't mind Lilly's little reprimands. It was a sign that she cared, and it had been a long time since she'd felt that kind of love.

"Oh." Riley pointed to the corner of the living room. "Since we had to replace the stainless-steel flue, we replaced the potbelly with a higher capacity woodstove."

"Where does this lead?" Lilly asked.

Kate swung the door open. "My new bathroom. Have a look. The laundry nook to the right connects to my bedroom."

"It's bright. That's a nice-sized shower." Lilly slid open the shower glass door. "I love the aquamarine tiles. They shimmer like flowing water."

Kate smiled as she turned to Riley. "Do I have to take a two-minute shower?"

"No. The propane heats your water."

Kate walked into the bedroom, and Lilly and Riley followed. The walls were drywalled and painted a lovely cream color. The trim around the windows looked like Douglas fir too. "I wonder where the crocheted blanket came from?" She smiled at Lilly.

"Oh, just an extra one. I thought it'd look nice in your room."

"It's spectacular. Thank you." Kate stopped in her tracks at the French doors that opened to a rosy-red wood deck. "What's that? A deck wasn't on the plans, especially one that large."

They stepped outside.

With a sweeping hand gesture, Riley said, "The wood's Western Red Cedar. It's aromatic with a natural insect repellent. And we can leave it unstained, or you can pick out a clear or color stain, and I'll do it later. Regardless, it won't warp."

"It does smell wonderful. Cedar sounds expensive. Was there enough money in the budget?" Kate put her hand above her eyes to block the sun as she peered into Riley's eyes.

"The budget covered the materials, but Megan, Hayley, and I did the work as a gift." Riley motioned. "You still have a small stone patio leading to and around the fire pit that you wanted."

"Thank you for such generous gifts. Everything is gorgeous." The kindness took Kate's breath away, but she hoped Riley didn't stretch her profit margin too thin. Kate didn't worry about Megan; she had family money and drove a new top-of-the-line Ford truck. Kate wiped some tears of joy away. "I'll thank Megan and Hayley next time I see them. They're incredible."

"Yes, they are. And here's your fire pit." Riley motioned for them to sit down.

"Where did the chairs around the fire pit come from?"

"Oh, I'm guessing Santa Claus." The skin around Lilly's eyes crinkled as she giggled. "I think he also dropped off a couple of bottles of wine."

"This is all so wonderful." Kate hugged Lilly and kissed her cheek. She turned to Riley and hugged her. The contact was electric, and her heart thumped loudly. She kissed Riley's cheek but forced herself to stand back. "Thank you from the bottom of my heart. I can't believe your crew finished all of this so quickly."

"Being able to start in July was great luck. Thanks to the crew and the extra help, this is the smoothest renovation I've ever done. The materials were all in stock, the deliveries were on time, and we didn't hit any glitches." Riley held up her hands and laughed. "Well, no glitches after finding the rot in the roof."

"To celebrate you coming home, we stocked your new fridge with some goodies." Lilly glanced at her watch. "I figure it'll be noon by the time Riley talks your ear off. Then you two can make a fire." Lilly pulled her sweater tighter around herself. "I'll make sandwiches, cut up some cheese and fruit, and pour some wine. It's gotta be five o' clock somewhere."

"I like your thinking." Kate winked.

Kate and Lilly sat while Riley served them chilled Pinot gris. Kate imagined Riley looking mighty fine in a black tux with a bow tie. Maybe shorts instead of slacks. Or better yet, tight boy shorts from TomBoyX.

Riley put the bottle down and lifted her glass. "Here's to wishing everyone a good year filled with fun and dreams."

They clinked their glasses together and said, "Cheers." Kate's heart raced as she sipped. This was no longer a crush. She wanted Riley. If Lilly weren't here, Kate would give herself to Riley freely. Except she couldn't give Riley the guarantee of staying. And that made her hesitate big time.

# Chapter Twenty-Six

*October*

AFTER PLACING HER WATER and lunch into her backpack, Kate rolled up a wool blanket and strapped it on top. She'd also packed a compass, topographic map, a knife, matches, and a flashlight. Not that she ever hiked far enough to get lost but keeping a few essentials always on hand never hurt. She stepped outside, took a deep breath, and enjoyed the refreshing cool air. Wispy clouds against the blue sky and a slight breeze made for a delightful day. Groves of quaking aspen broke the dominance of the evergreens on the hillside, and their bright yellow leaves glimmered like gold coins.

At her favorite spot, she spread out the blanket and laid down with her hands folded over her chest. The leaves against the backdrop of the sky were beautiful, but it was the sound they made that amazed her. When the breeze rustled the leaves, they trembled like thousands of fluttering butterfly wings. Their unique sound was like no other tree.

Her lunch was tasty, the scenery was gorgeous, and the weather splendid. And to top it off, her cabin was spectacular. She couldn't have asked for a more perfect home and setting. But she was lonely not seeing Riley and Lilly daily, and she missed Sherry and Max. Video chat through her new satellite service was fun, but Kate couldn't wait until they arrived for a visit. The problem was, visits always ended, and she'd be alone again too soon.

She had begun to think of Idaho in a new light, but she wanted more. And that more included Riley. But after the cabin reveal, she had only briefly seen Riley a few times. Megan had said they were slammed with projects. She hoped that was the true reason and not that she was only imagining and wishing for something more.

Kate tossed her trash into her backpack and hiked out of the grove and to higher ground. After nearly four months here, she was used to the elevation and didn't tire as quickly. She hiked for an hour or more every day now, but the loneliness overshadowed today's fun. She wanted someone who could share her adventures. And once again, her mind turned to Riley. "Good God, I'm already going crazy not sitting down to dinner with her every day."

Kate stared up at the sky then closed her eyes and soaked up the sun. A little voice inside warned her about getting her heart broken, while another pushed her to take the risk. She had to talk this over with Sherry, but it was another week before they arrived for their visit.

"I'm talking to myself like a lunatic again. Yep, I'm going certifiably crazy."

She headed back to the cabin after another fifteen minutes. "I'm baking cookies and vicariously living through characters on Netflix. Might as well get the most out of the satellite service I'm paying for."

Sadness settled in her chest. Cookies and TV weren't going to make her happy. Sure she had made friends, but the town was so small. Some days, she made it through without worry, but on a day like today, she was lonely. One thing was clear. If she really wanted Riley, then she'd have to take the risk and make a move.

\*\*\*

The week dragged on, and a rare storm dumped a mix of snow and freezing rain. Even that didn't tamp down Kate's excitement over Sherry and Max's visit. They had safely arrived in Boise before the storms rolled through and were due any minute. Kate stirred the stew on the stove, then strolled out onto the front porch and sat down in the rocker with a cup of coffee.

The sky was blue with popcorn-shaped clouds, and the temperature had significantly risen, melting most of the icy mixture. Kate had tried to clear off the walkway earlier, but there was only so much you could do with gravel. It was a total muddy mess elsewhere with patches of slush. She put her coffee down and smiled as a rental car drove up.

Max parked and Sherry jumped out of the passenger side. "How ya doing, grizzly mama?"

Kate ran toward her friends with open arms. "I'm so happy to see you guys. I've missed you so much."

"Same here." Sherry squeezed her tight. "But it's freaking freezing out here."

"What did you expect? You're in a dress with no coat, it's October, and I live at nearly eight thousand feet." Kate laughed as she rubbed Sherry's exposed arms.

"We stayed in a swank hotel last night. Max had arranged a couple of hours at the spa and a private candlelit dinner in our room." Sherry's face glowed. "We had their fancy buffet breakfast this morning. It was fabulous, but they had a dress code." She rolled her eyes. "Can you believe that? A freaking dress code for breakfast. They stopped Max and asked her to switch out her black jeans and tennis shoes for dressier attire."

"I kept my cool and politely argued and won." Max removed the suitcases from the car.

Sherry grinned. "I kept the dress on in the car so I could enjoy Max caressing my thigh."

"TMI." Kate stuck her fingers in her ears and grinned.

"Also, I didn't know who we'd run into." Sherry raised her eyebrow. "Is the cute builder here?"

"No, she isn't."

"But you're going to tell me all about her, right?"

"Yes, now get inside, Miss Troublemaker, before you freeze to death." Kate swatted Sherry's shoulder. "I'll help Max with the luggage."

"I'll gladly take you up on that." Sherry took a few steps backward and pivoted toward the porch.

"Be careful—"

Sherry lost her balance, caught her stiletto heel in the mud, and fell sideways. Kate and Max rushed to help her stand. Splotches of mud covered her, and one shoe was missing from her foot.

"I guess I'll be needing a hot shower." Sherry unceremoniously pushed in her boob that was about ready to pop out.

"I'm so sorry. The gravel walkway is usually sufficient, but it was one hell of a storm yesterday."

"It's all good. Mud wrestling's probably a sport around here." Sherry grinned.

"Let's get you cleaned up." Kate wrapped her arm around Sherry's waist.

"These are trashed." Sherry giggled and kicked off the other heel. "But

I don't care. I'm with my bestie."

They stepped inside, and Sherry gazed around at Kate's newly renovated cabin while Max unloaded the car. "Wow. That's all I can say. The photos of before and after looked terrific, but this is out of this world. I loved the vaulted ceilings. Oh, and you have a loft with an artistic staircase."

"Riley had the staircase custom built for me."

"Just a friend. Uh-huh." Sherry looked at Kate with a gleam in her eyes.

"Something smells good." Max dropped their luggage by the door.

"Vegetable stew. I'll put biscuits in the oven while you shower." Kate showed them where to find all the towels and toiletries. It wasn't long before Max came out dressed in sweatpants.

"You can take my bed, and I'll sleep here on my pull-out sofa." Kate patted the sofa cushion.

Max shook her head. "We're not taking your bed. The sofa sleeper is fine with us."

"Okay." Kate pointed to the sleeping bags and a tent next to the coat rack. "What's up with the camping gear?"

"We have to sleep under the stars at least one night."

Kate rolled her eyes and dropped onto the sofa. "Max, you're out of your mind. Sherry's not going to sleep outside."

Max sat beside her. "She promised to try one night. I figured we'd set up next to the cabin. That way, she can sneak back if she's unhappy."

"Want to bet on how many minutes it takes her before she comes running inside?"

"Hey, I heard that." Sherry emerged from the bathroom wearing jeans and a pink, blue, and white plaid flannel shirt. Pink fluffy slippers with bunny ears completed the look.

"Nice shirt." Kate smirked. "And what's up with the slippers?"

"I bought *one* flannel to blend in with the locals, and I like the slippers. They're warm." She plopped down between them and wiggled her toes. The bunny ears flopped. "Now spill the beans about this dashing builder, Riley."

Max shook her head and stood. "You two catch up. I'm going for a walk and to check out the rest of the property." She kissed Sherry and left.

"Come on. I've been good and haven't teased you for weeks. Don't torture me any longer." Sherry twisted to face Kate and swung her arm on the back of the sofa.

"We're only friends."

"And that adorable blush says you want a lot more."

"Yes. I admit it. But she's busy, and I didn't want to screw up our friendship. What if the winter's horrible, and I decide to cash in and leave by the summer? Riley deserves better than me treating her like a vacation fling. And you know my track record with women. Nothing lasts very long, except Audrey." Kate grumbled. "And that was a match made in purgatory."

Sherry made an X-sign with her two index fingers. "Don't mention her name again." She bumped Kate's leg. "Sweetie, you've had some missteps but don't give up on love. If you like Riley, then do something. Make the first move. Kiss her. What the hell are you afraid of? The Kate I know is not a chickenshit."

Kate hopped up and took the biscuits out of the oven.

Sherry threw her hands in the air. "A few dates and kisses could go either way, but you'll never know unless you try. Get off your ass before you go crazy sitting around alone in this cabin. And if you and Riley decide friendship is all it's going to be, then that's okay. Look at how our friendship grew once we split up."

Kate threw her head back and laughed. She dropped back down onto the sofa. "We were in college, and we were young and stupid."

"And blissfully having fun. Casual sex can be fun as long as both parties are honest about their expectations and boundaries. I say make the first move and see where it goes. Kiss her." Sherry lightly placed her fingers on Kate's arm. "By the way, I *am* meeting her, yes?"

"Yes. Max wants to go fishing, so I asked Riley to arrange the trip."

Sherry wrinkled her nose. "I'm meeting her, then staying here, right?"

"Wrong-o, missy. We're all going the day after tomorrow."

"I don't like fishing. Max has taken me twice, and I've never caught one. I'm staying in your comfy cabin."

"You always say, 'Think positive.' Take your own advice and come with us." Kate nudged her arm.

"Okay." Sherry bolted upright as if she'd had an idea. "I'll go, and if I catch a fish, then you take Riley aside and kiss her." Sherry tilted her head. "Be brave. You can do it."

Sherry was unlikely to catch a fish. But if she did, then what? It could be embarrassing and awkward if Riley rejected her. On the other hand, Kate's desire had been simmering on the back burner far too long.

"Okay, you're on."

# Chapter Twenty-Seven

RILEY'S ARRIVAL MADE KATE'S stomach erupt in butterflies. And every time Riley drew near, her subtle cologne drove Kate nuts. But it was Riley's muscular, flat stomach and strong arms and legs that made Kate quiver.

"Good morning." Riley waved.

Kate snapped out of her haze. "Hi. I'd like you to meet my best friends, Sherry and Max."

They piled into Riley's truck after the greetings. Sherry settled in the back next to Kate. She winked and mouthed, "Sexy." Kate swatted her leg, but she didn't try to stop the smile that came from thinking about how sexy Riley was. Max sat in the front with her digital SLR. As they traveled north, she snapped picture after picture.

"So, what do you think, Max?" Kate asked.

"It's different from other parts of the Rockies—unique and beautiful." Max grinned at Sherry over her shoulder. "Maybe we can stay a little longer than a week."

"Sure, when we hit it rich and no longer have to work."

"Smile." Max reached back and touched her knee. "Today's going to be a blast. And tonight, we'll have steelhead trout for dinner."

"Yes, and I have a feeling today is my lucky day. I'm catching my first fish." Sherry turned and gave Kate a wicked grin.

Unlikely as that may be, Kate felt giddy about kissing Riley. Sherry was right. One of them had to address the growing attraction soon, or it'd be a long, extra cold winter.

They met Megan, their guide for the day, at the river. Her family owned the land along the river, and her dad owned a fishing store in Stanley. Max grinned as Megan explained fly-fishing techniques and showed them all the gear, including the chest-high waders.

"You didn't say we were getting into the river." Sherry glanced at Kate with wide eyes.

"Are you chicken?"

Sherry put her hand on her hip. "Bring it on. If you can do it, so can I." She stepped forward to grab her waders and boots.

"One more thing," Megan said. "Kelly will be arriving soon to set up a picnic table and grill our lunch. We'll have barbeque chicken and whatever fish you catch."

"That sounds like heaven. Now let the fishing begin." Max grinned.

After an hour, everyone except Sherry had caught a couple of fish. The frustration shone in her face, but Kate didn't dare point out that it would help if she waded deeper into the river.

Sherry cast her line out again. "I got one. And he's a strong devil." She reeled and pulled. The steelhead thrashed out of the water, wriggling to get off the line.

"You can do it," Max yelled.

"Give the line some slack," Megan said. "Steelhead are strong. Let the reel's drag system wear the fish down. And walk a few steps into the river. You're in too shallow."

Kate counted two steps that Sherry took. She shook her head and grinned. Sherry fought gallantly. She reeled, then let the line go slack as Megan had instructed. The steelhead flipped, jumped, and thrashed. Sherry complained about getting tired, but she kept at it. And with every minute that went by, she inched further into the water.

"You can tell that it's a big fish from how the rod is bending," Riley said. "She was so hesitant, but she's one determined woman."

Kate nodded. "She's an amazing person who never gives up."

"Oh, my God. Look at that." Sherry reeled the tired fish in closer.

The fish appeared to have relented, but then in a flash, it darted away and sent Sherry splashing in the stream.

"Oh no, you don't." Sherry stood as she grappled with the rod and reel.

Max cheered. "That's it, sweetcakes. Hold on."

Kate couldn't believe Sherry was still fighting despite taking a bath in the icy water. Megan offered to take over, but Sherry wouldn't have it. She and the fish battled it out for another five minutes before the fish succumbed, and Sherry deposited it safely in the basket. With Max's assistance, Sherry walked to shore with her head held high.

"Let's weigh it." Megan pulled the fish out of the basket, and everyone gathered around, gawking at the whopper. Riley handed Megan the digital fish scale. "Twelve-point-four pounds. Congratulations, that's one of the biggest of the entire fall season."

"And you all didn't think I could do it." Sherry smiled and stood tall and proud.

"My oh so strong ultra femme. I love you." Max cupped her face and kissed her.

"How about a picture?" Megan asked.

Sherry made Max hold the fish while she pretended to touch it.

"Honey, tonight you get to massage my aching ass. And you!" Sherry pointed to Kate. "You lost the bet. Off you go."

"What bet?" Riley asked Kate.

"Just a small wager." Kate kept her gaze on Sherry and her fish, but Riley continued to watch her. Heat burned across Kate's face, and she knew it wasn't from the fire.

"Why are you blushing?"

Kate shrugged. "I'm not."

"Now I'm intrigued." Riley took a metal container out of her upper breast pocket. "Mint?" She offered the box to Kate.

"Thanks."

With the pictures over, Sherry sauntered up.

"Nice fishing for a beginner," Riley said.

"Why, thank you." Sherry turned to Kate. "I'm going to get into some dry clothes. Time for you to pay up."

"Later. Isn't it time for lunch?" Kate turned toward the area where Kelly was grilling.

"Oh, no, you don't. A bet's a bet."

"I have to hear this. What's the bet?" Max asked.

Everyone looked at Kate. There was no way she was getting out of it. She turned to Riley. "Let's take a walk."

"Okay."

Kate took Riley's arm and dragged her away. Excitement and terror rattled her brain. *Don't think. Just go with it.*

"Slow down," Riley said. "No one can hear or see us since you hiked practically into Wyoming. What do you want to say?"

"We're planning a hike in the next couple of days, and I was wondering if you'd go with us. And maybe you'd like to have dinner. Just the two of us. Not on the trail or fishing. A date in a restaurant. Or maybe at my house. I could cook for you." What a hell of a time to have diarrhea of the mouth. Kate's heart thumped in her chest.

"We're pretty busy. I'm not sure I can get away. How about next weekend?"

"That's great."

Riley took a step closer. "Was that the bet? Asking me out?"

Kate's heart went from thumping to galloping. They stood so close that she could smell the mint on Riley's breath and see the caramel streaks in her eyes. Her nostrils filled with the heavenly scent of Riley's woodsy cologne.

Riley rested her hand on Kate's arm as if teasing her to go further. The sensation through Kate's flannel shirt sent a jolt throughout her body. She trailed her fingertips down Riley's cheek, then cupped her chin and placed a tender kiss on Riley's soft, intoxicating lips. Kate's body tingled in places that hadn't for quite some time.

Slowly, she pulled back and searched Riley's eyes for a reaction. Riley hadn't pulled away but neither had she returned the kiss. Kate was beginning to panic when Riley reached out and cradled her hand. She rubbed her thumb over the top of Kate's hand and gazed into her eyes. The simple touch of Riley's soft fingers and the warmth of her eyes enthralled Kate. Slowly, she leaned in and kissed Kate, softly at first, then with an intensity that took Kate to dizzying heights.

Anxious to touch her, Kate slipped her fingers under the hem of her shirt and skimmed her fingertips across her stomach. Riley slid her hand down low on Kate's back, then brushed her backside. Every inch of Kate's skin was on fire.

"Where are you guys?" Sherry's voice boomed in the distance.

Reluctantly, Kate broke off. "The bet was the kiss."

"I'm not a big gambler, but I enjoyed that bet."

"Lunch is ready. Or have you found something tastier in the woods?" Sherry's laughter sounded closer.

"Looks like Sherry's advice is spot on, but her timing sucks."

Kate thumbed over her shoulder. "If we don't show up soon, she'll come looking for us. But I think there's time for one more kiss."

"Or two." Riley pulled Kate into her arms.

The kisses that followed eased Kate's worries. The delicious sensation of Riley's lips and hands sent a pleasant tingle down her body, straight to her clit. Damn, this woman could kiss, and Kate didn't want it to end.

\*\*\*

They had a date, and Kate was ecstatic all the way home. She waved goodbye to Riley as the setting sun slipped below the horizon, displaying reddish-orange colors across the wispy clouds in the sky.

"You ladies go relax on the back deck with a glass of wine. I'll put our things away."

"Thanks, Max." Kate turned to Sherry. "You get the wine, and I'll get the fire pit blazing."

"Deal."

Under the light from the crimson sky, Kate quickly built a fire and plopped down in a chair. Sherry handed her a glass of white wine and set a platter of cheese on a small round table between them.

"Thanks. God, I can't believe how tired I am."

"Me too, but I have to know the details in the woods."

"Our kiss was phenomenal."

Sherry bounced her legs rapidly up and down in celebration. "I told you. Those enemies-to-lovers relationships sizzle."

"Don't jinx me."

"She seems right for you. She's kind and considerate." Sherry put down her wine glass. "And she's a natural beauty. I think she'd look gorgeous in a suit or dress with her hair fixed up."

Kate nearly spat out the wine. "You'd never catch her in a dress or with a fancy hairstyle. And that's fine with me."

"Maybe not, but I'm just saying she's breathtaking. And she made that shack of yours into a gorgeous gem. That's some serious talent. And adding extras as gifts? Grab hold and make sure that kiss isn't the last."

Kate shook her head. "Oh, I promise that it won't be."

"Good."

They watched the flames dance as dusk slid into a clear night. Kate looked up. The stars here were so bright and peaceful.

"Kate, you know I miss you terribly."

"I miss you too. I thought I'd miss the pace of Chicago, but I've been glad to slow down. I think you were right about me being a workaholic." Kate pinched her thumb and index together and giggled. "Just a touch."

"You were, big time. But you're different now."

"Yeah, I'm no longer with those sharks that took over the firm."

"No, it's more than that. You seem happier than you have been for years."

Kate propped her feet up on the stone edge of the fire pit. "I thought I was nuts when I decided to give this place a try. I still get lonely now and then, but for the most part, it feels good."

"And why do you think that is?"

"The people in town are quirky but lovable. Dr. Allred has me hooked on genealogy research. And Lilly's become like a second mother. And Isaac—Father." Kate got up and poked the fire. "I wish he'd talked more. His letter was a shocker. It's strange how sometimes you learn more about a person in death than in life. But I have to admit, this whole place just seems to fit. Maybe it's my grandmother's spirit. Who knows?"

"Uh-huh. Is that it?" Sherry cocked her elbow on the chair's armrest.

"Riley. One kiss." Kate laughed. "Okay, several kisses."

"Oh, yeah. I knew you were in the woods a little too long. Things are looking up for you."

"Are you making wedding plans for me already?" Kate forced a giggle. "Let's see what the winter brings. I'm excited, but I hate snow. What if I can't make it through?"

Sherry shook her head and smiled. "Cuddle up with Riley in bed, and you'll make it through with flying colors."

"Oh, did I just walk into a personal conversation? I can leave." Max handed out the blankets.

"Thanks, Max. We just finished." Kate motioned for Max to sit.

Sherry put her hand on Max's thigh. "Honey, on a scale from one to ten, how compatible do you think Kate and Riley are?"

"You two do seem close."

"Ha, I told you." Sherry popped a cheese cube into her mouth.

"Yes, Momma Sherry. I'm going to date her, but let's not rent a U-Haul just yet."

"Hey, my intuition has got this." Sherry shook her finger. "And I bet you a spa weekend trip that you stay here."

"Don't push it."

"Are you scared, Ms. Minton?" Sherry said in her polished, professional voice.

# CABIN FEVER

"Nope."

"Then what's the problem?"

"Okay, it's a bet. Cheers!"

They clinked their wine glasses together.

All of the confusion and anger from the first days in Idaho had faded. And for the first time, Kate contemplated permanently living in the cabin. But she wasn't going to admit it to Sherry. She needed to make sure. Winter would be a serious test, and so would striking up a relationship with Riley. The former terrified her, but not the latter. Things were moving in the right direction, thanks to Sherry's nudge.

Kate leaned back in the chair and looked up at the beautiful night sky. A shooting star blazed across brightly, and the warmth of contentment spread through her as she made a wish.

# Chapter Twenty-Eight

RILEY SLID THE CELL phone into her pocket. "Can I have a word with you, please?"

Megan followed Riley outside. "What's up?"

"Puck was doing so good but showing up late this week is pissing me off." Riley put her hands on her hips. "It's nearly the end of October. We moved like a well-oiled machine with Kate's place, but everyone's slowed down on this project. Puck's a bad influence, especially on Charley."

"Despite her off-color jokes and sometimes lazy attitude, she's a damn good carpenter. I'll bring her in line."

As Riley's best friend, project co-manager, and often her voice of reason, Megan was right nine times out of ten. Riley begrudgingly admitted that they couldn't afford to lose Puck now that the three Challis workers had moved on to another project. "I'll give her one more chance. That's it. In the meantime, I'll look for another carpenter. It wouldn't hurt to have another helping hand because I'd like to cut my hours back." Riley rubbed her eye with the back of her hand. "Damn sawdust."

"Yeah, what else is driving you nuts?"

Riley jerked her head toward the truck, and Megan followed. Inside the cab, Riley sighed. "Kate. She's driving me crazy. Good crazy. Every time I'm around her, I get a little softer. In the woods after fishing, she kissed me, and I kissed her back. And when she asked me out, all I could do was grin and say yes."

Megan laughed. "And how is any of this bad?"

"It was terrific. It's just...I have trouble concentrating when I'm around her. Scratch that." Riley banged her hand against the steering wheel. "She's on my mind—a lot."

"Ah, the true root of the problem. You've fallen for Kate even before the first date."

Riley twisted toward Megan. "I don't know when, but somewhere along the line, my feelings shifted beyond friendship. And her kiss released all my bottled-up emotions." She took a deep breath and blew the air out with a whoosh. "Why does she have to be so sexy when she hikes or fishes? And damn, those light blue eyes are the color of icy glaciers; they're something else. And she's really sweet and fun to be around. I've wanted to kiss her for weeks, but she's the one that made the first move." Riley rested her head against the steering wheel.

"Why do you seem worried?"

"You know I'm not relationship material."

"That's self-pity crap. Your other girlfriends never tried to meet you halfway. They always wanted you to change and pushed you to move away from Merrick. And Beth was the worst of them all."

Riley cringed.

"Sorry, pal. But Kate is different."

Riley straightened up. "Kate's a good person." She swallowed and looked at Megan. "I told you the truth about going to Pocatello with Hayley, but there have been other times."

"Don't you dare date Kate if you want—"

"No." Riley shook her head. "I don't want to go back to meaningless hookups. But about two months before Kate came to town, I slept with two women from the bar. The thrill didn't last long before misery set in. I'm tired of being alone."

Riley tapped the steering wheel with her thumbs, and Megan slapped her hand on top to stop her.

"What if we start something, and the winter chases her away?" Riley asked softly.

"That's it? The great Riley is afraid of Ms. Kate. Say it ain't so?" Megan punched Riley's arm.

Riley swallowed. "In all honesty, a part of me is scared because I've never felt like this with anyone before."

"Relax. Don't be so hard on yourself. The way I see it, you scored big. But you have to give the relationship a chance, and you have to work at it." Megan pointed out the windshield. "Charley's coming this way." She shook her finger at Riley. "I think Kate's the real deal. Now, go pick up the lumber and supplies, boss."

Megan hopped out and gave a thumbs up before sauntering toward Charley.

As Riley drove off, her mind was partially focused on the unpaved road, but mainly on Kate. For as short as those kisses were, they'd unleashed a torrent of desire.

# Chapter Twenty-Nine

KATE WASHED HER HANDS and rushed to the living room. A ringtone on her MacBook signaled a FaceTime call.

"Hey, Sherry. Did you guys make it home okay?"

"Not yet."

"Okay. Did you make an exciting pitstop since you're grinning?"

Sherry stuck her hand in front of the camera. Kate's eyes widened at the sight of the large rock surrounded by an intricate pattern of diamond chips and another plain gold band. Then Sherry's ecstatic face popped back into the picture.

Kate finally shut her gaping mouth. "Is that two rings as in engagement and wedding bands?"

"Yes."

"Wow, you finally did it. Congratulations."

"Instead of flying back to Chicago, Max surprised me with a trip to Vegas and those gorgeous rings. She was so damn cute, getting down on one knee. I couldn't turn her down."

"Of course not. But getting married in Chicago would save you from your mother wringing your neck. You know she's been planning a huge wedding for you over the past year." Kate smiled.

Sherry's chuckle sounded genuine, then a little shaky. "Yeah. I'm not sure how I'm going to break that news to her."

"Hi, Kate." Max stuck her face in the camera.

"Hi, Max. A little piece of advice: don't be around when Sherry tells her mother. Hey, maybe go to Canada and hang out until she stops being mad."

They all laughed.

"Max's parents are a dream. They already know. I'll have Dad help me with Mom. Anyway, I just wanted to let you know."

"Congratulations. I'm happy for you both. You two are the best."

"Thank you. Anyway, we have tickets for a Cirque du Soleil show. Talk later. Bye." They both waved goodbye.

"Bye, guys."

She was so happy for her friends but longed for her own happily-ever-after. Could Riley be the one? Thoughts of Riley flooded Kate's senses since that day in the woods. She could hardly wait until Friday evening when Riley was taking her out to dinner for their first date.

# Chapter Thirty

Riley's resistance fell when Kate kissed her on that fishing trip, but tonight was their first official date. Excitement and nerves hummed through her body. She stood in front of Kate's door and glanced down at the crisp, forest-green shirt she'd teamed with dark gray dress slacks and a matching blazer. She swallowed and knocked, hoping for the best.

When the door swung open, her pulse double-timed. Kate looked stunning in a simple black dress that hugged her body in all the right places. A gold shawl draped over her shoulders and tied in the front revealed enough cleavage to make Riley drool. "You look spectacular."

"Thank you. And you look striking."

Riley smiled. She didn't dress up often, but it was worth it just to see Kate's glowing face.

"Are you going to come in?" Kate grinned.

"Yes, of course." Her gaze didn't leave Kate's, and she almost tripped over the threshold. Somehow Kate had turned her unrattled disposition into a nervous shish kabob. Dreams of kissing and touching Kate had run wild and consumed Riley, but she decided to play it slow. She'd never forgive herself if she screwed this up.

Tonight, she wanted to pamper Kate. Since Merrick didn't have any romantic dining choices, Riley had made a reservation at Michel's Christiania in Ketchum, one of the best French cuisine restaurants in the West. On the drive, she let Kate do most of the talking.

"You're a little quiet." Kate put her hand on Riley's forearm.

The softness of Kate's skin added to the flame flickering within. She swallowed hard and glanced over. Oh, how Kate's lips formed a cute yet devilish grin. Riley's gaze darted back to the road, and she jerked the wheel to bring the truck back from the centerline. "Sorry. Just trying to concentrate on driving. I think you'll like the surprise."

"Surprise? I thought dinner was at a French restaurant."

"There's something that I want to show you before."

When Riley pulled into the Sawtooth Botanical Gardens' parking lot, she cut the engine and leaned her arm on the back of Kate's seat. "We don't have much time as they close at sunset, and it's cold. But seeing the Garden of Infinite Compassion is worth the stroll."

They got out of the truck, and Riley guided Kate to a pavilion.

Kate stopped, and her face lit up. "Wow. That's a big Tibetan prayer wheel."

"Four hundred pounds. The Dalai Lama gifted it during his visit in 2005. It was hand-constructed by goldsmiths and painters in Dharamsala, India, with over a million prayers."

"The detail is exquisite. Good karma." Kate spun it clockwise. "The world would be a better place if people looked inside themselves first to begin positive changes. Too many people, like my brothers, rely on material objects and external validation for their happiness." Kate shook her head. "Listen to me. I even got caught up in that shit at one point."

"And is it better now that you live here?" She thought Kate was far more optimistic now than when she'd first arrived in Merrick but waited for Kate's answer with bated breath.

"It's growing on me, especially the people." Kate winked. "I miss larger cities from time to time. Ketchum and Sun Valley are nice, but I'd like to visit Boise when they have a major art show. Any chance you could take me?"

"Your personal guide awaits, madam." Riley bowed. The sinking sun's rays added warmth to Kate's beautiful features. She leaned in and placed a soft kiss on Kate's lips which turned into a deep tongue tingler. "Are you warm enough?"

"I'm getting a little chilled." Kate buttoned her coat.

"Let's go to dinner." Riley placed her arm over Kate's shoulders and was pleased when Kate leaned in and hugged her waist. They strolled back to the truck, watching the sunset.

At the restaurant, Riley ordered them an appetizer and let Kate pick the wine. When it arrived, she took a sip of the chardonnay. "You have good taste."

"Thank you. Is this restaurant one of your favorites?"

"It's one of Lilly's favorites. The chef and owner is Michel Rudigoz. He bought the restaurant in the mid-nineties. But his biggest claim to fame is coaching the US downhill ski team, including Picabo Street."

"Gold medalist, right?"

"Yep. Idaho born and raised just south of here. This place has a long history. It was known as the Christy and was one of Ernest Hemingway's favorite restaurants. Did you know that he finished his novel *For Whom the Bell Tolls* down the road at the Sun Valley Lodge?"

Kate tilted her head back and laughed. Riley had the urge to stroke her fingers down Kate's creamy, smooth skin.

"Riley Anderson. I never would have guessed you to be a Hemingway fan. I thought you were more into modern novels, especially lesbian novels."

"I read his books in school, but his enthusiasm for the outdoors hooked me." Riley sipped her wine and talked more about local history. Kate seemed to appreciate the natural beauty but had little background in how the West played a role in US history. Riley loved it all and wanted to share it with Kate. And now more than ever, she wanted Kate to make Idaho her home.

Kate drained her glass and ordered another. "Interesting local tales, but I'd like to know more about you. Tell me one big thing you dream about."

Kate's floral perfume filled her with desire. The temptation to snuggle Kate tight was overwhelming. Riley took a sip of wine and placed her hand on top of Kate's. She wanted to answer, "Have you stay here forever," but she shrugged instead. "That's a hard question."

"Be brave. Tell me a dream." Kate squeezed her forearm.

The innocent touch warmed Riley. "Okay, but it does involve history."

Kate hung her head with a fake grunt but then laughed and kissed Riley's cheek. "Just make it personal, please."

"I've never been to the ocean, and I'm curious about other cultures. I was a quiet student all through school and did okay. Then I got stuck with a Western Civilization class my senior year and thought it would be the most boring thing in the world, but Mrs. Karr made learning about ancient cultures exciting. Someday, I'd like to go to Greece and Italy, see the ancient buildings and ruins, enjoy the food, and relax on the beaches of the Mediterranean. There. It's a big dream that will likely never happen." She bit the inside of her cheek.

"Why do you say that? You seem like a person who could do anything you put your mind to."

"The cost alone." Riley took a deep breath. Some things were hard to admit, but she had to be honest if they were to form a deeper relationship. "I might own a business and co-own another with Aunt Lilly, but our margins are slim. I don't want to raise prices because we're better off than some of our neighbors. So my trips are shorter and planned closer to home."

"What if you shared that cost with a loved one or friends? You could put savings aside every year and go for a big event like your fiftieth birthday."

"Maybe." Riley picked up a piece of brioche toast with smoked salmon and topped it with a dollop of onion and sour cream dip. "What about you?"

"I also love to travel. I've been on a couple of fun weekend trips to Canada and eight states but half were for work, which isn't much fun. My favorite trip was to Mackinac Island."

While talking about summer sunsets on Lake Huron and horse and carriage rides, Kate drank her second glass of wine, then they each ordered another.

"And what about your dream?" Riley squeezed Kate's hand.

"My cooking sucks."

"What? You're too harsh on yourself. You never had the time before, and now with Aunt Lilly helping you, I find your cooking wonderful." Riley melted at Kate's smile.

"Wonderful, minus a few burnt dishes." Kate giggled. "Thank you."

"And your dream, please."

"I'd like to combine a trip with cooking lessons, preferably somewhere sunny and warm." She laced her fingers with Riley's. "I'd join you on a trip to Italy if you'd also take cooking lessons with me. But I can't believe you've never been to the ocean. Not even to the West Coast?"

"Nope. I've been throughout the Rocky Mountains and various state and national parks but never the ocean."

"Someday, I think you'll make it to the Med."

Kate moved her hand under the table and rested it on Riley's thigh, and heat pooled between Riley's legs. The waiter came by with another glass of wine for Kate, but she didn't remove her hand.

"Let's switch categories," Kate said. "If you could make one impact in the world, what would it be?"

"Are we out to dinner, or are you interviewing me?"

Kate laughed. "Come on. I've cracked your hard exterior and want to see inside."

Riley twirled her wine glass and cleared her throat. "A lot of good people live in Merrick and Idaho. But no matter how many times a person says they accept and love you, a few in the crowd always want things shoved behind a closed door. Hush, hush. Like the recent push to ban books from schools because they 'harm children.'" She gritted her teeth. "Did you know that Idaho's state legislature is considering a bill that would fine school librarians a thousand dollars and threaten them with a year in jail if they don't remove certain books?"

Kate shook her head. "That's ghastly."

"Lena and her cronies support the idea, but I was shocked at a few others. Hell, I knew when I was eight that I liked girls. And if a novel or memoir can mold a kid's sexuality, I should be straight, because I never had any gay books or saw any queer TV characters growing up. It was all straight people talking about how happy they were to get married and have babies." *And how queer people were an abomination.* Riley took a swig of her wine. After her father died, her mother removed the TV and books were mainly religious. Now wasn't the time to delve into those raw memories. "Anyway, we all deserve to grow up with the freedom to be who God made us. And we deserve to have a partner and family without society shaming us or making fun of us. I can't give my time, but I make contributions to organizations that fight for the rights of all Americans. We can't slide backward."

"Good may get knocked around, but I'd like to believe that the best in us always prevails. And right now, I'm having a delicious dinner with a smart and caring woman." Kate squeezed her thigh again, then removed her hand. "Thank you for sharing with me." She lifted her wine glass. "Cheers."

"Cheers." Riley's hand slightly trembled as they clinked their glasses together. If it hadn't been for Aunt Lilly, Uncle George, and her chosen family, she wouldn't have survived into adulthood. They saved her life and gave her the freedom to become who she was today. And it turned her stomach to think that others wanted to erase years of progress.

"Ladies, the mains should be coming out soon. Can I get you another drink or appetizer?" The waiter topped off their water.

"Thank you. I'll have a third glass of wine with dinner, please." Kate smiled at the server.

"A little more of the dip, please." Riley waited until he left, then leaned into Kate. "You're on your third glass already."

"Oops. Well, in my defense, it's good wine."

"Yes, it is." Riley liked a slightly inebriated Kate. She was more carefree and chattier but in a pleasant way. "And what impact do you want to make, Ms. Minton?"

"Promise that you won't laugh at me."

Riley held up her index and middle fingers together in the scout symbol. This should be interesting since she had never seen Kate drink this much.

"I'm still not sure about the winter, but I enjoyed the summer and fall. I thought living in the country was too quiet at first, but now I'm beginning to find more peace and enjoyment in nature."

Riley blinked. Interesting. Where was this leading?

"Almost all of the tourist activities are in Ketchum and Sun Valley. There's not much around Merrick. But wouldn't it be great if Merrick had a country retreat for city women of all ages and backgrounds. A place where women could come for a few days or a week to see a flip side of life."

"Who are you?"

Kate lightly smacked Riley's bicep. "I'm not joking. I'm not talking about anything elaborate, just some relaxation, easy hikes with picnics, that sort of thing. But if I ran such a place, my picnics would include wine and cocktails at sunset. Oh, and a good spa."

"You could open up a zipline course. Hayley could set you up. She used to be an instructor. Have you ever done it?"

Kate rolled her eyes. "No."

"I'd love to see you try. It's a blast. But unfortunately, the only zipline adventure parks are near Boise. We could take in the museums one day and zipline the next. And I promise I've only seen one wardrobe malfunction, but that lady wasn't wearing a bra and her T-shirt was skimpy."

Kate chuckled until tears rolled down her face. She looked adorable as she dabbed her face carefully, not messing up her makeup.

"I'd be the one who helped the proprietor find clients and advise on the spa and the menu. But I promise not to cook."

They were still laughing as the server brought their main course.

"Your glass of wine, ma'am." He grinned. "Enjoy, ladies. Can I get you anything else? More bread?"

"Thank you."

Kate cracked up again as the server walked away. "I'm getting drunk. Sorry, I was a little nervous and forgot how many glasses of wine I'd had."

"Nervous?" If only Kate knew how Riley had been earlier.

"I'm not nervous anymore." Kate clasped her hand around Riley's. "I like the soft side of you. You're a very compassionate person."

"So are you." She kissed the back of Kate's hand.

Riley had dessert and coffee to finish the meal while Kate had a dessert wine. They held hands on the way back to the truck. Kate tugged at Riley's hand. "Listen."

"I hear fifties' oldies."

"And look." Kate pointed.

Riley's head turned. "No. I'm not dancing, especially to music before Aunt Lilly's time."

"Oh, come on. I double-dog dare you. Where's your adventure to do something different?"

Riley protested as Kate dragged her inside and onto the dance floor, but it was hard to resist Kate's enthusiasm. She glanced around. "Half of these people are over sixty, and the other half are on life support."

"Stop it. That's not entirely true. Dance with me. I'll make it worth your while. Stay here."

"What?"

Kate rushed over to the DJ, stuffed some tip money in his jar, said something, and returned with a big grin. The following four songs were all slow love songs. They might not have been Riley's taste but having Kate against her body felt like heaven. It'd be a miracle if she didn't remove Kate's dress tonight.

Once the slow music stopped, Kate said, "Okay. You're off the hook if you want to leave." She turned to walk away.

"No way." Riley caught her arm. "It's just getting good with classic rock 'n roll. I love 'Great Balls of Fire.'"

Kate had rhythm. Riley not so much, but all she cared about was the smile on Kate's face. She threw in some ridiculous moves in the song's middle to get Kate laughing. They danced to six of Elvis' rock 'n roll songs then the DJ took a break.

"You're jealous of my style, aren't you?" Riley bumped Kate's shoulder.

"More like embarrassed." Kate giggled.

"What?" She laughed with Kate then pulled her in tight. "Take that back."

Kate's breath against her neck sent a delightful shiver down Riley's back.

"You're loads of fun, but do you want to expend all your energy? You have to drive us home and save a little for hugs and kisses," Kate said.

"Is that all?" She couldn't believe she'd been so bold to say that.

Kate looked at her. "We'll see."

They walked to the truck holding hands. Inside, she kissed Kate before starting the engine. When Kate's hands skimmed down her chest, her hammering heart tripled in beat. Riley gulped for air when they broke apart. "We'd better go before we get arrested in the parking lot for obscene public behavior." She drove well below the speed limit. The wine she consumed wasn't a problem since two hours had passed. But sexy Kate, twirling her fingers through her hair and stroking her thigh dangerously close to her center, was a distraction. The wine made Kate bold, and Riley liked this playful side, but they needed to slow down. "Whoa."

"What?"

"Any other time, I'd love your hand under my shirt but not while driving through the mountains. I'm going to have an accident. Let's wait until we get home. Please."

"Spoilsport."

The thought that Kate might be the one to capture her heart still scared Riley a tiny bit. Right now, she wanted to get them home safe and then rip Kate's clothes off. The truck's Bluetooth system lit up and caller ID showed a phone call from the Merrick Medical Clinic.

"What the hell? They're not open this time of night." Riley punched the button. "Hello."

"Hi, Riley. It's Dr. Allred. I wanted to let you know that Nathaniel brought Lilly in. Her blood pressure dropped, and she fell. Everything's okay, but we're running a few tests. She's confessed to forgetting her medicine on occasion. That's probably the cause, but I want to make sure."

"We're halfway home from Ketchum. I'll be there within half an hour."

# CABIN FEVER

"Okay. Drive safe."

Every muscle in Riley's body tensed. Aunt Lilly was her rock.

"I'll go with you."

Riley swallowed and nodded. She increased the truck's speed to the limit. Sixty-five was too damn young for a serious problem, wasn't it? She couldn't lose Lilly. She'd be lost without her.

# Chapter Thirty-One

LILLY'S MEDICAL SCARE HAD jarred them both, but the worried look on Riley's face had lasted for days and made Kate's heart ache. She knew what it was like to lose a mother, and Riley's aunt was all she had. Fortunately, it was nothing serious. She helped Riley nurse Lilly back to full health and establish a routine with her new medicine, but their time alone had been limited until today.

She glanced at Riley, who flashed a gleaming smile before turning her attention back to the road. It was their second official date, and they were hiking to Goldbug Hot Springs. It was an all-day affair, but one Riley had planned before Lilly got sick. Riley loved the outdoors and seemed excited to take Kate to Goldbug.

Along the way, Kate marveled at how the terrain changed. After Clayton, the hills were barren and brown, except along the river. Evergreen trees dominated the hillside as they neared their destination. Kate missed the aspens' shimmering, golden leaves. As winter had crept closer like a silent stalker, the aspen leaves had fallen.

Kate rested her hand on Riley's, gently rubbing her thumb back and forth. Riley lifted her hand and kissed the back of Kate's. God, she had half a notion to tell Riley to pull over and take her in the truck.

"There's a horse ranch nearby." Riley pointed at a sign. "Do you like horseback riding?"

"Love it."

"We'll have to go some time."

"I'd like that."

"You're in for a treat. We have more natural hot springs than any other state, but Goldbug is the one you don't want to miss."

Riley turned off Route 93, and it wasn't long before she pulled into a dirt spot off to the right of the road. They hopped out and strapped on their backpacks.

"It's not busy." Kate pointed to the one car. "Maybe we'll have the place all to ourselves."

"I wouldn't complain." Riley pointed toward the track. "The trail is flat at first but turns steep, and the last section is strenuous."

"Do you think I can't handle it? I should be fine with a little mouth-to-mouth resuscitation." Kate grabbed Riley's shirt and pulled her in for a tender kiss, then took off at a brisk pace.

"Tease. You'd better slow down and save some of that energy for our leisurely soak."

"Catch me."

They made plenty of progress before tackling the first leg of steep terrain. Kate stopped to drink some water.

"I have to admit that section was tough. But the view beats the StairMaster at the gym."

"Yes, it does. And you're only a tiny bit out of breath. Let me help."

Riley rested her hands on Kate's hip, then pulled her in for a long kiss. Kate's nipples hardened as Riley pressed her body against her. When their kiss ended, she rested her head on Riley's shoulder, out of breath and lightheaded.

"Are you sure about the mouth-to-mouth method?" Riley whispered in her ear.

"I think we should practice it more."

"Agreed. But let's get to our destination first."

Riley held Kate's hand, and they walked part of the trail together. They separated when it got steep again. The terrain leveled out once more, and they crossed a bridge over a ravine. Kate stopped Riley in the middle and held onto the bridge railing. The expansive valley spread out before them. The contrasting view of the evergreen trees against patches of rocky, barren outcrops was incredible.

"Are you sick of Idaho yet? I know you mentioned a retreat in Ketchum, but..." Riley crammed her hands in her front pockets.

The question took Kate by surprise. "I wasn't kidding about how a retreat would be cool. Yes, I'm dreading the brunt of winter, but I'll make it through—"

"My favorite winter sport is snowmobiling, and you need to learn in case you're snowed in. You'll love it." Riley smiled.

"Are you challenging me?" She tickled Riley's ribs and was rewarded with another bright smile. "If yes, then I'll be your best student. However, you didn't let me finish my sentence. I'll make it through with your help because I want to see a lot more of you." She kissed Riley then pulled her up the trail. "Right now, I'm dying to take a dip in Idaho's number one hot spring."

The first pool they came across was heart-shaped. They waved hello and tried not to gawk at the three couples in their birthday suits.

One yelled, "Go naked. It's the only way."

Kate's pulse increased. She had a bikini on under her clothes. Would she dare take it off? What about Riley? Did she bathe in the buff? The tantalizing thoughts nibbled at Kate.

Riley led them to a trail winding down the hill toward another pool. The water cascading into the pool drowned out the voices of the rowdy group from above.

"This one's small but a little deeper and more private, with room for us to sit under the rock ledge and waterfall."

Kate shimmied out of her clothes and sank into the clear waters of the natural pool. "This is great. It's warmer than I expected." The sight of Riley's body in a bikini top and tight board shorts made Kate's breath hitch. How long she would last before giving in to temptation was anyone's guess. "Have you ever gone naked?"

Riley grinned. "No, but your swimsuit doesn't leave much to the imagination." She placed her towel and bag nearby and laid back in the water.

Kate splashed water in Riley's face, then straddled her for a lavish kiss. She nibbled on Riley's lower lip and ran her tongue across it. Riley slid her hand down Kate's back to her butt. The jolt of arousal coursed from her core to her chest. She gently brushed her fingertips over Riley's breast and pinched her hard nipple.

Riley moaned. "Oh, God, I want your hands all over me, but we need to be cautious."

"Why?" Kate kissed her neck.

"Because I don't want someone to interrupt us. I don't want anyone else but me to see you naked. And speaking of that, you've seen me but I've yet to see you."

Kate sucked in Riley's bottom lip. "I guess you'll have to wait a tad longer." She slid off Riley and sat beside her. When Riley smoothed some loose strands of hair behind Kate's ear, her body came to life again. Never before had a woman's innocent touch so enthralled her. "Okay. I can settle for some hot kisses for now."

"I never get tired of kissing you. But I'm hungry." Riley grinned and stretched for her backpack.

"I can't believe you're choosing food over me. That's rude."

"You're too quick to judge." Riley removed a plastic container from the backpack. She placed a large strawberry between her teeth then turned and slowly moved forward until her lips and the strawberry were inches from Kate's mouth.

Kate bit the strawberry in half and chewed while gazing into Riley's eyes. Afterward, she pulled Riley in for a deep kiss. The taste of berry mixed with red hot desire was so erotic for such a simple gesture.

Riley broke the kiss and whispered, "Do you like my style of snacks?" She kissed Kate's neck tenderly.

"Uh-huh." Kate moaned when Riley brushed her fingertips down her torso and stroked the top of her chest without going underneath her swimsuit. "You're torturing me." They made out for several more minutes before Riley held her in a loving embrace. "It's beautiful up here. Thanks for bringing me."

"You're welcome. Want another snack?"

If it was anything like the last one, Kate was all in. She crawled over Riley and stood next to the bag. "Oh, it's freezing after being in the nice hot waters."

"Perks a person up." Riley stared appreciatively at Kate's chest. She rose and hugged Kate from behind. "Warmer?"

"Yes." She intertwined her fingers with Riley's and enjoyed the embrace. When she looked down at the bag again, her breath stilled at the sight of the butt of Riley's handgun tucked inside the folded towel alongside her pack. "Riley, why in the world—"

"What?"

Kate gestured to the gun. "Is that necessary? I thought mountain lions were nocturnal. I understand why you carry one for work with the break-ins. But we're on a leisurely hike, and it's daylight."

Riley put the gun back in the backpack. "You know I carry a gun. I grew up around them. And mountain lions do hunt mostly from dusk till dawn, but they also come out in the day if they're hungry. I'm sorry it makes you feel uncomfortable, but we're miles and hours away from help, and cell phone coverage is spotty to call in a rescue helicopter."

"Hayley alluded to another reason behind you always carrying a gun. Can you talk about it?" Hayley had given Kate the gist of the story, but she wanted to hear it from Riley. The sad look that came across Riley's expression broke Kate's heart.

"Maybe I'm a little paranoid, but when the mug shot of Steven Nelson's killer and his accomplices flashed on the TV, I swear they looked just like the guys who we took out on a guided snowmobile trip a few months before." The muscles in Riley's jaw twitched, and she ran her fingers through her hair. "And a married lesbian couple were murdered last year in southeast Utah. I keep my gun whenever I'm alone or off the beaten path."

"Thank you for your honesty." Kate wrapped her arms around Riley.

"I'm not a yahoo, Kate. I don't go shooting rounds into the air for fun, or threatening anyone, or killing animals unnecessarily. I just want to be safe. I want to keep *you* safe."

Kate brushed her hand on Riley's cheek. "Lilly said you're extremely safety conscious."

Riley rolled her neck. "You talked to Aunt Lilly about this?"

"Yes. It concerned me." Kate sighed. "Listen, I'm not going to own a gun or take lessons. That'd be a recipe for disaster. As long you don't shove me in that direction again, we'll be fine."

"Deal. So, you love horseback riding?"

Kate cocked an eyebrow at the way Riley always changed the subject around touchy topics like guns and her mother. She decided not to push. One heavy conversation was enough in one day. "I love horses but haven't had the opportunity to ride much. Do you have something in mind?"

"We won't have time to ride today, but the ranch has sleigh rides when it snows. The mountains and evergreen trees contrasting against the snow is so beautiful."

"I've never been on a horse sleigh ride."

"You're kidding," Riley said. "We have to make a reservation for Christmas before they're all booked up. They have a great restaurant too."

"Hey, if they're open for an early dinner, let's eat there."

"Why do you think I asked you to bring a change of clothes?" Riley smiled and looked very pleased with herself. "I made a reservation as a surprise gift. I suppose it wouldn't hurt to show up a little early."

"That's very thoughtful. Thank you."

Their conversation shifted to light-hearted stories. They lingered in and out of the pool, kissing, talking, and laughing. Kate's body ached to make love to Riley. It'd be late when they got home, but she still planned to ask Riley to spend the night.

# Chapter Thirty-Two

KATE ADMIRED THE HORSES in the pasture as Riley drove onto the ranch's property. "The coat on that Appaloosa is gorgeous."

"The Appaloosa is Idaho's official state horse," Riley said.

"Really? I always wanted an Appaloosa growing up."

"You lived in the third largest city in the country." Riley laughed.

"Hey, I had my dreams." Dreams that Kate had forgotten until they drove onto the ranch. She hated the old Western movies her father watched on VHS tape but loved the horses. The Appaloosa John Wayne rode in El Dorado mesmerized her. One Christmas, her father gave her a miniature replica of a barn and horses, which instantly became her favorite toy. When he left them, Kate threw the toy in the trash. How ironic that she now lived in a cabin out west that he had given her. The tug of curiosity about her ancestors was one reason Kate stayed, but Riley had quickly become the main reason. She made living here bearable.

"Penny for your thoughts?" Riley parked and leaned in toward Kate.

"Oh, sorry. I was daydreaming."

"We'll return sometime for a trail ride." Riley kissed her.

Kate gestured to her outfit. "I hope these black jeans are dressy enough."

"You always look breathtaking."

"Look." Kate pointed to a bronze statue of people riding in a horse-drawn buggy just outside the building. "It looks like the one that used to be in the barn. The museum's doing a great job of restoring it. I forgot to show you the pictures the curator sent me. We need to visit soon."

Riley opened the door, and Kate stepped inside. Massive timbers held up the high ceiling of the lodge lobby. There weren't many windows, but tableside lamps created a soft glow around the sitting area. Spotlights highlighted paintings on the walls and two colossal bronze sculptures of a cowboy on a bucking bronco and an Indian chief standing next to his horse. The place oozed with old charm and class. Giggling caught Kate's attention, and she turned to see two children in costume skip up to the front desk with their parents behind them.

"Trick or treat," they said in unison.

"I forgot it was Halloween weekend," Kate said.

"The best part is the restaurant has a separate room for children. We won't be disrupted by their party," Riley said.

"Do you not like kids?"

"Not on a dinner date. Or are you asking me something else?"

"Maybe. What do you think?" Kate giggled to hide the serious side of the question. She had often thought about being a mother, but the timing was never right, and she always seemed to be in the wrong relationship.

Riley blinked. "I haven't been around a lot of kids. Nathaniel was well beyond a tiny kid when he came to live with us. As for me, I never really thought about being a mom, and now that I'm forty..." She wet her lips.

"No worries. I was just curious. Shall we?" Kate gestured toward the restaurant.

Riley held out her arm and didn't say another word. The restaurant host wore dress slacks and a shirt and tie. He didn't blink at their outfits. Unlike the lobby, large picture windows edged the dining room. The host seated them at a table on the west side near the fireplace and handed them menus. It was a perfect view for the setting sun.

"I love their T-bone steak, their BBQ is good, and their fresh salmon is awesome." Riley rubbed her hands together. "How about fruit and a champagne to start off?"

"Yes, on the champagne. How about we split a T-bone and the salmon?" Kate folded her menu.

"I like your way of thinking."

After ordering, Riley talked about the history of this part of the Salmon River. Two waiters approached. One placed a platter of fruit in the center of the table, and the other presented a bottle of champagne to Riley.

"Thank you. I'll take it from here." Riley poured their glasses as the waiters retreated. "You can enjoy it as much as you want. I'll only drink one glass since I'm driving."

Riley passed her the glass, and their fingers touched. It was like an electrical current running through Kate. "Thank you for this wonderful surprise."

"You're welcome."

"Hey, there's something I'm curious about." Kate scooped up a strawberry with her spoon. "Riley is traditionally a male name. How did you get it?" She dropped the strawberry in her flute and took a sip.

Riley glanced away and bit her lower lip. She spun her glass by its stem, then in one swift action, she raised the glass and drank nearly half in one gulp. "My name has a good story and an unhappy one. Basically, I didn't like my name, so I changed it to Riley."

"I'd like to hear your story sometime if you feel comfortable sharing it."

Riley set her elbows on the table and took a deep breath. "My parents used to like all different kinds of music. Before I was born, one of their favorite songs was Rhiannon by Fleetwood Mac." Riley cleared her throat. "Yes, Mormons listen to popular music. My full birth name is Rhiannon Lucinda Anderson. I hate that name, but it turns out my father gave it to me. And he was a great dad." Riley chewed her lip. "Lucinda was his mother's name."

Kate coughed to hide her giggle. "I'm sorry, but you're definitely not a Lucinda. Maybe a Lucy."

The frown on Riley's face deepened, and she rubbed her neck. Before Kate could apologize, Riley picked up her spoon, scooped up a melon ball, and catapulted it toward Kate. It hit her chest and slid down Kate's low-cut shirt.

"That'll teach you to call me Lucy. Need help getting it out?" Riley grinned.

"Perhaps another time." Kate glanced around the room. "I should go to the restroom."

"This should shield you." Riley picked up the drinks menu and held it out.

"A dare?" Kate slid her fingers down her shirt, and Riley's gaze followed. She plucked the melon from her cleavage, and Kate held it like she was going to throw it back.

"Ladies, can I get you anything else?" the waiter asked as he approached.

Kate dropped the melon ball onto the side of her plate.

"No, thank you, we're fine." Riley waited until he'd left again. "You have the cutest blushes that I have ever seen."

"Finish your story, please."

Riley slowly buttered a slice of bread. "I like the name Riley, and when I moved to Aunt Lilly's and Uncle George's, they helped me legally change my name to Riley Lee Anderson. End of story."

"That was lovely of them." Kate had noticed that Riley's "end of story" was her usual abrupt conclusion to things she didn't seem to want to talk about, usually involving her parents. Stories about her father were positive, but tidbits about her mother were not. Whatever Kate felt about her dysfunctional family, Riley's situation seemed to have been worse. Kate didn't want to push further and cause any pain.

Their main course arrived, and Riley talked about all of the national parks she had visited. Kate hung on every word. It was as if they'd been dating for years. Kate enjoyed her dessert and coffee along with the music from two guitarists and a singer. She partially turned her chair to watch the trio and rested her hand on top of the table. During one slow love song, Riley caressed the top of her hand. She gazed at Riley and intertwined their fingers. The longing look they exchanged made Kate feel like they were the only ones in the room.

The waiter dropped off the bill just as the musical group took a break, and Kate snatched it up.

"You bought in Ketchum. Dinner's on me tonight."

"Thank you." Riley grinned widely.

"I'm paying for the bill, but I'd gladly entertain your other thoughts." Excitement and nervousness flooded her body with equal measurement as she waited for Riley's answer.

"I hope I'm not being too bold, but I'd like to spend the night with you." Riley cleared her throat.

"Do you need to text Lilly?" She put her hand on top of Riley's and smiled at her blush. It wasn't often she saw this side of her.

Riley leaned back, her face a deeper crimson. "I already told her we might spend the night out this direction since it was such a long drive to Goldbug."

"Oh, you're a bad one. I like that." Kate drained her glass of champagne and tossed cash on the table for the bill. "Let's go."

They approached the front desk. "Excuse me, sir. Do you have any vacancies?"

He placed his pen down and smiled at Kate. "The lodge is booked, but you're in luck. Someone just canceled a one-bedroom cabin facing the pond. Is that okay?"

# CABIN FEVER

"Perfect." She handed over her credit card.

They had been flirting for months, and Riley had been teasing her to the brink all day long. No one before Riley had ever made her feel so much. And right now, all she wanted was to feel Riley's naked skin against her own.

Riley wrapped her arm around Kate's shoulders and led her outside. "We don't have to do anything you don't want to. I'll take it at your pace."

"What are you saying? Do I get to dominate you?" Kate asked.

A laugh escaped Riley's throat. "If you can handle me."

# Chapter Thirty-Three

THEY WALKED DOWN THE softly lit path from the lodge to their cabin, and Kate's brain swirled. Riley wasn't like any other woman she'd dated. She could be reserved in one moment and cocky the next. Lately, Kate had seen a deeper side of Riley, a more caring and sensitive side that was sweet and charming. Now she wanted that physical connection. She wanted their first time to be perfect.

Riley unlocked the door, flicked the light switch on, and stepped back. "After you."

Kate looked around the bright room. The knotty wood pine floors looked brand new. "It's beautiful." A leather loveseat and a chair faced a woodstove. Two paintings of the mountains hung on the cream walls. She dropped the blinds and moved to the fireplace. "Let me get the fire going and get the chill out of the air."

"You're getting pretty good at lighting fires." Riley winked.

And she intended to set Riley ablaze tonight. Once the fire had caught, she closed the stove doors and watched the dancing flames through the heavy ceramic glass. When she stood, Riley was coming out of the bathroom.

"You're grinning. What's going on in that beautiful head of yours?" Riley rubbed her thumb over Kate's cheek.

"I'm not sure if I can handle you. It's my first time being a dominatrix."

Riley laughed. "I'd like to think the first time is the sweetest."

Kate's body tingled as Riley drew her in for a tender kiss. Riley traced her tongue over her lips, and her pulse shot through the roof. She returned Riley's kiss with hunger. When they separated, the look of desire was written on Riley's face.

"The room has a jacuzzi. Let's start there for a nice soak since we've had an active day."

Kate raised her eyebrow. "I thought I was in control." She smiled and brushed her fingers down Riley's arm. She headed to the bathroom, stopped at the threshold, and curled her index finger. "Follow me."

The spacious bathroom had a ledge and a large window with a frosted finish above the jacuzzi. But what Kate liked best was the look on Riley's face. The thought of dominating her was an incredible rush. She turned the faucets until the temperature was just right and poured in the cedarwood bath crystals she'd found.

"You're teasing me," Riley whispered, her voice hoarse.

Kate glanced up and smiled. "Impatience, that's a side of you I've never seen." She flicked water at Riley and stood. She inched her shirt over her head slowly, exposing her black lace bra she'd chosen especially, just in case she got lucky.

"Nice."

As Kate unhooked and let the bra drop, Riley sucked in a deep breath. She unzipped her black jeans and dropped them to the floor to reveal matching panties. "Do you like these?"

Riley nodded. Her steady, admiring gaze made Kate's nipples harden, and the wetness between her legs pooled.

"Sit." Kate pushed Riley lightly onto a teak bench next to the jacuzzi. She laced her fingers around Riley's neck and softly kissed her. "Care to help me take these off?" She hooked her thumb in the waistband of her panties.

Riley's breathing hitched, and she eyed Kate's breasts, which were inches from her mouth. "Uh-huh."

She put one hand on Kate's hip and grabbed her ass with the other. Riley gently kissed, sucked, and nipped at Kate's tender flesh.

"That feels oh so good. But that's not what I asked you to do. I want you to take my panties off with your teeth."

"Hm, I've never done that before." Riley lightly smacked her ass.

Kate wagged her finger in Riley's face and shook her head slowly. "*I'm* in charge." She moaned at the feel of Riley's lips against her stomach before she pulled down Kate's panties and laid tender kisses from her hips to her breasts.

Kate's breathing deepened when Riley sucked in a nipple and flicked it with the tip of her tongue. "Um, so soft and hard. Good." The electricity running through her went straight to her core, but she pushed back. "Plenty of time for that. Get undressed."

"Bossy." Riley rushed to take off her jeans and almost toppled over.

Kate placed her hand over her mouth to suppress her laughter, but a light snicker still escaped.

"Are you satisfied that you've got me so worked up?" Riley tossed her jeans aside.

"Quite pleased." Kate turned off the water and dropped in more bath crystals. She swished them around with her hand, knowing that Riley's gaze was all over her body. "What are you thinking right now?"

"You're driving me crazy. You're so beautiful. That doesn't do you justice, but I can't think of another word because my brain's on hold, and my body's on fire."

"Then hurry up." Kate eased down into the water.

Riley tore off the rest of her clothes and practically jumped into the tub.

Kate laughed. "Come here. Sit on my lap and put your legs around me." She sucked one of Riley's nipples into her mouth and her pulse skyrocketed at the taste of her.

"Keep doing that, and we're never going to get out of the tub," Riley said breathlessly.

"You like that, huh?"

"Yes."

"I love being in control of your strong body," Kate whispered as she trailed her hand up Riley's back and undid her ponytail. Riley's damp hair cascaded down her back. Kate slid her other hand beneath the water and between Riley's legs, eliciting a soft moan. She stroked around Riley's clit. When Riley leaned forward and playfully nipped at her lower lip, Kate pulled back. "In a hurry?"

"Yes, and you're in charge, but you're killing me."

"Kiss me." She continued to tease Riley's clit as they kissed.

Riley broke the kiss. "Please."

Kate entered her with one finger, then two, and started a steady but gentle rhythm while she caressed Riley's neck to her breast with her other hand. She sucked Riley's breast into her mouth and flicked her nipple.

"Come for me." Kate smothered Riley's breast with kisses while she pumped harder, her thumb still pressed against Riley's clit.

"Kate, oh..." Riley's breathing hitched, and her body quivered.

Kate eased her rhythm and kissed Riley's neck, tenderly nipping from time to time. "Did you enjoy that?"

"Yes," Riley whispered. "You're amazing."

"Good. Let's finish washing and get in bed. I want to see if your biceps are more than just for show." She grinned wickedly.

"Is that a challenge?"

Shivers ran down Kate's spine, and the hum between her legs intensified. She leaned into Riley. "Don't you think you can rise to it?"

"Bring it on." Riley squirted bath gel onto a sponge and washed Kate's chest and back.

"I like your hair down. It shows a softer, more vulnerable side of you." Kate ran her fingers through Riley's hair.

"When I'm not working, I'll wear it any way you like it. Now, close your eyes."

Kate's skin tingled as Riley delicately brushed the sponge over her face, neck, and ears. Riley turned on the hand shower turn and rinsed her head and chest. She patted a towel on Kate's face. Kate's body hummed with excitement, and she opened her eyes.

"I'm not finished yet." Riley smiled and squirted shower gel into her hands. She rubbed them together then glided her hands over Kate's breasts, lightly pinching Kate's hard nipples. "They're perfect."

In between caresses and kisses, they managed to finish washing. Kate needed to feel Riley's skin against her own and hastily toweled off. Riley stood and stared.

"What?" Kate asked.

Riley grinned, then snapped her towel at Kate's backside. "I'll caress and kiss it. But you have to catch me first." She sprinted to the bed and flopped down with a twist.

"Oh, that's war." Kate landed on top of Riley and pinned her arms down. The instant warmth as their bodies pressed together sent a tsunami of pleasurable waves crashing through her. But all she could do was stare into Riley's eyes. She kissed Riley's nose. "I love the warmth in your eyes."

"And yours are like magic, drawing me in." Riley played with Kate's hair. "I'm hooked on you, Kate. Your honesty, determination, and your passion. Just, wow." She grinned. "The sex is just the icing on the cake, but I'm still hungry."

"Uh-huh. I think you need to make amends for your horrific towel assault on me. My ass is still throbbing. And I have other places I'd like to throb."

"Oh, I can do that." Riley flipped their positions and kissed her.

Kate savored Riley's mouth like a warm, sweet dessert, then broke the kiss. "I need your kisses all over." She wrapped her hand around Riley's head and gently pushed her down.

"Delicate skin, so smooth and soft," Riley said between kisses.

"Stop talking."

"You teased me. Now it's my turn." Riley quirked her eyebrow.

"Please."

"What do you want? This?" Riley kissed her stomach and slid her hand down to caress Kate's inner thighs. When Riley's fingertips circled her clit lightly, Kate thought she'd die if Riley didn't hurry up.

"Can I taste you?"

"Yes." Kate opened her legs wider, and Riley traced leisurely strokes over her clit. God, this teasing was driving her insane. Then Riley picked up the pace and set a perfect rhythm. It wasn't long before Kate's muscles spasmed with pleasure. She balled the sheets in her hands as her body arched and her lungs gasped for air.

"Was that satisfactory?" Riley asked, though her grin showed that she already knew the answer.

"Oh, yeah."

"Any ideas on what to do next?" Riley crawled up beside her.

Kate took a deep breath and flipped her over. She took Riley like her life depended on it. It was a high to make Riley moan and squirm at her touch. And when Riley lay breathless, Kate watched her chest rise and fall. "Don't quit on me now, champ. Time to go again." Kate caressed and kissed every inch of Riley's body. When Riley screamed out, "There. Oh, yeah, don't stop," Kate couldn't resist a smug grin.

And when Riley took her again, Kate fell over the edge as Riley sucked hard on her breasts, stroked her clit with her thumb, and thrust her fingers inside, connecting to Kate's sweet spot. Her heart beat loudly and the tingling sensation pulsed and spread with each clench and release of her muscles until she thought she'd burst.

Every touch, sound, and reaction tonight had awakened Kate's mind and body with an intensity that she hadn't felt for years, if ever. And sometime in the dark of the early morning, Riley pulled her in. Kate cuddled into Riley's chest, listened to her heartbeat, and drifted off to sleep.

\*\*\*

Riley woke from the sunlight seeping beneath the edges of the curtain. Kate was tucked into her side, sound asleep, her head resting near Riley's breast. She had the urge to run her fingers through Kate's hair but didn't want to wake her. Instead, she took comfort in Kate's warmth and enjoyed the display of her naked, smooth skin. Touching Kate's skin had set hers on fire.

Last night had been phenomenal. Kate telling her exactly what she wanted was a huge turn-on. And Riley loved every second of Kate's take-charge personality. All of her previous lovers always wanted Riley to pamper them, wanted Riley to be in control. Sure, she liked the outdoors and fixing houses, but that didn't mean she fit into a perfect box labeled butch. She liked to receive just as much as she liked to give.

Kate tipped the balance of Riley's life but in a good way. Her smile, laughter, and even her nerdy genealogy talks captured Riley's attention. She wanted to be around Kate as much as possible. And now, with sex, Riley was in nirvana.

"Good morning." Kate stirred.

"Good morning." Riley kissed her forehead, then rolled out of bed and stretched.

"Oh, you are a goddess. I could look at your muscular, naked body all day," Kate said huskily.

"I know that look." Riley shook her finger. "I'll never forget the first time I saw it. Do you think Hank knew what he was doing?"

"Uh-huh, he sure did."

"I'm going to take care of morning business and freshen up." Riley gave Kate's ass a gentle smack.

"Shall we go to breakfast at the lodge, or will you be hungry after freshening up?" Kate rolled over on her back and laced her fingers behind her head.

"Oh, yeah, appetizers in bed." Riley ran to the bathroom. Connecting emotionally with former lovers was usually tough, but she felt no awkwardness with Kate. Instead, they just seemed to fit together as if they'd always been a couple. And from Kate's reaction, she felt the same way. God, how did she get so lucky? Then the literal million-dollar question slammed into her and made her chest ache. Would Kate eventually leave and return to Chicago?

Kate sauntered in soon after, and Riley pushed her worries aside. They quickly showered and got back in bed. She moaned as Kate kissed and nipped at her skin.

"I haven't tasted you yet. May I?"

"Take me." Riley threw her head back as Kate lowered her mouth. She ran her fingers through Kate's hair as Kate flicked her tongue over her clit. "Oh, yes." She arched her back in pleasure when Kate took her tender flesh gently between her teeth and sucked hard. "Yes, Kate. Don't stop." Minutes later, the buildup burst into sheer bliss, and her muscles quivered with delight.

"Happy?" Kate whispered.

"Immensely." Riley tugged her upward.

"Ditto."

She was about to make love to Kate until she saw the bedside clock. "What time is checkout?"

"I think the receptionist said eleven."

"Shit. It's ten-forty. We have to go."

"You're kidding." Kate's head whipped around to look at the clock. She grinned up at Riley. "Raincheck?"

"Oh, yeah." Riley clung to the positive. She didn't want to think about her past, and she certainly refused to dwell on the possibility of Kate returning to Chicago. This last twenty-four hours had been magical. Great sex and a happiness that Kate brought to her life. Riley was going to do everything in her power to make this relationship work.

# Chapter Thirty-Four

*November*

KATE GATHERED UP HER backpack and waved to the library staff, then she headed out the door. The snow flurries looked pretty earlier, but the wind had picked up, and her best coat didn't seem to be doing the job. She leaned into the gusts and picked up her pace. If the rest of winter was like this, it was going to be agony.

The warmth inside the café hit her as she stepped inside. Thank goodness for that blower above the door. "Hello."

"Good afternoon, Kate. Oh, my, you look frozen. Coffee?" Nancy slid a fresh tray of pumpkin bread into the display case.

"Yes, please, with a touch of pumpkin spice cream." Kate eyed the case filled with scrumptious treats as she inhaled the sweet autumn spices that filled the air. "And a slice of pumpkin bread."

"Good choice." Nancy chuckled. "Mind if I join you?"

"Please."

At two thirty on a weekday, the lunch crowd had dispersed, and the evening rush hadn't begun. Kate went over to her favorite booth, and Nancy arrived with their snacks.

Kate gave a thumbs-up while she chewed the pumpkin bread.

"I haven't seen you for days. How have you been?" Nancy asked.

"Everything's going great." Kate grinned. "And I'm enjoying getting outside. Riley took me to Goldbug Hot Springs last week. It was incredible." The heat she felt wasn't from the coffee as Kate raised the cup to her lips. Their lovemaking had replayed in her mind, and each time, Kate's body erupted in sensational tingles.

"That's the best one." Nancy gave a devilish grin. "When we were younger, Tom and I used to go skinny dipping there."

Kate quickly snatched a napkin and covered her face just in time as she spewed coffee out of her mouth. "Sorry." She coughed and thumped her chest with her fist. "I have trouble imagining your quiet, shy husband bathing naked."

Nancy smacked the table and chuckled. When she calmed down, she winked. "And we still do on a rare occasion."

Kate sat the cup down so fast that it sloshed over the rim. She grabbed a fist full of napkins, but her effort only spread the mess evenly across the table. "I'm sorry. I don't mean to be a prude."

"I understand." Nancy grinned. "It's unusual to see someone strut their stuff when they're in their mid-sixties and out of shape. But it's all in loving yourself, loving your partner, and confidence. I feel like the luckiest woman in the world because our love keeps growing. Tom is the love of my life."

"You two are a sweet couple." Kate shook her head. "But I'm going to turn bright red the next time I see him."

"He's seventy-two, so he's super reserved. But with me, he's open and charming."

"Sounds like he robbed the cradle."

"Thanks for that, but I'm only six years younger."

"No way."

Nancy grinned and puffed up her hair. "Speaking of togetherness, you and Riley seem to be hitting it off."

Kate couldn't help her big smile. "Yes, we've become close."

"Ha! I knew you two would be a good couple."

Kate topped off her coffee, stirred in some more pumpkin spice cream, and watched the swirling liquid. She was enjoying herself with Riley. She glanced up when Nancy placed her hand on top of hers.

"It's good to see Riley happy. There was a time that I thought I'd never see that day."

"What do you mean?"

"Oh, it's nothing." Nancy picked up the menu. "Hey, you've sampled so many of our specialties, do you have any favorites that haven't made it to the menu? I was thinking about adding a few new dishes." She scooped up a large bite of her bread pudding as she studied the menu.

Nancy was being as evasive as Riley. What the hell had happened to her?

"I have some great news to share with you. I'll be right back." When Nancy returned, she handed some computer drawings to Kate. "I'm toying with the idea of building a bed and breakfast. Tom's supportive, but

I'm still mulling it over."

Kate studied the drawings. "This looks fantastic."

"Don't say anything to Riley right now. I'll hire her, but I like playing with my computer home design software and mulling over the possibilities."

Kate nodded. "I promise. That would be great since we don't have any hotels in Merrick."

They finished their treats, and their conversation moved to Thanksgiving and Christmas. She'd once thought Idaho was too rough and wild, but now she didn't think she'd ever been more comfortable in her own skin. Riley and her beloved extended family made Kate's heart swell with joy, and she was looking forward to sharing holidays with them. And her sizzling relationship with Riley was like an early Christmas present.

# Chapter Thirty-Five

KATE CRAWLED OUT FROM underneath her warm blankets, pulled on her sweatpants, and wandered out to the kitchen. The coals in the cookstove weren't enough to make coffee and breakfast, and the wood racks were empty. *Damn it.* Riley had told her to keep her wood topped up inside. Swearing at herself, she slipped on her boots and coat and stepped outside.

"Holy cow." A few inches of snow covered the ground when she'd gone to bed last night. Now, at least a foot of snow covered everything. Thankfully, she'd picked up extra firewood with her truck last week. After starting the fire and the coffee, she heard a peculiar rumble. When it grew louder, she pulled back the living room curtain. A humungous tractor with a snowplow came to a halt, and Riley hopped out.

It had only been a couple of days, but Kate missed those soft and delicious lips. She swung open the door and grabbed Riley by her coat collar for a kiss. After a couple of minutes of splendid joy, Kate pulled Riley inside.

Riley held out a bag. "I brought an apple pie that Aunt Lilly baked."

"Thank you." She took the bag and placed it on the dining table. "What do I owe you for plowing? That monster probably guzzles gas."

"Nothing. The owner hurt his back last month. He asked me to plow his farm roads in exchange for letting me use it to plow wherever I needed. I still have eight more people that want their roads done, and I need to get it done before we get slammed again."

"Huh?"

"The weather channel is calling for another foot. Isn't that glorious?" Riley grinned.

Kate punched Riley's arm. "Stop teasing me."

"I swear it's true."

Kate flung back her head. "I'm not sure I'm ready for this."

"Have some pie. It'll help."

Kate poured their coffee while Riley sliced the pie before she settled on the sofa.

"Hey, isn't that one of your grandmother's journals? You haven't mentioned them lately. Did you ever figure out who she had an affair with?" Riley pointed to the journal on the coffee table and crammed a big bite in her mouth.

"Oh! I forgot to tell you." Kate placed their mugs on the table and snuggled up to Riley on the sofa. "I put the journals away and just got them out the other day. Grandmother Emmeline was clearly in love with JJ and getting it on. They were like two rabbits."

"Who's JJ?" Riley propped her foot on her knee.

"My grandfather's best friend, Jeremiah Jacobs."

Riley's mouth dropped. "Holy shit. I wonder if that had anything to do with the feud between the Jacobs' and Christensens." Riley bolted upright. "Didn't Howard give you that box?"

"Yep, but he doesn't know what's in it, and I'm going to tell him. He's probably heard the rumors."

"What if–"

"Two steps ahead of you. So far, no connections to the Jacobs' have appeared in my DNA testing, and I have matches on the Christensen side. So, Jeremiah isn't my grandfather."

"Oh, that's good."

Kate put her hand on Riley's thigh. "I'm so glad Sherry dared me to kiss you."

"Me, too." Riley placed her hand on top of Kate's and rubbed her thumb back and forth.

"You should probably know that Sherry and I dated in college."

"Really?" Riley's eyes widened. "Two high maintenance femmes. That must have been hard." She chuckled. "You were such a prissy princess when you got here."

Kate raised her eyebrows. "Damn right, I'm a princess, but prissy ain't me, sweetheart."

"You kind of were when you first got here."

Kate tilted her head. "Maybe. But I'm better now, huh?"

"You are."

Kate placed a soft kiss on Riley's cheek. "And how are my mountain skills now? Do I keep us warm enough in bed?"

"I'm so proud of how hard you work and play." Riley winked and shoved another bite into her mouth.

"Pie comes before a kiss. I know where I stand." Kate punched Riley's bicep.

With her mouth full of pie, Riley gave Kate a quick kiss. Kate shook her head and grinned, then licked the flavor of apples and Riley from her lips.

What a difference several months had made. The idea of selling and running back to Chicago after a year was slipping further from Kate's mind. It was both scary and wonderful to think how their relationship had gone from cold to a lukewarm friendship and now to lovers. Yet, they had so much to discuss and to consider. "Can we talk about a few things?" Kate swirled her spoon in her coffee mug.

"What's on your mind?"

Kate told Riley more details about her family and her father's standoffish personality. She told Riley about getting fired over her sexual harassment complaint and how she'd struggled to find another job in Chicago. She explained why fighting would be a lost cause but didn't reveal the details of the assault. It was too raw. Her father dying on the day she was fired was a double punch to the gut. And for the first time, Kate told Riley how Audrey had dumped her.

"I have some baggage." Kate shrugged. "Anyway, I just wanted you to know that I'm far from perfect."

"No one is. You've been through a lot." Riley wrapped her in a tight hug and kissed the top of her head.

Were her feelings for Riley just the rush of a new intimate relationship? Or was she falling in love? She wasn't sure but being with Riley felt warm and safe.

"You've had a lot with your mom too."

"That was years ago." Riley released her and pulled away. "Excuse me. That coffee has gone right through me."

Kate had hoped that by opening up, Riley would do the same. She'd have to try harder.

Riley came out of the bathroom and poured coffee into her travel mug. "I need to get back to plowing."

*What the hell? That's it?* Shaking off the thoughts, Kate decided to focus on the positive. "When will I see you again?"

Riley grinned. "We're going out in two days. I'll deliver your snowmobile and show you the basics. I promise to make it safe and gradually build up your skillset. Deal?"

"Deal, if you spend the night."

"Oh, you twisted my arm."

Riley had convinced her to try so many things that previously scared her, but Kate had ending up loving everything they'd done, even the fishing. Kate walked her to the door and pulled her in for one more hot kiss. "Come by early if you want breakfast and coffee."

"Any chance of pancakes and eggs?"

"Only for you." Kate gave Riley one last quick kiss and softly closed the door. God, she was addicted to this woman. She only wished that Riley would open up to her. For now, she'd focus on the present. And things were pretty damn good, especially the sex.

# Chapter Thirty-Six

KATE RACED TO OPEN the door. She was looking forward to today's outdoor adventure. Riley's enthusiasm had infused her like a magic potion, pushing her to try things she would have never previously considered. She opened the door wide with a big grin. "Hi." She couldn't get enough of Riley.

"Ready for your maiden snowmobile voyage?" Riley stepped in with her arms full of cold-weather gear. Excitement shone in her eyes.

"You mean my baby lesson. Geez, how much do I have to wear?"

"These will keep you nice and toasty. Don't worry if the pant legs of the snowsuit are too long. You can roll them up."

"Do I have to wear those clunky boots?"

Riley hitched her eyebrow.

"Okay." Kate pointed to the chair. "Put the gear down, and give me a kiss, please."

Riley wrapped her in a soft embrace and tenderly kissed her. Their kiss deepened, and Riley caressed the small of Kate's back. Kate moaned, and Riley pulled back.

"You promised me pancakes and eggs."

"I did. But I'm a little faint now. You'll have to serve yourself."

While they ate, Riley pulled out the manual for her snowmobile and started talking between bites. Kate held up her hand. "I'm a visual learner. Show me. Then I'll skim through it after our trip."

"Okay. It's not that hard if you follow my directions." Riley spooned more scrambled eggs onto their plates. "You'll need the extra energy. Trust me. Eat up."

After they cleaned the table, Riley motioned to their gear. "Time to suit up. You need to know the basics before everyone else arrives."

Kate wriggled into the winter gear over her regular clothes, and her body heated up fast. When she stepped outside, the cold air felt good.

"This is your new machine. It's last year's model, so I got you a bargain price. It's sweet." Riley mounted the machine and explained all the controls and buttons. "The handles have built-in hand and thumb warmers, but you may not need it on a day like today." She showed Kate how the throttle and brakes worked and demonstrated how to lean into curves.

"Now, you climb on."

Kate swallowed. The machine looked far larger than the ones she'd seen online.

Riley clipped a cord to her overalls.

"What's that?"

"If you fall off, then it activates the emergency button and automatically kills the engine. It's unlikely anything will happen because we're going to take it easy."

"Famous last words." A mix of anxiety and excitement flooded through Kate.

"Hop off. I need to familiarize you with more safety equipment."

Fear crept into Kate's bones when Riley mentioned avalanches. She showed Kate the emergency beacon and airbag, then talked about using a shovel and probes to dig out a victim.

"You look three shades paler than before." Riley put her hand on Kate's shoulder.

"Have you ever been in an avalanche?"

"No. No one in this group has. We follow the rules, take precautions, and always evaluate the terrain. The emergency gear is just in case." Riley kissed her lightly. "After learning the basics, you'll be able to ride to town with me. And if you want to join the Snow Hellcats, I'll teach you privately so you can ride more challenging trails with us."

Kate laughed. "Your group is called the Snow Hellcats? Should I be scared of all the ill-tempered women?"

"Nope. We're all laidback."

The faint rumble of the snowmobile engines grew louder. "I guess it's time to meet them."

Megan, Hayley, Charley, and Penny greeted her, and Riley introduced her to a few new faces—Lacey and Donna, who appeared to be a couple. Riley quickly went through the hand signals with the entire group, and everyone hopped back on their machines.

Riley grinned. "Don't forget." She clipped Kate's tether to the emergency button. "When we break, I'll show you a few more tips, and we can take it up a notch. Hayley's in the lead. I'll be last, and you'll be in front of me. Anytime you're uncomfortable, give the signal and stop, and I'll radio everyone. Are you ready?"

Kate flipped down the visor on the helmet and gave a thumbs up. With the neck warmer and helmet, she was happy that Riley couldn't see her swallow hard. As the sound of the machines roared to life and the group headed out, Kate said a silent prayer and gave the throttle a gradual squeeze. Within fifteen minutes, her confidence began to grow.

Hayley picked up speed on flat terrain, and Kate glanced at her speedometer. Forty miles an hour seemed like flying through space. They turned off into a meadow and slowed to a gentle stop.

Riley rushed up to Kate. "You look awesome. How do you feel?"

"Great."

"Let's take ten, and then we'll practice."

After their break, Riley talked her through some tips and demonstrated more maneuvers, including sharp turns and a few bumps.

"If you're moving along at high speed on the trail and hit a bump without notice, then it's crucial to balance your weight. It's better to learn here. Megan and I will practice with you. Ready to go?"

Kate nodded, and Riley rapped her knuckles on top of Kate's helmet then strolled back to her machine. Over the next hour, Kate surprised herself by learning to shift her weight correctly into high-speed turns. During the first couple of laps, she headed into the bumps slowly. Gradually picking up speed, she caught a tiny bit of air on the third lap, and her confidence tipped to the cocky side.

In the fourth lap, she accelerated toward the bump, and her snowmobile flew into the air then banged on the ground with a jolt. She was still upright, but it jarred her back to reality. She feared that she'd broken something on the snowmobile and quickly stopped several yards away from where the rest of the group was parked.

Megan rode up and flipped up her visor. "You looked good. But that was a little fast on the last one for a rookie."

Kate nodded. "Sorry, I got carried away."

Riley pulled up next and stripped off her helmet. "You were fantastic but keep the speed down. You're not an expert, and I don't want to see you crash."

"Sorry. I'm not sure I like the bumps. The weight of a snowmobile and speed is quite different from a mountain bike." Kate hoped she didn't look

ADDISON M. CONLEY

wimpy, but honesty was best.

Riley moved close to Kate. "You don't have to do anything that makes you feel uncomfortable. If you want to try again later, we can do that but slower."

The smell of Riley's woodsy cologne and her warm smile made Kate feel dizzy with desire. She wrapped her arms around Riley and kissed her. A wolf whistle pulled them apart.

Riley jammed her hands in her snow pants. "Forgot them. Your kisses are delicious."

"There'll be more later."

"I hope so."

The rest of the trail was more challenging. She was having a blast, but her body needed a break. They stopped in a clearing in the woods next to a snow groomer. Nathaniel was there, stoking a blazing fire, and the wonderful aroma of BBQ wafted in the air.

"Welcome, ladies." Nathaniel waved. "In about fifteen minutes, I'll have boneless short ribs, potatoes, and mixed vegetables ready for you. Have a seat."

Everyone thanked him.

"Good to see you, Kate." He thumped his chest. "I'm the honorary lesbian for the day."

Donna smacked the back of his head. "Geez, I don't know what my baby sister sees in you."

He jutted out his chin. "That would be my handsomeness, intelligence, terrific personality, and great sense of humor."

Donna rolled her eyes. "And a mild touch of bravado. You do know how to cook on the trail, though."

"Why, thank you, ma'am." He bowed slightly.

"Now help me and Megan with the snowmobiles. You brought extra gas, right?" Donna asked.

"Yep." He climbed into the bed and handed cans to Donna and Megan.

Kate leaned over to Riley. "Who's Nathaniel's girlfriend?"

"Brooke. She's nineteen, and Nathaniel's twenty-two. Donna's in her early thirties and a little overprotective."

"Where can I relieve myself?" Kate glanced around.

"Follow me, and I'll show you the best spot Mother Nature has to offer. I promise not to watch."

222

Kate was honestly worried about peeing her pants more than Riley seeing her. She almost did when Charley shouted, "Are you two off to the woods to make out?" Kate waved her off and put her arm through Riley's. "Charley seems a little immature. How old is she?"

"Twenty-four. She's got a kind heart, but Puck influences her. And as you've seen, Puck has no filter."

"Does Puck snowmobile?"

"Occasionally." Riley nodded. "This way."

After relieving herself in the forest, Kate played lookout while Riley took care of business. Luckily, Riley had a small bottle of hand sanitizer.

"I'm always prepared. Ready to go back?" Riley asked.

"Not yet." Kate stepped closer and kissed her. As the kiss grew more passionate, she melted. Her body tingled when Riley squeezed her ass.

"Wow. You *did* come out here to make out."

"Don't be a smartass, Charley." Riley took Kate's hand.

"Okay. But it's good to know. Otherwise, I was going to ask her out." Charley smiled broadly.

Kate cupped her hand around her mouth. "Not interested. You're barely above jailbait."

"Yeah, and she's more immature than Nathaniel," Riley said.

Charley put a hand over her heart. "Now, that's plain mean."

Riley led Kate back to the group. They washed up and took their seats. Nathaniel passed out drinks and food along with reusable wooden sporks. The meal was delicious, and the hot coffee tasted rich and heavenly.

Kate bumped Riley's shoulder. "I had fun today, more than I thought possible. If it hadn't been for you encouraging me, I never would have tried this."

"Do you still hate winter?"

"Not when you're around." She laced her fingers through Riley's and rested her head on her shoulder. The warmth of fire was nice, but the heat between them was better.

It was nearly seven p.m. when they returned to the cabin. They made a quick meal of sandwiches and salad, then showered and slipped into bed. The soft glow of candlelight filled the room. Kate skimmed her fingertips over Riley's breasts and torso, then rested her head on Riley's chest. "I love to hear the beating of your heart." Each swirl drew a delightful moan from Riley. She settled into her favorite spot between Riley's legs. They made love several times, and when they finally tired around two a.m., Riley fell asleep in Kate's arms.

She listened to Riley's slow, steady breathing and thought about their developing relationship. She admired Riley's intelligence, her love and respect for Lilly, and her caring nature for their friends and employees. And Kate missed her every minute they were apart.

*God, I'm falling for her.*

# Chapter Thirty-Seven

RILEY LEFT KATE'S IN the early morning. Hank was waiting for her just inside the door when she got home. She hoped his excitement didn't wake Aunt Lilly.

So far, Aunt Lilly hadn't said anything, although she probably knew. But she deserved to hear the news from Riley because the way she and Kate were heating up, the whole damn town would be talking about them soon.

As she fixed breakfast, she grappled with what to say. A little later, she heard Aunt Lilly slowly moving down the stairs as if her knee was giving her a problem again. Riley poured coffee for them and set the table.

Still in her nightclothes and robe, Aunt Lilly shuffled into the kitchen and yawned. She sat at the breakfast nook. "Good morning. What an unexpected pleasure."

"Good morning. I wanted to do something special for you. I'm baking strawberry muffins, then I'll fix us some eggs." Riley turned toward the sink and began washing the mixing bowl and utensils.

"Riley, dear. Your coffee's going to get cold. Or is this cup for someone else?"

"Nope."

"Then come sit and keep me company. It's rare that I don't see you running out the door in the morning, especially on the days that Kate works in the store."

Turning slowly, she smiled and slid onto a seat next to her aunt. The hot brew tasted delicious and gave her time to think but not much. She knew Aunt Lilly's facial expressions, and this one said she was waiting patiently for Riley to speak.

"Ah, so, I'm dating Kate. It's getting serious."

Aunt Lilly's half-smile turned into a full glow. "You mean, staying at Kate's isn't platonic? Well, my heavens, I wouldn't have guessed. Especially when you wear the same clothes as the day before." She laughed. "Looks to me like it's been serious for several weeks."

"What if she leaves?" Riley's shoulders sagged.

Her aunt patted Riley's hand then gently squeezed it. "You've had bad luck in the girlfriend department, but I don't think Kate will hurt you. About leaving...sometimes people feel they have a different path to follow. That's not always bad. Sure, it hurts like the dickens, but if Kate feels the need to go and you love her, then you've got to let her go. Just like I'll let you go, because I love you to the moon and back."

Riley's head bobbed up at the word love. Why did her heart beat faster every time she thought or heard the word love in relation to Kate? Was she falling in love with her?

"And it will hurt me like the dickens if you move to Chicago." Her aunt sipped her coffee and glanced over the rim.

"Fat chance of that. You know I'm not a city girl."

"The point is, we can't smother the people we love. We can't take away the things that make them happy or make them cut ties to others. That only brings unhappiness to everyone." She chuckled. "I'm amazed at how Kate has changed. Look at how she was when she first got here, but she's gotten the hang of it."

"Yeah, she's no longer a babe in the woods." Riley grinned. "Instead, she's a hot babe in the woods."

Her aunt smacked the back of Riley's head so softly that it was more of a loving pat. Riley picked up her cup and tried to hide her smile. Every time Aunt Lilly tapped her, it was followed by sound advice, and it was always precisely what Riley needed.

"Listen, my dear, I believe you should enjoy each other and follow your heart, but don't forget your ears and brain. Listen and learn from one another. Couples that do usually find a common path to follow. They make it happen. It's not always easy, and it's not always equally shared. Just as long as you both take turns working at it and carrying the load. Because it's no fun when it's one-sided all the time."

"I think we share pretty good." Thoughts of Kate's bossy times in bed made heat rise from her toes to the top of her head. The timer went off, and she jumped up. She struggled with the oven mitts. They fit her aunt's petite hands but were rather tight for hers. "I'll fix our eggs now." She placed the muffin pan onto the nearby countertop trivet.

"Let them cool. Sit. Keeping all your emotions inside isn't good." Aunt

Lilly patted the seat. "Tell me what else is on your mind."

Riley shuffled back and settled in the chair. "I don't want to leave you alone."

Her aunt rolled her eyes. "I've been alone before. Besides, you're not the only one sleeping with your significant other."

"Huh?" Riley bolted upright. "You're seeing someone?"

Aunt Lilly coughed and coffee dribbled down her chin, followed by a rip-roaring laugh. Finally, she was able to talk. "I'm sorry, but that's hilarious, dear."

"Okay, if it's not you, then who?"

"Give me a moment." She wiped her eyes with another napkin. "You should've seen the look on your face." She waved her hand back and forth.

"Stop teasing me. Who else?"

"I dropped by Nathaniel's apartment the other day, and Brooke answered the door in a robe. We talked later that day. She's thinking about moving in with him after the holidays. I was thinking how small the apartment is. Maybe I should offer them the basement."

Riley's mouth opened wider with each word.

"You know I've always treated Nathaniel like he was my own. I love that boy."

"You like taking on challenges."

"They're young, but she really loves him. And you know how goofy he gets around her."

"Yeah. But they're so young."

"George and I were too. And we had a lot more to overcome, but we made it work." Her aunt patted her hand. "And to finish up our conversation about you and Ms. Kate. I've always hoped you'd find someone around here. I saw more and more positive interactions with you two as she settled in. Don't be scared. Whatever happens is meant to be. You know how that line goes, 'It's better to have loved and lost than never to have loved at all.' Wouldn't you say so?"

"Who said that?"

"A British poet named Alfred Tennyson. Why the funny look? You know I read a lot. Besides, the best advice from literature will live throughout time and never wear out. Now, stop your worrying."

Riley nodded. "I'm starved. Time for eggs. And I need to let Hank back inside."

Aunt Lilly tugged on her arm. "Huskies like cold, especially Hank. Dear, I hate to intrude, but I feel you need another piece of advice."

Riley propped her face in the palms of her hands and stared at her coffee cup.

"Don't let the past hold you hostage. That's important. Another is talking about it with the one you love. You need to talk to Kate."

"I need time."

"You sure you're not stalling?"

Riley didn't answer. She hadn't touched that topic for years.

"Well, when the time is right, don't stay tongue-tied. Now, any chance of some bacon with those eggs? I feel like cheating on my diet."

"Yep." Riley kissed the top of her aunt's head and rose to finish breakfast. As she rattled the pans on top of the stove, she sniffled and willed back the tears. Just thinking about that hellish place made her sick, and the latest gossip from Lena's gang made it hard to forget. They gabbed about Riley's mom having a second daughter in her early twenties and being pregnant with a fifth child.

If Aunt Lilly knew about her sister, she would have told her. *Forget it. That chapter of my life is over and sealed.* Her mother hadn't contacted her, and Riley sure as hell didn't want to see or speak with her.

"Smells like the bacon is getting crispy," Aunt Lilly said.

"Yep. Almost done." Riley wiped her eyes with her sleeve, pretending the heat of the stove was getting to her. But sooner or later, she'd have to talk because the buildup of emotions was paralyzing her.

# Chapter Thirty-Eight

*Thanksgiving*

With her guests arriving soon, Kate scurried around in a panic, trying to pull together the final touches for Thanksgiving dinner. What in the world was she thinking offering to cook for six people?

"Oh, oh, hot." She dropped the cornbread in the cast-iron skillet onto a trivet. The edges appeared a little too crisp, but the center looked perfectly golden. A sweet smell wafted up. Next, she slid the green beans into the oven next to the sweet potato casserole. She shut the oven door and moved the pot of boiling potatoes over to a cooler position.

"I'm way over my head."

Kate had prepared a meal for three when she lived at Lilly's, but now she was attempting to fix dishes that she'd never cooked before. The squash soup had turned out well and was simmering on the back burner, but the saltiness of the sourdough, mushroom, and bacon dressing left something to be desired. Glancing around at the disaster zone that was previously her kitchen, she swiftly launched into cleaning mode.

Her phone buzzed with an incoming Zoom call, and she smiled. "Happy Thanksgiving, Sherry. How's the family?" Kate could see she was in her parents' backyard.

"Max is playing Xbox with our nephew, but I had to get some fresh air. Mom is driving me nuts. In front of the entire family yesterday, she said, and I quote, 'Now that you're married, when am I going to get more grandbabies?' Telling her that wasn't in our plans was no use. She keeps asking. So, I hope your day is going better than mine."

Kate laughed. "I'm trying to clean up the mess I call cooking before everyone arrives."

"Oh, please. I'm sure everything will be delicious." Something caught Sherry's attention, and she rolled her eyes. "Gotta go. Mom's calling me."

"Maybe she wants to show you the various artificial insemination procedures she's found on the web."

"Not funny." Sherry made a stern face, then cracked a smile. "Happy Thanksgiving. And tell your charming Riley that I miss you all. I was so happy you two finally got together. Bye, sweetie."

"I miss you guys too. Enjoy the married life. You deserve it. Bye." Seeing her friend over video chat wasn't the same as having her here to hug. A visit in the spring with Riley would be heaven.

Her guests knocked on the door, and she took a deep breath and yelled, "Come in. It's open."

"Happy Thanksgiving." Lilly swung the door open.

Hank came racing in and did his happy dance around Kate, then he looped back around Megan, who was carrying pies. Tom and Nancy brought a salad and deviled eggs. Riley came in last carrying a cooler, and Hank ran to her feet.

"Calm down, boy." Riley gave Kate a dazzling smile as she unpacked a shrimp cocktail tray, a cheese and cracker platter, and Lilly's famous bacon-wrapped brussels sprouts.

"Wow. Thank heavens we won't starve because I'm not on my game today." Kate sheepishly thumbed over her shoulder toward the stove.

"Nonsense, dear. Your cooking is wonderful." Lilly smiled. "But my nose detects a slight burning smell. Is everything okay?"

"It could be the fire that I see through the glass." Riley pointed at the oven.

"Oh, crap." Kate grabbed her oven mitts, flung the door open, and removed the sweet potato casserole with its marshmallows ablaze. The smell permeated every square inch of the cabin.

"Did you mean to flambé it?" Riley grinned. "Scrap it off and put new marshmallows on top. It'll be fine."

Kate's tension drained when Riley came behind her and massaged her shoulders.

"Relax. I'll finish this." She kissed Kate's cheek and removed her apron.

"Nathaniel's eating at his girlfriend's house. He wanted me to tell you that he'd stop another day for leftovers." Lilly hugged Kate.

"Happy Thanksgiving." Tom and Nancy greeted Kate with bear hugs.

Megan slung her arm around Kate's shoulders. "Don't worry. The leftovers won't last long between Riley, Nathaniel, and Hank. Now let's grab some appetizers."

# CABIN FEVER

Megan and Tom piled goodies on their plates. Nancy and Lilly giggled about something as they opened a bottle of champagne, and Hank wolfed down the meal that Riley had served him. Kate sat on the sofa and smiled at her dear chosen family, who were all foodies. She used to cook and bake sweets with her mom and a few friends during the holidays. But since her mom's death, Thanksgiving and Christmas had become just days to check off the calendar. And Kate had rarely accepted her father's invitation, because the tension between her and her stepmother always hung in the air. Sherry had often invited her, but Kate didn't want to crash her family gathering either.

"Sweetie, why the sad face?" Lilly sat down and placed a tissue in Kate's hand.

It was only then that Kate realized she was crying. The room stilled as everyone looked at her with concerned expressions. She wiped away her tears with trembling fingers. "My mom and I used to cook together. After she passed, I spent most of the holidays alone. This is the best Thanksgiving I've had in years. Thank you for coming tonight."

Everyone murmured their thanks for Kate inviting them, and Lilly bear hugged her. After feeling adrift with hardly any family ties, she was now filled with immense love for these people who had so willingly opened their hearts and homes to her.

"Now, how's that turkey coming along?" Lilly pointed to Megan, who was standing next to the oven. "I'll fill the water glasses." She rose and joined Megan and Nancy in the kitchen.

Kate hugged Riley. "Happy Thanksgiving." She never wanted to go back to the daily grind of getting up at five a.m., riding public transportation, working long hours, and skipping lunch just to get home late and do it all over again and again. Life was too short. Idaho might not be the easiest place to live, but Kate was happy here with her chosen family and Riley.

"Happy Thanksgiving," Riley whispered and kissed Kate's cheek.

The scent of the wonderful food filled the cabin. Riley was no longer hungry. She looked into Kate's tearful eyes, and her heart broke and her eyes misted. Everyone probably thought she was reacting to Kate, but that was only half of the reason. No one had a clue how Kate's words had dug deep.

"Dinner's done. I'll carve the turkey," Megan shouted.

Everyone pitched in, leaving Kate and Riley alone on the sofa. Kate kissed and hugged her and didn't let go. But Kate's affection didn't chase away Riley's invisible agony that twisted her stomach into knots. She swallowed and pushed the negativity away the best she could.

"Let's eat, lovebirds." Megan stood over them.

After everyone was seated, Aunt Lilly said a prayer, and each person said a few words of gratitude. Riley was the last to speak. She cleared her throat and raised her glass. "Here's to good food for the brood, and great friends and family despite my insanity. Now, my stomach's as big as the sky. Let's eat so we can get to the pie."

"Please don't write me a poem for birthday and holiday cards. I want you to save your best poetry for the big New York City publishing houses." Kate smirked.

Laughter filled the room. The merriment didn't show in her aunt's eyes as she glanced at Riley over the top of her water glass.

Halfway through dinner, Kate glanced down at Riley's half-eaten plate. "Did I mess it up too much?"

Riley rubbed her belly. "No. Your cooking is great. I was sneaking snacks before I came over." Thankfully, Hank whined, and she stood. "I need to take him out. Make sure to save some pie for me."

"I'll go with you."

Riley gently pressed down on Kate's shoulder. "No. Sit and relax. It's cold, and we'll be back in no time." She clipped on Hank's leash, tossed on her coat, and hurried out the door.

"Easy, boy."

Hank tugged on her arm, passing one tree up after another, sniffing until he found the right one. Riley chewed on her bottom lip. Every time Kate talked about her mother, she mentioned their tight bond. What would that even feel like? Riley kicked a rock.

"Are you done yet?"

Hank howled and yanked her along again.

The thoughts of those years in Arizona had faded into the background following three years of therapy, but that summer before her sixteenth birthday was one memory Riley couldn't shake. And every time Kate asked questions, a tiny piece of her wall fell. But overhearing Lena had triggered Riley big time.

She squeezed her eyes shut and clenched her jaw. Aunt Lilly wanted her to tell Kate, but she wasn't ready. So she did what she always did, avoided the subject and focused on something—anything—else. Tonight, it was food, wine, and games with friends. Tom was the designated driver, and she intended on taking advantage of that opportunity. But her therapist's warning was coming true: avoidance only worked so long. Her anxiety had worsened with the return of her distressing flashbacks and luckily only her aunt had noticed. She wiped her eyes.

Hank cocked his head to the side and looked up at her as he howled and whined.

"That's a new sound for you. Is that sympathy?" Riley tugged on his leash. "Let's go back."

He bolted and almost pulled her over.

"I swear, I need to buy some skis for our winter outings."

Riley stopped just outside the door. Despite her chest heaving, she couldn't seem to get enough air into her lungs. She spun around and sat on the porch steps. After a few minutes of controlling her breathing, she slowly rose. "Okay. Showtime."

# Chapter Thirty-Nine

*December*

"GOOD MORNING. I'M FULL of energy, but I can't resist your coffee and food." Kate grinned.

"How's it going? Seen Riley lately?" Nancy winked as she poured Kate's coffee.

"Yeah. I'm a little crazy about her."

"Like you could hide it." Nancy giggled. "You light up like a Christmas tree when she's around."

"True."

Nancy chuckled. "I've known her since she was a babe. She's a keeper."

Kate nodded and placed her order. Soon after, Howard stepped into the diner, and they exchanged a wave.

"Good morning, do you mind if I join you?" he asked.

"Please do."

"You look radiant. Merrick is obviously agreeing with you."

"It's the Christmas season, and it's my day off. You're not hunting me down, are you?" She laughed.

He smiled widely. "Nope, but I think your glow is more than holiday cheer. After six months, you seem to be fitting nicely into our little town."

"Merrick is growing on me." Kate couldn't wipe the smile off her face. With each passing day, the possibility of making Merrick her permanent home grew.

Her mind shifted to the journals. Howard hadn't mentioned the box since the day he'd given it to her. Did he know about the affair between her grandmother and his grandfather? She should let sleeping dogs lie. She smiled again. The longer she lived in Merrick, the more she picked up the regional jargon.

"Have you started decorating for Christmas?" he asked.

"Lilly and Riley are visiting me tomorrow for brunch. I'm cooking, and they're decorating. I don't know who should be more terrified, them or me."

He chuckled. "I'm sure your cooking is delicious."

"I thought so too until Thanksgiving when I burned the marshmallows on the sweet potato casserole *twice* and overcooked the turkey."

"Say, have you ever thought about a trip to Boise? Now's the time to go. The holiday light display and decorations at the Botanical Garden are out of this world. It runs through the first weekend in January."

"That's exactly where I'm going this weekend. Riley and I plan to visit a museum or two, but I'm really looking forward to the zoo. We're going to be able to see little Muffin, the bobcat baby that I found." The weekend after Boise, she and Riley planned to appear at the town's Christmas party. Lilly said almost everyone attended the party.

"Your take-out will be a few more minutes. Have a cup on the house." Nancy slid coffee in front of him and a glass of juice for Kate.

"Thank you, Nancy." He turned back to Kate. "That's exciting. You should visit the art museum. They have an exhibit of my grandaunt Mary's paintings and photos." He leaned back and looked proud. "Her friendship with your grandmother was a shining example to other family members to put disagreements aside. My cousin Diane's daughter, Chris, lives in Boise. She's also an artist and selected the pieces."

"That does sound exciting. Is Diane your cousin who lives in Oregon?"

"Yes."

"How's she doing after the car accident?"

"Good. She has a small limp, but that should get better with continued physical therapy."

"How many inches do you think we'll get?" She glanced out the window at the enormous snowflakes drifting delicately down.

"Whether it's six or eighteen inches is sometimes hard to tell. The weather's been wild lately, but Idaho folks are good with plowing. And a little birdie tells me you're mighty handy with a snowmobile."

"The narrow dirt road alongside the highway confused me when I first moved here. It never occurred to me that it was for snowmobiles."

They both chuckled. Nancy waved and set his bag on the counter.

"I should get back to work. Have a great day." He patted Kate's shoulder.

"You too, Howard."

Mary Jacobs' art display sounded like a perfect addition to the weekend trip. She couldn't wait to tell Riley. She finished lunch and thought again about her grandmother's journals. The last time she glanced through them was nearly two months ago. Other than the references to JJ, the entries on everyday life blurred together, and her interest had quickly dwindled. Maybe Mary's art would make Kate feel better connected.

"Can I get you anything else? A little dessert?" Nancy asked.

"I'm good, thanks. Although, the Thursday through Saturday roast turkey special for supper sounds yummy."

"Did you hear yourself? You said supper and not dinner. We'll make a local out of you yet." Nancy chuckled. "I heard Howard mention Boise. The light show is spectacular."

"Riley and I are going there this weekend."

"A little romantic getaway. How lovely." Nancy smiled widely. "And Mary Jacobs' art is wonderful. Her work has gotten more popular outside our state. You can even buy her prints online. She's our superstar. My grandparents, who started this café, knew her." Nancy's face glowed with pride. "Mary used to come in here all the time with Emmeline, your grandmother. They were best friends. Thick as thieves apparently." Nancy tapped her finger on the table. "My grandma taught elementary school part-time. She said the girls were her best students. When they were teenagers, Grandpop would talk history with them. Mary would sometimes paint pictures based on his stories. Grandpop didn't go past the sixth grade, but he loved books and would talk anyone's leg off about history." Nancy glanced up and down the street through the picture window. "There's so much history here. It's a shame that jobs are so limited. So many of our young folk have moved away for better opportunities." She sighed deeply. "Well, I best get back to work and let you go."

"I changed my mind. I'll take a dozen chocolate éclairs to go."

"You got it."

It was cold outside, but Kate stopped to admire the snow falling from the sky. She stuck out her tongue like a little girl and giggled. Maybe she could talk Riley into spending an extra night in Boise if she bribed her gang with the éclairs.

Kate dragged her feet through the fluffy snow. Suddenly, she stopped.

*Thick as thieves.* If Mary and her grandmother were so close, why wasn't Mary mentioned anywhere in the journals? She had skimmed through over half and couldn't think of one instance of seeing Mary's name. That didn't make sense. "Why didn't I notice that earlier?"

A honking truck startled her, and Riley pulled up beside her, grinning. "Hello. I'm new in town and was wondering if you could recommend a great spa."

Kate strolled up to the open passenger window and stepped onto the truck's running board. "Well, we have a small service in town, but I hear the best spa is in Boise."

"I might get lost. Do you have time to show me the way?"

"Uh-huh. What kind of other services do you require?" Kate twirled a finger in her hair.

Riley glanced down. "Is that a bag of food you're holding?"

"Talk about spoiling the moment. You're hopeless." Kate slid in and closed the window.

"Are you going to share with me?"

"They're chocolate éclairs for the workers, but if you promise to give me the best massage of my life tonight, then I might let you have one."

"Deal."

Kate couldn't get enough of Riley's smile, but it didn't take her mind off the fact that Mary's name was missing from the journals. She'd have to read more carefully and not rush through, but she had little time between now and the Boise trip. Maybe the Mary Jacobs art exhibit would hold a clue.

# Chapter Forty

KATE INSISTED THAT THEY leave for Boise at a reasonable time. They checked into their hotel, quickly showered for a romantic dinner, and afterward, they strolled through the Winter Aglow at the Idaho Botanical Garden. The festival and its 400,000 lights were spectacular, but the ride back to the hotel was delightfully electric.

Riley drove with one hand and caressed her thigh with the other. Occasionally, she explored between Kate's legs, adding fuel to the fire. And when Riley told her precisely what she was going to do when they got back, Kate couldn't wait to feel their bodies touch.

At the hotel, she grabbed Riley by the shirt collar and pulled her inside their room. The door slammed as she pinned Riley against the wall. Kate moved in for a kiss, but Riley pushed away from the wall, turned Kate around, and pressed her against the wall.

"I'm in charge tonight." Riley held Kate's neck firmly but gently. "Say it."

"You're in charge." Kate released a soft breath as arousal coursed through her from Riley's command.

Riley kissed her neck, gently at first, then she began to suck. Kate would have a hickey tomorrow, but it felt so good, she didn't care. Her breathing increased as Riley skimmed her fingertips down her body and traced lazy circles along her collarbone. She caressed Kate's nipple through her clothes.

"Do you like it?" Riley asked.

"Yes." Kate's clit throbbed.

Riley yanked Kate's shirt out of her jeans. She sucked harder on Kate's neck while slowly gliding her fingertips between Kate's stomach and her breast. A few strokes over Kate's nipple through her bra's fabric had Kate moaning with pleasure. She was almost to the brink when Riley pulled her hand away. Kate was going to protest, but the sound of her zipper silenced her. "Riley, I need your hand."

"What's that? Did you say please?" Riley cupped Kate's sex then withdrew her hand.

"Please."

"That's better." Riley continued kissing and sucking on Kate's neck as she pulled Kate's jeans down just enough for her to push her hand inside Kate's underwear. Her long strokes teased Kate more. "Someone's wet."

She kissed Kate hard as her fingers drove her wild with an increasing tempo. Kate couldn't get enough, especially when Riley moved down to bite her nipple. "Please take my clothes off."

Riley stopped. "Since you asked so nicely..." She pinned Kate's wrists to the wall with one hand and used her other to unclip her bra. "What would you like me to do?"

"Kiss me."

Riley arched her eyebrow. "Where? And don't forget your manners."

"Please. I need your mouth all over my body."

Riley smiled and lavished Kate with a mix of tender and intense kisses. Then she quickly peeled off Kate's jeans and underwear. She slowly walked Kate to the bed and pushed her back onto it.

Kate focused on the lustful storm in Riley's eyes.

"Scoot back and get comfy with the pillows," Riley whispered.

She crawled on top of Kate, her mouth and hands more commanding and forceful but never hurtful.

"Where do you want my mouth again?"

"Please...everywhere." Kate gently nudged her lower.

Her teasing flicks, hard sucking, and light nips drove Kate wild. Her chest heaved, and her heart pounded. "Oh, Riley!" She gripped Riley's head as she quickened her pace. Kate flung her head back as her pulse pounded so loud it thundered in her ears. Stars danced behind her eyelids, and she bucked underneath Riley.

Riley climbed up and laid beside her. She placed her hand over Kate's galloping heart. "I think someone's happy."

"Oh, yeah. Give me a few seconds, and I'll have my way with you."

"I think we should make this a contest until we're both exhausted."

Kate's eyes widened. "You're on." After barely catching her breath, she rolled on top of Riley.

Several hours later, they lay blissfully entwined. Kate was in heaven. She felt so much more than lust. Once again, the word love popped into her mind. Her feelings were at a level that she'd never experienced before, but prickles of fear rippled over her skin. If she said those three words too soon, it might scare Riley away. She glanced at the clock: three in the morning wasn't the time to figure it out.

"Kate?"

"Yes." Kate rolled on her side to face Riley. Moonlight shone through the crack in the drapes and highlighted Riley's chiseled features.

"You're the best thing that's ever happened to me."

"That's sweet, babe. You make me really happy." Kate cupped Riley's cheek and kissed her softly.

"Babe?" Riley raised her eyebrows. "I'll be your babe if you'll be my buttercup."

Kate giggled. "Buttercup?"

"Reese's peanut butter cups are my favorite, and you taste delicious from your head to your toes." Riley traced Kate's lower lip with her fingertip. "Plus, the wild buttercup flowers in Idaho are stunning, and their yellow petals are sunny and bright, just like you."

"Then I happily accept being called your buttercup. Goodnight, babe."

"Goodnight, buttercup."

She nuzzled into Riley's arms and smiled. No one could predict the future, but for now, her life seemed to be falling into place.

# Chapter Forty-One

"BREAKFAST WAS DELICIOUS. THANK you for this trip. It's a fabulous Christmas gift. The lights festival was spectacular." Kate dabbed her lips with the napkin, then entwined her fingers with Riley's.

"Were the lights the only spectacular thing last night?"

Riley's smile sent shivers down Kate's spine. God, those lips had pleasured Kate last night. "Our lovemaking was stellar as always. You drive me crazy with desire."

Riley picked up the menu and fanned herself.

The server brought a large to-go coffee for Riley and their check. Kate left money on the table. "Let's go. I can't wait to see little Muffin and Mary's work."

"Did you find any mention of Mary's name in the journals?" Riley asked as they walked out of the hotel restaurant.

"No. It's weird. I scanned through another chunk and couldn't find a single reference to her."

"Maybe you'll see something today in Mary's art."

Kate sighed. "Hopefully, but she's known for her landscapes."

"You drive while I finish my coffee. I don't want to spill it or get us in a fender bender." Riley tossed Kate the keys.

"Boise's population is less than one tenth of Chicago's, and I never drove in that city." Kate snickered. "But dodging the damn grazing cattle on the county back roads has sharpened my driving skills."

"See? You're an expert now."

Zoo Boise and the art museum were in Julia Davis Park. Riley had arranged for them to see Muffin shortly before the zoo opened. They met the caretaker, and she took them to the back of the exhibit where Muffin and the other bobcats were housed.

Goosebumps rose on Kate's arm and her stomach lurched as the bobcats growled and fought for choice cuts of their meal—rats chopped in half. "Do they spit out the bones?"

The woman laughed. "They eat everything."

Kate held onto Riley's waist for dear life. "Which one is Muffin?"

The woman pointed through the cage. "The feisty big one that's trying to steal a portion from the little one."

"Wow. He's gotten so big. He's as big as a grown house cat."

"We're guessing he'll be in the upper ranks, probably at least thirty pounds at maturity."

Little Muffin had gotten her through a tough period of loneliness, and Kate would be forever grateful. Her heart filled with happiness that he was safe and with other bobcats. She looked at the caretaker. "Thank you for taking care of him. We need to leave for the art museum but will come back another time."

Riley laughed as the door shut. "Never would have thought you'd be squeamish. Rats are a natural part of a bobcat's diet and essential for their growth."

"I loved seeing him, but next time, I don't want to see them eat." Kate thrust the truck keys into Riley's hand. "You drive now in case I need to roll down the window and hang my head out for fresh air."

"Or puke." Riley laughed again.

The art museum was around the corner. Riley read the first exhibit sign out loud, "Ms. Mary Jacobs-Dawson, 1899 to 1990, was one of Boise's most beloved artists. She owned a studio in Hyde Park, but her love extended beyond her work. For nearly fifty years, she volunteered her time to teach art to deaf children. The art museum would like to thank the family and friends of Ms. Mary Jacobs-Dawson for sharing this outstanding art collection. Special thanks to Ms. Jacobs-Dawson's great granddaughter, Boise's own Chris Reicher, a fine artist in her own right."

They strolled through the paintings, and Kate admired Mary's artistic flair.

Riley's mouth dropped. "Wow. This one is of Old Town." She pointed to the exhibit label below. "The 1920 Fourth of July parade in Merrick, Idaho."

"The shops look very different."

"Some buildings had to be rebuilt after the 1983 Borah Peak Earthquake."

Kate swallowed. "I thought you were joking about how bad that quake was until I looked it up on the internet."

# CABIN FEVER

At the next painting, Riley pulled Kate close and whispered, "A delightful painting of a stylishly dressed young woman, sitting in a two-seat buggy and preparing to go into town. Circa 1918."

As Kate examined the portrait, her heart thudded in her chest, and all other sounds faded in the background. "Oh, my God. That looks exactly like the wagon with the red-painted spokes that I donated to the museum in Merrick." She pointed to the woman in the carriage. "I think this might be my grandmother, Emmeline." She grabbed Riley's arm and pulled her past more landscapes until they came upon a large portrait. "That's my grandmother. I have the original black and white photo." Kate marveled at how the colorful oil paint brought the rendition to life. The dress material was dark maroon velvet with a white lace collar.

Kate tugged Riley along, searching for another, but the rest were all landscapes. And strangely, Mary's style changed drastically toward the end of her career. The few paintings from the last twenty years of her life were dark and stormy.

"Let's look at her photography." Riley led her into the next room.

The photos were all landscapes or pictures of animals, leaving Kate disappointed and a little heartbroken. As they meandered through the display, an opening to a smaller room caught Kate's eye. "In here." She grabbed Riley's shirt and pulled her along.

"Slow down. And watch it, or you'll rip my shirt off."

Kate read the placard before entering the room. "Ms. Mary Jacobs-Dawson took these photos from 1932 through 1978. These personal photos have never been seen by the public before. Although she died in 1990 at the age of ninety-one, she gave up photography in late 1978."

Unlike the previous exhibits, all the photos were casual portraits or small gatherings. Kate meticulously examined all the ones with female subjects. Flooded with emotion, Kate grasped Riley's hand and didn't let go.

"Buttercup, you're bruising my hand."

"My grandmother is in most of these photos, and the single portraits are only of her." The farther along they moved, Kate saw her grandmother's progression from a vibrant young woman riding horseback to an older adult with a cane by her side. She read the final exhibit card. "The last known photos, dated September 5, 1978." The month sent a chill down Kate's spine. "Grandmother died later that month." She looked up. Her breath stilled, yet her pulse ticked up. Was she truly seeing what she thought? "Riley?"

"Yeah?"

"What do you see?" Other people were milling about in the room, but Kate blocked out all noise. Lightheadedness took over, and she rested her head on Riley's shoulder.

"Ah, four photos taken in sequence?"

*Oh, my God. Grandmother, I can't believe you hid your secret for so long.* Tears formed in Kate's eyes. *It must have been so hard for you.*

"Can you give me a hint?" Riley asked.

"Look closely." Emotions choked Kate's throat.

The first photo was a closeup of a tearful Emmeline, though she smiled brightly. In the second, her arthritic-crooked index finger pointed to her chest. In the third, her arms formed a tight cross against her body with her hands closed. Her head was turned to the side as if she was hugging an imaginary figure. Another blissful smile played on her lips. The sign symbolized *love.* In the fourth, she pointed straight at the camera.

"My grandmother is signing 'I love you' to Mary."

"Holy cow."

After several seconds, Kate flung her head back. "I can't believe I missed it. We need to get home. I have to talk to Howard." She practically ran out of the room.

"Wait a minute. We weren't going home until after dinner."

"I don't know how, but JJ must be Mary." Kate continued at a fast clip.

"I can't believe I'm two inches taller and having trouble keeping up with you. Slow down. And why in the world would your grandmother use Jeremiah's initials instead of Mary's?"

Kate rushed down the museum steps. "Probably because it was a lesser punishment. Think about it. If anyone accused her of an affair with a man, it would be damaging. But finding her in a same-sex relationship would be complete devastation." As they got to their parking spot, she held her hand out to Riley. "Give me the keys."

"Oh no, you don't. I drive." Riley pulled her back before she opened the door. "Wonderful. We got a ticket."

Kate ripped it off the windshield and whipped her phone out of her pocket. "I'll pay it while you drive." She paid the ticket, then leaned her head against the window. Her heart ached. The anguish her grandmother must have gone through hiding her true love must have been enormous. How did Emmeline and Mary do it?

Suddenly, the strange letter from Kate's father made more sense. He alluded to something out of sorts and hoped she could untangle the mystery. He must have figured it out but refused to deal with it. Kate sighed. Howard was the last hope of finding out more.

# Chapter Forty-Two

KATE GRABBED RILEY'S ARM. "I have a better idea. Turn the truck around." She texted Howard.

"What are you up to?"

"Chris Reicher lives in Boise, right?"

"Please tell me that you're not thinking about paying her a visit."

"She's an artist who arranged the exhibit. How could she not know?"

"Okay. I agree it looks suspicious, but it's a big jump to Mary and Emmeline being lesbians. Best friends say they love one another all the time. And Howard doesn't have a problem with us being gay. Don't you think he would have told you if his grandaunt was a lesbian?"

"He might not know. Look, a few of the journal entries threw me for a loop. Something was off, but I couldn't put my finger on it. And it's pretty damn odd that I couldn't find Mary's name anywhere. They were best friends. Nancy called them 'thick as thieves.'"

Kate propped her feet on the dash. "It makes sense now. One of Grandmother's entries details her sadness at seeing JJ exchange wedding vows. I researched the date of Jeremiah's wedding. It was the same month but five years later than the date in the journal. I talked myself into thinking that he might have been married twice. With what we know now, Grandmother had to be talking about Mary. How in the world did my brain not process that big red flag?"

Riley squeezed her thigh. "Because the cabin was under renovation, and you were falling for my adorable personality."

Kate grinned. "Yeah, you were a pleasant distraction." Her phone pinged. "Chris' studio is in the building that once housed Mary's old studio. Talk about déjà vu." She typed the address into the truck's GPS.

Twenty minutes later, they were in front of the two-story brick building on North 13th Street in a section of Boise called Hyde Park. Quaint shops and restaurants lined the street and buzzed with activity, but the studio was closed. "Damn. Maybe, she's still inside." Kate pounded on the wooden door.

"Easy. You don't want to set off the alarm."

"She could be in the back where it's hard to hear." Kate rapped lighter this time.

"Can I help you?"

They looked to the right. A young woman wheeling a small cart full of groceries eyed them suspiciously.

"Hi, I'm Kate Minton, and this is Riley Anderson. We're looking for Chris Reicher."

"I'm Chris."

Kate swallowed. "I'm Isaac Minton's youngest. Well, he was born Isaiah Christensen. Howard Jacobs settled my father's estate, and we've become good friends. He recommended the exhibit. Mary's art is amazing, particularly the stunning portraits and pictures of my grandmother, Emmeline Christensen. I was wondering about their friendship."

"So much for subtlety," Riley muttered.

Chris smiled. "Any friend of cousin Howard is a friend of mine. If you guys help make the salad, you're welcome to stay for dinner." She unlocked the door.

"We don't want to interrupt," Riley said.

"No interruption. I'd enjoy the company."

They climbed two flights of stairs to get to Chris' apartment above her studio. It was an open living space, and the lounge's large picture window faced the restaurant across the street. Customers gathered in the adjacent garden around flaming outdoor heaters and a firepit. Evergreen trees decorated for Christmas provided a cheery atmosphere.

"Who needs a tree when there are several across the street? Just toss your coats next to mine." Chris pointed to the chairs at the kitchen island. "We can eat in the living room." She pulled out some panels that attached to the coffee table and extended the length. Then she adjusted it to just the right height.

"Is all the artwork yours?" Riley asked.

"Yes."

When Chris turned her back, Riley nudged Kate's shoulder and motioned to a painting. Bright rainbow splotches of colors surrounded a nude woman. Her body was angled with her chest pressed forward,

250

her arms stretched outward, and her fingers straight and tight together. Her head arched back, exposing her throat, but she wasn't in the throes of passion because her legs were together and straight, and her toes pointed.

"She's diving." Kate marveled at the exquisite detail.

"Yes." Chris smiled.

Riley cleared her throat. "I'll help with that salad."

Nerves kicked in during dinner, and Kate slid into idle chatter. Riley bumped her foot under the table, and she finished the sentence then stuffed some bread into her mouth.

"So, how long have you two been together?" Chris asked

Riley looked at Kate with a smirk. "Just a few months, but sometimes it feels like years."

Kate swatted Riley's shoulder as Chris laughed.

"What was your favorite part of my great grandmother's exhibit?" Chris sipped her wine.

This was her opening. "The four pictures showing Emmeline signing, 'I love you,' to Mary."

"Mine too. Did you know they were a couple before the exhibit?"

"No. Does anyone else in your family know?" Kate asked.

"My great grandmother told my mom before she died. Mom didn't want to tell anyone else. I think Howard and some other cousins would have handled the news, but Mom didn't want to upset the Dawson side of the family. They're still very prominent, and rich, and don't like controversy. Apparently, I'm enough controversy for now. But I make a good living, and I don't need their money or praise."

"It's sad that our society accepted Jeremiah taking the fall but would have punished two female lovers. Has your mother seen the exhibit?" Kate asked.

"Not yet, but she'll be here soon for Christmas." Chris grinned. "Mom only told me about it because I'm exactly like my great grandmother, Josie, except I consider myself genderqueer and not bi."

"Oh, she was bi? Wait a minute. Did you say Josie?" Kate leaned forward.

"Her full name was Mary Josephine. Professionally, she went by Mary, but her close friends and family called her Josie." Chris cleared her throat. "To this day, the Dawson side does not say Josie. My guess is they think it's not classy enough."

"Well, that confirms who JJ is in your grandmother's journals," Riley said.

"She left you journals?"

"Yes. I knew nothing until I arrived in Idaho." Kate quickly explained about the cabin, her father's letter, and Emmeline's journals. "When I heard about our family feud, I tried coaxing some information out of Howard. I got the impression that he's sad over everything that happened between our families."

"He's a good guy that takes everything to heart when someone is hurting. He probably didn't want to upset you," Chris said.

"Howard's been a gem. I'm surprised that Merrick has a lot of people that are gay-friendly. My father was never comfortable when I came out. Part of it was his quirky personality, but he was from an older generation."

"Some older folks are tight-lipped," Chris said. "They didn't talk about a lot of serious matters, especially sex and sexual preference."

"Yeah, my father could never say the word lesbian and simply referred to me as living 'a lifestyle.' Now that I know so much more, I'm pretty sure he suspected his mother was a lesbian." Kate took a sip of wine and swirled the liquid in her glass. "Wait a second. When you said Josie was bi, how do you know?"

"She wrote a letter to my mom." Chris raised an eyebrow. "Turns out my great grandfather knew all along about the love affair and let it go on. That's why Mom doesn't want to upset the apple cart. Imagine one of Idaho's most prominent families finding out one of their own condoned his wife's love affair with another woman. I put Josie's personal pictures in the exhibit because I'm tired of hiding. Josie was a phenomenal artist. It's time the world knew." Chris left, and when she returned, she held out an oversized envelope to Kate. "It's a copy."

Kate gently took the letter written by her grandmother's lover as if it were a fragile Japanese origami. How much did Josie write about her feelings for Emmeline? Kate's breath stilled as she carefully slid the letter out of the envelope.

# Chapter Forty-Three

KATE HELD THE LETTER between her and Riley and began to read.

My lovely granddaughter Diane,
I am so proud of you and your accomplishments, and now, you are a mother. Christine is so precious. As I held my beautiful great granddaughter in my arms today, happiness and sadness engulfed me. I looked into her sleeping, beautiful pink face, and it hurts to know my time is short.
But what hurts the most is that I have secrets buried deep inside that have nibbled on my soul for years. At the age of ninety-one, I thought they would die with me. But God calls on me to tell the truth. My dear granddaughter, I have chosen you to hear my story.
I fell in love with my childhood friend, Emmeline Davis. Yes, a woman. We had no choice but to marry men. Emmeline's marriage was arranged after her sixteenth birthday, and I married the following year.
Your grandfather was a cheery, easy-going man, handsome, and so intelligent. I don't know how to explain, but I loved him and Emmeline. He moved us close to his family in Boise soon after our marriage. Traveling back then was not easy. Emmeline and I frequently wrote to one another, and I visited Merrick as often as possible. I would often travel alone as your grandfather's medical practice grew.
In 1929, your grandfather discovered my letters. I was JJ, and she was ED. He naturally thought ED was a man and threatened to divorce and take our only child, your mother, away. I broke down and confessed. He gave me the silent treatment for days, and I just about lost my mind.
When the silence broke, he asked if I was confused. I cried hard

and said I could not bear to be without him or Emmeline. He asked more questions. In the end, he said that my relationship could continue as long as no one ever found out. Amazingly, our relationship never diminished and only grew.

I was heartbroken when he died in 1932. He was a good father and a good man. I remained in Boise near the Dawson family, who helped take care of us, and continued my discreet visits with Emmeline. No one ever guessed we were more than best friends.

A couple of years later, Emmeline's husband found a love letter she was writing to me and thought JJ was my brother. He confronted Jeremiah, who denied the affair.

Emmeline was ready to confess, but I told her I would tell him. Jeremiah and I were always close, and I could not see him in pain. When I laid my sins bare, Jeremiah was angry. I expected him to go straight to Papa and the Dawsons. I prepared to be disowned and for the Church to excommunicate me.

I worried about losing the house and your mother. And what would happen to Emmeline and her son? What if they put us in an asylum? Loving the same sex was considered a dreadful disease. I didn't sleep for nights.

Then Jeremiah came to me and told me he would confess to being Emmeline's lover. He ordered me to stay away from her and never speak of the matter again, all in the name of protecting our family's honor. I could not make that promise. I loved her so much.

Yet, the next day, Jeremiah told his lie. Our family was in pain, but they did not turn their back on him. He was their only son. To simmer down the feelings, Papa bought out Elijah Christensen's share of the businesses and paid him a hefty sum of money. Thankfully, Jeremiah's wife did not divorce him despite the ugly gossip in town.

Elijah continued to allow me to visit since he thought I posed no threat. I had to live with the guilt of destroying Elijah and Jeremiah's friendship every time I made the trip. But my love for Emmeline burned bright.

Yet, she was not like me. Emmeline did not love her husband and wanted to run away with me. That was not possible. We would have lost everything. I talked her out of it, but I could not stay away from her. My heart ached for her. And so, we continued to be secret lovers.

Even though I broke my promise, Jeremiah never revealed our true relationship to anyone, and Elijah never found out about us. He would often ask me to keep Emmeline company when he went on long hunting trips. I loved her till the day she died in late 1978. Then my heart stopped beating, and I nearly fell apart. Diane, I do not know how you will react to my confession, but I know you will not disown me. My darling granddaughter, I love you with all my heart.

Love always,
Grandmother Josie
March 1990

Kate was at a loss for words, and she handed the letter back to Chris. She picked up her glass and took a hefty gulp of water. "So your great grandfather shared Josie with Emmeline."

"Yeah." Chris grinned. "Some of the older folks can surprise you. I shared the letter because I thought you had a right to know. But it's up to my mom to tell Howard. And I have no idea why she hasn't yet. He's the most progressive on the Jacobs' side."

"I agree. I won't spill a word."

"I'll keep urging Mom to tell him. Who knows, maybe Howard will come to visit when Mom's here. Then she won't have much choice." Chris laughed. "I was never the quiet, obedient child."

"Thank you for your hospitality. It's getting late. Can we help with the dishes?" Kate asked.

"Oh, no, you're the guests." Chris waved her hands.

"It was a pleasure to meet you, and the meal was delicious." Riley stood.

"And the art exhibit and letter. Thank you again."

"You're welcome."

After they'd hugged goodbye, Kate clung to Riley as they descended the stairs. She was quiet as they walked.

"You okay?" Riley pulled her tighter and kissed her forehead.

"That was a bombshell. I understand better and feel closer to Father and Grandmother Emmeline than ever before. It's painful to think of the fear she must have felt. That makes her resilience to never stop loving Josie amazing."

Riley opened the door, and Kate climbed into the truck's passenger seat.

"We're going to be tired when we get back. Can you take an hour off tomorrow and cuddle in bed with me?" Kate stroked Riley's cheek.

"I'll take the entire morning off to cuddle with you, buttercup." Riley winked.

"Thanks, babe." She laced their fingers together, and Riley gave hers a small squeeze. What Kate had learned today was mind-blowing but having Riley at her side made the day more special. Kate smiled. She would have previously said that fate had brought them together. Now, maybe the ghost of her grandmother was the matchmaker.

\*\*\*

While Kate slept soundly, Riley lay on her back and stared at the ceiling. She rolled over and took in the beauty of Kate's face: her long lashes, creamy skin, and slightly parted soft lips. She was glad the trip to Boise had brought Kate happiness. Her grandmother's story was remarkable.

Right before Kate fell asleep, she talked about how her grandmother must have gone through enormous pain being forced into marriage to a man she didn't love while at the same time hiding herself and her true love from the world. It was all Riley could do to keep her composure. The topic of arranged marriages was like a razor to Riley's heart.

Tears welled up in her eyes, and she rubbed them away with the palm of her hand. *Forget it. Focus on Kate and the future.* She slid out from under the covers, padded into the bathroom and closed the door. The Christmas party was next weekend, three days before Christmas. Now was the time to be happy, but the past kept haunting her and the fear of Kate leaving grew within.

Riley pushed her sadness aside, washed her face, and tiptoed back to bed but couldn't sleep. She rolled on her side again to watch Kate. A tear rolled down her cheek. *I think I'm falling in love with you, Kate. Please love me back. Please stay in Idaho.*

# Chapter Forty-Four

TONIGHT, KATE WOULD BE on the arm of Riley to attend the town's Christmas party, which Lilly said hardly anyone missed. Kate shimmied into several slacks and shirts but didn't like the look. She tried on three dresses and debated whether they showed too much skin, but she wanted a little pizzazz. She slipped the dark green dress back on and turned at various angles to look at herself in the mirror. The dress hung just below her knees and hugged her hips. Lace covered her back, and the front dipped down to the V between her breasts. She smiled. *This is the one. I want to look special for the woman I love.* There were those words again.

As Kate fiddled putting on earrings, her phone buzzed with Joel's ringtone. She dropped the one earring that was giving her a problem and picked up the call.

"Hi, big brother."

"Merry Christmas, sis. What are you up to?"

"I'm getting dressed for a big Christmas party, but I can talk for a few minutes."

"How's the winter in the cabin? We haven't talked for a couple of weeks."

*Three, to be exact.* Kate had left voicemails for him a couple of times, but he only returned short texts, including at Thanksgiving. At least Joel called occasionally, whereas Karl and Roger hadn't contacted her once since their father's death. "It's good. I'm getting used to living off the grid."

"That's fabulous. We're finally getting the businesses straightened out. By the time we paid down the debt, the real value was only about half of what we thought. You should be glad you inherited money and the land and didn't have to deal with this nightmare."

"Yeah." Kate closed her eyes. On more than one occasion, their father had said that the car business was a man's world. That was one area where Isaac had never changed his old-fashioned thinking. That attitude meant Kate was entirely in the dark on the businesses. But if it was true that the business value was half of what they thought, then her inheritance was about equal to her brothers, and her father had known exactly what he was doing.

"So, sis. Only seven more months to go, and you can move back home. I have a job for you. Well, just until you find another paralegal position." His voice was high-pitched with excitement like a kid on a sugar high.

Kate could imagine him bouncing on his toes. "About that." She cleared her throat. "I'm considering staying in Idaho."

"For how long?"

"Merrick feels like home now."

"Huh?" He laughed. "You're joking, right?"

"No. I'm serious. It's peaceful and laidback."

"I thought it was too quiet and was driving you bonkers."

"It was at first, but I've adjusted. The folks are super kind and good neighbors. I don't miss the fast-paced city life or the noise anymore. And believe it or not, I'm enjoying several outdoor sports, including hiking and snowmobiling." She laughed. "Yeah, I know it's hard to envision me playing in the snow, but it's fun. You should come for a visit."

More seconds of silence passed. Kate had omitted her relationship with Riley. She didn't need her big brother thinking that Riley was the only reason for staying in Idaho.

"You still there, Joel?"

"Yeah, just stunned. I'm sorry, but I have to go."

"Me too. Love you, big brother."

"Love you, sis. And Merry Christmas."

*Merrick feels like home.* It had slid effortlessly out of her mouth like honey, with no hesitation and no worries. Why couldn't she say them to Riley?

Kate heard the front door open and shut.

"I'm a tad early. Take your time if you're not ready," Riley shouted from the living room.

She had given Riley a key. Their routine was beginning to feel like a long-term commitment. And for once, Kate didn't feel afraid. She waltzed out and found Riley stretched out on the sofa with her legs propped up, typing away on her phone. She looked fantastic in black jeans, black boots, and a cream button-down shirt. A red tie with Christmas trees and twinkling lights completed the look. Kate laughed.

"Don't be snickering at my stellar tie." Riley stood and slipped her phone into her back pocket. She looked at Kate and froze like a statue with her mouth agape.

"Is this too much?" Kate turned and showed the lace barely hiding her back. "I can change."

Riley's gaze slowly moved down Kate's body. "No way, don't change. You're totally mind-blowing, gorgeous. Although you make me want to skip the party and hit the hay."

"Would you like a glass of wine since alcohol isn't allowed at the party?" She needed one glass to calm her nerves and figured Riley did too. Stepping out in front of practically the entire town for the first time as a couple was a big deal, more so for Riley than Kate.

"Sounds good."

Taking more than her usual sip, Kate almost choked on the wine as Riley placed her hand on Kate's knee and skimmed up her dress.

"Keep doing that, and we won't make it to the party. Save the fireworks for later."

"We don't *have* to go," Riley said with a husky voice.

"Lilly will hunt us down if we don't show up."

"True." Riley removed her hand.

"It's going to be fun. Cheers." Kate grinned as they clinked their glasses together. Her thoughts drifted to Chicago. She no longer wanted to live there, but was she ready to commit to a life in the wilderness? The harshest part of winter was yet to come. If she made it through, and her relationship with Riley didn't falter, then surely it was meant to be.

# Chapter Forty-Five

THEIR BREATH HUNG IN the air as a crisp wind hurled them along. But the closer they got to the Christmas party, the faster Riley's heart beat like a drum. Hell, everyone had known she was gay for years, and thanks to Lena, they'd learned about Kate. And of course, with the numerous coffee and meal dates at the diner, they were the hottest gossip item around. But this was different. Riley had never taken anyone to a formal town event. And she wasn't sure how well they'd be received since a third of the town's folk were Latter-day Saints. Not everyone was as progressive as Dr. Allred and his family.

"Riley, where are you? You're all tense and out in the ether somewhere."

"Ah, sorry. What were you saying?"

Kate rested her head on Riley's shoulder. "You smell good. Just promise to hold my hand a lot. Somehow, that glass of liquid encouragement has had the opposite effect. I'm super nervous."

"It would be my pleasure to hold your hand." Riley placed a kiss on Kate's hand, swallowed, and silently chanted, *I can do this.*

They entered the high school gymnasium with Kate's arm tucked inside Riley's. Multi-colored lights twinkled on the ten-foot Douglas fir in the center, and Christmas music softly played as people danced in an area between the tree and the stage. People sat at tables set along the side of the hall with colorful red and green tablecloths. Christmas decorations and more lights hung from the ceiling and walls throughout. A sign indicated that food and additional tables were in the adjoining room.

When a couple gave them an odd look, Riley waved. *Relax.* Most people are likely curious and mean no harm. Aunt Lilly sat off to the right with Tom, Nancy, and Howard Jacobs. Dr. Allred, his wife, and most of his adult children were present with their spouses and a gaggle of grandchildren. Oh, God, they'd have to pass them to get to her aunt's table. She hadn't seen his sons and daughters for years. All but two daughters had moved out of town.

"I guess we're going to make a big splash."

"Yep." *Now or never.* Riley forced her legs to move. "Merry Christmas." She hoped the soft glow of the Christmas lights hid her blush.

Dr. Allred jumped out of his seat and hugged them, glowing like they were one of his children. As he introduced Kate to his family, Mrs. Allred smiled and reached out with a shaky hand from her wheelchair. Riley saw her occasionally, but sadly Parkinson's disease had severely affected her mobility.

Riley leaned over. "Good to see you."

"You too, dear." She gently brushed her fingertips along Riley's cheek. "You make a lovely couple."

"Thank you." That lifted Riley's spirit. As they continued on to her aunt's table, she relaxed into the warmth of Kate's arm in hers. After hugs and kisses from Aunt Lilly and Nancy, Tom shook Riley's hand and kissed Kate's offered hand. They exchanged hugs and greetings with Howard.

"This is my cousin, Diane, from Oregon. She's Chris's mom," Howard said.

"It's a pleasure to meet you. I understand you enjoyed my Grandmother Josie's art show last weekend and had a lovely visit with Chris." Diane smiled.

"The letter was an astonishing eye-opener. My grandaunt lived a remarkable life." Howard lifted his glass of punch and slightly bowed his head.

After more conversation and fantastic food, Kate rose and held her hand out to Riley. "Let's dance." When Riley hesitated, Kate said, "You danced with me in Ketchum."

Riley rose with a forced laugh, and Kate pulled her along to the dance floor. They arrived as a slow number began. Kate draped her arms around Riley's neck and pulled her in cheek-to-cheek.

"You're tense. Why?" Kate whispered in her ear. "We won't be the only gay couple here. Megan and Hayley are arriving later with their girlfriends.

"Yes, a lot of people here don't dance this close." *Especially how you're pressed against my body.* Riley ignored the prying eyes of other curious couples. She breathed in Kate's perfume, a floral scent that reminded her of the time they cycled amongst the wildflowers. Their relationship had blossomed so fast that she worried it was all a dream.

"May I cut in?" Nathaniel asked.

"Rockin' Around the Christmas Tree" began to play.

"Be my guest." Riley stepped back.

Nathaniel and Kate twirled around, laughing as "Have a Holly Jolly Christmas" by Burl Ives played next. More than once, Nathaniel stepped on Kate's toe. While they giggled and danced, Riley's anxiety built and constricted her body. What if she'd ruined Kate's life? Merrick didn't have big museums, fancy art galleries, or fine-dining establishments like Chicago. About the only change around was the diner menu. What about Kate's friends? Would Kate visit Sherry and decide to stay? What about her brothers? Would they talk her into leaving?

Her short, rapid breaths soon made her lightheaded. Her aunt's voice played in her head, *Now, honey, stop your fretting. Thinking about woulda, coulda, shoulda won't do you any good. You'll make yourself sick chewing on possible outcomes and jumping to conclusions.*

"Looks like Kate's part of the family."

Tom's words sent the hamster wheel in Riley's head to a screeching halt. When she turned to meet his solemn face, he'd straightened up a little but was still leaning over her. He was so freaking tall. She knew how to read him, but most people mistook his serious expression and nature. His mouth barely curved up when he smiled, and he was a man of few words, but that was just Tom.

"Yep, looks that way."

They turned back to watch Nathaniel and Kate as another fast tune kicked off. Tom draped his arm around Riley's shoulder, which he didn't often do. They stood silent for several seconds before he faced her. She took a deep breath.

"Family is everything. I think Kate was meant for you. Enjoy and cherish each other and drop your worries. We've got your back."

Riley teared up, and he engulfed her in a hug. She buried her head in his chest. "I love you guys."

He kissed the top of her head and rubbed her back, and it felt so damn reassuring.

If anyone had told Riley back in the spring that she'd meet the love of her life, she would have immediately dismissed the idea as crazy. And there was that word again—love. *Oh, God, I do love her.* Riley was excited and petrified at the same time. Was it too soon? And could she even tell Kate?

# Chapter Forty-Six

*Christmas Eve*

HAVING KATE SPEND CHRISTMAS Eve with her at Lilly's was a gift. With Kate's head resting on her shoulder, this was the happiest holiday Riley had ever had. She glanced at the clock. Down to a minute before Zooming with Sherry and Max. She almost didn't want to share Kate, but her friends meant so much to her and were fast becoming some of Riley's favorite people too.

She kissed Kate's forehead as they sat upright in the bed, propped up against the headboard. "Are you awake? It's time."

"Just relaxing in your arms." Kate looked into her eyes. "I could never get tired of snuggling with you."

Riley rested the laptop on her legs, slightly turned so Kate could see. She connected the call, and Max picked up from their living room, but Sherry was nowhere in sight.

"Merry Christmas, Max," Kate said.

"Happy holidays." Riley waved.

"Merry Christmas, guys. I gave Sherry an early gift. She should be here any minute." Max looked away then back at them. "She's hanging up her coat now."

"Kate said you're having a hard time deciding where to go for Christmas," Riley said.

"We're getting up early and driving to my parents. We'll get there before noon, spend about four hours there, and then drive back to have dinner with Sherry's folks. It'll be a long day, but it'll keep everyone happy."

Sherry sat down, holding a very fluffy, orange-haired dog that licked her face. The dog turned and pawed Max. "Meet Bella, our new baby girl," Sherry said. "Isn't she adorable? Sorry I'm late. I took her for a walk and forgot the time."

"She's gorgeous. Is she a Pomeranian?" Kate asked.

"A spoiled Pomeranian." Sherry laughed. "You're so precious, aren't you?"

All Riley could see was Bella's backside as Sherry nuzzled her face with the pup.

"Ah, that's cute," Kate said.

Sherry turned the dog back around. "Max brought her home yesterday." She grinned and glanced at Max before turning back to Kate and Riley. "I texted Mom that we had a baby girl surprise."

Kate raised her eyebrow. "I hope you clarified that. You know how your mom gets carried away."

"Nope. I'm torturing her." Sherry's eyes widened. "You were right. Mom did print out web documents on IVF."

Riley burst out laughing, and Kate smacked her on the leg and gave her a look. But Riley saw Kate wasn't doing a very good job of holding back a smirk either. "Sorry, Sherry. With all the stories about your mom, I have to meet the matriarch of your family someday."

"Oh, you must visit. We'd love having you."

"Kate's been after me. Maybe this spring." Riley hugged her.

"That'd be great. We can go to a Cubs baseball game. And if you visit before the end of March, we could catch a Blackhawks hockey match," Max said.

Sherry kissed Max's cheek. "I think we've been to half of them. What are you two doing tomorrow?"

"We're at Riley's aunt's," Kate said. "Let me tell you, Lilly is an awesome cook. She's been stuffing us for days."

"Ah, much more laidback and relaxing. I'm envious. But I *am* looking forward to seeing my mother-in-law's face tomorrow." Max smiled at her wife. "She's going to kill you for that text. Hell, she's probably already picked out a baby dress."

"Serves her right for constantly nagging us." Sherry giggled. "I hate to cut this short, but we have to go. I have a Zoom scheduled with my cousins soon, and Ms. Bella needs to be fed. Have a Merry Christmas."

Kate and Riley said, "Merry Christmas," and everyone waved.

"So, did you mean what you said?" Kate softly kissed Riley's lips.

"What?"

Kate tickled her ribs, and Riley squirmed and giggled.

"Say it?" Kate didn't let up.

# CABIN FEVER

"Yes, I will try my best to carve out a week so we can go to Chicago."
Kate beamed and gave her a passionate kiss.

"My Christmas wish is we both have a nice long night in bed. I want
to take pleasure from every inch of you." Riley tucked Kate's hair behind
her ears.

"Then what are you waiting for?"

Riley pinned her down and slowly remove Kate's clothing, kissing her
exposed skin as she went lower and lower. She loved being with Kate, the
taste of her, and the relationship that they were forming. For once, all the
scattered pieces of her life were coming together.

# Chapter Forty-Seven

*Christmas Morning*

KATE FORCED HER BLEARY eyes open and sniffed the air. *Cinnamon buns.* Waking up Christmas morning with Riley sound asleep curled up tight against her was wonderful and Kate would love to linger any other day, but not today. She glanced around the room and saw Hank sprawled out in his doggie bed, softly snoring. Slowly, Kate slid out of bed. By the time she had dressed, Riley was awake.

"I like you better without clothes." Her feet dangled off the side of the bed, and she grinned broadly.

"Merry Christmas to you too." Kate bent over and kissed her cheek. "I think Lilly would appreciate some help in the kitchen. Don't you smell the buns?"

"Yes. But I'd rather enjoy your buns?"

Kate gave her a gentle slap.

"Ouch." Riley pouted.

"I didn't hit you that hard, you big baby. See you downstairs." Kate practically floated down the hall and stairs in a cloud of bliss. "Merry Christmas, Lilly. Riley will be down soon. What can I help you with?"

"Merry Christmas, dear. Scramble the eggs, please." Lilly was busy stuffing the turkey.

Kate washed her hands and got busy with breakfast.

"Ah, turkey. Don't let Kate near the bird, or we won't have dinner tonight." Riley walked in, smirking, with Hank at her side.

"But Lilly does cook the best out of all three of us." Kate kissed Lilly's cheek.

"Suck up."

Kate flicked some water at Riley.

"Hey. Now, don't go messing up my kitchen, you two. Or you might not get your present."

Riley made toast, set the table, and poured juice and coffee. Lilly washed up and placed the cinnamon buns on the table, and Kate spooned out scrambled eggs. As everyone buzzed around, Hank made a pitiful howl.

"We're not going to forget you." Kate patted Hank's head and put food into his bowl.

Once they sat, Lilly held out her hands and Riley and Kate took them. They both bowed their heads in respect for her and her faith. "Dear Lord, we give thanks for this time to be together. I'm so grateful for my niece, Riley. And thank you for bringing Kate into our lives. We give thanks for this joyful holiday when we can celebrate our Savior and his love for us. With joy, we pray. Amen."

Kate smiled at Riley, remembering her earlier confession that she was agnostic. Riley confided that she attended Lilly's church occasionally only to make Lilly happy.

"It's almost present-opening time," Riley said.

Lilly patted her mouth with a napkin. "Just because you gobble your food doesn't mean the rest of us do. I ought to get you one of those anti-gulp bowls like Hank's with all those swirls."

"I'd like to see that." Kate snickered.

The other thing that Riley and Kate had talked about was the difference in their Christmas traditions. The Smith and Anderson families were frugal. Children received two or three presents while the adults typically received one. It took forever for Kate to decide what gift to give Riley. One thing they still hadn't talked about was Riley's mother. Kate figured the relationship was too painful to talk about but hoped Riley would open up one day.

They went to the living room with another cup of coffee to exchange gifts, and Kate could barely contain her excitement. Riley insisted Lilly open her box first.

"Oh, my, Lord. Feel how soft this is, Kate." Lilly's mouth hung open when she looked at Riley. "Is this merino wool?"

"Yes. Feel free to crochet me a sweater." Riley grinned.

"I hope my gift is that luxurious." Kate winked at Riley and handed her box to Lilly.

When Lilly popped the lid, she chuckled. "Four colors from Riley and four colors from you. Guess I'll be making a new round of scarves and sweaters. I love it, girls."

Riley appreciated the new boots Lilly gave her. Then she opened Kate's.

"I hope it's the right kind." Kate held her breath.

"It's perfect." Riley showed the fishing reel to Lilly.

"Sorry that you'll have to wait to use it."

"What are you talking about? With enough layers, winter fly-fishing is fantastic. I'll show you." Riley bumped her knee. "And you have to try ice fishing."

Kate put up her hand. "Oh, no. Snowmobiling is all I can handle in winter."

Lilly cleared her throat. "Riley, please help me with Kate's gift."

They left the room, leaving Kate confused. When they returned, each held the end of a colossal rectangular object. The present, wrapped in a jumble of different Christmas paper, was so large that they shuffled their feet in tiny steps. Lilly beamed as Kate tore the paper away.

"It's gorgeous." Kate's eyes popped, and her mouth gaped. "Is Mary Jacobs-Dawson the artist?"

"Yes." Lilly wrapped her arm around Kate.

Kate shook her head slowly. "I appreciate the sentiment, but I'm not sure I can accept this. I've seen the resale values on the web. This is like buying me a car."

"Well, yes, but I didn't pay full retail value. You see, I asked Howard where I could buy a small, framed print for your Christmas present." Lilly glanced at Riley with her eyebrow raised. "I had to do it at the last minute because someone dropped a crystal vase that was to be your present."

"Guilty as charged." Riley blushed.

"Howard insisted that I take one of the paintings from his office. Well, dear heavens, I couldn't do that. Then he said he had the perfect one at his house and that it would make his heart sing if I gave it as a gift from both of us. When I offered him money, he shook his head and said a donation to charity would do. So, you see, I couldn't refuse."

"Thank you. Howard is a great guy. I'll call and thank him later." Kate drew Lilly and Riley into her arms, and the three admired Mary's art. Her breath hitched. "The tree groves are different, but I recognize the hills and the cabin. That's my cabin—the Christensen cabin." She was bowled over with emotion and wiped tears from her eyes.

ADDISON M. CONLEY

"I'll help you mount it on the wall." Riley gently rubbed her back.

"What'd you get Kate, dear?" Lilly sat back down and sipped her coffee.

Riley handed Kate a small thin box. She unwrapped the gift and looked inside. She glided her fingertips over the leather-bound journal. "Thank you. It's exquisite."

"Oh, and this. It's still one present since they're a set." Riley retrieved a small wooden rectangular box from under the tree and handed it to Kate. "It's not an expensive one, but it's pretty."

Kate flipped the lid open, removed a gorgeous fountain pen, and rolled it between her fingers. "It's perfect. I'll think of Grandmother and you every time I write with it." She kissed Riley's cheek and put the pen back in its box. "This is the best Christmas I've ever had." Tears rolled down her face.

"May every year keep getting better, dear." Lilly lifted her cup.

Kate jumped up and hugged Lilly, then Riley. "Thank you for making everything perfect." She lingered in Riley's arms, desperate to say *I love you*, but she couldn't quite do it just yet.

# Chapter Forty-Eight

*January*

RILEY PUSHED THE DRAWING back across the table to Megan and slurped up the last of her root beer. "Looks fantastic. But why are we delaying? Everyone had three days off with the New Year's holiday. Let's get rolling."

"The basement renovation is the only project right now, and it's easy-peasy. The house is the client's summer retreat, and they won't be back until May." Megan shrugged and smirked.

"Make some room, ladies," Nancy called out as she stood at their booth with her arms full.

Riley and Megan quickly made space.

"More refills?" Nancy asked.

"Yes, please," they answered in unison.

Riley took a bite of her Reuben sandwich and moaned. She tapped the drawing that had been pushed to the side and raised her eyebrows at Megan. "Something's going on. What is it?"

Megan's grin widened. "My sister has campground reservations right outside Zion National Park next week. I want to meet her. Hayley wants to go too. Nothing's going on around here the first two weeks of January. Let's close, and then you and Kate can join us?"

"Which sister?" Riley asked just as Megan scooped a large spoonful of shepherd's pie into her mouth.

Megan had two brothers and three sisters, but only Megan and her brothers had stayed in Idaho. They were all good folk, but Megan's sisters were a mixed bag.

"The cool one in Santa Fe. Come on. Except for the holidays, we've been working our butts off since June."

"I don't know." Riley frowned as she swirled a fry in ketchup. "We should find another project. And don't you dare!" She pointed her finger at Megan, who was about to squirt soda out of her straw at Riley.

"You're no fun. When was the last time you were at Zion?" Megan rested her chin in the palm of her hand.

"Okay. If Lilly and Tom don't mind me taking off, then I'm in. But I'm not sure about Kate. We haven't slept in a tent yet." The fry that Riley had slathered in ketchup dripped onto the table as she held it in mid-air. "Ah, I mean—"

"Yeah, I know what you mean." Megan laughed. "I thought you've been acting all blissful since that October kiss. How is she in—"

"Kate." Riley jumped up but caught her knee on the table. She rubbed it hard. "Great to see you. I didn't think you were coming into town today. Sit down."

"Hi, Kate." Megan waved over her shoulder and wiggled her eyebrows.

Riley gave her a *don't you dare* stare.

"Hi. I came into town for Howard." Kate stole a French fry off Riley's plate. "I see you're planning your next project."

"Yeah, but we're taking time off to go camping. Wanna come?" Megan asked.

Kate blinked at Megan and turned to Riley. "It's January and bloody cold."

"No problem. You and Riley can zip your sleeping bags together and—" Megan squeezed her eyes tight and grimaced. She reached under the table. "Damn, Riley. Did you have to kick my shin so hard?"

"If that's the only way to stay warm," Kate said and smiled.

"See. She wants to come." Megan's hand flew up. "Don't kick me again. Pun not intended. Well, maybe a smidgen. Anyway, it's fifty degrees in Zion. Perfect weather." Megan smiled.

"How cold is it at night? And what about snow? I'd love to get away from the snow drifts around here." Kate looked between them.

"A little snow, glistening in the canyon and on top of the towering cliffs. It's gorgeous and makes the park very photography friendly. Best of all, it's not crowded." Megan sounded excited.

"That didn't answer my question about the temperature."

Riley cleared her throat. "Around twenty-five degrees at night."

"But we have extra cold-weather gear." Megan smiled. "Come on. You'll love it."

Kate didn't look convinced. "Zion National Park in Utah, right?"

"The one and only." Riley cupped her hand alongside her mouth and yelled, "Hey, Nancy. Kate needs some French fries. She's eating all of mine." With her other hand, she squeezed Kate's thigh under the table and was rewarded with an appreciative smile.

"I'll have the club sandwich on wheat with fries. Water is fine. Thanks, Nancy." Kate smiled.

"Coming up." Nancy placed a glass of water on the table and left.

Kate grinned. "Zion would be perfect. I just got an email from another distant cousin. My great grandfather was her second great grandfather. She lives near Kanab in southern Utah and invited me to visit."

"Kanab? That's near the border with Arizona." Riley's throat went dry.

"Yes. Didn't I just say that, goofy?"

"What does she do?" Riley found it hard to speak. Her throat felt like sandpaper.

"She works with pre-school children."

"Did she send you a picture?" Riley muscles tensed.

"Geez. Let it rest." Megan threw a crumpled up napkin at Riley. "Don't be suspicious of everyone that lives in southern Utah or northern Arizona. Kate's Zoomed and emailed with other distant cousins. They seem normal."

Kate laughed at Megan. "What are you talking about?"

"Nothing. She's talking about nothing," Riley said as she glared at Megan.

Kate turned to Riley. "So, if I go camping with you, will you please drive me to meet my cousin?"

That took Riley's breath away and not in a good way.

"It's a little out of the way, but I promise to make it up to you. Please." Kate cupped Riley's face.

Riley still didn't answer until Megan lightly kicked her under the table. "Sure."

Kate leaned in and kissed her cheek softly.

"I'm off to the bathroom. It's getting too mushy for me." Megan laughed and left the booth.

"Does public affection still bother you?" Kate asked.

"Not at all. I've just got this project on my mind. That's why I'm in a funky mood." Riley glanced down at the drawings, hoping Kate would stop the questioning.

"Can I kiss you again?"

"A small kiss. I don't want to cause anyone a heart attack."

Kissing Kate felt so comforting. She deserved to know about her past, but Riley just couldn't bring herself to share it. Every time the subject rose to the surface, all the oxygen whooshed out of her body, and her heart lodged in her throat. Shoving the topic off to a later date may not be the best plan, but that's all Riley could handle at the moment.

# Chapter Forty-Nine

RILEY'S RELATIONSHIP WITH KATE kept getting better and better, like a fairytale dream come true. Kate didn't grumble about the long drive to Zion National Park or the camping. For four freezing nights, they nuzzled up to one another with their sleeping bags zipped together and happily fell asleep in one another's arms. During the day, they enjoyed leisurely hikes through the canyon.

Today was different. Riley's muscles ached from tension as she drove to Kanab. Everyone Kate had contacted so far had resulted in more information and a positive outcome. This cousin lived too close to Arizona, and an uneasy feeling rumbled through Riley's body. Still, she'd promised to take her.

Kate yawned and stretched in the passenger seat. Admiring Kate's beauty, Riley pushed aside her worries. "Coffee not strong enough today?"

"Yeah, we might have to make a pit stop for a second cup." Kate tipped her travel mug and took a healthy swig.

"Sure." Riley grinned. Sleepy Kate looked gorgeous. The way she curled her lips over the coffee travel mug made Riley want to turn around and take her back to the tent and stay in the sleeping bag all day.

The truck thudded. "Sorry about that pothole." Riley gripped the wheel and focused on the road. "Did you spill your coffee?"

"Nope." Kate reached out and twirled a finger through Riley's hair. "Pay attention."

"Keep doing that, and I'll pull over and have my way with you." She loved Kate's throaty laugh. "Are you going to give me more directions? Does your cousin live in the village of Kanab or on a nearby farm?"

"I'm sorry. I thought she was in Kanab, but I got it wrong. Her place is forty minutes into Arizona on the eastern side of Kaibab National Forest, Happy Canyonland Ranch. Funny name, huh?"

Riley slammed on the breaks.

"What the hell?" Kate braced herself on the dashboard.

"You're not going to visit this woman." Riley turned the truck around.

"What's wrong with you? Now I *do* have coffee spilled all over me."

Riley clenched her jaw. How stupid could she be to come this close? And what did Kate even know about someone she'd met through a genealogy website?

Kate grabbed Riley's shirt sleeve. "Slow down, or we're going to have a real emergency. Answer me. What the hell's going on?"

Riley turned off Route 89 and headed back toward the campground. She stared forward, silent. *No, no, no.* She couldn't do it. She couldn't go back anywhere near that place.

"Riley, you're speeding, and you're scaring me."

"You're not going there. End of story." Riley barely slowed down and waved her pass as they approached the campground entrance.

"You're acting like a crazy person. Why? Talk to me." Kate placed her hand on Riley's arm. "Slow down!"

Riley slid the truck to a halt on the icy parking space in front of their campsite.

"Whoa. What's up?" Megan asked as she approached.

"No way in hell." Riley slammed the truck door and tossed Megan the keys, then marched past her toward the trail leading from their site to the ridge.

Dawn was breaking and the campfire was lit, a beautiful scene except Kate's nerves were shredded by Riley's wild reaction. She was angry and bewildered as she watched Riley retreat. She sat in the passenger seat trying to tamp her emotions, then finally hopped out and faced Megan. "She went fucking berserk on me for no damn reason." Kate pointed toward Riley as she walked further out of sight.

"Take some calming breaths."

Kate put her hands behind her head, closed her eyes, and breathed deeply. When she relaxed, she told Megan the story.

Megan frowned. "Nothing in Kanab would set her off. Tell me about your cousin."

"She lives in Arizona. That's where I told Riley we were going when she freaked out." Kate leaned against the truck.

"Ah, that explains it." Megan hopped up on the hood. "Near Kaibab National Forest?"

"Yeah." Kate shifted her weight from one foot to the other.

Megan waved for Hayley's attention. "Go check on Riley, please." She looked back at Kate. "It's not my place to tell you."

"Megan, I need to know. Please. What set her off?"

Megan twisted her mouth and jumped off the truck. "Let's sit down."

"I need another cup of coffee." Kate filled her travel mug with a shaky hand, then plopped down at the picnic table. The gravity of the situation hit her smack in the chest. Calm, cool, collected Riley wouldn't flip like a switch without a good reason. "Megan, I remember her mother moved to Arizona. Does it have something to do with that?"

"This cousin of yours wouldn't happen to live at Happy Canyonland Ranch, would she?"

Kate nodded.

"Shit," Megan muttered.

"I've hardly ever heard you cuss."

"Her mother lives on that ranch. It's home to fundamentalists who broke away from the Church of Jesus Christ of Latter-day Saints. They're *very* different than the Mormons in Merrick."

Kate picked at a piece of wood on the bench. Things were starting to fall into place. "Maybe my cousin isn't part of that."

"*Everyone* at Happy Canyonland Ranch is a fundamentalist."

"Fundamentalist in what context? Like Lena?"

"Lena is like Belle in *Beauty and the Beast* compared to the people at this ranch. They believe the nineteenth-century teachings and that everyone who doesn't obey their interpretation of Jesus Christ should be punished. Women wear dresses to their ankles and marry as young as sixteen. They're subservient to their husbands and help raise the children as a collective with their husband's other wives."

"Polygamous families? But isn't that illegal?"

"Yes, but it still happens. The LDS Church disavowed multiple marriages by 1900, but the fundamentalists think the church made a mistake and view themselves as the divine chosen ones. At least, those at Happy Canyonland Ranch aren't as extreme as the Warren Jeffs' group."

"Who's Warren Jeffs?"

Megan raised her eyebrow. "A leader of an extreme fundamentalist group located in Texas. Jeffs is serving a life sentence for two felony counts of child sexual assault. They convicted him as the organizer of sexual, religious rituals with young girls. One of the accusers said her abuse began when she was eight years old."

Kate covered her mouth with her hand and closed her eyes. Any person that could do that to a child was a monster.

"Anyway, Riley doesn't talk about her time away from Merrick at all."

Kate's eyes opened wide. "Riley lived there?"

Megan nodded. "For two years. She came back right before her sixteenth birthday and lived with Lilly and George."

Appalling was the first word that came to Kate's mind, followed by barbaric and a string of other words that made her blood boil. Emotions swirled in Kate's brain as she pieced Megan's words together. "Are you saying that her mother took her to this cult and tried to marry her off?"

Megan sighed. "That's my guess, but I don't know for sure. No one does, really. When she returned to school, she was quiet and withdrawn. And although the kids teased Riley about her clothes, Lilly never made her wear dresses." Megan smiled brightly. "Riley rocked up in jeans and joined the basketball team the next year. That's where we became close friends. It's not too hard to tell who plays on the same team."

"And she's never told you what happened to her at the ranch?"

Megan shook her head. "Not one word. She acts like it never happened, but she does go crazy if it's brought up. I suggest you ignore your cousin's emails."

"I'll block her." Kate picked up her phone. "Done." She sucked in a breath and looked at Megan. "That's such an awful story. Thank you for telling me."

Megan nodded. "Riley's a good person, Kate. She's rock solid, but this tiny glitch messes with her. I'm sure she'll talk to you in time."

Kate wasn't convinced. "She hasn't with you, and you're her best friend."

"Yeah, but I'm not the one she's falling in love with." Megan tilted her head. "Is the feeling mutual?"

"Yes."

"What about Chicago and your former life and friends?" Megan folded her hands.

"I don't want to hurt Riley, and I didn't want to rush things." Kate toggled the opener on her travel mug back and forth. She looked off in the distance for a brief moment and bit her lip. "I think Merrick is the right place for me, but I need more time. Until I can answer that, it wouldn't be fair for me to make a promise." *Bullshit. You feel love. Why can't you tell Riley how you feel?* Kate saw the concern in Megan's eyes. "Please don't say anything. I'll talk with Riley when I'm ready. Trust me. I'm not going to hurt her."

"Okay. But I think she's already fallen for you and is just too chicken to say it."

Hayley ran up to them. "She's sitting on top of the ridge."

"She won't do anything stupid, will she?" Kate jumped up.

"No, Riley's not suicidal." Hayley guided Kate back to her seat. "When she gets in this mood, she doesn't talk for hours. Then she'll act like everything is normal. It was Arizona, wasn't it?"

Megan nodded. "I've already given Kate the gist."

"Okay. Let's go hiking. I'll grab my bag." Hayley thumbed over her shoulder.

"We just can't leave her here. It just doesn't feel right." Kate tried to bite down the fear, but it rose anyway.

"After a while, she'll be fine," Hayley said.

Megan pointed over at the creek. "There's a nice spot a couple hundred yards up. It might do you some good to stretch your legs. Or we could hike when Riley returns, if you'd prefer that?"

"You two go. I want to wait here for her." Once they'd left, Kate got up from the bench and paced back and forth. The group Megan described sounded extreme compared to the conservative Mormons in Merrick. Her heart shattered for what Riley must have gone through. She wanted to throw her arms around Riley and comfort her but out of respect, she waited.

# Chapter Fifty

RILEY DREW HER KNEES to her chest and wiped the tears from her face. She didn't know how long she'd been sitting here. Thankfully, Hayley hadn't put up a fuss about leaving her alone. After being friends for so long, she and Megan knew Riley's moods and didn't question her. But now there was Kate. How much should Riley tell her? Some things were best left in the past, but she couldn't stop the memories from invading her present.

"Goddammit." She stood and kicked a rock off the ledge, then took off. Her legs burned as she pushed her body down the hill. Closer to the camp, her heart beat faster, and she stopped to control her breathing before continuing.

"I'm sorry if I scared you." Riley sat down beside Kate at the picnic table, not quite ready to face her and see the judgment in her eyes.

"I was worried about you." Kate rested her hand on Riley's thigh. "Megan told me a little. I didn't know that my distant relative was a fundamentalist. I'm so sorry."

Every muscle in Riley's body grew rigid. She hated thinking about the ranch. She closed her eyes and gritted her teeth. When Kate's arms wrapped around her middle, it took all her strength not to crumple.

She kissed Riley's cheek and whispered, "I'm so sorry."

"Thank you." Riley's voice cracked. "For what it's worth, I looked in the rearview mirror to make sure no one was behind us. But it's no excuse to go ape shit and leave you without any explanation."

"I'd probably go crazy too if it were me." Kate rested her head on Riley's shoulder.

They sat in companionable silence for quite some time. Riley just couldn't bring herself to talk. It hurt too much.

"Thank you for inviting me on this trip," Kate said after a while. "The cream, pink, and red rock layers along the canyon walls are phenomenal. I've had a great time hiking here, even with the snow."

Riley breathed a sigh of relief that Kate had switched to a neutral topic.

"Yeah, each place in the West has a unique beauty and story, but Zion is one of my favorites."

"Riley, I want to experience fun things like this trip with you. We haven't been together very long, but I'm kind of crazy for you." Kate twirled her fingers in Riley's hair. "I know it's hard and painful to talk about your past, but please know that if you ever want to open up, I'll be a careful listener."

"Maybe someday. I just can't talk about it now. Where's Megan and Hayley?" Riley rose and looked around. "Let's not waste a hiking day." She grabbed her daypack and took off.

Physical exertion is what she needed, not talking about the fucking ranch. But she feared the dreams and flashbacks would only intensify now that Kate knew some of the facts. She stabbed her trekking pole into the ground and hastened her pace. Not today. No fucking way was she going to talk about it today.

\*\*\*

For the remainder of their camping and hiking, it was like there was an ice shield between them. No matter what Kate did, Riley barely returned affection. She hugged her at night, but the laughter and lovemaking were gone. During the day, Riley pushed them to hike longer as if physical exertion distracted her from the emotional pain. They left for home, and Riley insisted on driving straight through, only stopping for lunch and bathroom breaks. With the traffic through Salt Lake City, it took them almost nine hours to get home, and Riley was silent most of the way.

Kate worried about Riley's behavior. Things would only get worse if she bottled things up and isolated. She was willing to give Riley some time, but it hurt.

When they arrived at the cabin, Kate jumped out and jerked her bag from the truck bed. She wanted to get dinner out of the way and slip into bed. Riley helped her light the fires in the woodstoves without a word. Over the past three days, Kate's empathy had gradually slipped away, and her patience had worn thin with Riley's silent treatment.

"Riley, I'm willing to give you time, but if our relationship is going to survive, you need to talk with me."

"Another time. I'm exhausted."

Kate bit her tongue. They did need to rest after the long trip. "All right.

What do you want for dinner? How about salmon and rice?" She added a drizzle of olive oil to a pan.

"I should go and check on Lilly." Riley moved toward the door.

The words took Kate's breath away. She dropped the pan, and it rattled on the stovetop. "You're going to leave? Why?"

"I have to work tomorrow, and I don't want the project falling behind."

It hurt when Riley wouldn't face her. "Babe, don't go." Kate hurried to Riley and pulled her into a hug. "Have you ever seen a therapist?"

Riley's arms fell from their embrace. Kate cradled Riley's cheeks with her hands, trying to make eye contact.

"Yes. It's been a while," Riley whispered.

"I think it'd do you some good to try again. Don't give up. Sometimes it takes time to click with the right therapist."

Riley nodded. "I need to go."

Reluctantly, Kate let her leave. She wanted to soothe Riley and be by her side, but Riley had thrown up an invisible wall. Out of deep concern, she called Lilly. Their brief conversation didn't leave her any less concerned. When she asked about the ranch, Lilly grew quiet for several seconds. Then she said Riley had suffered trauma but didn't elaborate. Although Kate didn't know what Riley had gone through, it must have been horrible for her to keep a secret for so long. Kate could only hope that Riley would share her story with time.

\*\*\*

"Did you miss me, boy?" Riley patted Hank's back as he howled. "Hi, Aunt Lilly." She headed upstairs.

"Come here, please."

Riley sighed and trudged into the living room and sat next to Aunt Lilly on the sofa. "What's on your mind?"

"Kate called," she said softly. "She cares about you, honey, and she's a good woman. Don't let her slip through your fingers."

"I know you both mean well, but I need some rest and time to think." Riley swallowed.

"You should go back to therapy." Aunt Lilly laid her hand on Riley's back and gently rubbed.

"That's none of Kate's business."

"Kate didn't mention that in her phone call. *I'm* saying it. Over the past few years, your fits of isolation have increased any time someone mentions your mom or Arizona. Have you ever stopped to think how that may have contributed to your relationship issues? You haven't had the best girlfriends, but it takes two to tango. And I certainly don't think Kate is one of the bad ones. But from what she told me and how you're acting with me now says you've slammed the door to the world. Don't withdraw. This world may not be perfect, but we're your family. So, please consider going back to therapy."

"I'll think about it." Riley teared up when Aunt Lilly squeezed her hand.

"We're all getting old, honey. You need to trust someone else before it's too late and you're all alone."

"Stop talking like that." Riley flung her arms around her. She couldn't bear to think of losing her.

"Well, it's true, though I might live to a hundred just to push some sense into your stubborn head. But we never know when our number is up. You have to make the best by living in the moment."

Riley lingered in the embrace for several minutes of silence, feeling like a little girl again, safe in her aunt's arms.

"Do I get a lollipop, like when I'd fall and skin my knee?"

Aunt Lilly pulled back. "I'll give you a pop on the back of your head, how about that?"

Riley chuckled. "I love you, Aunt Lilly."

"I love you too. Now, get some rest. But you get out of this mood and make up with Kate." She tapped Riley on the nose like a bad dog. "The sooner, the better."

"Yes, ma'am." In a daze, Riley shuffled away. So much had happened in the past three days. Her stomach hurt, and her mind was spinning out of control with jumbled thoughts. Hank, who was usually energetic, seemed to notice her shift in demeanor. He matched her slow pace to the bedroom, where she popped two Tylenol PM tablets and flopped on the bed.

The memories kept assaulting her from every corner of her mind, and she tossed and turned. She finally got up and began playing her favorite video game. Several hours later, she crawled back in bed. The game had only provided a temporary pause. Hank nudged her as she cried into her pillow.

# Chapter Fifty-One

IN THE TWO WEEKS since returning from Zion, Riley had seen Kate only once. Yesterday, she'd dropped by to ask Kate to babysit Hank for a few days because she was so busy with her new project. In her heart, she knew Kate was well within her rights to say no, but she couldn't resist Hank and had agreed. The tension in the air between them was barely tolerable. Riley had ignored her aunt's advice, stuffed her emotions deep inside and walked away. This morning, she had decided to tell Kate tonight, but after a trip to Nancy's, she was sick to her stomach.

"Fuck it." The gravel flew as her truck wheels dug into the hill going up to the construction site. She swung into a parking spot. "Charley, pass out the lunch sacks," Riley yelled and headed toward the ladder.

"Wait a minute." Megan ran up and grabbed her arm just as she got to the first rung. "I think you should take the rest of the day off. You've been out of sorts since Zion."

"With the new snowstorm in the forecast, we need all hands on deck. You even asked Nathaniel to help out today. I'm going to get that upper level started." Riley shook out of Megan's grip and hurried up the ladder.

"Harness in," Megan said.

The project had morphed from a simple renovation to a new second level and addition, and that meant a ton of work. With the unpredictable winter weather, they needed to move fast. The floor joists needed additional nailing. If Riley could get that done, they might be able to finish laying the subflooring today. She worked while trying to keep thoughts of Kate and all the shit from Arizona out of her head. She ignored Charley and Nathaniel when they climbed up and started laying the subfloor.

"Fuck!" Riley growled.

Nathaniel ran over. "Oh, shit, you nailed your foot to the joist."

Charley strolled up and bent over with her hands on her knees. "Looks painful." She popped her bubble gum inches from Riley's face. "I'll take that." She removed the nail gun from Riley's hand.

"Everyone, take a break. Charley, send Hayley up." Megan glared at her from a few feet away. After the place cleared out, she leaned over Riley. "Way to go, idiot. How did you do that?"

"Don't cut my boots. They were my Christmas gift from Lilly." Riley could feel the blood oozing between her toes.

Megan used a hammer to slowly pry the nail from Riley's foot.

Riley gritted her teeth at the pain. "Stop, stop, stop."

"Candy ass. How else do you think I'm going to get it out?"

"Just give me a minute." Riley took a deep breath. "Okay, go."

"Need help?" Hayley asked. Penny was by her side with a first aid kit. Riley hadn't heard them arrive.

"Penny, hold her. Hayley, steady her boot. I need to get some leverage to pull the nail the rest of the way out." Megan looked at Riley. "I'll make it as quick as possible."

Riley stifled a scream as Megan tugged hard. Several moments later, Megan pulled the nail out.

"Thanks, guys. Go on and finish your work." Megan opened the first aid kit.

Riley removed her boot and sock and poured water on the wound. "I'll be fine. I don't think it hit the bone." She grabbed the gauze out of Megan's hand, slapped it over her bloody foot and squeezed tight.

"Looks like the nail went between the big toe and the next one. You're lucky you didn't do more damage. Why are you wearing simple boots and not your steel-toed ones? You know you're not supposed to work without them," Megan said, clearly angry.

"I forgot the steel-toed ones."

"Obviously." Megan sighed. "Look, all this crap with your mom and Arizona is eating you up. Whatever's still haunting you, I think your load will be a little lighter if you tell someone. And that someone needs to be Kate. She's hooked on you. Don't shut her out."

Riley put her head in her hands and swallowed the lump in her throat. "But Kate didn't come here to stay."

"Huh? Did she tell you that?"

"While I was waiting for our take-out, Howard's secretary and that yackety-yak chick from the bank came in. They sat down and didn't notice me nearby. The bank chick said Kate had to live here for a year then she'd inherit a half-million dollars."

"That's a nice chunk of change if it's true. But so what?"

"So what? Don't you see? She came here for the money. And there's more. Kate was inquiring about an appraisal on the entire property." Riley smashed her fist down on the wood. "She must be selling."

"What did Kate say?"

Riley stared at the blood that had already soaked through the gauze. "I haven't talked to her yet."

"You idiot. That's not fair. You should have at least called." Megan leaned closer until they were nose to nose. "I understand you've had more than your share of bad luck, and you're scared—"

"I'm not scared." *More like fucking terrified.* Her tough act was just that—an act. What had worked for her in the past failed her when Kate came along. Now, all of her energy was sucked up in a whirlwind of feelings she couldn't stop. Hiding the pain that bubbled up inside and threatened to spill out had become exhausting, and after Zion, she didn't know how much longer she could keep it together. "I'm not scared." As if repeating it might make it true.

"Yeah, right. You have everything under control most of the time, but you can say stupid stuff and act like a little kid." Megan gripped Riley's chin so she couldn't avoid eye contact. "I think Kate's the real deal, and there's plenty of affection between you two. And how many of your other girlfriends interacted with our sports group? How many could handle a mountain bike and a snowmobile like Kate? She's a charger and always gives it a try."

Riley gave a quick smile. "Yeah, she is pretty good."

"But more importantly, Kate enjoys being around *you*. Don't throw that away. You need to work this out."

Riley swallowed. Maybe now it was time to open up a little, at least about her feelings for Kate. "No one has ever affected me like she does. I'm mush around her." Riley wiped the eyes with the back of her hand. "I think I love her. But I'm sure as shit not moving to Chicago. I don't know where that leaves us."

"Don't jump to conclusions."

"But why did she ask for an appraisal?"

Megan sighed. "For someone so bright, you're acting stupid right now. Talk to her." She shook Riley's shoulder. "If you don't, and you throw this away, it's all on you. And whatever went on in Arizona is unfinished business you need to deal with."

Riley buckled under the truth. "Maybe."

Megan stood. "Get out of here. You're a danger to yourself and everyone else. And look at your damn foot." Megan kicked Riley's foot, and she winced. "I hope your tetanus shot is up to date. Go to the clinic first, then go see Kate."

They had only argued a handful of times and never like this. Riley stood and ignored her throbbing foot. She was lucky it was her left foot, and she could still drive. "I'm sorry. You're right."

"Yes, I am," Megan said softly and jabbed her finger in Riley's chest. "I know my real friend is in there somewhere. She knows what to do." Megan quickly hugged Riley and patted her on the back.

The pulsating pain grew worse as Riley drove to the clinic. She hobbled inside and took a seat while Dr. Hubert talked to the receptionist.

"Ah, Riley. I hear you had a little accident." Dr. Hubert crossed her arms.

"Yeah. Are you ready for me?" Riley glanced at a man thumbing through a magazine.

"Dr. Allred will be taking care of you today. Sue will take you back."

"Guess you've been busy since he usually leaves by one." Riley rose.

"No, we haven't been busy. He was leaving early today to visit his son, but he canceled when Megan called. He insisted on seeing you."

Dr. Hubert's smirk told Riley this would be no ordinary visit. "Okay." Riley took baby steps and followed the nurse down the corridor and into the examination room. What did Megan say to get him to stay?

Dr. Allred came in, leaned against the supply table with his arms folded, and watched

the nurse take Riley's vitals. "Thank you, Sue. I'll take it from here. Good afternoon, Riley."

"Good to see you, Doc."

He examined Riley's foot and washed it with water and antiseptic. She gritted her teeth through the tetanus and antibiotic shots. After gently bandaging the wound, he placed an open-top, protective boot onto her foot.

Dr. Allred was usually a softie, but he didn't hold back when he had something on his mind. Today, the silent treatment killed Riley about as much as her foot. And why was his face so expressionless? And why had he insisted on tending to her?

"That should do it. Clean it every morning and at night." He handed her a box of gauze and three bottles. "The liquid is antiseptic. The pills are ten days of antibiotics and a week's worth of pain pills. But only take those if regular pills don't ease the pain. And take them with food."

"Can I have one now? My foot is throbbing."

"Just a minute."

He left and returned with milk and a granola bar. She swallowed the pill with a gulp of milk and munched a bit of the granola bar. "Is that it?"

He held her gaze. It was a look that Riley recognized. She was about to get a lecture.

"Do you know what hurts a lot more than that nail going through your foot?"

"No." Riley swallowed.

"Seeing Kate cry."

"She talked to you?" Riley never thought Kate would confide in Dr. Allred, yet he seemed to have a superpower that made people comfortable in conversations.

"I knew something was bothering her, and I heard you all took a trip to Zion National Park two weeks ago."

"What did she say?" Riley looked down.

"She said you've been withdrawn and using work as an excuse not to visit. She may not recognize your emotional avoidance as a coping mechanism, but I do. And as we've discussed before, it's an unhealthy choice." He gently placed his finger under Riley's chin and lifted her head.

Tears sprung up in her eyes as she met his gaze.

"What did I tell you years ago, and that I have to keep reminding you?"

He waited for her to respond. When she began to cry, he wrapped his arms around her. "I said that you're a beautiful child of God, and there is nothing wrong with your soul. But Riley, dear, you're becoming a prisoner of your own making by hiding from the ones you love."

"I know. It's just so hard." She leaned into his body, and he held her tighter. Dr. Allred had always been there for her and Aunt Lilly. He cared for her dad in his dying days and Uncle George. And he was the one who'd freed her from Happy Canyonland Ranch.

"You just have to start somewhere. Just a little bit, and the words will begin to flow." He stood back and looked up at her. "You can't drive after taking the pain medication. So, you'll ride with me."

"Where to?" But Riley knew the answer.

"Come on. Doctor's orders."

She shuffled along, barely able to see through her tears. Dr. Allred opened the car door for her, and she slowly slid in. Confronting her demons that haunted her was one thing. Explaining to Kate why she was a total, fucked-up mess was another. Given the state she was in, she wouldn't blame Kate if she wanted to leave.

# Chapter Fifty-Two

THE SAME OLD, SICK feeling rolled through Riley when they pulled up to Kate's. She glanced at Dr. Allred, her throat too dry to speak.

"You can do it." He patted her shoulder.

She hobbled out of his car and up to the cabin door. She wanted to bolt away, but Dr. Allred waved and drove off, leaving her stranded. On the other side of the door, Hank whimpered as if in pain. Why did she ask Kate to babysit him for a few days? She rested her forehead against the door. "Because part of me set myself up for this moment."

The door popped open. Hank rushed out and nuzzled her with his nose while Kate stood back, looking beautiful as ever but also looking pissed.

"How has my best boy been?" Riley asked. "Sorry, boy. I don't have any treats."

"It's nice to see you. I didn't expect you until tomorrow." Kate walked over to the kitchen. "The heat's escaping. Please come in and shut the door."

Riley noticed the coolness in her voice. After softly shutting the door, she rubbed Hank's ears and scratched below his chin. *What do you think, boy? Will she forgive me?* He whimpered again and tilted his head to the side. "Guess you're telepathic." Riley lumbered over to the island where Kate was chopping vegetables.

"I called you this afternoon, but Megan answered your phone." Kate didn't look up from the chopping block.

Riley patted her pockets. Sure enough, her phone wasn't there. "Sorry."

Kate pointed at Riley's foot. "I see you have a new fashion accessory."

"Busted." Riley nodded. "It'll be okay. Can we talk?"

Kate's hand stilled. "If you're going to say more than two words, then yes." She tossed the vegetables in a container and threw them in the refrigerator.

Riley hobbled over to sit, bumped into the coffee table, and collapsed onto the sofa. "Sorry. I'm tired."

"Three words isn't much of an improvement. I've heard them a lot recently but sorry doesn't mean anything unless the behavior changes."

*Ouch.* "You have a right to be mad at me. I withdrew, and I'm sorry."

Kate eased down but left some distance between them. She crossed her legs and leaned back. Her posture and solemn face made Riley swallow.

"Why didn't you tell me?" Riley's voice cracked.

"Tell you what?"

"About the big, fat check you get after living here for a year." *Shit, I'm deflecting again.*

Kate sucked in a breath and sighed. "Riley, money has no bearing on my feelings for you—"

"Your leaving will kill me. Please don't sell. Please stay in Merrick."

"What are you talking about?"

Riley had never begged anyone before, but the words popped out of her mouth like they had a life of their own. She picked up a tissue and dabbed her eyes, then stuffed it in her cargo pants pocket. "The bank chick, the one with the bad hair dye that blabs all the time...I overheard her conversation with Howard's secretary about an appraisal. Why are you selling? And why didn't you tell me about the inheritance?"

"I'm not selling." Kate partially turned and rested her arm along the back of the sofa. "But let's back up. I'd like a little more from you than 'I'm sorry' again." Kate sucked in her lower lip and sighed. "You've been a big influence on me wanting to make Merrick my permanent home, but our relationship over these past few weeks has gone downhill fast. You're acting like a stranger, and I can't be in a relationship alone." She ran her fingers along the back of Riley's hand. "Give me a reason to stay. Talk to me as the partner I thought I was to you." Kate scooted closer and caressed Riley's cheek. "Please tell me what's going on in that head of yours."

Emotions surged in Riley, bursting through her weak defenses. Sadness for her half-sister and anger at her mother all mixed together and made her sick to her stomach. She leaned in and sobbed in Kate's arms for what seemed like an eternity while Kate held her.

"Babe, I don't know what happened, but I want to help." Kate rocked her back and forth. "You're an awesome person. You're kind, smart, fun to be around, a true friend, and a gentle lover. You're so many wonderful things. And I want you as an equal partner, but you have to trust me. Whatever is bothering you has been a wedge between us. Don't let that happen. Talk to me."

Riley withdrew from Kate's arms and lowered her head between her knees. "My mom..." The deluge of memories flooded in, and the image of her mother popped into sharp focus. Tears ran down Riley's cheeks. "She was always stricter than Dad. When he died, she changed so much. Then she married this fundamentalist, and we moved to Arizona. I was only thirteen and hated wearing dresses even in Merrick, but we had to wear them there." Riley had to pause. It hurt so bad.

Kate rested her arm on Riley's shoulder.

"Dreams and ambition were for boys. Every day, girls were taught that our purpose in life was to get married, have kids, and follow our prophet. One freaking guy they called a prophet surrounded by six they called bishops. It was their interpretation of the Bible and the Book of Mormon. It was nothing like the church in Merrick. Slipping up on any little thing brought punishment. I felt like I was dying. And when I thought it couldn't get any worse, I turned fifteen." Riley wrapped herself again around Kate and cried. It took several minutes before she could go on. "They began to groom me to marry this man, James, the following year."

"Oh, sweetie, I'm so sorry." Kate kissed the side of her head.

"I think my mom knew I was different even before she caught me kissing another girl." Riley wiped her face with her sleeve. She laughed without humor. "I think I wanted to get caught, hoping that they'd kick me out. But they didn't." She sat up and looked at Kate. The understanding and compassion she saw there enabled her to continue.

"They tied me to the bed in the attic and only let me up to go to the bathroom and eat. My mom, stepdad, and some elders would have a group prayer for me three to six times a day. I really wanted to die, but I got angels instead. Dr. Allred showed up with a nurse. Somehow, he convinced my mom to let me go to the hospital where they helped me escape. While he talked to my mom, the nurse led me to Tom and Nancy. They took me to Aunt Lilly and Uncle Harold, who were waiting nearby. There was a small fight to try and get me back. I'm not sure how, but thankfully it failed."

Kate rubbing her thumb over her hand felt so good. Riley wet her lips.

"I'll never forget the thing Dr. Allred told me that day. He said, 'You're a beautiful child of God, and there is nothing wrong with your soul.'"

"He's such a good person. I'm so thankful they were all there for you."

The story drained Riley, but somehow, she had room for more tears. The gentle touch of Kate's fingers at the base of her neck were a comfort.

Kate kissed her cheek, tears and all. "I'm so, so sorry. Thank you for trusting me and sharing your story with me."

"I guess I should be grateful they didn't beat me. My physical punishment was less than some girls."

"Binding you to the bed is abuse. And I have no fucking words for them preparing you for marriage at sixteen." Kate thought of her grandmother's arranged marriage. How anyone could coerce and brainwash a young girl like that made Kate sick. "I'm glad they didn't break you and thankful for everyone getting you out." She glided her fingers through Riley's hair. "You're stronger than you know."

"Thank you. I don't feel that strong." Riley gave a half-smile. Years back, her therapist had said that the shame that consumed her would gradually go away, and that she'd feel so much better if she could spill the dark secrets inside her. Living with Aunt Lilly and Uncle George and surrounded by Dr. Allred, Tom, and Nancy was a safe space, but releasing her emotions to another person outside their circle had lifted a heavy weight off her shoulders. Why on earth had she taken so long to tell Kate? "It hurts to talk about it, but I was also afraid. Afraid that you'd think I was too damaged to waste your time on."

"I care deeply for you. Burying that kind of pain is a normal reaction to that kind of trauma."

"It usually doesn't affect me, but sometimes, it gets through, and I just cry." Riley wiped her tears with the sleeve of her shirt. "Sorry I've been an ass the past couple of weeks. Every time I thought about telling you, I got physically ill. Do you still want to be with me, or have I messed everything up?"

Kate kissed Riley's cheek. "Of course I still want you. And you're not damaged goods. It's okay to be strong and still cry or ask for help."

She leaned her head on Kate's shoulder and drank in the comfort and peace for several minutes. "There's more. I found out through Lena's big mouth that I have a younger half-sister. And Lilly doesn't know because she would have told me. I just...I can't deal with it. Please don't say anything."

"I won't." Kate smoothed her hair.

After a few minutes, she straightened up. "So what's the deal with your inheritance and the bank?"

"I receive the extra money and the property after I've lived here for a year. When I first arrived, I intended to sell at the end but then I met someone very special." Kate smiled and traced her fingers down Riley's jawline. "Hayley has been talking about starting an adventure company, and I was checking the property value for a loan."

Riley frowned as the pieces started to come together. "That's been a dream of hers for years, but how did you get involved?"

"I've been looking at her plan since you introduced me to the Snow Hellcats and somehow got me to love snowmobiling." Kate smirked. "Hayley and I are thinking of starting with snowmobile tours next winter, followed by a zip line and obstacle course the following year, and maybe ATVs in the future. And since the bank's assistant manager races snowmobiles, we had him come out. We poured on the charm, and he feels the property would more than cover the loan amount."

"But why a bank loan?"

"We're talking at least a quarter-million-dollar startup and the same the following year. Equipment, salaries, training, insurance, licenses, a professional company to plan and build the zip-lines, advertising, etc. Hayley doesn't have much money saved, so I'll be the main owner, but I'm low on cash right now. Then I don't want to drain all of my inheritance money. Plus, it typically takes a few years for businesses to become profitable. The financials should be settled by the summer, which would mean we could place an order for the snowmobiles to arrive by October."

"Where are you going to put them?" Riley was finding it hard to breathe. Kate's dream was a huge undertaking.

"I'll store them in the barn to save money, although that means my poor truck would be out in the open." Kate stuck out her bottom lip then broke into a smile.

"I could build an extension." Riley had employed Hayley for eight years. She was a good person and knew the outdoors. As long as Kate could manage and do the accounting, maybe they could make it. "And if you need any help with the books, just ask. I like Uncle George's ledger, but then I turn around and input the data into business software."

"Now, you're talking like a caring partner." Kate smiled and lightly punched Riley's shoulder. "As long as you don't sulk away and stop talking for days, I think I'll keep you."

"I'm counting on that." Riley interlocked her fingers with Kate's. "What about a place to stay? Tourists don't like to stay in campgrounds in the winter, and there are no hotels in town."

"Not yet."

Riley's eyes went wide.

"That's where Nancy comes in. She's been saving to build a B&B in the vacant lot next to the café. She likes our idea and thinks we could work together."

"Holy cow." God, how could Riley have been so wrong? She looked into Kate's eyes, and for the first time, her heart wanted to burst from love and not pain. Her throbbing foot dragged her back into reality.

"You look like you're about ready to crash. How much sleep did you get last night?" Kate asked.

"About four."

Kate rolled her eyes. "No wonder you had an accident. Let's get you into bed."

They made slow progress to Kate's bed. Riley kissed her and curled up with the pillow. "That pain pill Dr. Allred gave me is making it so I can barely keep my eyes open. Goodnight, buttercup."

"Babe, move over a little. I'll take a nap with you."

Hank jumped up on the bed.

"No." Kate pointed to the big, plush dog bed on the floor. "Out, Hank. I paid a fortune for your new bed."

Hank whined and looked away from Kate. He snuggled his head against Riley's chest and stretched his body out to take up the rest of the bed. Riley laughed.

"Fine. No treats for either of you tomorrow," Kate said.

"Come on, Hank, get up." Riley pushed him out of bed. Kate took Hank's place and cradled Riley in her arms. "Thank you."

"You're welcome, babe."

Riley closed her eyes. *I love you, Kate.* She didn't have the strength yet to speak the words out loud, but she would soon.

# Chapter Fifty-Three

THE FOLLOWING DAY, KATE fixed breakfast while Riley slept in late. She came into the kitchen, stretched and yawned.

"Good morning. You're all dressed. Maybe you should take the day off." Kate finished plating their meal.

"Morning." Riley pressed her body against Kate's back and wrapped an arm around her robe-clad body, kissed her head, then slipped a hand underneath and caressed her breast. "You're tempting, but I do have a full schedule. Here, let me help."

Kate missed her touch when she stepped away to grab the salt and pepper shakers and coffee. Although Riley seemed back to normal, Kate was hesitant to break the mood and remained quiet as they ate. But the thought had been gnawing away at her. She cleared her throat. "I was thinking that maybe I should give up my genealogy research."

Riley laid down her fork. "Why? It was only one crazy cousin. The one in Portland seems sane. You came out to her, and she didn't have a problem. Just promise me to be careful. Ask questions and exchange pictures. If they don't want to share, then they're probably hiding something."

"I promise." Kate squeezed her hand.

"Good. I don't want you to give up researching your family because of me. It hurt like hell to tell you about my mother, but it was also a massive relief." Riley kissed her hand. "How about you drive me to work, and then you can go to the library? You're making such progress."

An hour later, they kissed goodbye, and she watched Riley hobble into the hardware store. "Stubborn woman. She's worse than me." Kate stepped inside and found Dr. Allred perusing the newspaper. "Good morning." She tapped him on the shoulder.

"Kate. Lovely to see you."

She was shocked when he hugged her tightly since a handshake or a gentle one-arm hug was his usual greeting. She squeezed back, cherishing the gesture. "Thanks for dropping off Riley last night. Can we speak privately?"

He nodded and looped his arm in Kate's and guided her to the conference room.

"Riley told me about her ordeal in Arizona and your daring rescue. Thank you so much. I already admired you, but my appreciation has grown tenfold. It hurt to see her in agony, but I think that sharing her story has helped to release some of her pain. She means so much to me."

He patted her hand. "It's hard to hear, but you're right. More sorrow can come from burying one's pain and ugly secrets."

"How in the world were you all able to keep it a secret and out of the newspapers?" Kate bit her lip. "It's a federal crime to take a minor child from her parents over state lines without permission. In the eyes of the law, you kidnapped her. Didn't Riley's mom come after you?"

After a deep breath, he sighed. "We could have been neck-deep in legal problems, but I wanted to stop that from happening. I took photos of the marks on Riley's wrists and ankles. When Tom and Nancy took her home, I stayed behind and drove back to the compound to deliver them. I made it clear that I'd spend my wealth fighting them."

"And they caved?"

"Not as easily as I'd hoped." He cradled Kate's hand in his. "Riley's stepfather was a tall man and he tried to intimidate me. He threw the photos back in my face and said they had every right as parents to educate Riley against the dangers of homosexuality and to restrain her from running away. Twenty-five years ago, many judges would have backed the parents, so I told a few little white lies." He looked down and swallowed before looking back up. "They were arranging for Riley to marry a man named James. He was in his late twenties, and the marriage was supposed to happen after Riley's sixteenth birthday."

"She mentioned that." Kate gripped Dr. Allred's hand, bracing herself for what he might say. When he hesitated again, Kate's stomach dropped.

"They left Riley to spend the night with him, and he touched her. But I implied that he'd done more than that, that he raped her. That's when they backed off. They didn't want an investigation into them and their religious cult."

Anger churned inside Kate's gut. How could any parent do that?

He shook his head. "I struggled with the idea of reporting them, but with an investigation and a trial, there'd be media swarming around Riley.

And Lilly, George, and I believed it would have done more harm forcing her to testify against her mother and stepfather. She was too fragile."

"I think you did the right thing."

"Lilly and George's guardianship was swift and informal. They saw her bruises and knew that story, but Riley didn't want them to know what James had done. I'm only telling you because I think you're strong enough to hear it."

"Thank you for trusting me."

"I believe God helped us."

Dr. Allred's revelation had shocked her so much that she hadn't felt the tears sliding down her cheeks until he took out a tissue and gently wiped them away.

Merrick had what she needed—lots of people that loved her. They had become her family, and this was her home. Now, she just needed to find the courage to tell Riley how much she loved her.

# Chapter Fifty-Four

*February*

OVER A FOOT OF snow had fallen over the first two weeks of the month. Another four inches of fresh snow added to the total overnight. The flurries finally ended by breakfast, and Kate was looking forward to playing in the powder today. She carefully inspected her safety items and packed them in a bag. Besides loving her jobs with Howard and Lilly, she also loved playing in the snow with Riley. "Babe, I'm packed and ready. How long does it take to bandage your foot?"

"Done." Riley strolled out of the bathroom in bright pink long johns.

Kate grabbed her side and bent over, snickering.

"Don't laugh. They were on sale for half price."

The hum of snowmobiles sounded in the distance. "Cute, you look pretty in pink." Kate slipped into her exterior cold-weather gear. She swung the door open as Megan walked onto the porch. "We'll be right there. Riley's a little slow today."

Megan glanced around Kate to Riley. "How's the foot, Ms. Pig-headed?"

"Never better," Riley said.

They got Hank settled and locked the door. Most of the construction gang were present, and she was happy to see Penny, Donna, and Lacey. Nathaniel's presence took her by surprise. He stood beside a stunning young woman that looked a lot like Donna.

"This is Brooke, the world's most amazing girlfriend." He swung an arm around her and kissed the top of her head.

"Pleased to meet you, Brooke." Kate waved.

Puck introduced two newbies as Alisha and Bev. "They're part of our group but moved to Sun Valley near the hoity-toity crowd." Puck grinned.

Alisha smacked Puck's shoulder. "We're not rich. Jobs are hard to find around here." She turned to Kate. "I'm a restaurant manager, and my wife is a massage therapist. There's more money in Ketchum and Sun

Valley, which means better profits. Plus, we love skiing and get a discount through our employers. But we miss everyone in this club."

"It's time for the rules." Megan passed out maps while Hayley stepped up and reiterated safety rules and precautions, then ran through the route.

Kate unfolded her map and examined the contours on the topographic map. They were higher elevations with steeper slopes than she'd previously ridden. Riley had said today would be more challenging. But as Kate stared at the map, she questioned her ability.

"Don't worry." Riley gave her a hug and kissed her forehead. "We'll take care of you."

Everyone buddied up to check each other's emergency equipment, and to make sure everyone had brought extra clothes and lunch. Hayley and Riley put first aid kits in their snowmobiles.

They rode down the snow-packed road and headed into the trees, with Megan leading. Kate loved the rush of wind as she blasted through the powder. Weaving in and out of the evergreen trees was thrilling.

After about an hour, they entered a clearing and cut their engines.

"I'm climbing that hill." Puck revved her engine, then took off doing a wheelie.

Riley shook her head at Kate. "No wheelies for you. But I'm impressed with how well you're doing."

"I second that." Penny clapped her back and held out a granola bar for her and Riley. "You sure you've never done this before."

"Thanks. If I had known how much fun this was, I would have booked snowmobile tours years ago." Glancing up the hill, it didn't look that bad to Kate. She turned to Riley. "Let's hit the hill after our snack?"

"Ah..."

"It's not that bad of a hill." Hayley joined them. "Most of us like the jumps and wheelies. Riley's probably the best jumper here. But Puck sometimes takes it over the limit, and we have to slap some shit out of her."

"Riley?" Kate tilted her head.

"Okay, your skills have improved enough to give it a try." Riley took a deep breath. "But no wheelies or jumps. And only one person on the hill at a time. No exceptions. And don't take it too fast."

Riley spread the word that Kate was going up next. When Puck returned, Kate raced up the hill. She descended and raced back up again twice.

"Good job." Penny gave Kate a thumb's up.

"Thanks." Kate took her place in line when Megan signaled for everyone to regroup. As they took off into the trees, she screamed, "Yahoo," even though no one could hear her. The grove of trees gradually narrowed. In a tight turn, the snowmobile dipped toward a tree, and she smacked into a branch and fell from her snowmobile. She sat up, dazed.

Riley pulled up in her snowmobile and pulled Kate out from underneath the branch. "Does anything hurt?"

"Nothing hurts except my pride."

After Riley checked her extremities, Kate stretched her arms and legs.

"You sure you don't have any numbness or tingling?" Riley asked.

"Plenty of tingling. Better check my torso and massage my body." Kate grinned.

"Yeah, you're in one piece." Riley cleared her throat.

"I don't understand. I swore I only hit the outside of a branch." Kate looked at the snowmobile stuck at a funny angle and now partially buried in a subalpine fir's heavy undergrowth

"It's my fault. I forgot to tell you about tree wells." Riley sighed.

"Huh?"

"The snow isn't so compact around the base, and a pocket of loose snow forms. Getting close, even to the edge, can cause you to tip towards the tree."

"How the hell do I get my machine out?"

Megan and Riley grabbed the skids and tried to yank the snowmobile out of the bank, but they could barely move it. "Stand back." Riley hopped onto Kate's snowmobile, counterbalanced her weight away from the tree and plowed through the branches. Ends snapped off as they smashed into her body and the face shield of her helmet. She motioned to Kate. "Everyone hits tree branches now and then. The closer you are to the tree, the harder it is to maintain balance. Bail out if you even come close to a branch."

Kate nodded. "I guess I also got a little too big for my britches."

"Riley, you might have to spank her when you get back."

"Shut up, Puck, and go back to your position," Riley said over her shoulder.

"Okay. I'll do it if you're unwilling."

A few choice curse words almost slipped out of Kate's mouth. Puck had frayed her nerves today too.

"You're doing great, but please take it easy," Riley said softly. "I do like all of your limbs and digits functional."

"Yes, ma'am. Ditto."

Kate trudged a few feet through the deep snow to her snowmobile and yanked the power cord. As she took off, she thought about her relationship with Riley. They spent most of their nights together, going back and forth between houses. Kate had begun to think about more permanent arrangements. They weaved in and out of the denser grove of trees, then climbed in altitude. Kate was exhausted and happy when they reached the next level clearing.

"Time for lunch," Hayley said.

Everyone except Nathaniel and Brooke gathered around and traded their goodies. Giggles from Nathaniel and Brooke drifted in the air. Lost in each other's eyes, they exchanged a kiss then divvied up their lunch away from the group.

Donna groaned. "My baby sister is smart but acts like a newborn puppy around him."

"They're cute together, and Nathaniel's a good guy," Kate said.

"Yeah, but she's just out of high school. I wish they'd take it slower."

"Stop staring, mother hen, and let's get back to enjoying this ride." Riley clapped Donna on the back.

During lunch, Kate unfolded her map and pointed ahead. "Hey, these peaks look crazy, but the terrain leading up to them seems gentle."

"Some of us will play on it but not you. You need more experience first." Riley was clearly serious.

"I agree with her. I'll hang out with you, Kate," Penny said.

"And no highmarking!" Riley shouted to everyone as she walked over to Megan.

"What's highmarking?" Kate asked Penny.

"A contest to ride up steep slopes as far as possible without the engine crapping out or rolling over. If you screw up, you have to buy the group a round of drinks."

Hayley strolled up. "Riley's ultra-safety conscious, and today, she's right. All that fresh powder on top of the wet snow is too dangerous."

"We're hanging back here in the trees," Nathaniel said over the radio.

"You'd better not sneak off and make snow bunnies. I'm not ready to be an aunt," Donna said into her mic.

"Listen up. I'll go first to check the stability and radio the status," Megan said. "Donna and Lacey, team up with me. Alisha and Bev, you're with Puck. Hayley, Charley, and Riley, you'll go last. No hot-dogging, Puck." Megan's half-serious warning drew a giggle from Puck. "I mean it. Follow the rules."

"Sure, captain." Puck gave a mock salute, then rummaged through her lunch bag and pulled out a second double-decker sandwich.

Her attitude irritated Kate's cheerful nature. Last month, Puck had pushed too far, and Riley had threatened to kick her out of the club. According to Hayley, Megan usually kept the peace between them on construction sites.

Kate watched Megan, Donna, and Lacey ride up to a flat knoll. It looked to be about three thousand feet below the crest of the steep slope. Megan did a couple of solo runs on the steep hill, while Donna and Lacey stayed on the knoll.

"I gotta take a dump. My dinner last night is ripping through me." Puck wandered off.

Kate bit her tongue. *If Puck wasn't feeling well, why did she show up today?* Puck's negative side outweighed her sane and funny moments, which were few and far between. She wasn't sure why Riley and the rest of them put up with her.

"The bottom three quarters is stable," Megan said over the radio.

"Let's play it safe," said Riley. "No higher than the middle. Again, folks, no highmarking, and only one at a time."

"Okay. Midway. Got it," Megan said.

After four runs apiece, Megan, Donna, and Lacey headed back to the bottom. Lacey ripped off her helmet, rolled her fist in the air, and whooped. "That was awesome."

"Totally," Donna said.

"Time for the next group," Hayley said.

"I've changed my mind. I don't feel as confident on this slope," Bev said.

"Where's Puck?" Megan looked around.

"Right here. Mother Nature called," Puck said.

Kate saw Riley's jaw tighten, but she didn't say a word. Alisha and Puck rode up to the knoll. Just as they stopped, Puck turned around and headed back.

"Puck, what's wrong?" Megan asked on the radio. After no reply, Megan repeated herself. Nothing. "Goddammit. She doesn't have her radio on."

"She's probably taking another shit," Hayley said as they watched Puck ride to the edge of the trees.

Alisha took off and only did the lower quarter.

"I'll go up." Riley yanked her cord and zoomed up.

Just as Riley stopped at the knoll, Alisha turned her snowmobile around and stopped.

"What's wrong?" Kate tried to hide her concern in her voice.

"She slowed down before making the turn. Something must be wrong with her machine." Penny watched through her binoculars.

The radio chirped. "This damn thing won't start," Alisha said.

"I'm on my way," Riley said.

Kate's throat tightened as Riley rode up to Alisha and traded snowmobiles with her. Something didn't feel right. While Alisha rode down to the knoll, Riley unlatched the hood of the broken machine.

"Riley will radio if she needs help. She's pretty good with repairs in the field." Penny clapped Kate on the shoulder.

The words had barely gotten out of Penny's mouth when Puck whizzed out from the trees and up the hill. She didn't stop at the knoll and blasted past Riley, climbing higher and higher.

"What is she doing?" Megan grabbed the radio and yelled, "Alisha, get to the side, out of the chute. Riley, hurry!"

"Puck's fucking crazy," Penny said. "The upper part is too unstable."

Kate glanced at Penny, whose eyes were wide. When she looked back, Puck had reached the top and raised her arms in triumph.

"Oh, thank God." Kate breathed a sigh of relief.

"Come on, Riley. Get out of there." Megan radioed again.

The urgency in Megan's voice sent chills through Kate. "They're safe, right?"

A low rumbling sound like thunder rolling through the mountains began and grew louder.

"Avalanche! Avalanche! Avalanche!" Megan screamed.

Everyone ran to their machine and took off while Kate stood frozen, watching as the snow to the right of Puck slid slowly down like a shimmering wave. "We have to help Riley."

"Get on!" Megan grabbed Kate and pulled her toward her machine.

The rumble grew to a roar as Megan raced toward the side and out of the chute. Kate glanced up the hill. The snow was flowing like a tsunami. "What can we do?" But her voice was silenced by their machines and the snow racing toward them. Megan stopped on higher ground off to the side, and they both took out their binoculars. Somehow Riley was on the front of the wave.

"She started the snowmobile, and she's riding it. Come on, Riley," Megan said. "You can do it."

A wave of dizziness hit Kate as she watched the unfolding horror barrel down on Riley. The surging snow snapped trees like they were little twigs, and Riley was barely in front of the avalanche. Then she was gone, swallowed up like a rag doll.

*I love you. Don't you dare die on me.*

# Chapter Fifty-Five

"OH, SHIT." RILEY YANKED once. Twice. The machine came to life, and she hit the throttle. *Faster. Faster. God, please. I don't want to die.* She had experienced plenty of avalanches from a distance and knew the sound. The roar of this one told her all she needed to know; she was screwed. She tried desperately to outrun the killer nipping at her heels, a killer that could travel twice the speed of a snowmobile. When the roar grew to a crescendo, Riley yanked the ripcord of her avalanche airbag. Within seconds, the wall of snow engulfed her and tore her from the snowmobile. Like a monstrous ocean wave, it tumbled her down the chute. She waved her arms in hopes of creating an air pocket.

Everything stopped. Silence.

The snow penetrated Riley's helmet and settled around her mouth and face like a thick, heavy scarf. She struggled to breathe but couldn't.

*I love you, Kate. I love you, Aunt Lilly.* Everyone's faces zipped through her mind. Riley thought of her accomplishments. Mistakes. Hard work. All the things she should have done or done differently. *Kate.* What she said and what she hadn't said. Her feelings. *I love her so much.*

Riley knew the snow would soon create an ice shield from the heat of her breath and choke off the remaining oxygen in her body.

*Please, dear God. No. There's so much more I need to do.*

\*\*\*

"No, no, no," Kate screamed as the snow roared down and consumed Riley. Tears stung her face, and she fell to her knees.

"Everyone, switch your beacons from the transceiver to search mode," Megan shouted on the radio.

"I called for a rescue chopper," Hayley said. "They're nearby. It won't be long."

"Let's go." Megan yanked Kate up off her knees.

Kate switched her beacon to search and sat behind Megan on the snowmobile. She saw Bev parked near her partner Alisha, who had gotten tossed off Riley's snowmobile while trying to outrun the danger. Alisha was okay, but Riley's snowmobile was twenty feet up the hill, half-buried and pointing up at the sky. Everyone else moved higher toward the vicinity where someone had last spotted Riley. Nathaniel and Brooke came from the other side.

Megan gave the signal to stop. They hustled and formed a spiral pattern, a body's width apart from one another and began searching to pinpoint the strongest signal. Kate's transceiver wasn't getting much of a ping. She kept wiping away her tears, determined to carry on.

"I have a strong signal over here." Nathaniel pushed a probe down perpendicular to the slope. "No positive strike. Give me another one." With a positive third and fourth probe, they determined how her body was laying and the depth. "She's shallow. Just under two meters."

Kate joined Nathaniel. She didn't know what to do.

"Start over there." He pointed. "We don't want to collapse any air pockets."

He chopped at the hard chunks of snow on one side of the probe site while Kate worked the other. Everyone else started digging around another probe. The snow had compacted like concrete. It was like nothing Kate had ever experienced.

*I love you. Don't die.*

"We're going to get her out," Nathaniel said.

Nathaniel worked methodically and swiftly. His determination inspired Kate to dig faster. When the orange stripe of Riley's avalanche airbag peeked through, Kate tossed aside her shovel and shouted for help. Nathaniel and Kate dug out Riley's face using only their hands while everyone else unburied her body. Riley had a pulse but wasn't breathing.

Seeing Riley's unconscious body shocked her to the core. Nathaniel scooped the snow out of Riley's airway and started resuscitation breaths.

"Come on, babe, breathe." Kate eyes filled with tears.

Hayley pushed Kate out of the way and began chest compressions. Off to the side, Kate rocked on her heels as tears streamed down her face. Riley had told her that most avalanche victims died from asphyxiation rather than hypothermia. *Come on, babe. Live. I need you.*

Megan pulled Kate up and wrapped her in a big hug. "She'll make it.

# CABIN FEVER

We found her quickly."

Kate nodded. She turned away and saw Puck just feet away. "You bitch! You stupid fucking bitch!" She lunged toward her.

"Whoa." Megan grabbed her. "This isn't good for anyone. Let's finish the rescue. We'll deal with her later. I promise."

"I'm so, so sorry. I didn't mean for this to happen." Puck walked away and sat in the snow, sobbing.

Kate rushed back to Riley and kneeled again next to her. "Babe, I love you." The sight of Riley's white face and blue lips scared her, but she reached out with a trembling hand and smoothed her hair as Nathaniel gave Riley mouth-to-mouth. For a brief second, Riley's mouth moved, and her eyes fluttered, but then there was only stillness.

"Hang on, Riley." Nathaniel resumed mouth-to-mouth breaths until Riley opened her eyes. "Damn, it's so good to see you!" He was inches from her face.

"Ew. Why are you kissing me?"

He laughed.

"You're going to be okay, babe." Kate leaned in and kissed her.

"I'm tired and so cold," Riley said.

"We're going to take care of that." Hayley quickly checked Riley's extremities. "Okay, time to wrap you up and get you out of here."

The helicopter landed, and two crew members took over. Within minutes, they were gone. Kate fell to the ground and buried her head between her knees. Fear consumed her that Riley wouldn't recover or that she'd die in flight to the hospital. Her trickle of tears turned into a raging sob. Megan and Hayley came to her side, but their voices sounded distant. They pulled her up. Her body was so tired and heavy, and the tears wouldn't stop.

"Come on, Kate. We have to get to the hospital. Have faith. She'll be okay." Megan rested her forehead against Kate's. "You can do it. We're going to put you on the snowmobile. Hold tight to my waist."

Kate could only nod. With Hayley's help, she straddled the snowmobile behind Megan and held on for dear life as the machine whizzed away. And every second, she prayed and hoped for Riley's safety.

# Chapter Fifty-Six

THE COLD WAITING ROOM at the trauma center chilled Kate to the bone. She sat in silence with Lilly. Their hands clasped together was their lifeline, clinging to hope that Riley would fully recover. After nearly an hour sitting around, Kate grew impatient. She was about ready to leap out of her chair and rip someone's head off when a doctor approached them.

"Mrs. Smith?"

"Yes." Lilly sprung to her feet like a young jackrabbit.

For a short, older woman, the move surprised Kate.

"Riley is stable, but we want to keep an eye on her for the next couple of days. If nothing changes, then she can go home."

Lilly shouted, "Oh, thank the Lord." She threw her arms around Kate, and they rocked back and forth.

"She's lucky and blessed to have good friends. I hear you all ride with emergency gear, including avalanche airbags. They're an expensive piece of equipment but essential for backcountry adventures. You all can be proud. Getting her out in under fifteen minutes saved her life."

"Can we see her now?" Lilly asked.

The doctor nodded. "She's in a deep sleep with the medication. I'll let you visit her briefly, but she needs to rest. No trying to wake her."

"Let's go see our girl." Lilly's eyes lit up, and she lovingly squeezed Kate's hand.

"I'm sorry," he said. "It's the hospital's policy to allow only the next of kin inside the intensive care rooms."

Lilly scowled at him and stepped into his personal space. "No." She shook her finger up at him. "Kate and I are her family. We're going in together."

The doctor had to be at least a foot and a half taller than Lilly. His eyebrows shot up, but then he smiled. "You only have ten minutes. You can see her again at ten in the morning."

Lilly nodded, and they followed the doctor to Riley's room. Megan had booked two nearby hotel rooms by the time they'd returned to the waiting room, but Lilly didn't want to leave the hospital.

"Auntie." Kate cradled her hand. "This waiting room is freezing, and we can't see her until tomorrow. I'm about ready to fall over." Kate gestured toward Hayley, who was stretched out in a chair and snoring. "And she's going to have a sore neck tomorrow."

"You just called me Auntie. That's lovely."

"Riley's in good hands. We need some sleep. Please." Relief flooded through Kate that Riley was alive, but new tears sprung to her eyes. She didn't know that much about avalanches, and it bothered her that the doctor didn't say if Riley would suffer any long-term damage. Not being able to breathe for almost fifteen minutes couldn't be good.

Lilly reached out and wiped the tears from Kate's eyes. "Okay, dear."

It was close to eleven p.m. when they checked in. Kate was so drained of energy that she struggled to take a shower before face planting into the bed. She drifted off.

"It's too early. Let me sleep." Kate pushed the hand away.

"Honey, it's morning. Wake up. We can go see Riley in the hospital." Lilly shook her again.

Kate opened her eyes wide, and the memory of what had happened yesterday flooded into her brain. She threw back the covers. "I'll wake Megan and Hayley."

"I've already called them. They're meeting us for breakfast."

Kate glanced at the clock. The hospital was within walking distance, and they had plenty of time. Downstairs, Kate picked at her food. She was anxious to hear a full report on Riley's condition.

When Megan and Hayley went to get seconds, Lilly squeezed Kate's hand. "I know you and Riley love one another. I don't have to hear the words. I can see by the way you look at each other."

"I do love her, but we haven't said it." Kate put the fork down and sighed, feeling guilt that she had waited so long. "I told her on the mountain before she regained consciousness. Then the helicopter came and whisked her away. I'm going to tell her once we get to the hospital."

"I think that'd be lovely." Lilly patted Kate's hand.

Kate didn't care who was in the room. She was going to pronounce her love to Riley. And if the trauma caused any secondary health issues, she'd be by Riley's side to help her through them.

# CABIN FEVER

***

Riley woke from the medication cocktail early in the morning. She vaguely remembered being wheeled out of the ICU onto another floor. The other bed in the room was empty, so everything was nice and quiet. She took off her fingertip monitors and wheeled the stand with the IV bag into the bathroom. Before returning to bed, she stood at the window and looked out into the moonless night. The light pollution obscured the stars.

"You're not supposed to get out of bed on your own," said the nurse and forced Riley back to bed.

By breakfast, a new nurse named Lindsey showed up. If Riley had to guess, Lindsey was *family*. The doctor explained everything, and Riley zoned out over the boring medical details. All she cared about was that she hadn't died or suffered any brain damage, and life should be normal soon.

As he stepped toward the door, he turned to the nurse. "She can take a shower before her visitors arrive."

Excitement shot through Riley, realizing Aunt Lilly and Kate were close by. She tore the covers back. "Lower the bar, please."

"Easy."

Lindsey let her take ten minutes to shower and dress. Riley found it annoying that she stood outside with the door cracked.

"Shit, this thing's hard to tie," Riley muttered as her fingers fiddled with the hospital gown.

"Need help?" Lindsey cracked the door wide.

"Nope." Riley shuffled out with the back open and brushed her aside. She sat on the edge of the bed and took in Lindsey's short haircut, stylish and nearly buzzed on one side, and the bottom of a tattoo peeking out from her nurse's smock. *Yep, she's a soft, baby dyke.* She figured Lindsey couldn't be more than twenty-five.

"Lie down, Miss Stubborn. I need to check your fluids."

Riley grimaced when Lindsey inserted a new needle into one of the dual IV ports.

"It's a saline drip. Rest and don't get out of bed, or we might have to give you some sleep meds." Lindsey also placed the gadget back on Riley's index finger.

"Is that irritating thing necessary?"

"Yes. It sends your heart rate and oxygen saturation levels to our workstation. Don't argue. I can be wicked." She pointed to a button. "Press and call if you need me."

Riley stared at the ceiling, then flung her arm over her face and closed her eyes. There was so much more she needed to say to Kate. But did she have the guts? Her train of thought had been clear just before the accident. She had everything in line and her words planned out but now she couldn't think logically. Had the drugs affected her reasoning?

"Shit, my bag's in my truck, back at the house. Maybe this is all the sign that I need to wait." *You're scared because you've never said these words to anyone other than family.* The sad fact settled into her chest. She'd never wanted to say those words before. But Kate was different. She had a gigantic heart and a smile that melted Riley's defenses. Yet, every time Riley thought about saying I love you, her mouth stayed shut like it was crammed full of peanut butter. Not to mention her stomach flipping and twisting into knots.

And what would Kate think if she said it? They were practically living together. But that didn't mean marriage anytime soon. Right? "One step at a time."

She flipped on the TV and found her favorite renovation show, *Maine Cabin Masters*. This would help get her mind off the situation. Twisting herself into a pretzel over every little "what if" would do her no good. What would be, would be. Wasn't that what Aunt Lilly said?

# Chapter Fifty-Seven

KATE DREW A DEEP breath at seeing the doctor standing at the nurse's station. The four cups of coffee she'd downed this morning had only heightened her anxiety.

"Good news, ladies. Ms. Anderson is recovering nicely. All of her tests are in and show no brain damage. We moved her to room 2458. That wing allows up to four visitors per room."

"Oh, thank you!" Lilly flung herself forward and embraced him. "Come on, girls. No time to waste." She turned on her heels just as swiftly and took off for the elevator.

When they got to Riley's room, Lilly was the first to embrace her. Kate moved to the other side, entwined her fingers with Riley's, and kissed her forehead. Megan and Hayley waved from the foot of the bed, and the chatter began.

"You scared the living crap out of us. Thank goodness for Nathaniel," Megan said.

"His beacon found you first. That boy sure did rise to the challenge," Hayley said.

"He jumped right in without any hesitation and saved your life with mouth-to-mouth." Kate smoothed back Riley's hair.

"I wondered why he was giving me sloppy kisses."

Everyone laughed.

Riley's face hardened. "I know Puck didn't mean it, but she's careless. No one will trust her after she ignored safety protocols. She's out of the club and tell her to pack up her tools. She's fired. I don't care how good she is at carpentry."

"Done," Megan said. "But you need to calm down. They can probably hear you down the hall, and that thing is beeping faster." She pointed to the monitor.

Kate gave Riley a lingering kiss and hugged her tight. "I love you."

Riley's arms dropped from her neck, and Kate leaned back, hurt and confused. She had whispered it in Riley's ear and hoped for the same in return. Didn't she feel the same? No one seemed to notice the awkward moment between them.

"I remembered you kept a bag with a change of clothes in your truck," Megan said. "You'll need it when they release you." She placed Riley's duffel bag on the side table.

Riley stared at the bag, and a serious expression clouded her face. The room was quiet, and everyone seemed to be waiting for her to say something.

The silence was too much for Kate. *I've screwed up.* She walked toward the door and motioned for Megan and Hayley to follow. "I'm going to grab a coffee. Join me and give Lilly some time alone with Riley."

"No, don't go. Please."

Kate turned around.

"Please." Riley's eyes were wide, and her gaze locked onto Kate's. "Megan, hand me the bag?"

"You're not supposed to dress until—"

"Just give me the freaking bag." Riley lowered the bed railing and swung her feet over the bedside.

"Young, lady, I don't—"

"Aunt Lilly, how do you think I go to the bathroom?" She took the monitor off her index finger, rummaged around inside the bag, and then tossed it aside. She walked toward Kate with one hand holding tight to the IV stand, and the other holding up an oblong, red velvet case. "I was going to give you this after snowmobiling. I love you too."

Relief and happiness flooded Kate's body. "Oh, babe."

Kate kissed her, and as their kiss grew passionate, Megan and Hayley wolf whistled.

"This is a touching scene, but I have to say that you've scarred me for life with your ass hang out the back of your robe," Megan said.

"And I took a picture." Hayley chuckled. "Just kidding."

"Shit." Riley thrust the jewelry box in Kate's hand and hastily wrapped the flimsy robe around herself. "Sorry." She looked back at Kate. "Why don't you open your present now?"

Kate swallowed at the creak of the hinge, and her hand trembled as she removed a gold bangle with dazzling sapphire stones. She turned it in her fingers to read an inscription on the back, *Love, Riley.* She gently rubbed the bangle as she fought to hold back the tears.

"Is it too much?" Riley asked.

"It's perfect. I love you."

Riley kissed Kate's forehead and placed the bangle on her wrist.

Kate had never expected such a gorgeous, luxurious gift. She kissed Riley and hugged her tight. Over Riley's shoulder, Kate saw the biggest smile on Lilly's face. Megan and Hayley cheered and gave thumbs up.

"This is lovely, and I hate to dampen the mood." A tall, young nurse came into the room and pointed her finger at Riley. "You're not to get out of bed without notifying us." She took Riley's arm. "Back into bed with the monitors back on."

"Yes, Nurse Lindsey." Riley glanced around. "Don't leave me alone with her. She might beat me up."

"I will if you continue to defy orders." Her stern look softened after reconnecting the monitors, and she turned to Kate with a warm smile. "You're a lucky woman. I wish you all the best. But you need to keep an eye on this one." She thumbed over her shoulder. "I think she needs a strong upper hand." She winked and chuckled as she walked out.

"Oh, that one's got some spunk in her. I wonder if she's into women," Hayley said.

"Dream on. She's too young." Megan snickered.

Kate moved to Riley's side. She rested her hand on Riley's forehead and gently kissed her lips. "Thank you for the gift. I'll cherish it, but the most precious gift you've given me is your love. I love you with all my heart, Riley Anderson."

"Riley, dear, you should move in with Kate," Lilly said. "You're always worried about her being alone."

Kate shook her head. "You shouldn't be alone in that big house, Lilly."

"I'll spend half the week at Kate's, and she can spend the rest of the week with us until you've decided on the basement," Riley said.

"Oh, I'll be sprucing up the basement and turning it into a couple of bedrooms." Lilly looked at Riley. "But don't worry, dear, there'll still be room for your workshop."

"So, Nathaniel and Brooke are moving in?" Riley asked.

Megan and Hayley turned toward Lilly as if they'd just been told aliens had landed on earth. Kate blinked at Riley.

"Yes." Lilly bit her lip. "I wish Brooke hadn't been out snowmobiling."

"Why?" Riley asked.

"Oh, forget I said that." Lilly took off her glasses and rubbed the bridge of her nose.

"Oh, no, you don't. Why?"

"I told you they were thinking about living together." Lilly folded her hands in front of her, and her thumbs twitched together.

"That doesn't answer the question. And why *bedrooms* plural?" Riley asked.

"Relax, babe. Your heart monitor just increased its beeps."

"I can't believe I let that slip. I must be getting too darn old." Lilly sighed. "She's pregnant. But don't say a word. They were going to tell Brooke's family tomorrow night."

"Oh. My. God. Donna's going to kill him," Megan muttered.

Hayley cleared her throat. "Got any other news, Lilly?"

Lilly smiled brightly at Riley. "They mentioned making you a Godmother."

"Well, that's guaranteed to screw up the kid." Hayley laughed.

"Nah, I'm sure Riley's good with kids. Don't you think so, Kate?" Megan winked.

"I'm sure she'll be fantastic." Kate smiled.

"See." Megan held out her hand and tilted her head at Riley. "When are you two having your first kid? You know forty is the new thirty."

Kate's breath stilled, and she looked at Riley, who was equally speechless. They'd danced around the topic after Goldbug Hot Springs but becoming mothers was unlikely.

"End of jokes. Kate and I will decide if we get married and have children. We'll make those decisions without being pressured." The serious tone in Riley's voice, along with her finger pointing, shut Megan and Hayley up. "Would you pour me a glass of water, please?"

While Riley gulped down the water, Kate wished she had a glass filled with a good stiff drink. She'd once mentioned her dream of adopting or fostering an older child to Audrey who instantly said, "Hell no. You're crazy." Even if Riley didn't want kids, she'd be more empathic in her response than Audrey. And Riley wouldn't belittle her. But did she still want a child?

"Ah, I don't know what meds they gave me, but I was so thirsty. Thanks."

"You're welcome." Kate took the glass.

# CABIN FEVER

"And just a little clarification for you two clowns." Riley pointed at Megan and Hayley again then kissed Kate's hand. "If we ever have kids, Kate will be the one to carry the baby. I can see her now with a cute baby bump cooking me supper." Riley and her friends laughed.

Kate lightly smacked Riley's hand. "Oh, you think that's so funny. Just wait. Paybacks are hell."

Nurse Lindsey entered with a wheelchair. "Ladies, I hate to break up the party, but the doctor has ordered one more test. We have to take our rising star away. The waiting room is more comfortable. I'll let you know when we're done."

Kate kissed Riley on the cheek. Riley held her for a brief minute and whispered, "Guess we still have things to discuss. You know, right now, you could ask for the moon, and I'd say yes. I love you so much."

"Love you too." Kate left, grinning. She was grateful that the avalanche hadn't caused Riley any permanent damage. As for kids, Riley's last words implied she was open to discussing the matter. Their relationship was different than any other Kate had experienced. Even the words *I love you* didn't adequately describe how deeply she cared for Riley.

# Chapter Fifty-Eight

*March*

AVOIDING THE STEAM RISING from the opening of her insulated mug, Kate carefully sipped her chamomile tea in front of the fire pit. She crossed her legs and leaned her head back to watch the fading sun. The sky had been a brilliant cobalt blue with a few popcorn clouds, a perfect picture of nature's beauty. Kate heard the click of the door and turned. "Hey, babe. Thanks for doing the dishes."

"No problem. Thanks for cooking my favorite dinner." Riley snuggled up next to her and placed a blanket over their laps. "It's freezing."

"Freezing but beautiful." Maybe instead of tea, a good dose of Riley was what she needed. "The wind died down. Why in the world did my ancestors build up so high?"

"Probably for logging and mining." Riley pulled her in tighter.

They sat for several minutes. Kate enjoyed Riley's affection and the gentleness of her thumb delicately rubbing over the top of Kate's hand under the blanket.

"I love you. I'm lucky you're my partner." Kate kissed her. They cuddled together in silence and watched the flames lick up into the sky.

"I have some good news. Well, sort of," Riley said and giggled.

Kate sat up. "And what does that mean?"

"Donna's no longer threatening to kill Nathaniel for impregnating her baby sister. And Lilly's over the moon because Brooke's having twins."

Kate chuckled and slapped her hand on her thigh. "That's good news for her, but how about Brooke? And is Donna in a state of shock?"

"Donna hasn't gotten out of her state of shock, but Brooke is as happy as Aunt Lilly."

They laughed. When their excitement died down, only the crackling of the burning wood and an owl hooting pierced the quiet night.

"Let's go inside for a minute. I have something for you." Kate tugged

Riley to her feet.

"Is it chocolate chip cookies?"

"Nope." She pulled Riley along.

"You baked a cake?"

"Funny lady. Are you always thinking about food?" Kate opened the door and gestured for Riley to go first, then smacked her ass when she walked by.

"Are we experimenting with spanking tonight?"

"Shut up and sit down." Kate took a gift bag out of the closet and handed it to her.

Her heart raced, waiting for Riley's reaction.

Riley popped open the box. When she looked at Kate, her sparkling eyes and smile made Kate's heart sing.

"These are gorgeous. Such exquisite detail."

"The band is white gold. The curled half-heart is fourteen karat yellow gold accented by a diamond." Kate swallowed.

"I love how they match up to make one heart." Riley put the jewelry box down and smiled. "Are you asking me to marry you, Kate Minton?"

"Yes. We don't have to rush, but I want to marry you. Waking up with you and going to sleep at your side is heaven. I'm so happy with you, and the thought of ever losing you scares me."

"You're not going to lose me."

Kate blew out a long breath. *She nearly had.* "The accident scared me. I need you by my side."

"Kate, you've got me." Riley stood and placed a kiss on Kate's nose.

"So, will you marry me?" Kate rested her forehead on Riley's.

"I'd be a fool to pass you up."

She took out the ring and slipped it onto Riley's left hand, and Riley did the same for her. The kiss that followed grew in intensity. Kate's heart pounded against her chest. "I'd like a summer wedding when the wildflowers are in bloom. Nothing fancy. Is that all right?" She played with Riley's hair.

"Whatever you want, my buttercup."

Kate wrapped her arms around Riley and kissed her neck. "Have you ever wanted a child?"

Riley leaned back with a serious look on her face. "Do you?"

"Never mind. It's the wine from dinner talking."

Riley put her finger under Kate's chin. "I'll seriously consider it if that's what you want. But we're in our forties. Don't you think it's a bit late to be caring for a baby?"

Kate cleared her throat. "There is an alternative."

"And that would be?"

"We could be foster parents to an older child in need." She couldn't read Riley's expression. "Marriage is a big enough step. I was talking maybe in the future, with an emphasis on *maybe*."

"A year ago, I would have told anybody that there was no way in hell I'd ever want to be a mom. But you've made me question everything. If we did, I could close the loft in for a second bedroom."

Kate's heart filled with joy. She wrapped her arms around Riley, snuggled into her neck, and whispered, "I love you so much."

"I love you too." Riley held out her hand, examining the ring. "I never dreamed I'd ever be in this position. Even when same-sex marriage became law, I never thought I'd get married." She brushed her hand down Kate's cheek. "You make getting up every day worth it. And you're pretty handy with a snowmobile." Riley grinned wickedly. "Like that time you almost hit the tree."

Kate cocked her eyebrow. "I hit the outer branches, which I've since seen Penny and Megan do. But no more risky backcountry rides on steep slopes. I can't bear the agony of losing you in the snow again."

"Agreed." A mischievous grin spread across Riley's face. "So, you're not sick of me taking up half the space in your cabin?"

"Nah, I think I'll keep you." Kate twirled a strand of Riley's hair. "And if I ever get mad at you, I'll throw you in the barn with your tools. You can build me a jewelry box or something to win back my good graces."

Riley smiled, then kissed her again. "Deal."

# Epilogue

*Twelve Years Later*

KATE SMILED AT THE scene before her. Riley stood behind Amelia and had to catch hold of their daughter several times when the stronger fish almost toppled her into the river.

"Grab him, Mom," Amelia shouted as the tired fish came into range.

The fish splashed them before Riley got it into the basket, and they both laughed, then waded onshore.

"I caught a big brook trout, Momma."

"I see." Kate smiled and grunted as her ten-year-old jumped in her arms. At seventy-eight pounds, Amelia was no longer their little girl. "I love the hug, but you're a little too big to run at me full force. And you got me wet." She kissed Amelia's forehead before letting her go.

"Sorry." Amelia took off her waders.

Kate spread out a blanket, and Amelia plopped down between them with her eyes downcast.

"Momma?"

"Yes, dear." Kate brushed Amelia's hair behind her ears.

Amelia glanced over at her mom, and Riley nodded. Amelia sighed. "I've told Mom, but not you."

Kate pulled her chin up. "I know that look. Honesty, please."

"I punched Tony Dixon in the nose."

Kate's gaze darted to Riley, then back to Amelia. "Why?"

"He said you and Mom were disgusting lesbos. I tried to be calm, but he wouldn't shut up. So I punched him. We both have after-school detention on Monday."

"I'm sorry he said hurtful words, but even the smallest violence can spin out of control. And I'd be heartbroken if he'd punched you back and broke your lovely nose." Kate swiped her index finger down Amelia's nose. "You should have handled it with words."

"I did." Amelia swallowed and looked at Riley. "Do I have to say it?"

Riley narrowed her eyes. "Yes."

Amelia hung her head again, and Kate waited patiently.

"I have detention the whole week because I called him a stupid fucktard."

"Amelia Emmeline Josephine Anderson. For that, I agree that you deserve detention. Don't say anything like that again."

"Okay," Amelia said with an edge to her voice.

Good God, despite not being their natural child, Amelia had both their qualities, but she took after Riley in the cockiness department. "Can you please say it with more sincerity?"

"Yes, Momma. I won't say it again."

"Go transfer your fish to the cooler." Riley handed the basket to Amelia.

When Amelia was out of earshot, Riley turned to Kate and whispered, "I agree with the punishment and everything you said. But that kid is trouble. Maybe he'll shut his trap now."

Kate didn't have time to answer as Amelia returned and plopped down between them.

"Are you going to give me extra punishment? Please don't take away my ATV trip with Auntie Hayley next weekend."

Hayley and Megan had become like second moms to Amelia. Since the adventure company startup, Hayley handled ATV and snowmobile operations, while Kate dealt with management. They'd just bought kid-size ATVs and planned their first easy trip for ten and up with two local teachers. They intended to teach ecology along the way.

Riley wrapped an arm around Amelia and kissed her cheek. "We still need to talk, but if you help out with extra chores, I bet Momma will let you go on the trip."

"Please." Amelia clasped her fingers together.

Kate nodded.

"Thank you."

"Do you know what day it is?" Riley asked.

Amelia scrunched her eyebrows. "July the 15th. It's not my birthday. It's Momma's next week." She dropped her hand in Kate's hair and rubbed rapidly, messing it up. "Momma turns the double five. How does it feel to be an old lady?"

"Oh, missy, you're walking on thin ice." Kate smiled. "Back to today. It's

330

an extraordinary day. Mom and I adopted you exactly eight years ago. You've made us very happy and proud. I love you, Amelia." She kissed the top of her head.

"I love you to the moon and back, Princess Leia." Riley kissed her cheek.

"I love you too. You're the best." Amelia crossed her arms. "But Mom, could you please not call me Princess Leia in public? It's embarrassing."

Kate suppressed a laugh.

"Sure, baby buttercup." Riley grinned.

"That's worse. Stop teasing me." Amelia punched Riley's arm.

Kate thought back to when Amelia came into their lives and smiled. Amelia's birth mother had died in an auto accident, leaving the toddler an orphan. Adopting and raising her had been more work than they'd ever imaged, but she had enrichened their lives so much.

Nathaniel pulled up in his SUV, and the sound of giggles filled the air.

"Violet and Vivian!" Amelia waved.

Nathaniel leaned out the window. "Are we on time?"

"Yep," Riley said. "Megan and Hayley are coming later."

The twins, who were a year and a half older than Amelia, jumped out and ran up with their golden retriever.

"Don't I get a greeting and hug?" Lilly shouted to Amelia.

"Hi, grandauntie." Amelia gave her a gentle hug, then went back to giggling with the twins.

"Good morning, ladies." Brooke strolled up with five-year-old Nathaniel Jr. "How are we ever going to survive the teenage years?"

Lilly chuckled from behind. "With a lot of luck."

Kate knelt to Nathaniel Jr.'s level. "How are you doing today, little man? I see you've got your crayons."

"I'm good, Auntie Kate," Nathaniel Jr. said. "I'm going to color a picture of our truck."

Nathaniel let out a loud whistle, and the chatter stopped. "Amelia, your moms asked me to bring someone for your special day. Check the cargo space." He motioned toward their SUV.

Amelia's long legs propelled her to the truck's rear compartment in the blink of an eye. Neither Kate nor Riley ever ran track, but Amelia talked nonstop about joining the cross-country team when she moved to middle school next year.

"It's a husky!" she yelled.

The dog bathed her in kisses and made noises almost like talking to her.

"Moms, she talks like Hank." Amelia grinned from ear to ear.

"Bring her here." Riley waved. The dog practically dragged Amelia along.

"She's a sixth-month old, thirty-pound ball of excitement." Riley rubbed her jowls just like she used to with Hank.

Kate teared up thinking about him.

"We better train her. What do you say if we adopt her on your special adoption day?" Riley put her hand on Amelia's shoulder.

"Really, Mom?"

"Yep, and thank Momma. She drove to Wyoming to get her."

Amelia lunged at Kate again, thankfully with a little less force, and wrapped her arms around her neck.

"Thank you, Momma."

"You're welcome." Kate held Amelia as long as she could. At two inches shy of five feet, Amelia would soon surpass her height. She was thrilled to see Amelia's coming transformation from a child to a young woman. "You have to name her. Got any ideas?"

Amelia broke away and hugged the dog. "Isn't Hank a nickname for Henry?" She stroked the dog's back. "I miss him." She looked at her moms, "Let's call her Miss Henry."

"Sounds lovely." Riley kissed Kate. "Momma baked your favorite cake for lunch."

"Chocolate with peppermint icing?"

"Yep." Kate smiled.

Amelia ran off to set up the picnic table with the twins. Nathaniel supervised the girls while Brooke sat next to Lilly, and Nathaniel Jr. colored. His tongue stuck out to the side as he concentrated.

"I can't tell you enough how happy I am." Kate wrapped her arms around Riley's waist and squeezed gently. "Sure, we have challenging days, but I wouldn't trade this for the world."

"Same here, buttercup." Riley gave a lingering kiss.

"Ew, Moms. You need to come up for air. That was way too much." Amelia rolled her eyes dramatically.

They both laughed. Dear Lord, she was growing up fast, and the physical and emotional changes of puberty were just around the corner.

Kate didn't know if she was ready, but she and Riley had agreed to do everything in their power to let Amelia express herself and be who she wanted to be. All they cared about was that she grew up to be a happy, kind, and respectful person.

"Moms, come on. I want to eat so I can get to the cake."

"Can't argue with that logic," Riley said.

"She's just like you in the eating department."

"Yes, but she's got spirit and beauty like her momma. We're so blessed." Kate watched Amelia interact with their extended family. "Yes, we are."

Unlike the childhood experiences they'd had, she and Riley worked hard to ensure Amelia's life was filled with love. Kate had gotten closer to Joel, but nothing had changed with Karl and Roger. And they all were sad when Sherry and Max had to cancel their visit at the last minute. Kate was proud when Amelia said over the phone, "I'll miss you, Aunt Sherry."

Riley rubbed her shoulder. "You and Amelia make me so happy. I love you."

"I love you too, and I intend to keep making you the happiest woman in the world." Kate's eyes watered with tears of joy.

"I intend to beat you in that contest." Riley cupped her hand over her mouth. "Hey, everyone. I have an announcement."

The chatter died down, and Riley led Kate over to the group.

"Even though Aunts Sherry and Max couldn't make it today, Aunt Sherry will have time next month. So, I bought us tickets to fly out and visit with them and Uncle Joel." Riley rubbed the top of Amelia's head. "And we can go to all those museums you want to see."

Amelia's eyes lit up. "And a Cubs baseball game too?"

Riley nodded, and Amelia hugged them both.

As Amelia chatted excitedly with the family, Riley whispered in Kate's ear, "I hope you like the surprise. Hayley said she's got the adventure company all under control."

"Of course, I love it. And thank you; I know you feel uncomfortable in the city, especially in large groups crowded into small spaces."

"Minus the crowds, the Field Museum is awesome, but it warms my heart to see you and Amelia having fun and being happy."

"Well, you won the contest this year for making me the happiest, but I'm fighting to win next year." Kate smiled and smoothed her fingers along Riley's jaw then tenderly kissed her. They'd both won the jackpot.

# What's Real?

Sawtooth Valley and the name of the mountains and hiking trails are real. The towns of Ketchum and Sun Valley and the historical facts about Ernest Hemingway are real, but most of the setting is from my dreams.

The town of Merrick, Idaho, Kate's cabin, and her vast amount of land are solely my imagination. The privately owned land in the Sawtooth Valley is mainly agricultural and off the major highway. And I don't think there is any private land deep in the Sawtooth National Forest. Riley's crew, composed of nearly all lesbian workers, is my imagination. Hey, it's called fiction for a reason.

Idaho has a lot of wild animals. In the book, Riley tells a story of a woman who went out to stop a stray dog from fighting her dog. When she picked up the stray, it turned out to be a junior mountain lion. That's a true story from a newspaper. And Goldbug Hot Springs is one of the many awesome hot springs in the state, although I didn't have time to visit during my 2021 trip.

It's true that Idaho is the second largest concentration of Latter-day Saints (often called Mormons) after Utah. Mormons live throughout the state, but most have made a home in the southeast corner of the state. I have a friend who grew up Mormon in SE Idaho. She had terrific stories of snowmobiling. And while the church doesn't like the term Mormon, my friend and others still use the term.

The Mormons moved westward to escape intolerance and physical violence. I wanted to touch on religion, not in a bad way, but in a good, loving way. The folks in my imaginary town are of mixed faith and peaceful. And while I like to put my characters on a roller coaster, Kate finds a home in Idaho with her chosen family and falls in love with Riley. Riley's mother is the one nemesis in the book.

Riley's mother's conservative religious group is imaginary. However, I did base her group's beliefs on Warren Jeffs' group, the Fundamentalist Church of Jesus Christ of Latter-day Saints (FLDS). The FLDS church is real.

Please do not confuse the FLDS with The Church of Jesus Christ of Latter-day Saints, whose members are often called Mormons. The Church of Jesus Christ of Latter-day Saints considers the FLDS church heretical and believes FLDS members are misguided people.

The FLDS members see Warren Jeffs as their prophet, even though he is now a convicted child rapist in federal prison. Twenty-four of Jeffs' 78 wives were underage. You can find info on the web and YouTube on Warren Jeffs and the FLDS. Netflix has a new documentary entitled *Keep Sweet: Pray and Obey*. Besides polygamy, Warren Jeffs taught that non-white people and gays were evil. Riley's mother thinks the devil is in Riley for being gay.

My novel setting is in Custer County. The ethnicity of the county is 93.9 percent white. The book's imaginary town is located in Custer County. The U.S. is a big country with vast areas with no major cities. Before I began work on the novel, I envisioned the primary setting with the main character that was a city slicker from Chicago. Unlike Custer County, Chicago is very diverse. The main characters, Kate and Riley, are white. Kate's best friend and former lover, Sherry, is Black, and Max is of mixed ethnicity. When Sherry and Max visit Kate in Idaho, they're just another couple visiting. Real life is complex and sometimes painful, but we have to try to make things better.

When I was young, maybe seven or eight, I asked the simple question, "Why can't Black people marry white people?" My adoptive father became angry, and I got in trouble. Sadly, some people still fear anyone different than them. Women still have to work harder than men to prove themselves, and people of color work harder to prove they are just like anyone else. It's not fair. We've made progress, but this world has a lot of work to do.

I didn't mention much about the native Americans in the book. Our country has, as have other civilizations, committed past sins. For the U.S., we stole the native American's land and replaced their culture with our own, which was rooted in European culture. And yes, we did far worse things.

Please remember, *Cabin Fever* has some truths, but it is a fictional romance with a happily-ever-after (feel-good) ending. I wish we all had HEA endings in real life. Despite all the world's turmoil, I still believe most people have love in their hearts.

If you've enjoyed the book, please leave a review on Amazon or Goodreads. Reviews are the lifeblood of authors.

Love and peace to all,
Addison

Email: addison.m.conley.author@gmail.com
Facebook: https://www.facebook.com/AddisonMConley.Fiction.Author/
Twitter handle is @NeoTrinity13

## What's Your Story?

Global Wordsmiths, CIC, provides an all-encompassing service for all writers, ranging from basic proofreading and cover design to development editing, typesetting, and eBook services. A major part of our work is charity and community focused, delivering writing projects to under-served and under-represented groups across Nottinghamshire, giving voice to the voiceless and visibility to the unseen.

To learn more about what we offer, visit: www.globalwords.co.uk

*A selection of books by Global Words Press:*
Desire, Love, Identity: with the National Justice Museum
Times Past: with The Workhouse, National Trust
World At War: Farmilo Primary School
Times Past: Young at Heart with AGE UK
In Different Shoes: Stories of Trans Lives

*Self-published authors working with Global Wordsmiths:*
E.V. Bancroft
Valden Bush
Addison M Conley
Emma Nichols
Dee Griffiths and Ali Holah
Helena Harte
Dani Lovelady Ryan
Karen Klyne
AJ Mason
James Merrick
Ray Martin
Robyn Nyx
Sam Rawlings
Simon Smalley
Brey Willows

# Other Great Butterworth Books

**Let Love Be Enough** by Robyn Nyx
When a killer sets her sights on her target, is there any stopping her?
Available on Amazon (ASIN B09YMMZ8XC)

**Lyrics of Life** by Brey Willows
Sometimes the only way to heal someone's heart is with a song from your own.
Coming June 2023 (ISBN 9781915009265)

**An Art to Love** by Helena Harte
Second chances are an art form.
Available from Amazon (ASIN B0B1CD8Y42)

**Of Light and Love** by E.V. Bancroft
To have a future, they must let go of the past.
Available from Amazon (ASIN B0B64KJ3NP)

**Zamira Saliev: A Dept. 6 Operation** by Valden Bush
Will the ghosts of their pasts drag them into a dark dead-end?
Available from Amazon (ASIN B0BHJKHK6S)

**The Helion Band** by AJ Mason
Rose's only crime was to show kindness to her royal mistress...
Available from Amazon (ASIN B09YM6TYFQ)

**Caribbean Dreams** by Karen Klyne
When love sails into your life, do you climb aboard?
Available from Amazon (ASIN B09M41PYM9)

**That Boy of Yours Wants Looking At** by Simon Smalley
A gloriously colourful and heart-rending memoir.
Available from Amazon (ASIN B09HSN9NM8)

**LesFic Eclectic Volume Three** edited by Robyn Nyx
Download for free from BookFunnel